the Legacy

Center Point
Large Print

Also by Michael Phillips and available from Center Point Large Print:

Secrets of the Shetlands Trilogy
The Inheritance
The Cottage

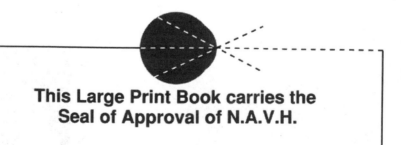

This Large Print Book carries the Seal of Approval of N.A.V.H.

the Legacy

SECRETS *of the* SHETLANDS
VOLUME 3

MICHAEL PHILLIPS

CENTER POINT LARGE PRINT
THORNDIKE, MAINE

This Center Point Large Print edition
is published in the year 2017 by arrangement with
Bethany House, a division of Baker Publishing Group.

Scripture quotations are from the Revised Standard
Version of the Bible, copyright 1952 [2nd edition, 1971]
by the Division of Christian Education of the National
Council of the Churches of Christ in the United States of
America. Used by permission. All rights reserved.

This is a work of fiction. Names, characters,
incidents, and dialogues are products of
the author's imagination and are not to be
construed as real. Any resemblance to actual events
or persons, living or dead, is entirely coincidental.

The text of this Large Print edition is unabridged. In other
aspects, this book may vary from the original edition.
Printed in the United States of America on permanent
paper. Set in 16-point Times New Roman type.

ISBN: 978-1-68324-474-5

Library of Congress Cataloging-in-Publication Data
Names: Phillips, Michael R., 1946– author.
Title: The legacy / Michael Phillips.
Description: Center Point Large Print edition. | Thorndike, Maine :
    enter Point Large Print, 2017. | Series: Secrets of the Shetlands ;
    book 3
Identifiers: LCCN 2017018761 | ISBN 9781683244745
    (hardcover : alk. paper)
Subjects: LCSH: City and town life—Scotland—Shetland—Fiction. |
    Shetland (Scotland)—Fiction. | Large type books. | GSAFD:
    Christian fiction.
Classification: LCC PS3566.H492 L43 2017b | DDC 813/.54—dc23
LC record available at https://lccn.loc.gov/2017018761

This is a series about generational legacies, those that extend in both directions. As I have written these stories, my thoughts have been filled with influences that have come down to me from my own parents and grandparents and ancestors even further back, including their Quaker heritage. And I am constantly reminded of those who have followed, namely Judy's and my sons and grandchildren, and whatever my life has been and will be capable of passing on to them.

More than two decades ago I dedicated books of a series to our three sons. They were young, and my father's heart was filled with visions of the years ahead we would share together. Now they are grown men. Whatever legacy a father is able to pass on to his sons looks much different to me at today's more mature vantage point from which to assess life's unfolding and progressive journey—both mine and theirs.

Therefore, to our three sons and the men of spiritual stature they have each become, I gratefully and lovingly dedicate the volumes of this series.

the Legacy
to
Gregory Erich Phillips

CONTENTS

Tulloch Clan Family Tree 12
Map of Whales Reef, Shetland Islands 14

Part 1

1. The Laird 17
2. Exciting Opportunity 21
3. New Leaf 23
4. Setting Sail 31
5. An Interview to Remember 36
6. Surprise Reunion 42

Part 2, 1924
A Legacy Begins—*The Adventure*

7. Shattering News 51
8. At Sea 55
9. A Grandmother's Blessing 60

Part 3, August 2006

10. The Cottage 69
11. The Chief 77
12. The Mill 81

Part 4, 1924
A Legacy Begins—*The Meeting*

13. Dangerous Wiles
14. Laird and Chief

15. Old Friends in New Times 100
16. Mid-Atlantic 103
17. The Mission 108
18. Morning and Evening 115

Part 5, August 2006

19. A Cousin in Trouble 123
20. Newcomer to Whales Reef 128
21. The Gun 134
22. The Rumor 138
23. Walk on the Island 143
24. A Talk Between Friends 147
25. A Sermon to Remember 150

Part 6, 1924
A Legacy Begins—*Island Explorations*

26. A Gray Day 161
27. Stone of Antiquity 168
28. Herbs on the Moor 173
29. Cottage of Intrigue 178
30. Dinner at the Hotel 185
31. A Walk in the Moonlight 188
32. Ambition, Character, and Fathers 193
33. Two Life Stories 197

Part 7, August 2006

4. New Friends 207
   Frantic Request 213
   A Foursome 218
   Excited Call 221

Part 8, 1924
A Legacy Begins—*The Friendship*

38.	Strange Sensations	229
39.	Memories in Many Directions	231
40.	Gone	236
41.	Whence and Why Come Change?	241
42.	Coffee, Larks, and Snails	245
43.	The Cliffs of Noss	250
44.	Sumburgh Head	254
45.	Picts, Peat, Puffins, and Porpoises	258

Part 9, August 2006

46.	Maddy's Adventure	269
47.	Tennyson's Ridge	274
48.	What Manner of Shepherd	281

Part 10, 1924
A Legacy Begins—*The Island*

49.	The Whales Fin Inn	289
50.	Tea and Wildflowers	292
51.	Fish and Chips	299
52.	Lunch at the Muckle Stane	310
53.	The Angels' Harps	315
54.	Laird and American	321
55.	Husband and Wife	327
56.	A Warm Twilight	33˘
57.	Supper at the Cottage	3˘

Part 11, September–October 2006

58. The Scent of Autumn 345
59. Return Engagement 349
60. The Photo 354
61. Unexpected Visit 360
62. Witness 372
63. Homecoming 377
64. A Pitlochry Proposal 384
65. Changing Horizons 392

Part 12, 1924
A Legacy Begins—*The Visit*

66. A Scotsman in America 399
67. The Pennsylvania Railroad 409
68. Volunteer Laborer 421
69. Journal of Love 433

Part 13, Winter, 2006–2007

70. New Adventures Ahead 439
71. The Redemption of Hardy Tulloch 444
72. A Pennsylvania Christmas 453

Part 14, 1924–1953
A Legacy Begins—*The Letters*

73. Renewed Memories 463
74. Centering Roots 468
. Quandaries of Change 473
   Relinquishment and Grief 484
   The Wood and the Land 486

78. Silence   492
79. Deception   496
80. Heart of Division   499
81. The Dark Years   502
82. Reunion in Kirkwall   507
83. Christmas and a New Year   517
84. Offer of a Secret Mission   521
85. The Shetland Bus   525
86. Serious Interviews   550
87. Passing of an Era   566

Part 15, May–June 2007

88. The Locket   569
89. Nostalgic Memories   577
90. A Laird's Secret   582
91. The Wedding   593
92. Swing Time   599
93. The Legacy   604
94. Ending Fragments   611

Whales Reef Tulloch Clan Family Tree
(Descended from Highland Clan Donald)

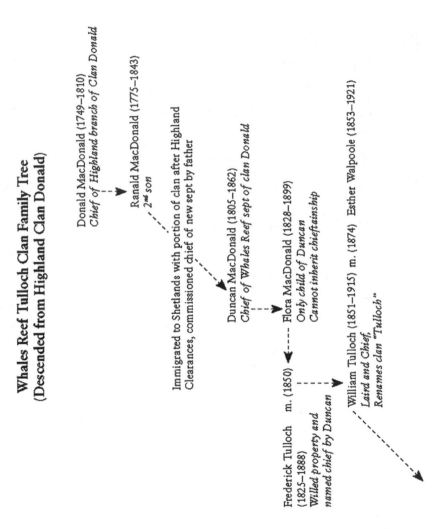

Donald MacDonald (1749–1810)
Chief of Highland branch of Clan Donald

Ranald MacDonald (1775–1843)
- 2nd son

Immigrated to Shetlands with portion of clan after Highland
Clearances, commissioned chief of new sept by father

Duncan MacDonald (1805–1862)
Chief of Whales Reef sept of clan Donald

Flora MacDonald (1828–1899)
Only child of Duncan
Cannot inherit chieftainship

Frederick Tulloch   m. (1850)
(1825–1888)
Willed property and
named chief by Duncan

William Tulloch (1851–1915) m. (1874) Esther Walpoole (1853–1921)
Laird and Chief,
Renames clan "Tulloch"

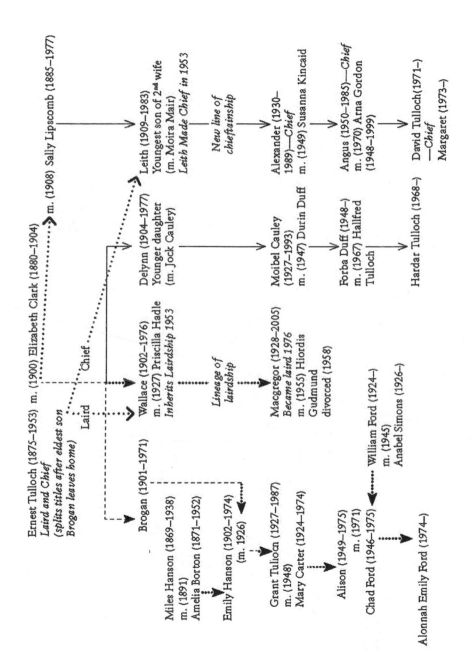

Ernest Tulloch (1875–1953) m. (1900) Elizabeth Clark (1880–1904)
Laird and Chief
(splits titles after eldest son
Brogan leaves home)

m. (1908) Sally Lipscomb (1885–1977)

Leith (1909–1983)
Youngest son of 2nd wife
(m. Moira Mair)
Leith Made Chief in 1953

New line of
chieftainship

Alexander (1930–1989)—*Chief*
m. (1949) Susanna Kincaid

Angus (1950–1985)—*Chief*
m. (1970) Arna Gordon
(1948–1999)

David Tulloch(1971–)
—*Chief*
Margaret (1973–)

Delynn (1904–1977)
Younger daughter
(m. Jock Cauley)

Moibel Cauley
(1927–1993)
m. (1947) Durin Duff

Forba Duff (1948–)
m. (1967) Hallfred
Tulloch

Hardar Tulloch (1968–)

Chief

Wallace (1902–1976)
m. (1927) Priscilla Hadle
Inherits Lairdship 1953

Lineage of
lairdship

Macgregor (1928–2005)
Became laird 1976
m. (1955) Hiordis
Gudmund
divorced (1958)

Laird

Brogan (1901–1971)

Miles Hanson (1869–1938)
m. (1891)
Amelia Borton (1871–1952)

Emily Hanson (1902–1974)
(m. 1926)

Grant Tulloch (1927–1987)
m. (1948)
Mary Carter (1924–1974)

Alison (1949–1975)
m. (1971)

Chad Ford (1946–1975)

William Ford (1924–)
m. (1945)
Anabel Simons (1926–)

Alonnah Emily Ford (1974–)

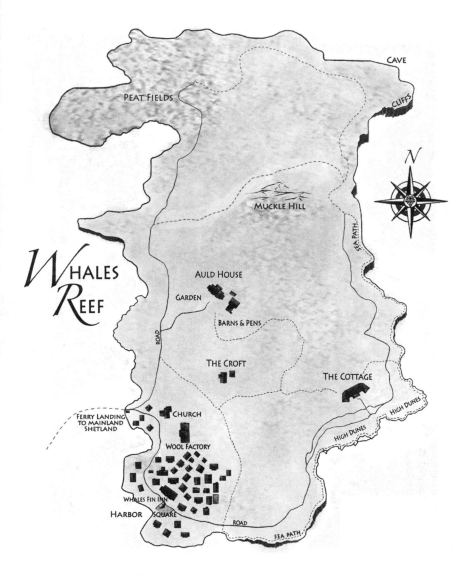

PART 1

1

THE LAIRD

AUGUST 2006
WHALES REEF, SHETLAND ISLANDS

Loni Ford, heiress to most of the land surrounding her on this remote island in the Shetlands, set down the book in her lap and breathed deeply of the fresh morning air.

The unbelievable change that had come to her life began two months ago with the fateful letter from Shetland solicitor Jason MacNaughton.

Dear Miss Ford, *she had read,*

Last year in the small Scottish fishing village of Whales Reef in the Shetland Islands, Mr. Macgregor Tulloch passed away leaving no will and no immediate family. After an exhaustive search . . . we finally have been able to locate . . . you as the closest living heir to Mr. Tulloch's estate.

The last thing Loni had expected was for th island and village of Whales Reef to exercise su magic upon her that she would fall in love v

17

them. The contrast could not have been greater between her fast-paced life in Washington, D.C , and the peaceful setting in which she now found herself.

As she explored the island and met villagers and familiarized herself with the Cottage, discovering books and heirlooms and photographs, Loni slowly found new places coming to life within her. The land and surroundings, the people and history, the traditional Scottish music, even such simple things as plaids and tartans and oatcakes, tugged at her soul with emotions altogether new. She had grown up knowing almost nothing about her roots. Suddenly she had more family connections than she knew what to do with.

From the antipathy in which she was held at first by those who considered her an American usurper to old Macgregor's inheritance, gradually the people of the island warmed to her presence. They began greeting her with smiles and bows and curtseys. She stood nearly a head taller than all the women, and several inches above most of the men of the island. What could be more logical in their legend-steeped minds than that she was an ancient Norse goddess or Scottish queen, the Auld Tulloch's long-lost heir in whom the Scots and Norse strains had come to rest? They invited er into their homes for simple meals around peat es and tea made the old-fashioned way, with er boiled in a black kettle hanging from an iron hook in the fireplace. They told stories of the old times, about grandparents and aunts and uncles and dead bodies and hidden rooms and legends. Each contributed its share in beguiling Loni into the complex tapestry of island life.

Perhaps most surprising, after a rocky start, Loni's perceptions about clan chief David Tulloch became more personal. The whole island now suspected how things stood between their new American laird and their chief.

Loni smiled at the thought. During those first days with David, she had made a fool of herself more than once. Yet their relationship had blossomed like a slowly unfolding flower of subtle hues.

She glanced down at the heather and wool ring on her right hand. Did she dare hope it signified more than mere friendship?

Now here she was calling the island Cottage "home," while her modern apartment in Washington, D.C., sat vacant, and her office on the seventh floor of the prestigious Capital Towers building was occupied by a temp who had taken her place as Maddy's assistant.

The only question now was, how long would the fairy tale last? What lay over the horizon of her future? What *would* she do about her job in D.C.? Could she find a way to balance her life *there* and her life *here* as the new "laird" of Whales Reef? For a few more days at least, Loni was content to live in the glow of the dream.

She had grown to love every inch of this small island in the North Atlantic. She had adopted David's custom of starting each day walking its bluffs and moors and coastlines. The two did not often encounter each other during their solitary morning rambles, though each occupied the other's thoughts. David's early excursions from the Auld Hoose on the other side of the island had usually concluded before hers began. The sea air had not succeeded in making her quite such an early riser as he.

Her favorite place to come and read, when it was not too cold, was the large flat rock on which she now sat, mostly sunk into the peat turf of the surrounding landscape.

She looked about . . . quietly, peacefully, drawing in several long draughts of the crisp morning air, then returned her attention to the book in her lap. She smiled as she remembered opening it a month before to see in careful script, *The Journal of Emily Hanson.* On the next page were the words with which Emily had begun her tale so long ago.

I am so excited! A month ago I learned of an opportunity to travel to the Shetland Islands . . .

How different, Loni thought, from her own first thoughts of coming here. She was discovering every day how similar she and her great-grandmother actually were, and how parallel had been their sojourns in this place.

Her thoughts drifted back in time to her great-grandmother's unlikely adventure.

2

EXCITING OPPORTUNITY

JUNE 1924
NEW YORK HARBOR
NEW YORK CITY, UNITED STATES

A young woman stood at the rail of the Norwegian ocean liner *Viking Queen*. Her final good-byes said, Emily Hanson thought fondly of her farewell three days earlier with the dear woman who had helped make this trip possible.

"Good-bye, Grandma," said Emily. "This would not be happening without you."

"You just have the time of your life in Scotland," replied Grandma Hanson with a hug and a smile. "And don't forget to write down everything," she added, pointing to the wrapped package in Emily's hand. "Remember what I told you about when I was your age. This next month will change your life."

"Thank you, Grandma. I will remember."

Emily knew she was not the adventurous type. But this was a rare opportunity such as might never come again. She was determined to make the most of it. When the dean of her college told her about traveling to the Shetland Islands as a companion for her aunt, Emily knew immediately that the main objection would come from her father.

"My father is planning for me to spend the summer with my elderly grandmother," she told Dean Wilson. "She lives only three miles from us in Burlington. He feels that she should no longer live alone, that she needs someone with her."

"Ah, yes . . . I see," replied the dean. "Well, family concerns always weigh in the balance. However, you will discuss the trip with them?"

"Of course. And my mother can be very persuasive," Emily added with an inward smile.

Tingling with excitement, Emily telephoned her parents that same evening. The moment she heard of it, Emily's mother had no intention of allowing anything to stand in the way of such an opportunity. Discussions and plans followed, as did a meeting between Emily and Dean Wilson's aunt, Harriett Barnes.

All that remained was for Emily to apply for a passport. An experienced traveler, Mrs. Barnes took everything in hand and saw to all the necessary arrangements.

"I know you will take good care of our daughter,

Harriett," said Mrs. Hanson, shaking the hand of Emily's temporary guardian one last time before the older woman left the three Hansons alone beside the ship for their final good-byes.

"I will, Amelia," replied Mrs. Barnes with a twinkle in her eye. "But don't forget, it is Emily who is supposed to be taking care of me!"

"From what short time we have known one another, I have the feeling you can take care of yourself."

Mrs. Barnes laughed. "You are right. There is not much I haven't seen in my years of travel. I am just glad to have Emily with me. She is a delightful young lady. I anticipate that we will become great friends."

3

NEW LEAF

AUGUST 2006
WASHINGTON, D.C.

At length Loni closed the journal, pulled her sweater more tightly around her shoulders, rose, and made her way back toward the Cottage. Bringing her reflections back to the present, her thoughts strayed, not back in time ninety years where they had been occupied with Emily's story but across the Atlantic five hours. Her boss and best friend would be up with her morning's first cup of coffee and expecting her call.

In Washington, D.C., Madison aka "Maddy" Swift sat at her desk, anticipating her call with Loni between 5:30 and 6:00. She sipped on a second cup of coffee and found herself growing uncharacteristically thoughtful. She had been pensive ever since her return from the Shetlands. She was beginning to understand why the small island of Whales Reef had taken such hold on her friend. Her reflective musings often revolved around her brief visits with crusty old Dougal Erskine. Suddenly she had been a girl with her grandfather again, thinking of things she had not experienced in years. Her visits to the family farm in central Virginia now came racing back out of the mists, stirring long dormant whispers of wistful nostalgia.

It wasn't only Dougal Erskine, however, and his sheep and adorable little Shetland ponies, or even the pastoral setting of Loni's "Cottage" that had Maddy's thoughts meandering along the byways of her past. Her conversation with Loni about her brief foray into the mysterious world of love had unsettled her more than Maddy would have thought possible.

She had tried desperately to put it out of her mind. She had come to terms with her life. She was a businesswoman, not a romantic. She was chunky. She knew that. No man ever looked at her twice.

She didn't care. She was a single career woman. She liked her life.

Why, then, had the Shetlands taken such hold of her? What was gnawing at her, making her long for something she knew she didn't have?

Maddy was happy for her friend. Yet watching her talk with David and laugh and walk about the island at his side raised the discomforting realization that perhaps she hadn't dealt with the realities of her own life as thoroughly as she had assumed. She couldn't erase from her mind the sight of Loni and David sitting in front of the fireplace, talking like they had known each other all their lives. What woman didn't long for such a friendship with a man?

Maddy glanced around her office—tidy, organized, businesslike. She was at the top of the investment world. Speaking engagements and job offers came in almost daily. But you couldn't snuggle up at night with account ledgers and a computer.

Was it too late for financial whiz Madison Swift?

Too late for what? She didn't even know what she meant.

She glanced at her watch, then logged into

Skype. A few minutes later Loni's face appeared on the computer screen in front of her.

"Hey, girl!" said Maddy. "You must have found a high-tech site for Skyping."

"Believe it or not, I'm calling from home," replied Loni. "You know, the Cottage."

"The twenty-first century comes to Whales Reef. I'm shocked!"

Loni laughed. "I had BT out to set up my internet two days ago—the British version of AT&T. I'm connected to the world again! Sort of intrudes on the old-fashioned feel of the place. But I don't suppose it could be helped."

"Tycoons have to be connected."

"You and that tycoon talk! I tell you, I'm just Loni Ford."

"I thought you said over there you were Alonnah."

"Oh, yeah—I forgot. Still haven't quite figured all that out. But a tycoon I'm not."

"Give yourself time!"

A thoughtful expression stole over Loni's face.

"What?" said Maddy.

"I don't know—just pensive, I suppose," replied Loni. "Being here does that to me. I was just rereading the first pages of my great-grandmother's journal again a few minutes ago, about when she first came here. I get goose bumps whenever I open her journal, as if I'm reading about myself. You know, like Dick Van Dyke said

26

in *Mary Poppins*, 'What's going to happen has all happened before.' It's that same kind of weird—as if I'm reliving her life."

"Sounds spooky, girl—a bit too much reincarnation for my taste!"

"I don't mean it like that!" laughed Loni. "It's just . . . I don't know, I can't explain it. But what is that you're wearing," she said. "I don't recognize it."

"It's new," said Maddy. "I'll model it for you," she added, rising from her chair and taking a few steps back.

"Whoa . . . Maddy!" exclaimed Loni. "A dress! I thought you had sworn off dresses for life. The blue is perfect on you. And so early in the day."

"I've got a breakfast meeting."

"It's lovely—what's the occasion? An important new client?"

"No, routine stuff."

"Why the dress then?"

"I just thought about what you said when we were in New York about my having nice eyes. I shouldn't have given you a bad time about that. You were just being nice. I'm sorry."

"Hey, forget it. Nae botha, as they say here."

"Maybe you were right. What would it hurt for me to look more feminine? I bought it yesterday—on an impulse, I suppose."

"Maddy, I'm shocked!" laughed Loni. "Is this really Madison Swift talking?"

"Maybe the new Madison Swift. If the Shetlands can change you, why shouldn't some of it rub off on me? Actually, there's something I wanted to ask you."

"Sure."

"Are you sitting down?"

"I am."

"Promise you won't laugh."

"Okay. What is it, Maddy?"

"What's the name of that gym where you work out?"

Loni stared back, speechless.

"You're not kidding?"

"I thought it wouldn't hurt to lose a few pounds."

"It's Capital Fitness Center. But why this—?"

"No questions," interrupted Maddy. "I might not stick with it, so let's just leave it at that."

"Fair enough. But Hugh's a member. That's why I joined. You're likely to run into him if you go between six and eight after work."

"I'll avoid that time slot! I might stop in and sign up this morning before my resolve fades. Have you heard anything from him, by the way . . . you know, after the ring episode?"

"Not a thing, but how would he contact me? By the way, don't give him this number or tell him my email's back up and running. Have you heard from him?"

"No. Though my temp said a guy who sounds

like it might have been Hugh was here looking for either of us when I was in Scotland with you."

"I'm not surprised. Knowing Hugh, I can't imagine him not trying to bowl me over with chocolates and flowers trying to change my mind."

"Chrysanthemums, no doubt."

"Probably," laughed Loni. "Let's just say it is probably a good thing I'm five thousand miles away. He's had everything his way for so long I doubt he'll give up without trying to talk me out of my decision. But he knows nothing about David."

"That will shock him—Oh, I almost forgot," exclaimed Maddy. "Guess what—big news. They finally announced the opening of the New York branch."

"And?" said Loni excitedly.

"As you always said, they offered me a vice-presidency to head it up."

"Maddy, that's great—congratulations!"

"Thank you."

"And you told them yes?"

"Provisionally. I didn't want to commit myself until your future clarifies somewhat. I have a couple months to make a decision. They're planning a big launch for the first of the year. I always said we'd do New York together. But now you've gone and fallen in love with a Scotsman

"But you'd take the job even if I couldn't go with you?"

"I don't know, Loni. We're a team. Let's just say I'm considering the options. Meanwhile, they're already interviewing for my replacement here in D.C. Interested?"

"No way. I wouldn't want the job if you weren't around."

"The word is they're looking at an independent consultant from outside. But I gotta run."

"Congratulations again."

Loni turned off her computer and smiled. She could still hardly believe it—Maddy in a dress and signing up at a gym!

Unconsciously she looked up at the clock on the wall. By this time tomorrow she and David would be on their way to Lerwick on an errand that would be anything but pleasant. Whales Reef was still rocking from the shocking developments of the previous week. As laird and chief of the small island clan, she and David had to do their best to help the authorities get to the bottom of the scandal.

Hopefully they would find some answers in the Shetland capital.

She sat a few more minutes, slowly growing pensive again, then picked up the journal and walked into the Great Room and began reading where she had left off before the chat with

Maddy. Again the eerie feeling of déjà vu stole over her as she continued reading about her great-grandmother's departure from New York ninety-two years before.

4

SETTING SAIL

JUNE 1924
NEW YORK HARBOR
NEW YORK CITY, UNITED STATES

From where she stood at the rail of the massive ship waving down to her parents, Emily knew her mother was crying. The occasional movement of her gloved hand to her eyes was indication enough.

Miles Hanson, however, was unlikely to be shedding tears on this day. Emily's father prided himself on his level-headed business sense. The banking executive and his wife, Amelia, had raised their seven children in a large Colonial house on twenty wooded acres outside Burlington, New Jersey. The tract had come down to him as a portion of an originally much larger grant of land to the well-known Woolman family, from which Miles Hanson had descended through one of the Woolman daughters.

Like many Quakers, Emily's father had sound

31

business instincts and had done well for himself. In his mid-fifties he had risen to the echelons of bank upper management. He was also a stern traditionalist. When his wife, choosing a suitable moment four years earlier, had informed him that Emily wanted to attend college, his first response was that his own alma mater, Haverford College outside Philadelphia, did not admit women and so the thing was impossible.

He was soon to discover that his wife and daughter were well ahead of him. They had already investigated several other Quaker institutions. With his other sons and daughters marrying and leaving home, the idea of Emily flying from the nest at such a young age was a blow to Miles Hanson's well-ordered world.

Among America's Christian denominations, Quakers had always been at the vanguard of progressive thinking. Had it not been his own ancestor, Quaker John Woolman, who had awakened the American conscience against slavery fully a century before the Civil War? Quakers, too, were socially ahead of their time in respect of women and their standing in the world. Yet these were uncomfortable times for men like Miles Hanson. Quaker women were speaking up and making their own decisions.

In spite of his reservations, therefore, his wife and daughter and mother made all the arrangements for Emily's adventure.

● ● ●

"Well, young lady," Hanson had said stoically a few minutes earlier, "it would seem that the time has come for you to get aboard. You don't want to be left behind."

"There is little danger of that, Daddy. Not with Mrs. Barnes watching out for me."

"Yes, well, I just hope she is a worthy chaperone. You will encounter many worldly influences. Do not be swept up in them."

"I won't, Daddy," said Emily. She gave him a reassuring smile. "I hope you will not worry about me."

"It is a father's responsibility to protect his children. I only fear that in this case, I have not been given— ."

"I know you didn't want me to go, Daddy," interrupted Emily. "But I thank you for allowing me to," she added quickly. "Good-bye, Daddy." She wrapped her arms around his waist and laid her head on his chest. "I love you."

On her part, Amelia Hanson was full of more emotions than she could define. They were things her husband could never understand about what it meant to be a woman in the 1920s. This opportunity for Emily represented more than merely a trip across the Atlantic. On her shoulders she carried the dreams and aspirations of a rising generation of women who were bursting the bonds of former barriers. Amelia Hanson knew she would never set eyes on Europe. But her daughter was on her way to do just that. Like Emily, she had dreamed of going to college. But in the late nineteenth century in her family, such had been unthinkable. Now Emily was poised to graduate from Wilmington in another year. Through Emily, perhaps some of Amelia's own secret dreams would be fulfilled.

She had said good-bye many times since Emily first left for college. But today's parting was different. Her daughter was setting off for a different part of the globe. Who could erase the memory of the *Titanic* from twelve years before? Putting Emily on a train for Ohio was not the same as sending her off on an ocean liner.

All these thoughts lay hidden in Amelia Hanson's heart as she now said farewell to her youngest daughter.

"You're not going to cry, are you, Mama?" Emily said.

"Certainly I'm going to cry!" replied Amelia. "Do you think I am going to send my youngest daughter halfway around the world and keep my tears inside? I will cry all the way back to Burlington!"

"Oh, Mama," said Emily. She tried to laugh but was close to tears herself. "There is nothing to worry about."

"It's just that you will be so very far away."

"I won't be gone even so long as when I leave for college."

"My brain knows that. But a woman's emotions are not ruled by her brain. All I can think is that five thousand miles of dangerous ocean will be between you and me. What if some dashing Englishman sweeps you off your feet? What if you forget all about us and begin talking with a British accent?"

"No dashing Englishman will pay the slightest attention to me," laughed her daughter.

"Don't be too sure, Emily. Still, the mother in me hopes you are right."

"You don't want me to be an old maid, do you, Mama?" teased Emily.

"Of course not, dear," smiled Mrs. Hanson. "But neither am I quite ready yet for you to be swept off your feet."

"I think I have enough of Daddy's stoicism in my blood to keep my wits about me.—Oh, there's Mrs. Barnes waving frantically. It's time for us to walk up the gangplank for the last time.—Good-bye, Mama."

Mother and daughter embraced.

"I love you, Emily."

"I love you too, Mama. Thank you for everything. And thank you for the book."

"Times like this, away from home in a strange place, are perhaps the greatest opportunities for spiritual growth that come to us."

"Thank you, Mama. Most of all, thank you for believing in me."

"I do believe in you, Emily. Good-bye . . . and have the time of your life."

Emily was too young to fully grasp the emotions for one like her mother watching her daughter take such a giant step into the unknown. Yet she sensed that something bigger than her own life was at stake.

A thunderous rumble from the ship's horn suddenly drowned out all the shouts and final farewells. Emily felt a tremor beneath her.

They were under way!

5

AN INTERVIEW TO REMEMBER

JUNE 2006
WASHINGTON, D.C.

The Capital Towers building maintained an exercise room on its ground floor, with showers and locker rooms. However, Maddy had no intention of allowing anyone in the building to see her trying to exercise for the first time in her life. Capital Fitness was only a few blocks away. She would undergo the humiliation there.

Twenty minutes had proved more than enough for her first session several hours after her breakfast meeting. By then she was sweating like a cow. The idea of dressing again for work was hopeless, unless she took a cold shower and that was equally against her principles as exercise. She had to sit around cooling off for twenty more wasted minutes before showering and returning to work.

On the second day of her foray into this brave new world of fitness, therefore, she changed in the locker room at work and walked to Capital Fitness. Forty minutes later the return walk to Capital Towers helped her cool off. The walk to and from her workout—so-called, though for Loni it would hardly qualify as a warm-up—would be an added concession to her revamped daily regimen, if she could just manage to sneak in and out of the building without being seen in the hideous lavender sweat suit she'd grabbed off a clearance table.

Forgoing lunch for the gym, arms, shoulders, back, and legs rebelling at the torture to which she was subjecting them, and starving on top of everything else—the salad she'd had the night before, and a bowl of fruit and yogurt that morning, were hardly enough to keep a sparrow alive!—Maddy slipped through the doors of Capital Towers and quickly made for the narrow corridor leading to the lockers.

The lobby was unusually deserted for one o'clock. Two men in dark suits stood with their backs turned at the bank of elevators. Maddy walked by on the opposite side of the lobby. The *ding* of the elevator drew her eye. The men stepped inside and turned.

Suddenly Maddy's knees buckled, and her throat went dry. There was no mistaking that face or that smile!

The doors glided into motion. He glanced her way. As quickly as their eyes met, the doors closed. Praying he had not recognized her in such a ridiculous getup, Maddy hurried from the lobby.

Five minutes later she sat on a bench in the locker room, still in her gym suit, perspiring again, though not from a stair-stepper or elliptical machine.

Get yourself together, girl! she said to herself. *Whatever you thought you saw was just your imagination. Get off your duff, put on your professional mojo, and go back to work. The exercise endorphins are playing tricks on your brain!*

Only moderately successful in heeding her internal pep talk, Maddy managed to make herself presentable and returned to her office.

A message was waiting on her phone. She eased her aching body behind her desk with a sigh. She knew she had reached the moment of truth in this lunchtime resolve. For the price of a chocolate croissant across the street she would chuck the whole thing, forget the gym, give her sneakers and sweats to a thrift shop, and be done with it.

She pressed Play on her answering machine.

Miss Swift, it's Lucy up on the tenth floor. Mr. Chalmers would like to see you at two o'clock. He wants you to meet one of the finalists he's interviewing for your position.

Maddy glanced at the clock on the wall. One-twenty. That would just give her enough time to make a couple of calls and bone up on the précis she had been preparing outlining her responsibilities in case it was needed. Company President Adrian Chalmers had been with Capital just three years but was determined to make his mark. The New York expansion had been one of his goals since his first day in the building. After announcing her selection to head up the new division last week, he had asked Maddy to help with the final vetting process in the hiring of her replacement.

She emerged from the elevator on the tenth floor at one-fifty-seven.

"Hello, Miss Swift," said Chalmers's executive assistant as Maddy walked into the presidential suite. "You may go right in."

Maddy crossed the reception area, opened the door, and entered the inner sanctum of power—a room so large, with original art on the walls and four-foot brass and copper sculptures in opposite corners, that it could house five offices.

"Ah, Miss Swift!" said Chalmers, rising from behind his intimidating six-by-four-foot desk. "Come in—good of you to join us."

Out of the corner of her eye, Maddy saw the navy blue suit she had noticed at the elevator downstairs. She would recognize the profile of that head and face even had a hundred years passed. Momentary faintness again threatened her. She struggled toward the empty chair beside Chalmers's guest, hoping he would not remember her.

"Sit down, Miss Swift," said Chalmers. "I would like . . ."

The man's head turned.

". . . to introduce—"

"Madison!" exclaimed the newcomer, leaping from his chair. "Madison Swift . . . it *is* you!"

Maddy found herself caught up in an embrace that nearly squeezed the air out of her lungs.

"Miss Swift, meet Tennyson Stafford," said Chalmers, laughing at the spectacle. "I gather the two of you already know each other!"

"I apologize, Mr. Chalmers," said Stafford, stepping back as he sent his eyes over Maddy's face with a smile. He resumed his seat, and Maddy sat down beside him. "Not very professional of me, I admit. I hope that outburst won't cost me the job. But yes, Miss Swift and I worked in the same office some years ago—though I assume from the dazed expression on her face that she does not remember me.—"

Again he turned toward Maddy.

"Madison," he said, "it was in Atlanta, at Southern Securities . . . we were both wet behind the ears and just getting started. I'm sure you don't—"

"I remember you very well, Tennyson," said Maddy, trying to sound calmer than she felt. Suddenly her recent exercise rushed back over her. In seconds her dress felt drenched. She hoped her face wasn't as hot and red as the rest of her. She was too young for hot flashes, but this definitely qualified! He was even more handsome than she remembered. "Actually," she added, "I'm surprised you remember *me*. I was just a kid, but you were a rising star."

"I was probably too ambitious for my own good back then," laughed Stafford. "Now here we are again and *you* are the star and I am the lowly interviewee hoping for the position you are leaving behind. When I heard Mr. Chalmers say Miss Swift, I couldn't believe it. I had no idea I was applying for *your* job."

"Well, this little reunion should make the transition smooth and pleasant," said Chalmers. "Have no fear about your spontaneity, Mr. Stafford. We like to think of Capital Investments as a family.—Lucy," he said into his intercom, "if you wouldn't mind bringing us three espressos."

41

He rose, motioning to Maddy and Stafford. "Come," he said as he walked out from behind his desk, "we will be more comfortable over on the couches. Coffee will be along in a minute."

The rest of the awkward interview passed in a blur. Maddy remembered almost nothing that was said. Forty minutes went by as Tennyson and her boss talked about hedge funds and what mergers were on the horizon and the price of gold and inflated real estate values and indexed funds and IPOs and the future of the NASDAQ.

6

SURPRISE REUNION

When the meeting was over, Maddy and Tennyson Stafford left the presidential presence and walked through the reception area without speaking. Maddy had recovered her equilibrium, though now that they were alone together her mouth again went dry. They made their way to the elevators. Fortuitously there were no others waiting. Slowly the doors closed behind them.

"So . . . alone at last," said Stafford. "What's your floor?" he asked as he pressed the button for the ground floor lobby.

"I'm on seven, but I'll see you out of the building," replied Maddy.

"Gosh, Madison—it is so great to see you," said Stafford, beaming. "I really can't believe it. You look good! I love your dress—blue, my favorite color. And you've obviously done well for yourself. Who's the star now!"

Maddy laughed. "I don't know about that. But yes, I've been fortunate."

"How long have you been here?"

"Twelve years. I came straight from Atlanta. What about you? You'd landed a cushy position in Chicago, last I knew."

"Yeah, it was okay. I was there four years. But I didn't like the city, and the grind of office life wasn't for me."

"What did you do after that? Your name hasn't come up in my circles."

"I went into business for myself as a private investment consultant. I've been specializing in what you might call unusual opportunities for investors who want a more hands-on experience— adventurous, you might say . . . personal . . . out of the mainstream."

"I'm afraid you've lost me," said Maddy. "I take it you're not talking about blue chips and banking and utilities or municipal bonds?"

"Not exactly!" laughed Stafford. "I offer investors the chance to experience their investments."

"Have you been in Chicago all this time?"

"Oh no—I was anxious to get out of there. I set up my new company in Alaska."

"Alaska!"

Stafford laughed. "It fits the adventure image. People love it."

The elevator reached the ground floor, and they stepped into the lobby. A grin slowly crept to his face.

"That wasn't you I saw a couple hours ago, was it," he said, "in the gym suit?"

"I'm afraid it was," replied Maddy with obvious embarrassment. "I'd just come from the gym."

"An athlete, are you? We'll have to go for a run together sometime."

They moved slowly toward the main doors, then gradually came to a stop and continued talking in the middle of the lobby.

"Tell me more about your adventurous investments," said Maddy, anxious to get off the subject of going for a run.

"Let's say a guy wants to invest in timber in the Northwest," answered Stafford. "I put him with a dozen others who are interested. Then I organize a backpacking expedition into the wilds of Canada or Washington or wherever. We fly into some remote location that is included in the portfolio. We use experienced guides and bring along a gourmet cook who can do his thing over coals. It's pretty high end, not your run-of-the-mill backpacking thing—comfy tents and cots . . . I spare no expense. These guys are all millionaires and you've got to treat them well while giving them the flavor of roughing it. By the end of a week, they are the best of friends. Most important, they have hugged the trees and forded the streams they are thinking of buying. The investment has become personal. So much the better if they've seen a bear or bald eagle. They're personally *invested* in the investment. They're buying forests they traipsed through and slept in."

"What a fantastic idea."

"I use the same strategy for all my investments—a copper mine in the Southwest, we ride in on horseback and explore old abandoned mine shafts. Transportation, I'll put the men at the controls of an eighteen-wheeler or a locomotive pulling a hundred freight cars. Conservation, we'll go out and count the spotted owls in Oregon or endangered pandas in some remote part of China. I'll take them anywhere in the world. If some local investment group is considering investing in a bond measure to build a new football stadium, I send every one of them out to interview neighbors and business leaders and the players themselves. What do players want, how will the community be impacted? By the time that stadium is finished, these people truly own it personally, even though it may be only one tenth of a tenth of a percent. Oil exploration, we go to Scotland and spend a week on a North Sea oil rig. Grain or beef or soybean futures, we'll head for Iowa and I'll put them on a combine or tractor in the middle of a wheat field."

"How ingenious! How did you think of all that?"

"I don't know," laughed Stafford. "I always had an outdoor streak in me. This is my way to marry business with pleasure, I suppose. Now people come to me with *their* investment ideas. I don't have to send out a prospectus. They come to me and say, 'We're thinking of such-and-such an investment—how can you make it personal, get us involved, help us know up close and personal whether we want to pursue it or not?' As you would expect, I have a very select client list."

"I've never heard anything like it."

"It's not without its dangers. We were doing a mountain climb in Nepal and wound up in the middle of a flare-up of hostilities between two local tribes. One of the groups thought we were spying for their enemies and took us prisoners. It was frightening to say the least, but we survived it and were eventually released. Needless to say, that was an investment opportunity that did *not* materialize. My clients never wanted to see that part of the world again!"

"What sort of investment took you to Nepal?"

"Don't ask!" laughed Stafford. "Not one of my greatest triumphs."

It fell silent for a moment.

"I'm not making the same money I might on Wall Street," said Stafford more seriously. "But I love what I do. And my clients are so appreciative they keep coming back."

"Except the Nepal group!"

Stafford laughed. "Believe it or not, they did come back . . . but for something a little safer—telecommunications."

"What was your hands-on adventure then?"

"I put them into a television station and had them run it for a week. Under the supervision of professionals, I made one a producer, several became the news crew, a couple had to go out and sell advertising, two reporters went out and tried to find news stories that no one else had. Another had to assess the ratings and make programming decisions, and I put three on the air in front of the camera—a weatherman, an anchor, and a woman who was an accomplished chef I put into a cooking show. They all had a ball."

"And after all this, now you want to reenter the investment mainstream again?" said Maddy.

Stafford thought a moment. "I still have my consulting business. But my parents live in Virginia. They own a small horse ranch where I grew up. They are getting to the age where I have to think about the future. I felt it was time to settle down a bit so that I'm nearby as they get older. I'm an only child. They have no one else."

"Very admirable."

"It's the right thing. Too many these days get so caught up chasing dreams they forget life's most important priorities. I've chased a few of my own. And I have more that beckon. But I will never forget how much I owe my folks. They gave me life, put me through college, supported everything I've ever done. Not only that, I love them. I'll always be there for them. If that means taking an office job, that's what I'll do."

"You sound like a friend of mine. My assistant, actually—though she's in Scotland at the moment."

"Vacation?"

"No—family roots, an inheritance that came to her . . . long story."

"Well, I shouldn't keep the high-flying investment analyst Madison Swift from her appointed rounds," said Stafford. "I can't tell you how good it is to reconnect with you. You wouldn't—"

He paused, then smiled.

"—I know it's probably presumptuous, and maybe you already have plans—power lunches with clients and all that," he added after a moment. "But is there any chance you'd have lunch with me tomorrow? I'm not flying out for several days—I'm going to spend a little time with my folks. I'd love to catch up more and find out what you've been doing since I last saw you."

"I have no plans," smiled Maddy. "Nothing big on the agenda. I'd like that."

PART 2
A Legacy Begins—
The Adventure
1924

7

SHATTERING NEWS

OXFORD, ENGLAND

In the Oxford boardinghouse that had been his home for most of the last four years, a young Scotsman of twenty-three sat dejectedly staring into the fireless grate across his floor.

For one who had spent much of his sojourn at the great university garnering for himself a reputation as the life of any party, he had never felt more despondent in his life. He took a swallow from the glass in his hand. Even his favorite brandy tasted bitter.

He lifted the single sheet of paper in his left hand and glanced over the letter again. A second reading, however, did not change its unambiguous message.

. . . regret to inform you that your services will not be required.

Three weeks ago, with jubilant utopian farewells to his fellow graduates, he had been all optimism. Life was ahead of him with all its possibilities.

His father and stepmother had come south to England for his commencement, to witness the culmination of their financial investment in his

51

youthful preparation for man's estate. Not that he had given his father much of a return. He was reasonably intelligent. But he had certainly not distinguished himself, though he had not divulged to his father that he had barely squeaked through his final term.

Yet the elder Tulloch professed himself proud of his eldest son's accomplishment, shaking Brogan's hand enthusiastically with affectionate esteem at the conclusion of the ceremony. It was just like his father, thought Brogan, forever praising him even though they both knew there was precious little about his academic career that could be considered praiseworthy. And Sally, beaming as she embraced him, acted as proud as if he were her own son.

He had been hanging around Oxford, biding his time with nothing to do ever since, waiting for the job to come through. If his bags weren't exactly packed, in all other respects he was ready. He planned to depart for India the moment word came through confirming his appointment to the diplomatic staff of Lord Hartwell, whose son, his best friend at Oxford, had recommended him for the position.

Morose thoughts came sweeping over him as he gazed at the letter—not even signed by Lord Hartwell himself.

This was the final disillusionment. The ultimate humiliation. The unmistakable confirmation that despite having a degree in hand, he had no future to look forward to.

He had banked everything on this job. Bertie Hartwell told him the thing was in the bag.

Bertie's father had no doubt investigated his son's friend more carefully than either hoped he would. He shuddered to think what might be contained in the so-called letters of "recommendation" had any of the Oxford faculty been asked for an academic reference on one Brogan Tulloch, Esquire, of the Shetland Islands.

A more important question than how it had happened bore the practical consequences of his sudden predicament down upon him with crushing force: What was he to do now?

He had no job, no prospects, and a dreadful academic résumé.

The thought of returning to Shetland was intolerable in the extreme. Mortifying. Embarrassing. Slinking back with his tail between his legs to take refuge under his father's roof.

The doors to the wider world of opportunity had been slammed in his face. His family was not of the wealthy aristocratic class of southern England. Brogan knew that his father did not possess the wherewithal, nor the inclination to *keep* supporting him beyond making him welcome at the family home.

He did not relish the thought of hanging around for another twenty or thirty years—the failed eldest son loitering about the old homestead until he inherited the lairdship.

If he would be laird of his father's estate someday, that day would not come anytime soon. His father was in the prime of his life. He had to find something to occupy himself besides kicking about the island among his father's sheep. The thought of mucking out the cattle and pony pens did not hold quite the appeal now as it had when he was a boy.

Perhaps he could wrangle his way onto the Hotel staff. What better than for the laird's son—donning the outer crust of the gentleman aristocrat to welcome its guests and give them the thrill of brushing with the local nobility.

None of the Hotel's visitors need know that his father wasn't technically of the aristocracy. That he was called *laird* and was also *chief* of their small Highland clan was enough to impress the Germans, Norwegians, and especially the Americans who came to the island. As for the English, they had their noses too high in the air to be impressed by anything.

He cringed at the thought of asking his father to use his influence to get him even a low-level position like assistant to the *maître d'hôtel*.

He would talk to Craig first.

8

AT SEA

OFF THE EASTERN SEABOARD
OF THE UNITED STATES

As the *Viking Queen* steamed out of New York Harbor and gradually left land behind, Emily gazed out across the Atlantic, filled with feelings she could not define. Suddenly she was alone. She had no one to depend on but herself. Yet the last three years away from home had given her confidence that she *could* depend on herself.

She had never done anything that could be called dangerous. The most daring thing she had ever done was confide to her mother four years ago that she wanted to go to college.

Her three years at Wilmington College had prepared her for this moment. It was invigorating to stretch the legs of her personhood.

As she continued to gaze toward the unknown before her, Emily's thoughts turned pensive.

An observer would have found her a study in contrasts, a personality still being molded. She had grown up as a dutifully obedient daughter. She had followed the religious instruction of her parents. She was outspoken but not loquacious, witty though with occasional bite to her words, an easy conversationalist but not chatty. She held well-reasoned opinions yet felt no need to persuade others to her points of view. She revered tradition while welcoming the future. She was studious but not highbrow, bright but not haughty, logical without being pedantic, spunky but not overbearing.

One of the greatest character strengths within the developing personhood of young Emily Hanson was humble curiosity.

She was hungry to *learn*.

Life presented her infinite interest. The natural world—from plants to animals to the mysteries of the heavenly spheres floating in the vast universe—were the canvas of her intellectual musings. If she possessed a scientific bent, it was science suffused with just enough philosophy to keep her asking *Why?*

Though she had selected the animal kingdom as her chosen field of study, her greatest interest was *people*. Why men and women became the individuals they were—each with a unique combination of strengths and weaknesses, some with spiritual inclinations, others with no interest in life's higher purpose—these represented to Emily the secret of existence.

The inner stories of those around her thus presented Emily with life's most fascinating mystery. *Why* were people growing in the directions they were growing, for good or for ill? How had their life choices set their steps moving in those directions?

Emily was herself on the continuum of growth as well. Many *hows* and *whys* yet had to reveal themselves in her own development. She had not yet set out to define *herself*.

What could be said about her with confidence was that she was moving in good directions. Yet Emily, too, had weaknesses that only time would reveal whether she would turn to strengths. As most character flaws are the mirror images of potential strengths, she could be impatient with personal lethargy, as she perceived it, in those too content with themselves to hunger and *grow*. She had little tolerance for self-satisfaction. If she possessed another fault, she was annoyed by rudeness. On the other hand, she was occasionally prone to speak her mind somewhat too hastily without considering the consequences. Some of her instructors at Wilmington called her feisty. Whether that quality would develop into a character strength or a character flaw would, again, take years of growth to determine.

An hour or two later, Emily was seated in a deck chair. Sleepily Mrs. Barnes at her side awoke from a nap.

"I must have dozed off," she said. "How long was I asleep?"

"About an hour, I think," replied Emily.

"I am a little chilly. It must be the sea breeze."

"Shall I fetch your coat?" said Emily, beginning to rise.

"No, dear. I'll be myself in a few minutes. The air is bracing," she added, drawing in a deep breath. "I love sea travel. What is that you are writing?"

"My new journal," replied Emily. "My grandmother gave it to me for the trip."

"Read me what you have written."

Emily flushed. "I would be embarrassed," she said.

"Nonsense. We are good friends by now. I have the feeling that by the time that journal is filled, it will be a most interesting book."

Emily laughed. "It will just be my own thoughts and feelings."

"As I say, a most interesting book. Now . . . read to me your first page. I promise I will not ask you to read me another word from it."

"All right," said Emily. She turned back to the first page, hesitated a moment, then began. *"I am so excited!"* Emily read. *"A month ago I learned of an opportunity to travel to the Shetland Islands."*

Emily glanced at Mrs. Barnes. "I was so nervous when Dean Wilson called me to her office," she said. "I thought I must be in trouble for something, although I couldn't imagine what."

"From what my niece has told me, that is

unlikely. She says you are a model student. Go on."

"At first Daddy objected to my going. But as it turned out, Grandma Hanson was the most enthusiastic of all about the trip. She told Daddy that I was going and that was all there was to it."

"Good for her!" exclaimed Mrs. Barnes.

"She said that I would be following in her footsteps."

"What did she mean?" asked Mrs. Barnes.

"My grandmother had left home, too, though she was even younger than me. What she did took far more courage than I have."

"What did your grandmother do that was so adventurous?"

"She was a nurse during the Civil War."

"Oh, my—that *was* dangerous."

"She was only eighteen when she began. She showed me her journal of that time. That's when she gave me this book and said that it was now my turn to write about my adventure.—Oh, and let me show you these."

Emily reached beneath her chair and picked up two other books.

"Dean Wilson gave me this for the trip too," she said. "It is Edith Holden's *Country Diary of an Edwardian Lady.* She thought I would enjoy her naturalist reflections and drawings and might do something similar myself. And my mother gave me this other book, a signed copy of Hannah Whithall Smith's autobiography."

"Who is Hannah Whithall Smith?"

"A Quaker lady," replied Emily. "She was an author who lived in Philadelphia. My parents and grandmother knew her, though she is dead now. She is the author of *A Christian's Secret of a Happy Life*."

"What an interesting title. I would love to meet your grandmother," said Mrs. Barnes. "She sounds like a fascinating woman—a woman activist before anyone had even heard of suffragettes!"

Emily laughed. "When we get back to the States and life returns to normal, I will make sure you have that opportunity."

"But be prepared, dear," said Mrs. Barnes. "After an adventure like you are about to have, life never returns to normal. The adventure becomes part of you forever."

9

A GRANDMOTHER'S BLESSING

THREE WEEKS EARLIER—MAY 1924
BURLINGTON, NEW JERSEY

Three weeks prior to Emily's departure, eighty-two-year-old Wilhemina Hanson stepped out of the Burlington taxi and walked to the door of what had once been her own home. No one, least of all the son whom she did not want to know of it, would have suspected the purpose of her morning call.

"Wilhemina . . . good morning!" exclaimed Amelia Hanson when she opened the door and saw her mother-in-law on the porch, holding a book in her hand and wearing her finest dress and hat. "Come in . . . Emily is just home from college. She will love to see you."

The older woman followed her daughter-in-law inside.

"Hello, Grandma," said Emily, walking into the living room. "It is wonderful to see you again." She hugged her grandmother affectionately. "I was planning to come into town to visit you today."

"I'm afraid Miles isn't home," began Amelia as the three generations sat down together.

"I didn't come to see Miles," rejoined the elder Mrs. Hanson. Her tone was emphatic. "I intentionally waited until I knew he would not be home. I do not want him putting in his two cents' worth after hearing what I have to say. I came to see the two of you. So make me a cup of tea, Amelia. We Hanson women must have a serious talk."

Emily and her mother exchanged curious glances. They knew Miles Hanson's mother to be a woman who spoke her mind. But they had never seen her quite like this. Amelia rose.

"Now, Emily," said Mrs. Hanson, "while your mother is fixing us tea, tell me all about college.

You have just completed your third year . . . did you receive all A's again?"

"Almost, Grandma," replied Emily, smiling sheepishly.

"I understand you will be writing a paper next year. What will you write about?"

"I have been studying the birds of the North Atlantic and their migratory patterns, habitats, and the evolutionary implications of weather and locale in intraspecies development."

"They don't promote evolution at your college?" said Mrs. Hanson in alarm.

"No, but in my field of biology it always comes up since evolution is all the rage in the secular academic community. Our professors try to keep us aware of current thought."

"Well, it is far beyond me!" laughed Mrs. Hanson. "But we women of the family are all very proud of you—soon to be a college graduate."

"Thank you, Grandma. What about you? I haven't seen you for months."

"Nothing much changes for one my age. I miss your grandfather, of course. But widowhood is in the nature of things for most women. It is our cross to bear."

A few minutes later, Amelia returned with a tray. As soon as the three were seated again with teacups in their hands, Mrs. Hanson launched into the purpose for her visit.

"I want to know about this trip of yours," she

said, turning to face Emily. "Miles says you might not go."

"I, uh . . ." began Emily, glancing nervously toward her mother. "Daddy thinks it best that I stay in Burlington for the summer."

"Why would he think that? Opportunities like this don't come along every day."

"Miles wants Emily to stay with you for the summer, Wilhemina," said Amelia. "He says that you do not like being alone."

"Pshaw!" exclaimed Mrs. Hanson in an annoyed voice. "What docs he think, that I am so infirm that—?"

Mrs. Hanson paused and thought a moment.

"Actually," she said in a softer voice, "I'm afraid it might be my own fault. I have probably conveyed to Miles that it is lonely with his father gone."

"You must come live with us, Wilhemina," said Amelia gently. "With Emily away at college, there is more room than we know what to do with."

"I appreciate that, Amelia, dear. But I am not quite ready yet. I may be eighty-two, but I can take care of myself. My greatest fear in old age is becoming a burden to you and Miles."

"You are always welcome. We would love to have you."

"You are such a dear, Amelia. But there is time to think of that when the need arises. However, I came here to talk about *you,* Emily," said Mrs.

63

Hanson, turning again to Emily. "Do you know what I did when I was your age?"

"You were a nurse, weren't you?" answered Emily.

"Yes," nodded Mrs. Hanson. "And I was younger than you when I began. I was only eighteen when the Civil War broke out. The moment the reports in the newspapers began coming about the desperate need for nurses, I knew I had to go. It was something I *had* to do."

"*How* did you know that you had to do it?" asked Emily.

"I had always wanted to be a nurse. Had I lived in these modern times when women are doing so many exciting things, I think I would have gone to college with hopes of becoming a doctor. What a thrill it gives me just to think that I *might* have been able to do such a thing. It is too late for me, but it is not too late for you to fulfill *your* dreams."

Emily could not help laughing at her grandmother's enthusiasm. "Thank you, Grandma. Did you tell your parents what you wanted to do?"

"Oh, yes. My father said no."

"What did you do?"

"I wanted to be honoring and respectful of the Scripture about obeying your parents. But I went anyway. I packed a suitcase and told my parents that I was going to the hospital in Philadelphia to ask if they could use my help. I said that I did not want to do it behind their backs, but that I was determined to go."

"What happened?"

"Reluctantly, and silently, my father took me in the buggy to the train station to see me off. As I was leaving he gave me forty dollars, then hugged me and kissed my cheek . . . and that was it—I was off to the war. I saw things no one should ever have to see. I met so many interesting people it would fill ten books."

"I would love to hear every bit of it!" said Emily. "You are amazing, Grandma."

Mrs. Hanson laughed. "I still don't know if I did the right thing," she said. "I was a pretty independent girl. I suppose I have always been too independent for my own good," she added, laughing again. "But my father and I had many a laugh in later years over my impulsivity. When it was over he confessed himself proud of my desire to help people and for the lives I may have helped save."

Mrs. Hanson paused. "This book," she said, holding up the volume in her lap, "is the journal I kept during those years. That was a time of great change and growth in my life. I would not trade those years for anything. You know, I'm sure, Emily, of the Quaker tradition of keeping journals. It is something Quakers do. I want to leave my journal with you between now and the time for your trip. I want you to see what life-changing experiences come to a young woman who ventures into the unknown and seizes opportunities that come."

She handed the book to Emily.

"Thank you, Grandma. It will be a privilege to read it."

"The long and the short of it is this," said Mrs. Hanson. "You *have* to go on this trip that has been offered to you. It is time for you to follow in my footsteps."

She paused and became thoughtful. The room was silent for fifteen or twenty seconds. At length Emily's grandmother continued.

"I know how much Miles loves you," she said. "Your father is just trying to love you in the best way he knows, just as my father did. Fathers are protective of their daughters. It is a sign of their love for us. And God bless them for being good fathers. However, that does not change what we have to do. My opportunity came. Now it is your turn."

PART 3
AUGUST 2006

10

THE COTTAGE

The island of Whales Reef, two miles wide and four miles long, sat across an isthmus of less than two miles that separated it from the so-called mainland. Along with the three larger islands of Shetland, Yell, and Unst, Whales Reef was one of a hundred mostly uninhabited smatterings of rock and land that made up what were known as "the Shetlands," that northernmost archipelago of Great Britain sitting in the North Atlantic some two hundred miles north of Scotland proper. In addition to being the most remote realm of the United Kingdom, the Shetlands were known primarily for their unique species of flora and fauna. The whole world was familiar with the fabled Shetland pony—of which there were dozens of varieties. What was less well known outside the select circle of British naturalist studies were the several hundred bird species indigenous to the Shetlands. Scientifically this was a far more significant fact, with far-reaching evolutionary implications, than was the existence of the miniature species of pony that so captivated the horse-loving world's fancy.

Economically both indigenous birds and

Shetland ponies were dwarfed in importance by the development and breeding during the previous quarter century of Shetlands' own unimproved breed of sheep. Though not so visually unique as the Shetland pony, the Shetland Dunface and related strains produced a wool of short length and fine fiber which rivaled the expensive merinos from New Zealand that had taken the wool trade by storm. Shetland wool now offered a lower-priced alternative. The hardiness of the Dunface had resulted in an explosion of interest in the breed.

Whales Reef in particular was renowned for its prized wool. The island's wool factory had become a thriving concern, producing a great variety of goods and employing anyone on the island who wanted a job. Fishing had once dominated the fiscal outlook of Whales Reef. For the last twenty years, however, wool had driven that economy, and contributed in no small measure to the uniqueness of the "Whales Weave" brand of handcrafted wool products.

"Good morning, Isobel," said Loni as she walked through the Cottage's back door into the kitchen after her morning walk.

"Good morning, miss. I'm just setting out tea and oatcakes and digestives for elevenses. Saxe and Mr. Erskine will be in directly if you would like to join us."

"Thank you," replied Loni. "I would love a cup of tea."

As they were speaking, the housekeeper's brother could be heard descending the back stairway.

Loni and Saxe sat down at the table in the breakfast room while Isobel set out cups and saucers, milk, silverware, plates of oatcakes and biscuits along with butter and various jams. They were joined a few minutes later by Dougal Erskine, the estate's gamekeeper, who left his rubber boots outside the door and came inside in thickly wool-clad stocking feet. To say that the housekeeper joined the other three for tea would be misrepresenting the facts. She scarcely occupied her chair for more than sixty seconds before jumping up to replenish someone's cup or add more biscuits to the platter or refill the teapot or water cooker in the kitchen.

"We are all doing very nicely, Isobel," said Loni, "if you would like to relax and enjoy your tea."

"Telling my sister to relax will be speaking a foreign language to the lass, miss," said the elder of the two Mathesons. "She's not happy unless she is busy."

"Is that true, Isobel?"

"Aye, miss. Idle hands as they say."

"Well as I told you before, things are different in the United States. We aren't used to people doing for us what we can do ourselves. I know you have plenty to keep you busy, Dougal, with the animals and grounds. But, Isobel and Saxe, please do not feel that you have to wait on me."

"Oh, we have much to do, miss," said Isobel.

"I realize that. Still—"

"I have my chickens, miss."

"Of course."

"And the laundry and cleaning."

"I understand."

"And the windows and floors and silver to polish and glassware and cabinets to dust."

"You are very diligent and I appreciate that. Yet it would warm my heart to see you in the Great Room reading some of the books on the shelves."

"Oh, miss, I couldn't do that," exclaimed Isobel.

"You and I have had tea there together."

"That was a special occasion, miss. It wouldn't be fitting to be there alone."

"Why is that?"

"It just would not . . . it wouldn't be *right,* miss."

"Since it is my house and they are my chairs and books, I would *like* you to use the Great Room and read the books. And while we're on the subject, do you suppose the three of you could get used to calling me *Alonnah* rather than *Miss*."

They stared back as if she were speaking in Greek.

"It is a simple request," laughed Loni.

"We'll try, miss," said Saxe softly while Isobel went to see about something in the kitchen.

"Hae ye heard fae yer friend Maddy?" asked Dougal.

"She and I had a Skype conversation yesterday morning," replied Loni.

"What's that, miss?"

"Skype?"

"Aye."

"It's like a video telephone call."

The two men stared back with blank expressions.

"Our computers have little cameras inside them. When we telephone from our computers, we can see each other."

"Weel, 'tis a mystery to me," said Dougal. "But gie her my regards."

"I will, Dougal. You and she certainly hit it off."

"The lass said I put her in mind o' her grandfather. She was jist like a lassie wi' the lammies an' the wee ponies."

A few minutes later, Loni left the breakfast room and walked up the wide semicircular staircase from the expansive entryway to her favorite room in the house, the study of her great-great-grandfather Ernest, the man known as the Auld Tulloch. The room had come to symbolize the heart and soul not only of the Cottage but of the spiritual life of the island.

The more she read of Ernest's letters and pondered his treasured books and gazed upon photographs of his smiling face, the more curious she became about his sojourn as a farmhand in turn-of-the-century Prussia, and of his exploits during the second of the two great wars in the Allied cause.

After an hour in the study, Loni returned downstairs, left the Cottage, and struck overland across the moor toward the village of Whales Reef. The springy turf beneath her feet provided a grassy blanket overspreading the vast riches of peat beneath it. All around as she walked, the island's treeless moors were vibrant with heather's blossoms of purple and white.

Loni had not yet spent a winter in the Shetlands, nor was she sure she wanted to. So far north, the months of December and January were long, dark, and cold. To stay warm, the sheep for which the island was known wore thick coverings of prized wool that would in future years colorfully adorn men and women the world over as sweaters, mittens, scarves, and caps. Before then, however, their coats served the more utilitarian purpose of keeping their owners thickly blanketed through the biting winter months.

The humans of these regions had a more difficult time of it. Yet they too survived. An ingenious protection against the cold had been discovered millennia earlier by the men of antiquity. Endowed by their Creator with no natural protection against the elements, and with the thinnest skin in the animal kingdom, they found the potential of warmth buried beneath their very feet. If the humans of the islands could not grow insulating coats, they could excavate from the earth a miraculous subterranean substance capable of producing warmth through fire.

As autumn gave way to winter, the nuanced colors of the tiny heather blooms on Shetland's moors slowly faded, returning the subtle blossoms of majestic purple to the bowels of the earth. In its own yearly death, season after season dying upon itself, layer adding to compacted layer, century after century, millennium after millennium, the decayed heather was invisibly transformed beneath the surface, then excavated, cut, dried, and stored to keep the fires of the Shetlands burning hot and bright. If four walls and a roof could be built to surround and enclose their fires, the human population could thus be kept alive through the harsh conditions that came when the sun went south for the winter.

Indeed, the Shetlands were the repository of more peat per square inch than anywhere in Scotland. Peat warmed not only their homes, it fueled the fires of island hearts. Behind every cottage on Whales Reef stood a winter's store of "peats." These black brick-shaped chunks of living earth would keep their fires blazing until a new supply was harvested for the next year. Shetlanders would have little use for an American *wood*shed. But a supply of peats protected from the rain, whether in a shed or stacked beneath an overhanging projection of barn roof, was as vital to survival as a milk-producing cow.

Loni recalled her first morning in the Cottage. She had been so proud to make a fire with the wood David had provided. At the time she had no clue what the odd-looking dark bricks beside the grate even were. Dear old Sandy Innes had shown her how to build a peat fire and retain the life of its hot glowing embers through the night. David later told her of the mystery of the heather, a few tiny blossoms of which now encircled one of her fingers, and the inseparable intertwining mystery of heather and peat which gave a regal tradition to the highlands of his Scottish ancestors.

She had since grown to love the glowing oranges and reds of a peat fire no less than the spectacular display of the heather beneath her feet which produced it, and to relish in the aroma of the white smoke trailing up from the chimneys of nearly every cottage in the village she now approached on this chilly August morning.

11

The Chief

David Tulloch's first order of business when he arose, on most mornings about six o'clock, was to kneel in front of his fireplace, poke about among the bed of embers carefully blanketed the night before so that the insulated core would retain its heat. Exposing them, he leaned over the hearth and gently blew until tiny fingers of orange and red flickered brightly to life. From his store of dry, brown, earthy bricks dug, cut, and dried from the island's moors, he now added a fresh supply to the glowing nest.

After a little more coaxing, the peats were able to take care of themselves. David rose from his knees and went to the kitchen. There his ancestors would have repeated the same ritual to stoke their kitchen fires back to life. David merely flipped on the electric kettle on his counter to boil water for his morning tea.

Every house and cottage on the island, from the humblest to the two Tulloch homes, had been outfitted with radiators and oil burners. The twenty-first century had made inroads everywhere, aided in this particular region by North Sea oil and government subsidies. Even on the remote

Shetlands, nearly every dwelling now boasted all the modern conveniences—running water, indoor plumbing, electricity, telephones, and oil heat. Internet service, however, remained sketchy and incomplete.

In spite of such conveniences, most Shetlanders were traditionalists. Many of the radiators sat cold most of the year while smoke from peat fires rose daily from their chimneys. A hot peat fire provided more than mere warmth. In its subtle way, its heat also conveyed the message, *Fire still burns at the heart of the universe to warm the souls of men.* Not that most islanders thought about God these days any more than people anywhere. Their affinity for the glow and aroma of a peat fire was rooted more in the tradition of their ancestors than the Father whom the Auld Tulloch's favorite Victorian Scotsman called "the fire core of the universe." Yet truth is truth, to whatever depth men and women are capable of perceiving it. Thus the fire of peat signified many things to many people.

David's daily routine consisted of a cup of tea early, followed by his customary walk over the island. It was now about nine as he walked back into the Auld Hoose, set his *Times* from the village down on his kitchen table, and prepared a fresh cup of tea. A few minutes later he walked into the great room where the warm fireplace full of glowing peats greeted him. With tea in hand, he eased into the familiar soft brown reading chair, much of its leather cracked from the years of use.

David sipped from his cup, then picked up one of several books from the reading table beside him. He gazed contentedly around the room. His eyes drifted leisurely up and down the wall adjacent to the stone fireplace. It was housed from floor to ceiling with books. He was usually reading several titles at once—devotional, theology, or history comprising his usual fare. He had picked up one of the Scotsman's novels the night before. He had read the volume several times and knew it well. It was, in David's opinion, one of the best from the pen of Huntly's favorite son. Though in truth the Shetlands represented the *lowest*-lying region in Scotland, its remote islands had much in common in essential character with the Highlands where the small Whales Reef Tulloch clan had originated. When he immersed himself in one of the author's Highland tales, David invariably felt that he was reading of his own ancestral homeland. With relish and anticipation, he opened the old treasured volume and read:

A rough, wild glen it was, to which, far back in times unknown to its annals, the family had given its name. It lay in the debatable land between highlands and lowlands; most of its inhabitants spoke both Scotch and Gaelic; and there was often to be found in them a notable mingling of the chief characteristics of the widely differing Celt and Teuton. It was a solitary, thinly peopled region, mostly of bare hills, and partially cultivated glens, each with its small stream, on the banks of which grew here and there a silver birch, a mountain ash, or an alder tree, but with nothing capable of giving much shade or shelter. From many a spot you might look in all directions and not see a sign of human or any other habitation. Even then however, you might, to be sure, most likely smell the perfume—to some nostrils it is nothing less than perfume—of a peat fire, although you might be long in finding out whence it came; for the houses, if indeed the dwellings could be called houses, were often so hard to be distinguished from the ground on which they were built, that except the smoke of fresh peats were coming pretty freely from the wide-mouthed chimney, it required an experienced eye to discover the human nest. . . .[1]

---

1. From chap. 1 of George MacDonald's *Castle Warlock*.

12

THE MILL

Loni made her way through town, greeting villagers as she went, popping in for a word or two at each shop, stopping in at the Whales Fin Inn to exchange a few words with the men around the tables and ask about the weather and fishing, before disappearing behind the counter into the kitchen for a visit with Audney and Evanna Kerr. Leaving the inn, she turned off the main road and continued into the wide driveway up to the Whales Reef Woolen Mill, one of the assets she had inherited from the late Macgregor Tulloch's estate.

As a young teen working in her grandfather's furniture showroom, she had dreamed of a future in the business world. She had never anticipated owning a thriving manufacturing and wholesale business specializing in the woolen products known as Whales Weave.

Maddy called her a tycoon. The idea of such a label made her laugh. Yet she was determined to do her best for the mill's employees.

Loni walked through the large door and inside the largest structure on the island. The busy sight of looms and spinning wheels and knitting circles did not fail once more to delight her.

Seeing their new laird, the women throughout the room ceased their activities and broke out in smiles as they came forward to greet her. As it gradually quieted, their gazes followed one of their number now threading her way through the group. "Let me see yer ring, lassie," said Odara Innes.

"From what I have been told, you helped David make it," said Loni, holding out her right hand.

"Oh, aye—but seein' it on yer finger's a different thing."

Every woman in the mill clustered about, most not standing as high as Loni's shoulders, admiring the exquisite ring made of interwoven heather and delicate strands of white sheep's wool. The unique ring was the talk of the female element of the small community—each had her own theory of what it might signify.

Soon the ladies returned to their stations. Loni made her way through the room, examining every pattern emerging under their skilled hands, and the threads being spun and the tartans being woven, asking questions and listening to animated explanations. Though the Shetlandic accent was still a struggle for her, she understood enough to nod and exclaim in the right places. For their part, the ladies tried to speak "English" to their new laird, though their efforts succeeded only in ameliorating perhaps ten percent of the incomprehensibility of their native dialect.

Looking at her watch, Loni realized she needed to get back to the Cottage. She and David would be leaving for Lerwick in less than an hour.

She said her good-byes and walked toward the door. Behind her the buzz of activity resumed.

Loni turned one last time and glanced back. The hum of spinning wheels made music in her brain. Gradually out of the mists of the past came faint echoes of an orchestra and a ballroom filled with guests . . . couples dancing . . . waiters scurrying between tables . . . festive merrymakers enjoying an exotic adventure to the northernmost reaches of the British Isles.

It all came to life in her mind's eye just as she had read of it in the old journal when this very building had been a luxury hotel.

With reminders of her great-grandmother's first hours in Whales Reef, Loni closed the door behind her and slowly walked away. It was hard to imagine this as the same place, so changed now after all these years, where the one-time young heir to the Tulloch estate had spent so many of his leisure hours.

PART 4

A Legacy Begins—
The Meeting
1924

13

DANGEROUS WILES

WHALES REEF
SHETLAND ISLANDS, SCOTLAND

London journalist Robert Glendenning gazed about the ballroom of the Whales Reef Hotel, wondering what could possibly have brought this many Englanders so far into the wilds of the north.

Glendenning was accustomed to exotic locales. It was his business to follow "the story" wherever it led. But as he stood at the bar observing it all, he shook his head at the delicious inconsonance of a luxury hotel populated by England's privileged classes on such an out-of-the-way island.

The faint odor of fish still lingered in his nostrils, mingled with the aroma of the sturdy Scottish peasantry after laboring all day to pull their cash crop from the ocean. Less than an hour before, he had been standing in a frigid summer twilight on the quay of this island's harbor, chatting with a handful of fishermen. Most had just docked and were on their way home for a supper of beer, potatoes, and fish from their day's catch.

The musicians in the corner opposite him broke into a spirited Charleston. Quickly the dance floor filled with high-stepping heel-kickers. By this time tomorrow, they would be onboard the *Peregrin* on their return voyage to England.

The journalist turned to see a youth striding toward him.

"Mr. Glendenning," said the newcomer with a smile.

The Londoner eyed the young man with a curiously observant expression. "You seem to know me," he said, "but I confess I have no idea who you might be. I detect the accent of a Shetlander. Yet your brogue has clearly been softened with influences . . . hmm, would I be wrong in suggesting Oxford?" he added.

The young man laughed. "Very good! That is exactly right. I recently finished my fourth term. I am Brogan Tulloch. My father is laird of Whales Reef."

"I am pleased to meet you," said Glendenning, offering his hand. Several minutes of small talk followed.

"You, then, I take it, will one day be laird yourself," said the journalist.

"And chief," young Tulloch added with a wry smile. "As important as it sounds, however, we are not technically of the aristocracy. We of our tiny clan are out of step with the rest of the Shetlands. But indeed, one day the two dubious and anachronistic titles will fall on my head!"

"Your tone contains the hint of mystery between the lines. Perhaps I will find a story there."

"I shall await your findings with interest," laughed the young heir. "Just so long as you leave me out of them."

"You've no inclination to be the subject of my reportage?"

"I doubt you will find anything mysterious to report. I am neither more nor less than what you see. But what are *you* doing here, Mr. Glendenning? Or are you a simple bird-watcher who came to the Shetlands as an amateur naturalist?"

Now it was Glendenning's turn to laugh at the image. "No, I'm a thoroughgoing city man," he answered. "Not that I don't enjoy the occasional stroll along the sea. And I can appreciate a beautiful sunset as much as the next man. However, my main interest is people. What will be my story when all this is over, I yet have no idea. The mystery has yet to reveal itself."

"There you go hunting for mysteries again," laughed Tulloch.

"You don't find the people of your island intriguing?"

"Not as much as the Hotel's guests."

"I'm sure it is a novelty to your visitors to have a future laird and chief liven up the party. Do you ever wear a kilt?"

"Wouldn't be caught dead in one!" laughed Brogan.

"And with the young ladies who make up such tours as these, does romance ever result?" asked Glendenning.

"Let me just say," answered Brogan with a smile, "that I never miss the first and last evening of every tour. Alas, by tomorrow the Hotel will be empty, the island quiet, and I will be left to my own devices until the next group arrives."

"How long will that be?"

"A few days, a week at the most."

The journalist and son of the laird were interrupted by a silky feminine voice.

"Not dancing this evening, young Brogan?" purred a woman at Tulloch's elbow.

He turned. "Ah, Priscilla—I did not expect to see you here."

"It is *Lady* Priscilla to you," rejoined the woman with a flirtatious twinkle in her eye.

The two men found themselves gazing upon a devilishly beautiful woman a few years older than Brogan himself. The two had known each other for years. The former Priscilla Morrison had grown up in Whales Reef, not exactly as the most common of commoners, but a commoner nonetheless. Her social standing as daughter of the postman was but one or two rungs up the ladder from that of the fisher girls whom she despised. She had always determined to "marry up," and had used her good looks to begin surveying her marital options at a young age. She now had everything she had dreamed of—money and the dubious title of *Lady,* which she assumed for herself, though her older husband, who did wear a minor honorary knighthood, was not technically a lord.

Contentment, however, had not accompanied her rise in the social scale. She found herself plagued by silent regrets that she had squandered the best years of her young womanhood too hastily. Handsome and eligible squires were suddenly popping up around the Shetlands everywhere. Even the vague thrill of being addressed as *Lady Priscilla* had worn off and could not keep the wistful regrets at bay.

Yet the stigma of divorcing poor old Sir Horace, as he would surely be viewed if she dared such a thing, would ruin her reputation throughout the islands. She must make the best of it. This she did by keeping an active social calendar, most of it without the encumbrance of a doddering husband at her side. If tongues occasionally wagged at the coy smiles she flashed toward young men, who were still toddling around in diapers when her twelve-year-old molars were coming in, most such gossip never came within her hearing anyway.

"Aren't you going to introduce me, Brogan?" said Sir Horace's young wife, flashing a seductive look in the direction of the journalist.

"Of course. Glendenning, meet *Lady* Priscilla

Hadle.—Priscilla, may I present Mr. Robert Glendenning from London."

"Charmed, my lady," said Glendenning.

"Thank you," replied Priscilla. "You are a long way from home, Mr. Glendenning."

"One of the hazards, or perquisites, however you see it, of the journalistic life."

"A journalist—how fascinating. I would love to hear all about it. Perhaps you and I can get together later."

She began to move away. "Take care you don't drink too much, Brogan," she added with another bewitching smile.

Glendenning followed her with his eyes. "An extremely beautiful woman," he remarked.

"A viper," rejoined Brogan. "Watch yourself is my advice."

"Married?"

Brogan nodded. "She married a wealthy old landowner from mainland Shetland."

"Married or not, you can take it from me—that is a woman who is *looking,* if you know what I mean. The gleam in the eye is unmistakable. And unless I miss my guess, she is looking at *you.*"

Brogan laughed. "My father said the same thing when I was barely sixteen. I thought little of it at the time. He was concerned that she was trying to worm her way into our family and get her hands on his inheritance."

"Was she?"

"Who knows? She was a vixen all right.
father warned me about her, and she hated r
for it. But she's married now. That danger h
passed."

"If you say so," rejoined Glendenning. "So
when does the next tour arrive?"

"I can't recall exactly. If memory serves, there
will be some Americans in the next group. That
always proves interesting. Whatever they say
about us Scots, our accent is nothing so grating
as *American* English. But friendly chaps, and
invariably good for a laugh or two."

"What do you do all winter?" asked Glendenning. "I assume there are no tours. Does the
Hotel shut down?"

"It's not quite so bad as that. We have an
occasional group during the winter months—
the most adventurous types. But it does become
deathly quiet, desolate, and cold—a positively
dreary place."

Again a woman's voice interrupted their
conversation.

"You weren't with us today, Mr. Glendenning,"
it said. They turned to see a stout white-haired
woman, pearls hanging from ears and neck,
approaching. She was a walking mass of lace and
crepe displaying most of the colors of the rainbow,
her flowing dress, cut lower than her size and age
was well able to justify, presented the image of a
galleon coming toward them under full sail. "We

a whale's spout in the distance! It was so
iting."

"I'm afraid I wasn't up to it," said Glendenning.
But may I present Mr. Brogan Tulloch, the future
chief of Whales Reef."

"Charmed, dear lady," said Tulloch.

"It is a thrill to meet you, Mr. Tulloch," she said.
"Your island is so deliciously forlorn. You must
love living here."

"So one would think," rejoined Tulloch. "Forlorn it is indeed."

"Will your father be in attendance this evening?
I so hoped to meet an actual Scottish chief."

"That is unlikely. I'm afraid he doesn't go in
much for socializing. I fear you will have to
satisfy yourself with the heir apparent."

14

LAIRD AND CHIEF

A greater contrast could scarcely be imagined
between the glamorous opulence inside the
Whales Reef Hotel and the village of stone
houses and thatched roofs down the hill, whose
island inhabitants earned a hard-won living from
the sea. The narrow streets were pervaded with
pungent reminders of fish, faint wafts of salt
spray, and a whiff now and then of manure from

the animal byres attached to most of the cottag[...]
Overspreading all, the ubiquitous aroma of pe[...]
smoke filtered up from dozens of chimneys int[...]
the evening mist.

On a rise above the village, in what the Shetlanders call the Summer Dim, walked a man whose very gait seemed vaguely to suggest that he was out of step with his times. As his walking stick probed the soft peat-layered earth beneath his feet, he thought again how he loved his land, this island, and its people.

He was laird and chief of the small village clan who called this island home. Yet the glitter of the modern hotel below him was an anathema to everything held dear by the eldest offspring of the great William Tulloch. The son had done his best to honor the memory of his father. But the two men possessed far different values and bore diametrically opposite outlooks on life.

Ernest Tulloch, son of the Great Tulloch, as the late William was now called, made his way along the treeless ridge that overlooked the village. The spire of the church rose into the evening sky to his left. The great hotel—brainchild of his father, tourist destination for the southland's would-be naturalists, and watering hole of his eldest son—sat below him a little farther on. Beyond both, growing inland and up from the harbor as if it were a living organism, spread the irregular streets, dirt lanes, and alleyways of Whales Reef. In spite of

fact that the longest day of the year was only
ew weeks away, a nightly chill and biting wind
ersisted regardless of the advancing season.

He bundled up and went out most evenings
after supper before returning inside to spend a
few moments at his son Leith's bedside. There
he quietly talked over the day, then tucked the
rapidly growing boy in with a hug and a few
words of prayer. The pleasant nightly exchange
filled his father's heart with love for his youngest
son. Yet in his reflective moments he also found
himself wondering how much lasting benefit
it would produce in his son's heart toward God
or himself. Twenty years from now, would the
nightly tenderness between father and son be long
forgotten to the latter? Would his son still consider
him his friend and ally and protector? Would he
still be all that the word *father* meant to his son
once that son entered manhood?

He had tucked in Brogan and Wallace for
years in the same way, softly kissed their rosy
cheeks, and listened to their precious prayers of
childhood. Where was his fatherhood in their
lives now? There was Delynn to consider as
well. It was different with a daughter. It was too
soon to know in which directions the winds of
the future would blow in her life. The delicacy
and softhearted affections and special bond with
their fathers dwelt a little longer in the young
lives of daughters before taking flight into the

great beyond of adulthood. Sons, how
were anxious to be *men,* with all the rights
privileges thereof, and were quick to lose sight
the fact that to be a true man required learning t
be a true son.

After his final visit each evening to Leith's
bedside, he sat down with Sally before the fire
to enjoy the remainder of their evening together
in the company of books and quiet conversation.
Occasionally Wallace and Delynn joined them.
They were old enough, however, usually to prefer
the solitude of their own quarters or activities with
friends to the company of father and stepmother.

Sounds of gaiety rising from the Hotel intruded
again upon Ernest's thoughts. The knowledge that
his own son was at this moment probably more
than halfway toward intoxication filled him with
emotions too painful to contemplate.

Forty-nine-year-old Ernest Charles Tulloch was
an enigma to everyone who knew him other than
his wife, perhaps most of all to his two eldest
sons. The youngest, their soon-to-be fifteen-year-
old half brother Leith, had not yet arrived at an
age to begin wondering who and what his father
was, and what fatherhood and sonship meant. He
was an enigma because the currents that flowed
deepest in him were hidden from view. They
were currents of spiritual personhood not easily
understood by the most discerning of observers,
rarely plumbed even by friends, certainly not by

97

l acquaintances, and perhaps least of all by a
n's offspring. In that curious heartache that in
many ways defined the human species, the very
ones who should know a man best often knew him
least.

Ernest, however, was a man at peace with
himself, with the world, and with his God.

Instinctively his steps brought him to the church.
The rectangular stone edifice with its high steeple
pointing to the heavens stood above the village as
a sentinel of stability, tradition, and history. Two
more fitting symbols of the times could hardly be
imagined, thought Tulloch, than this church—now
cold, empty, and silent—and the Hotel, brightly
lit with music and dancing, which symbolized the
rollicking, decadent worldliness of this decade
they called the Roaring Twenties.

With reverent step he walked across the churchyard, then through the black iron gate, freshly
painted a week before, and began to meander
into the cemetery behind the church. Some of
the timeworn markers were so old that the names
and dates had been completely obliterated by the
northern winds and rains. Even unreadable, the
headstones were nonetheless venerable to him.
Those who lay below were members of that great
cloud of witnesses now looking down on those
who came after them.

Ernest was a man who valued the past, valued
the heritage of his forebears both temporal and

spiritual. He knew that much of what he was a man had been nurtured into him by the influenc of others. The histories of their lives had give him the opportunity to choose wisely the course of his own character. Thus, even nameless, these saints of the past were precious to him, and he honored their memory.

After walking thoughtfully through the cemetery, he closed the gate behind him and made his way across the moor above the village to an expansive manor house, home to the laird and chief.

The secret errand also on his mind—which would bring him outside again hours later after his household, the entire village, and presumably even the merrymakers in the Hotel were sound asleep in their beds—would have to wait until there was no possibility of his being seen by another soul.

The mysterious summons had arrived two weeks earlier from a man he had not seen in twenty years. He had, however, followed the rise of his onetime friend's career in Britain's political and military circles with keen interest. Whereas few outside the Shetlands had ever heard of Ernest Tulloch, his friend's name was known throughout the country.

His former friend was not a man whose summons one took lightly.

15

OLD FRIENDS IN NEW TIMES

The echo of the clock on the downstairs mantel was dying away after chiming half past two o'clock. Ernest Tulloch slipped from beside his sleeping wife, tiptoed out of the room to don the pile of clothing he'd prepared earlier, and proceeded down the wide staircase.

He crept from the house. The island was deathly still. With stealthy step he inched across the entryway, careful not to let his feet crunch on the gravel, then along the drive and to the road. There he quickened his step and hurried toward the village.

One never knew about fishermen. They might be about their business at any hour, day or night, if they thought the fish were running. However, he had made a few casual inquiries earlier. From the sound of it, no one would be out at this hour. He left the road some two hundred yards before reaching the outskirts of the village, crossed a dune of sand, then descended a rocky slope to the seashore. He turned to his right and hastened toward the small harbor.

Every boat sat moored securely in the protected

waters. He walked across the cement quay to the end of its outermost barricade. A small dinghy awaited him. He climbed down to it. The moment he was aboard, the man inside shoved them away from the wall with an oar.

For perhaps five minutes he rowed hard against the incoming waves. When he judged it safe he set the oars aside. Two quick yanks of the starter rope fired a small engine to life.

As they sped away, Ernest saw the silhouette of the yacht anchored offshore. When it had arrived off Whales Reef, he had no idea.

No words were spoken during the brief voyage. Twenty minutes later, the passenger climbed a rope ladder and aboard the yacht. He was led across the deck, down two flights of stairs, and finally to a closed door. He turned toward his guide, who merely nodded. Tulloch opened the door and entered.

"Hello, Ernie," said a gravelly voice from inside. Slowly he closed the door behind him.

Tulloch smiled. "Even if I didn't know your voice," he said, "the aroma of your cigar would betray you from thirty yards. Haven't given them up yet, I see."

"I enjoy them too much."

"It is good to see you again, Winston," said Tulloch as the two longtime friends shook hands.

"And you, Ernie. Sit down."

The two men chatted for several minutes, catching up briefly on the twenty years that had passed since their youthful affiliation.

"A drink, Ernie?" asked his host. "Cognac . . . tea, perhaps?"

"Nothing, thank you. I hope to get a few more hours' sleep later. I know the light out belies the fact, but this is the middle of the night."

"I'd forgotten what it is like in the Shetlands at this season."

"The best time of year to be a Shetlander. But obviously you didn't come here for the midnight sun," said Tulloch. "So what brings the Chancellor of the Exchequer to these remote waters? Have I overdrawn my account?"

Churchill laughed. "It's the country's chequebook I have to watch," he said, "not yours."

"If I didn't know better, I would think you had been reappointed to the First Lord of the Admiralty."

"I am afraid not," said Churchill. "My stock is still low in Whitehall."

"Yes, I was sorry about your defeat for Commons two years ago."

"Ah, well—things have a way of working out. I doubt Parliament has heard its last from me."

"Are you thinking of another run?"

"Perhaps one day. Not immediately. It may be that I can do more good in the Cabinet than as a back-bencher, or even as a front-bencher.

"Is that the capacity in which you requested to see me?" asked the Shetlander.

"Not technically. I am here as a patriot, as one who loves this nation. I come to you, as I said, because I know I can trust you."

Churchill paused and drew in a deep draught from his cigar while gathering his thoughts.

16

MID-ATLANTIC

While Ernest Tulloch listened to his old friend Winston Churchill lay the groundwork for the secretive mission he hoped the Shetlander would accept, far to the west and four hours earlier than the Greenwich clock, the guests of an ocean liner were getting ready for after-dinner dancing. It was their second evening aboard the *Viking Queen* bound from New York to Glasgow. In their shared stateroom, Harriett Barnes had been doing her best to persuade young Emily Hanson to join her downstairs.

"The dancing is probably already under way," she was saying.

"Mrs. Barnes," laughed Emily, "I don't know how to tell you this—but I've never danced with a boy in my life. Wilmington is a *Quaker* college, emember. We don't dance, though my mother did teach me the waltz."

"But what could be a more perfect setting for romance than this?"

Emily laughed again. "Romance is the last thing on my mind," she said. "I cannot imagine ever marrying. But if I should meet someone, I hope it will be a young man who is interested in me as a person, not someone I met on a dance floor."

Mrs. Barnes gazed across the room at her young companion.

"Well," she added with a smile, "I will enjoy myself even without you. It might be different had I not discovered Kathryn among the guests," she went on. "She and I have known one another for years. We will get along famously together, so you are excused. Just so long as you grace me with your company at meals and for the occasional promenade about the deck."

"I promise."

Mrs. Barnes walked from the stateroom, leaving Emily alone. An hour later she closed her journal and set her pen aside. Again she was reminded of her grandmother's words about journaling, and that she was not only following in the footsteps of George Fox and John Woolman, but also of Quaker women like her own grandmother and Hannah Whitall Smith. She took out the copy of Mrs. Smith's autobiography, signed to her mother.

Emily opened the famous journal, read by so

many thousands around the world, especially
since Mrs. Smith's death thirteen years ago. She
began to read again the familiar words that, except
for dates and marriage and a few details, Emily
could almost have written about herself.

> My parents were strict Quakers, and until
> my marriage at nineteen, I knew nothing
> of any other religion. I had an absolutely
> happy childhood and girlhood . . . My
> diary, kept from the time I was sixteen
> years old, shows that I thought so then.

What would she say of her life, Emily wondered,
looking back on her own life? *Would* she marry?
What would the next fifty years bring in her life?
And if her mother and grandmother were right,
what adventure awaited her on the other side of
this great ocean called the Atlantic?

Again her attention was drawn to the words in
front of her.

> Next to the influence of my parents upon
> my young life, *Emily continued,* was the
> influence of the religious Society of which
> I was a birthright member. I do not think
> it would be possible for me to express in
> words how strong and all pervading this
> influence was. Every word and thought
> and action of our lives was steeped in

Quakerism . . . Daily I thank God that it was such a righteous and ennobling influence.

But . . . the Quakerism of my day did not achieve its influence by much outward teaching. One of its most profound beliefs was in regard to the direct inward teaching of the Holy Spirit to each individual soul . . . The Quakers accepted as literally true the declarations of the Apostle John that there is a "true Light which lighteth every man that cometh into the world"; and their fundamental teaching was that this "Light," if faithfully looked for and obeyed, would lead every man into all truth . . . They taught us to listen for and obey the voice of God in our souls . . .

When the Bible was read to us . . . especially on "First Day" afternoons, very little explanation was ever attempted but instead a few moments of profound silence were always observed at the close of the reading, in order that the "Inward Light" might, if it should be the Divine Will, reveal to us the meaning of what had been read . . . Strong was this feeling among Quakers . . . Our teaching was to come to us, not from the lips of human teachers, but from the inward voice of the Divine Teacher Himself . . . Their preaching therefore was mostly composed of exhortations to listen for this "inward voice," and to obey it.[2]

Mrs. Smith's words could have been written about her own upbringing, thought Emily.

She set aside the book and picked up her journal again, though her thoughts remained pensive. She was not in the mood to write more this evening.

Why did Quakers keep journals, Emily wondered. If you were famous, they were published and people read them. But why did ordinary people keep journals if nobody ever read them but themselves? Who would ever read the words of her journal that she had begun two days ago?

She knew what her grandmother would say— she was writing it for *herself*. Her thoughts and feelings and experiences were no less priceless that no one might ever know of them.

They had eternal value because they were *her* thoughts and feelings and experiences.

---

2. Both quotes are from Hannah Whitall Smith's spiritual autobiography *The Unselfishness of God and How I Discovered It*, 1903, chapters 1 and 2.

17

THE MISSION

On the yacht anchored a mile offshore from Whales Reef, the reunion between the two friends of the Boer War had turned serious.

"What it boils down to," said Churchill at length, "is that grave dangers are afoot, both on the Continent and at home. I need a man I can trust implicitly."

"Why me, Winston? I must say, this cloak-and-dagger business is a bit much for a country laird like me. I have never been involved in politics."

"Because, *Captain* Tulloch, if I may use the name by which I first knew you, I do know I can trust you. I once trusted you with my very life. I would have to wait to find out whether such a level of trust was merited in another man. I already know that about you."

Another pause followed.

"These are perilous times," Churchill began again. "They are more perilous than most in Britain or the United States have any idea. Our booming economies belie undercurrents of discontent, even a sense of grievance and dormant anger in other parts of the world."

"I take it you are referring to the Continent—Germany in particular?"

"Perhaps," replied Churchill. "There are some who view Germany with concern. Frankly, my worries are focused farther east."

"Russia?"

Churchill nodded. "Versailles may have brought an end to the war, but it solved little. The pride of the German people was sorely aggrieved. And if there is one thing we can be sure of—the Germans are a proud people . . . dangerously so. Old animosities die hard. We only succeeded in making them hate us and the French more than ever. I have little doubt that a day will come when Germany's leaders will seek to exact revenge for the humiliation of that treaty. For now, however, Germany has been put in its place. It could not pose a threat if it wanted to. The Bolsheviks, however, with their revolutionary expansionism represent a more serious threat. They are a warlike and conquering people. I do not think they will rest until they have overrun all of Europe."

"Do you see such a thing as imminent?" asked Tulloch.

"Probably not. Their revolution is less than a decade old. It takes time to fill masses with propaganda, to fire industry, to raise armies. But mark my words, by the mid-thirties, 1940 at the latest, the tramp of Russian boots will echo from the east, and all of Europe will tremble."

He rolled what was left of a cigar around in his mouth. Exhaling, he filled the air around his head with smoke, then grabbed the stump from between his teeth and continued.

"Good times have a strange effect on nations," he said. "Prosperity breeds a liberal tolerance that is blind to realities. I do not mean liberalism in its strictly political sense, but socially. Traditional values and norms are cast aside. A spirit is growing in Britain today that is an unseen cancer eating away at our foundations— tolerance for anything and everything. And it has a political component as well. We see tolerance in the government toward the Moslems, tolerance toward these warmongering Bolsheviks, and far too much misplaced sympathy for our recent enemy Germany. My fear is, when the day comes and Russia marches west, or should Germany rise out of the ashes of its defeat, or even should the ghost of Mohammed rise from his grave in a new Islamic caliphate, that there will be much sympathy for their causes in this country. The old Ottoman Empire may not be as dead as people think. God forbid that those three races ever join forces. Western civilization would be doomed. Even now such sympathies are gaining ground. There are moles and spies everywhere. We uncovered many of them in the war. But we have no idea how many may still be among us."

Again Churchill paused and had a go at what remained of his cigar.

"I still fail to see what all this has to do with me," said Tulloch.

"I know that you will not be swept into the tolerance of the times," answered Churchill. "You have a sound head, clear focus, and keen insight. I came to you because I want you to go to the Continent for me—unofficially, of course."

"What—why . . . to do what?"

"To report back to me your sense of the mood of the country, of the German people, of its leaders, and Poland . . . Russia if you could get there."

"But I'm no politician."

"I don't want a politician. I want *you,* Ernie. I want your insight."

"There must be dozens of people more qualified for such an assignment."

"Not for what I need. You, I believe, spent time in Germany as a young man—do you still have contacts there?"

"Yes, some close friendships."

Churchill paused and stared intently into Ernest Tulloch's eyes. "You may not know it, Ernie," he said, "but back in our army days, you were seen as something of a mystic."

Tulloch laughed. "I have no idea what you're talking about!"

"You were quiet. You kept to yourself. You didn't go out drinking. I never saw you look at a woman. Yet you possessed something the men admired—a spiritual grounding, if that is the right word. I never heard you talk about things of faith. But we all knew that deep inside you were a spiritual man. You saw *into* things. You were able to probe people and situations like no one I've ever known. You were a man of few words. But when you spoke, your words counted. I always valued what you had to say."

"You are more flattering than I deserve, Winston."

"You know that flattery is not my style," rejoined Churchill. "I speak the truth. And now I need you to suss out these Nazis and the other splinter groups in Germany. Are they connected in any way with the Bolsheviks or Moslems, or likely to try anything such as what happened in Russia? Are my fears of a Russian military build-up well founded? I want to know what *you* think is in store on the Continent. I don't want diplomatic double-talk. I need to know what your gut says. You might sense what I'm looking for simply by walking the streets. You have instincts. What is the mind-set? Is the mood fertile for revolution? Is some new German Bismarck on the horizon? What do the Germans think of the Bolsheviks? Will Communism sweep west and bring Germany into its revolution? These are the questions that may determine Britain's future."

"What do you have in mind?"

"Would it raise suspicions for you to visit the Continent?"

"I can't imagine why. The von Dortmanns are dear friends. The old farmer himself is aging. His son is now in charge of most of the day-to-day operations. A visit to see his father before he gets much older would be the most reasonable thing in the world. He also has a cousin by the name of Heinrich von Dortmann, of the low aristocracy actually, a baron whom I have only met once but who struck me as astute both spiritually and culturally."

"Do you have business that would also give you cover?"

"I sell some wool in Germany, and a few sheep and ponies on occasion. I've never had dealings in Russia."

"Hmm, that is unfortunate. But you would be able to travel about easily in Germany. As I recall, you speak fluent German."

Tulloch nodded. "I also have an old friend who recently received a post at the University of Munich as a professor of history. He is a loyal Scot and a keen student of history. I could pay him a visit as well."

"Do you trust him?" asked Churchill.

"I would trust him with my life."

"And the others?"

"I would say exactly the same."

"Not a soul, however, can know that I have anything to do with it."

"I understand. I will see what I can arrange."

"I am also interested in Norway," Churchill went on. "On the world stage, Norway tends to be overlooked. Its location, however, as well as yours here in the Shetlands, as a navy man has always intrigued me. If Russia begins building up its navy, it will have two doors to the world. The first is through the Bosporus from the Black Sea, and thus the importance of the Moslem connection and the Turks. The second is from Barents through Norway's northern waters. Obviously the Shetlands sit at the strategic heart of a potential early-warning network. If there should ever be a war involving the Bolsheviks, I am convinced that the Shetlands and the Norwegian coast may play a vital strategic role in naval intelligence."

The two men sat a few moments in poignant silence.

"I'll ask you the same question I did about Germany, Ernie," said Churchill at length, "—do you have any contacts in Norway?"

"Quite a few, actually."

"Good. I want you to spy out the land, as it were, perhaps begin setting up a clandestine network of people we can trust, whom we can call on when the time comes. I don't know where all this will lead. I simply know we must be ready."

18

Morning and Evening

Several days had passed since Brogan Tulloch's conversation with journalist Robert Glendenning. The Londoner and tour group with him had vanished, leaving the island bereft of activity. Boredom, his frequent companion these days, had dogged Brogan's steps ever since.

At long last, two new busloads from Lerwick had come over on the four o'clock ferry the previous afternoon. The night of their arrival, however, had been disappointing. A lecture had been on the docket rather than music and dancing. With nothing else to do, the son of the laird had had rather too much to drink.

He dressed the following morning and made his way downstairs about ten. In his present condition, the voices of his father and stepmother in the breakfast room were more than he could bear. The thought of tea was intolerable. For reasons that would have been a mystery to him, he went out into the morning.

He struck out northward from the house. Twenty or thirty minutes later, Brogan approached the high cliffs of the northeast extremity of the island. On a day like this, when he was not so

115

steady on his feet, he wouldn't dare go near the edge. When he and Wallace, after swearing each other to secrecy, had dared walk to the edge of the Great Cliff and had cast their eyes down the fearsome cliff, they knew that if he ever learned of it their father would blister them in the righteous indignation of love's fury.

The cave of their boyhood adventures was worn into the same expansive wall of granite about a quarter mile west where the bluff sloped with a less dangerous incline toward the sea. Their discovery of the cave, too, they cherished for several years as a secret between them. By the time they were teenagers, however, they spoke of it openly. The subject of exactly when and how they had first discovered it did not come up, and Ernest was wise enough not to inquire into the matter too deeply.

Suddenly ahead Brogan saw a girl seated near the edge of the bluff. What was she thinking!

On wobbly feet, he made his way forward and called out a warning.

"Ho, I say there!" he said. "You need to get back."

A sudden flurry of orange, black, and white exploded into the air nearby.

"Now look what you've done!" she cried, turning around. "You scared them off!"

"It's only a few puffins," laughed Brogan, wincing from the echo between his temples. "This ruddy island is full of them."

"Not so close as those."

"Well you obviously had a nice look. But you need to come away from that cliff."

"It may take days to get so close again. Why did you come barging up and yelling like that?"

"I was worried that you were so close to the edge."

"I was managing just fine until you came along."

Not necessarily expecting praise for, as he saw it, saving her life, Brogan was nevertheless put off by the girl's contemptuous attitude toward his attempted chivalry.

"Look," said Brogan, "I realize from your American accent that you are probably a visitor here, staying at the Hotel no doubt. But you really need to get back."

A testy exchange followed in which the tempers of both came close to the boiling point.

At length the girl had had enough. "Thank you for your concern and consideration," she said with sarcasm. "Good day to you, sir," she added, then turned and tromped off.

Brogan stood staring angrily after her a minute more, then glanced along the coastline in the direction of the cave. Whenever twinges of inner disquiet gnawed at him, whispering that he was wasting his life, disappointing his father and in grave danger of becoming a complete wastrel, his steps drew him unconsciously to the pleasant days of boyhood. The cave reminded him of happier times, romps and explorations with his brother, of secret pacts and imaginary battles and voyages to faraway lands.

But his head was still throbbing. He couldn't think about all that right now. And he couldn't trust his knees to navigate the narrow path from the bluff down to the cave. If he tried it in his present condition, it might well be *his* body, not the girl's, they found on the rocks below.

Finally, his irritation from the interview subsiding, he turned and wandered back the way he had come.

By evening Brogan had recovered from his headache and strode into the Hotel about eight o'clock. A small band was already in full swing. As the ballroom gradually filled, a diminutive young woman at the bar caught Brogan's eye. He sauntered toward her.

"The Hotel keeps several excellent local whiskeys on hand," he said, "if you might care to join me?"

She turned toward him with a momentary smile but then walked away. Taken off guard, Brogan went after her. He caught her as she was sitting down next to an older woman.

"I did not mean to be forward," he said. "I only wanted to ask if I might be permitted to ask you to join me for a drink. I am Brogan Tulloch, son of the chief of Whales Reef."

The girl looked up with the hint of a smile.

"I confess myself confused," she said playfully, "why the son of the chief would want to have a drink with an American who speaks with such a grating voice."

Brogan's jaw dropped.

"You!" he said, struggling for words.

"As you can see," rejoined the girl, "I was in no danger. I must say, it is nice to know your name at last.—Mrs. Barnes," she went on, turning toward the woman beside her, "may I present Mr. Tulloch."

"A pleasure, Mrs. Barnes," said Brogan with a smile. "May I welcome you to Whales Reef. And perhaps I might make a request?"

"Why . . . of course."

"Would you be so kind as to introduce me to this witty young lady beside you? When we encountered one another earlier we did not exchange names."

"Oh . . . I see," said Mrs. Barnes. "Then, Mr. Tulloch, may I present my traveling companion, Miss Emily Hanson."

"Miss Hanson," said Brogan with gentlemanly grace, "it is a pleasure. And now that I am in my right mind, I hope you will accept my sincere apology for my behavior this morning."

While his son was mixing with the guests at the Whales Reef Hotel, in his upstairs study in the

119

Cottage Ernest Tulloch had just completed letters to his friend Alexander MacAlaster in Munich, and to the two von Dortmanns in that region of northern Germany formerly known as Pomerania, informing them of his proposed visit to the Continent. Then followed another in a similar vein to Nils Larsen in Trondheim.

PART 5
AUGUST 2006

19

A COUSIN IN TROUBLE

LERWICK, SHETLAND ISLANDS

Loni Ford and David Tulloch walked into the jail of the Lerwick Sheriff's Court in the Shetland capital a little after one o'clock. Ten minutes later a guard brought their mutual third cousin Hardy Tulloch into the visitors' room.

His face was unshaven, his hair disheveled, and his clothes a mess. If possible he wore a surlier scowl than usual as he glared at them.

"What are ye doin' here, David?" he said in an unfriendly tone. "I hae no interest in seein' ye . . . or yersel' either, Miss Ford."

"Please speak to the lady respectfully, Hardy," said David.

"Bah, David! If ye came tae insult me, ye can jist gae yer way. I'll finish wi' ye when I'm oot o' here, an' I winna be so easy on ye as last time."

"From what I understand, you may not be getting out for a while, Hardy. The charges are serious."

"An' ye're lovin' yer chance tae gloat. Ye always had it oot for me. Dinna deny it."

David sighed at his cousin's belligerence, but did not reply.

"I'll ask ye again, David, what are ye doin' here? I'm in no mind tae see either o' ye."

"We came to ask if you needed anything, Hardy—a change of clothes, books perhaps . . . anything at all," David replied softly. "Mostly we came to see if we could help you."

"Now I know ye're lyin', David!" spat Hardy. "You wouldna lift a finger tae help me." Almost the moment the words left his lips, what small remaining spark of conscience he still possessed shifted about uneasily at the memory of David's role in rescuing the *Hardy Fire* earlier that year.

Loni could take his rude bluster no longer. She stepped forward and stared Hardy straight in the eye. Whether Hardy had ever been confronted so forcefully by anyone other than David in his adult life was doubtful. He was accustomed to seeing fear in faces that looked into his and watching strong men cringe in his presence. That this American who stared down at him from a height advantage of two inches with flashing eyes, who was a woman at that and showed no sign of weakness, was a new experience.

"Hardy," she said emphatically, "if you really believe that, you are a bigger blowhard than I took you for. This man would give his life for you. From what I have been told, he and Noak Muir and several others *did* risk their lives for you. We came here because we want to help, just as David said. I have had enough of your rudeness to last me a long time. Now either speak respectfully or we *will* leave. As I see it, you don't have many friends. You are in trouble. You could go to prison for the rest of your life. David is probably the best friend you have right now. So sit down, Hardy!"

Whether he was quivering in rage, or in shock to be spoken to in such a manner, Hardy made no further outburst. He slouched into the chair beside him and sat like a pouting child. Loni and David took chairs on the opposite side of the table. They allowed the ruffled feathers of their cousin's pride to settle a few moments.

"I would like to know what happened, Hardy," said David at length.

"Nothin' happened."

"You're in jail for a reason, Hardy. The whole village saw you and Jimmy Joe McLeod arguing. You threatened to kill him. The next thing anyone knew, he was dead."

"It wasna me."

"The last anyone saw you, you were running after his car."

"You mind the day, the rain started fallin' like Noah's flood," said Hardy. "Aye, I was angry. The man was a double-crossin' liar. I dinna deny I wasna angert enough tae wring his neck. But then I went home like everyone else when the rain came pourin' doon."

"None of the men who followed you out of town saw you coming back to the village."

"I'd run oot past the landin' toward yer place by then. When the rain burst doon, I ran back ahind the village o'er the moor atween the Croft an' the kirk—'twas the shortest way."

"You saw nothing more of McLeod?"

"Naethin'."

"Did anyone see you on your way home?"

" 'Twas rainin' like the de'il. Wasna a body oot by the time I came up ahint the kirk."

It was silent a minute.

"You and I have had our differences, Hardy," said David after a few seconds. "You're too proud for your own good. You can be a mean-spirited rascal, and your temper's your own worst enemy."

"How dare ye talk tae me like that, David!" growled Hardy, half rising from his chair.

The guard across the room saw the movement and took a step toward them. But it was Loni who intervened.

"Sit down, Hardy!" she said in a commanding voice. "Why does it anger you to hear the truth? Your temper *is* your own worst enemy. You are one of the worst braggarts and windbags I have ever met. Can't you see that we want to help you and that David wants to believe you?"

Hardy slumped back like a wounded bear.

"I was going to say, Hardy," David went on,

"that if you tell me you didn't kill Jimmy Joe McLeod, I will believe you. Having known you all your life, I fear that you probably are capable of it. You are a big, strong, angry man." He hesitated a moment. "*Have* you ever taken a life, Hardy?" David added seriously.

Hardy glanced away. Both Loni and David saw the expression that flitted momentarily over his face.

After a second or two he turned back to David.

"I was in the Gulf War," he said.

"Of course. I remember. It must have been dreadful."

"Isna a time I want tae think aboot."

"Did you kill Jimmy Joe McLeod?"

Hardy hesitated briefly, then looked David straight in the eye. "I didna."

"Then that's good enough for me," said David, rising. Loni stood beside him. "We will see if we can find out more about the charges," David added, "and what evidence there is against you. So . . . is there anything we can do for you, anything you need, anything you would like us to bring you?"

"A change o' clothes would be welcome, if ye dinna mind," answered Hardy, not exactly humbled, but a little chastised. "My cottage is open, ye ken."

"A book to read?"

"If ye hae any ye think I might like . . . I ne'er

read one o' yer's, David, that ye wrote. I might like tae hae a look."

"I take that as a compliment, Hardy," laughed David. "I will see what I can do."

"But mind—I said I'd hae a look, not that I'd promise tae read it."

"Understood, Hardy!" laughed David again.

He and Loni walked across the floor as the guard unlocked the door.

"Uh . . ." they heard Hardy's voice behind them. They paused and turned.

"Sorry I spoke rudely, Miss Ford," said Hardy. "I, uh . . . thank ye for comin'."

"Of course, Hardy," said Loni. "We will see you again soon."

20

NEWCOMER TO WHALES REEF

WHALES REEF, SHETLAND ISLANDS

While David Tulloch and Alonnah Ford were engaged with their cousin Hardy in Lerwick, the Rev. Richard Sinclair stood at the Arrivals gate of the Sumburgh airport holding a computer-printed sign that read *Lincoln Rhodes*.

He had been contacted to transport the Shetland visitor to Whales Reef for reasons having nothing to do with Jason MacNaughton, David Tulloch, or Loni Ford. Dickie had been apprised of the man's mission, and, as had been the case during Loni's first visit, before they were halfway to their destination the two men were talking like old friends. In his mid-thirties, Rhodes was half a generation younger than his colorful taxi driver. Despite the difference in their ages, however, both men soon sensed a kindred spirit. Thoroughly engrossed in the young man's story, Dickie found himself wishing the drive were longer.

As they left the ferry landing and he took in his first glimpses of Whales Reef, unlike Jimmy Joe McLeod, whose ill-fated sojourn in the Shetlands had begun and ended with antipathy for the place, young Rhodes gazed about the quaint fishing village with an expression of delight.

"I have one request to make," he said as they pulled up in front of the Whales Fin Inn.

"Of course," said Dickie.

"Please do not divulge my identity or purpose on the island. There is obviously one other who knows, and I am scheduled to meet with him privately tomorrow. But I would prefer to get to know the rest of the community and its people without the inevitable baggage of my position."

"Hae nae worries, Mr. Rhodes. Yer secret's safe wi' me."

Dickie turned his taxi around and drove back to the ferry where he had asked the captain to wait for him. Carrying his single bag, Lincoln Rhodes walked through the door of the pub and inside the small village inn. His casual clothes betrayed nothing of his profession.

Glancing about, he nodded with a friendly smile toward two groups of men seated at two tables, and walked to the counter where the man behind the bar greeted him.

"Good afternoon," he said. "I believe you have a room booked for me. I am Lincoln Rhodes."

"Aye, Mr. Rhodes," said Keith Kerr, "we been expectin' ye. I'll get my daughter tae sign ye in an' take ye upstairs."

Disappearing through the swinging door toward the stairway, he reemerged a moment later, followed by Audney.

"This is my daughter, Mr. Rhodes. She'll take care o' ye."

"Thank you."

"I'm pleased tae make yer acquaintance, Mr. Rhodes," said Audney, extending her hand across the counter. "I'm Audney Kerr. I've already got yer name in oor register. An' hoo long will ye be stayin' wi us?"

"I'm not sure exactly. At least the rest of the week."

"That's fine. We're nae too busy at the minute. Ye're welcome as long as yer business keeps ye. What is yer business, if ye dinna mind my askin'?"

Her guest smiled. "I don't mind your asking,"

he said. "But if *you* don't mind, I would prefer not answering you yet. Do you mind being patient a few days for your answer?"

"Sounds mysterious!" laughed Audney. "I dinna mind. But ye canna stop me fae tryin' tae guess what brings ye tae sich an oot o' the way place."

Now it was Rhodes's turn to laugh, already taken with the spunky daughter of the inn's owner.

"Will ye be wantin' supper wi' yer room, Mr. Rhodes?" asked Audney.

"I will, thank you. And after I've put my bag away, I think I need to sample this beer your sign boasts as the best in the Shetlands."

"Ye winna be disappointed, at least 'tis what the men say. I'm nae fond o' beer mysel'. Noo," Audney added, coming around from the counter and bending down to pick up the suitcase on the floor beside their guest, "I'll show ye til yer room."

Rhodes moved quickly and took hold of the handle. "You don't think I would let a lady carry my bag," he said.

"Jist part o' the service, Mr. Rhodes."

"That is very kind. But it goes against the code," he said, lifting the suitcase. "Lead on!"

"Well, I winna contest the point wi' a man who knows his manners," laughed Audney. She turned and led him through the door she had just come through and up the stairs. "There's one room we're keepin' vacant at the minute," she went

131

on, "where the man was stayin' that was killed recently."

"A man was killed here—in the Hotel?"

"Nae in toon . . . oot on the bluffs. Fell off the cliffs, wi' a little help. The police hae been snoopin' aboot a few times an' told us tae keep the room as it is. But ye can hae yer choice o' any o' the others."

The men of Whales Reef were always happy to drink as much of Keith's brew as someone else would pay for. Two hours later, therefore, standing beers for the men about the place, and employing shrewd questions designed to elicit more information than his listeners realized they were divulging, Lincoln Rhodes had formed a surprisingly accurate picture of what had taken place on the day when Jimmy Joe McLeod had stormed away from the town square and not been seen again until Noak Muir's crew spotted his body on the reefs at the foot of the North Cliffs. Opinion varied widely on what had happened, and what had been Hardy's movements after racing on foot after McLeod's Range Rover. Once the storm broke, no one had seen Hardy the rest of the day.

The village men found the newcomer personable and down-to-earth. After reflection they realized that he listened more than he spoke. He was interested in everyone about him, and drew from each as much as they were willing to tell. He never spoke of himself, however. It was much the same during the supper hour, during which he made many new acquaintances with similar result. By day's end, though he had met probably two dozen or more of the villagers, and would surprise them in coming days by calling every one of them by name and remembering much they had told him about themselves, not a man or woman in Whales Reef knew a thing about the young man called Lincoln Rhodes.

Questioned, Audney told of her brief conversation with their guest and his reluctance to divulge his business. He was no Shetlander, that much was plain, probably not even a Scot. His tongue was hard to place, most said, though one added it reminded him of a man he had once met from London. He was about five-foot-ten, well built and tending toward stockiness, with powerful forearms and shoulders, not the sort of man you would want to tangle with. At the same time, his carefree, friendly, and gentle manner gave the equal impression of a man who wouldn't hurt a fly.

One thing all agreed on was that his eyes were always probing. When he asked a question, though his smile was disarming, his expression was searching between the lines for clues to what was not being said as much as what was. One came away with the unnerving sensation that he had been able to look inside and know what you were thinking. If he struck the people of Whales Reef as mysterious, it was no more than what Audney had said immediately upon making his acquaintance.

Based on his keen interest in the murder, by the next afternoon it was all around the village— for its men loved to speculate as much as its women—that the guest at the inn was none other than an undercover detective sent by Scotland Yard to investigate the Texan's death for reasons involving an Arab spy network that Hardy had somehow gotten mixed up in.

21

THE GUN

Upon their return from Lerwick, David and Loni went straight to Hardy's cottage. Loni stopped as they crossed the threshold, reeling from the overpowering aroma of fish. Having grown up the son of a fisherman, David scarcely noticed. He glanced over at Loni. Her eyes were watering.

"Would you rather wait outside?" he laughed. "I forget that you're not used to the extent to which fish dominates our lives here."

"I'm okay," said Loni. "I will have to get used to it eventually. But it is strong! Let's open the windows."

"I doubt Hardy washes his clothes as often as

might be the case if he had a wife looking after him. He takes them to his mum who has a washer. Someone who is out on the sea most days isn't even aware of the smell. But we'll see if we can find something clean and dry to take him."

They walked through the kitchen and sitting room, where shirts and trousers were thrown over backs of chairs and lying in heaps on a couch that appeared a repository for clothes more than any other purpose.

"Hardy doesn't employ a housekeeper, I take it," said Loni, pulling up a window and leaning out for a breath of fresh air.

"I don't think so," laughed David.

He led the way into the single bedroom where, if possible, the aroma was yet more pungent.

"I'm surprised his mum hasn't been in to tidy up," said David. "I should call on her and tell her we've seen Hardy." He paused and smiled. "Though she's hardly the doting type. Sometimes she gets more irritated at Hardy than all the rest of us put together! She's probably furious at him for getting himself into such a mess. Still, I should pay her a visit."

"I will make up Hardy's bed," said Loni, opening another window, "and leave you to do what you need to do. Maybe I'll wash up his dishes and tidy up the kitchen . . . with the outside door open."

A few minutes later, with a fresh breeze coming

through the door, Loni stood at the sink. David walked in from the bedroom holding a couple of shirts, a pair of trousers, socks, briefs, and what appeared to be a new pair of sneakers that Hardy might find more comfortable than the boots he was presently wearing.

"You found him a clean wardrobe, I take it," said Loni.

David set the armload of clothes on the table. "Look what else I found," he said, folding back the gray T-shirt in his hand to reveal a black revolver.

"A gun!" exclaimed Loni. "I didn't think people in the U.K. were allowed to own guns."

"They're not. Some sporting rifles are allowed but tightly regulated. But after the Dunblane school massacre ten years ago, handguns were outlawed. Hardy could get into trouble for this, all the more so if it had something to do with McLeod's death."

"Do you think it's the gun that killed him?"

Holding the pistol carefully with the shirt, David lifted the barrel to his nose.

"Captain Hastings always smells the gun to see if it's been recently fired."

"Who's Captain Hastings?"

"Never mind," laughed David. "Dumb joke—an Agatha Christie character."

"Has that one been fired?" asked Loni.

"I don't have a clue!" laughed David. "I have

136

no idea what it should smell like either way. Honestly, I know nothing about guns. But I can't figure out why the police haven't searched here and already found it."

"Maybe they did and that's why it's such a mess."

"Then why is the gun still here? Surely they would have found it."

"Maybe the smell drove them away."

"There is that!" chuckled David, wrapping the gun back up in the shirt.

"What will you do with it?" asked Loni.

"For now I'll take it with me since Hardy's cottage is unlocked, just in case there is some funny business afoot. I'll take it to the police, though in which direction it may point we can't yet know. They will want to check for fingerprints and to see if it's been fired recently. They'll be able to see if the bullet that killed McLeod came from this gun—another bit of trivia I've picked up from detective films."

"A movie buff, are you?"

"A little," smiled David.

"Will Hardy get in trouble for having it?"

"Probably, though I doubt it will be more than a fine. It will obviously be confiscated, and Hardy will hit the roof when I tell him I gave it to the police. But it's better than a charge of murder."

"Unless the gun *has* been fired recently," said Loni, "and actually implicates him."

"That's true," said David seriously. "Then I will have given the police the evidence to hang him with. Let's just pray Hardy is telling the truth. With him, to be honest . . . I'm just not sure what to think."

22

THE RUMOR

Audney Kerr was out of the inn when Lincoln Rhodes came down for his tea and breakfast on his first morning in Whales Reef. He was in and out most of the day, walking the village, visiting its shops and the woolen mill, familiarizing himself with the southern end of the island with extended visits to the church. He enjoyed himself again visiting with the village men in the pub through the late afternoon and into the dinner hour. Everyone was friendly and talkative, showing him a curiously deferential level of courtesy. While some of the women eyed him cautiously, he chalked this up to the natural wariness of any community toward strangers. As yet he had no inkling of the rumors swirling or how quickly, fueled by his curiosity about Hardy and the murder, they were taking on a life of their own.

He descended the stairs and walked into the common room a little before eight the next morning. Audney was busy serving breakfast to three other guests.

"Mornin' tae ye, Mr. Rhodes," she called across the room. "Sit where'er ye like. I'll hae yer tea in a jiffy."

He was finishing his cooked breakfast when Audney came by offering him more tea.

"Actually, yes—thank you," he replied to her question. "I do tend to enjoy my tea in the morning. Would you join me, Miss Kerr?"

The room suddenly rang with Audney's laughter. "If any o' the regulars were tae hear ye callin' me *Miss Kerr*, they'd wonder who ye was talkin' aboot. I'm just Audney tae the folk o' Whales Reef."

"Well then, Audney . . . would *you* like to join me?" repeated Rhodes.

"Don't mind if I do, Mr. Rhodes. I'll jist fetch a fresh pot."

She reemerged from the kitchen a few minutes later bearing a pot, sat down opposite their guest, and poured out two cups.

"Are ye ready tae tell me what brings ye til Whales Reef?" said Audney.

He smiled across the table. "All in good time."

"Will ye at least tell me where ye've come frae? Folk is sayin' London."

"People are talking about me, are they?"

"Oh, aye. It isna that we git many strangers, though a fair number o' bird-watchers are always aboot, ye ken. But no one takes ye for such as that. They canna help bein' curious."

"Then I will divulge this much—I grew up in Edinburgh."

"Did ye noo—I wouldna kenned it fae yer accent."

"I've worked to soften my street twang, or *Reekie spik* as we call it. And I've traveled a good deal. That tends to take the edge off. But what about the fellow that was here a month ago I hear everyone talking about—the Texan who was killed? Were people curious about him too?"

"Oh, aye! He was a big blusterin' chappie. I didna like him much, God rest his soul. But he was free wi' his talk, an' folk didna hae time tae git curious—he answered a' the questions afore they was asked."

"And the man they say killed him?"

"Hardy?"

Rhodes nodded. "Do you know him?"

"Aye. Everybody kens Hardy. I ken him better'n most."

"In what way?"

"He fancied me an' kept sayin' he would marry me."

"And on your part of it?"

"I wouldna marry Hardy in a million years. He an' I didna exactly see eye tae eye on the matter."

"What do you think, then—is he guilty?"

"I wouldna tell ye if I thought so. Whatever I

think o' Hardy, I wouldna betray the trust o' one o' my own fae the island. But tae be honest, I rightly dinna ken. Hardy's a mean one, there's nae denyin' it. But murder . . . I canna believe it. Or maybe I just dinna want tae believe it."

"Would you take me to the place where it happened?" asked Rhodes. "It appears a pleasant day. You could show me some more of your island."

"Weel o' course ye'd be wantin' tae see the spot, wouldna ye?"

"What do you mean'?"

"I hae two ears, Mr. Rhodes. Though ye haena told me yersel' who ye are an' what ye're doin' here, a' body kens it weel enough."

"Oh, they do! And just what am I doing here?"

"I hardly need tae tell ye yersel' that ye're a detective investigatin' the murder."

Rhodes stared back as a slow grin came to his lips. "I see," he said slowly. "And just who would I be investigating for?"

"Dinna make sport o' me, Mr. Rhodes. For Scotland Yard, as ye ken weel enouch yersel'. Ye're here investigatin' the oil spy ring the Texan was involved wi'."

Lincoln Rhodes could contain himself no longer. He burst into a roar of laughter that could be heard halfway to the mill. A few heads on the street outside turned toward the pub, thinking David must be inside. His was the only laughter they knew of that carried so far.

"I'm sorry," said Rhodes, still chuckling. "I would never make sport of you, Audney. But I couldn't help laughing at the conclusion the good people of your community have drawn."

"But it's true?"

"I'm afraid I must fall back on my previous commitment—that I will divulge everything when the time is right."

"Ye're a stubborn one, I'll say that for ye."

Again Rhodes laughed. This girl was delightful. "You may be right," he said. "Though I hope I am not, as the saying goes, too stubborn for my own good. I hope I have good reason for holding my tongue.—So what do you say, Audney Kerr . . . will you show me your island?"

"Weel, Mr. Lincoln Rhodes," rejoined Audney with fun in her eyes as she replied in kind, "I'll be happy tae act as yer tour guide. It'll hae tae be after lunch—till then I'll be helpin' Mum wi' the preparations for the day."

"That sounds perfect. I have some writing to do in my room, which may take me most of the morning."

"Ye're a writer too, are ye?"

"Just a few thoughts I need to organize."

"For yer investigation aboot the island an' its folk, nae doobt."

Again he smiled. "I suppose you might say that," he replied.

23

WALK ON THE ISLAND

Several hours later Audney Kerr and Lincoln Rhodes left the village and were walking along the western road of Whales Reef past the ferry landing. They chatted easily, Audney telling the island's visitor some of its history, especially about the mill and its origins as a luxury hotel. She also filled him in on their new laird. Soon they came to a gravel drive that led to the right.

"Hae ye met oor chief yet?" Audney asked.

"I haven't," replied Rhodes.

"Then I'll introduce ye. This leads til the Auld Hoose—the chief's house. The laird bides in what we call the Cottage—oor new laird, the American lady."

They turned along the drive and continued into the precincts of the Auld Hoose. There they found David, dirty and in a full sweat, in the garden in front of the house. He saw them coming, set aside the shovel in his hand, and strode over the upturned earth to meet them.

"What ho, Audney!" he said, coming toward them. "—Hello," he added, extending a hand to the stranger beside her. "I am David Tulloch. I apologize for the dirty hand."

"Nothing to apologize for," said Rhodes, giving David's hand a firm shake. "Honest toil, honest dirt. I am Lincoln Rhodes."

"Mr. Rhodes is oor guest at the inn, David," said Audney. "I wanted him tae meet ye.—David is oor chief, Mr. Rhodes."

"I am pleased to make your acquaintance, Mr. Tulloch," said Rhodes.

"And I yours . . . and please, it's *David*."

"Thank you. I hope you will return the favor and call me *Lincoln*. So, what are you working on here? Not exactly the time of year to be planting a garden."

"I'm afraid the plot has rather gotten away from me—I'm trying to reclaim it."

"Few things are more satisfying than getting one's hands in the dirt."

"If you stay long enough," laughed David, "I may put you to work."

"I would happily consent."

"As I understand it from the village grapevine, however," rejoined David, "you have more important things on your mind than my overgrown garden. You are, I take it, the man causing such a stir by trying to get to the bottom of what happened out on the bluffs."

"That's where I'm takin' him," said Audney. "He wanted tae see where it happened."

"Examining the scene of the crime, eh?" said David.

Rhodes smiled humorously. "You strike me, Chief . . . er, David, as one who knows it's not always wise to believe everything you hear."

"A statement which hints at mysterious undercurrents," rejoined David.

"No comment. However, I might take the liberty of canvassing your opinion—do you think the man called Hardy is guilty?"

"I don't know," answered David seriously. "There's no doubt he's one tough bloke. Audney knows that as well as anyone. But I do not want to believe he's a murderer."

"As chief, what is your role in the affair? Do you occupy the position of magistrate on the island?"

"Nothing like that. The police in Lerwick are handling the case. They have consulted me, but purely in an unofficial capacity."

"Have you spoken with the other Mr. Tulloch?"

"I have, yes. Miss Ford—our new laird—and I paid him a visit on Monday."

"And?"

"He assures me he's innocent. I honestly don't know what to think."

"I see. Well, we had better get on with our excursion. But don't be surprised if I show up one day with my work duds on and tell you to hand me a spade."

"I will look forward to it!" laughed David.

Audney and Rhodes returned to the western

road and were soon walking north toward the peat bogs.

"A personable man, your chief," said Rhodes.

"Aye—everyone loves David. Weel, everyone except Hardy."

"They don't get on?"

"They're cousins an' hae been rivals since they were wee tykes. I was in love with David once, an' that's angert Hardy e'er since."

"In love . . . but . . ." He allowed his voice to trail off in unspoken question.

"He wasna in love wi' me," said Audney. "He would hae married me if I'd let him. But I kenned there was another waitin' for him. An' noo he's found her . . . oor new laird, I mean."

"And yourself?"

"I'm still waitin'."

Twenty minutes later the two stood at the northern extremity of the island overlooking the sea from a height of a hundred and fifty feet.

"That's where the Texan was found, doon on the reefs," said Audney, pointing over the precipice. "Must hae been a terrible thing tae fall fae so high . . . though they're sayin' he was deid afore that."

"How could that be?"

"They say he was shot," replied Audney. "That's why they're sayin' it's murder."

24

A Talk Between Friends

"Do ye mind if I ask ye a question, Miss Ford?" asked Audney as she and Loni sat chatting over tea and biscuits in the breakfast room of the Cottage. Loni had invited Audney for afternoon tea. She was delighted to find that she was not quite as reluctant as Isobel Matheson, and with a little encouragement was *almost* able to meet her on the equal footing of friendship.

"Please, Audney, aren't we beyond the *Miss Ford* now?" said Loni.

"What do ye want me tae call ye then? I'd feel strange like callin' ye by sich a fancy name as . . . Alonnah, as they're sayin' ye're called." As she said the word, she glanced away sheepishly, as if she had committed a social blunder simply by uttering Loni's given name.

Loni laughed. "What if I tell you what people at home call me? No one here calls me by my nickname. But I would like it better than the Miss. So why don't you call me *Loni*."

"Wouldna ye think me presumin'?"

"That is the last thing I would think. We Americans are not so much bound by social conventions. I would be honored, in fact, for you to call me Loni. It shows that we are friends."

"But ye're the laird."

"That doesn't make me a different person."

"Folk here that's entitled tae it *want* other folk lookin' up til them. It's different than it used tae be, o' coorse, wi' lords an' ladies an' the like. Still, everyone kens their place, if ye know what I'm sayin'."

"The very thought of being considered higher than someone else makes me cringe."

"Ye Americans are a strange lot, if ye dinna mind my sayin' so."

Again Loni laughed. "Well, if it's thinking no one's above anyone else, then I don't mind being thought of as a bit strange. But I don't want you thinking of me as the *laird,* but just as a friend."

"I'll try. 'Tis kind o' ye."

"All right, then. With that settled, what was it you wanted to ask me?"

Audney looked away. Loni detected a slight reddening of her cheeks. After a second or two Audney glanced about as if by force of habit thinking she was in the common room of the inn with listening ears nearby. Even though they were alone, she lowered her voice to just above a whisper.

"What do ye think o' Mr. Rhodes?" she asked softly.

Loni took in Audney's words without divulging her curiosity at the reason for the question.

"He seems friendly and personable," she replied. "He and David are certainly hitting it off. That must say something."

"How do ye mean?"

"Just that David is a keen judge of character. If David counts him a friend, then he must be a man of worth."

"Aye, but David is acceptin' o' everyone."

"True, but in this case I'm sure it's more than that. I think they're on their way to becoming friends. That's just my take on it. So to answer your question," Loni added obliquely, "I would say that if there wasn't already a man on this island I had taken a fancy to, our mysterious visitor might possibly catch my eye. Of course, I would want to know a little more about him first. It might be scary to fall in love with a detective . . . though I suppose exciting in a way. Why do you ask?"

"Oh, naethin'," replied Audney, blushing again. "It's jist that he's bein' right friendly. An' who wouldna notice sich a good lookin' bloke. That's why I wanted tae know what ye thought o' him."

"Well, from the little I have seen of him, I like him . . . and you're right, he is *almost* as handsome as David," added Loni.

Audney was not anxious to pursue the matter further. She now diverted the conversation into other channels. "What hae ye heard fae yer friend Miss Swift?" she asked.

"Actually, she's gone off the radar," replied Loni. "It's not like her. She hasn't answered my emails for several days."

"Do ye think somethin's wrong?"

"I'm sure not. But the last time I talked to her she was behaving very strange—wearing a new dress and talking about working out. *Something* is going on. I'm just not sure what."

Loni smiled, then began to chuckle lightly. "This island seems to do strange things to visiting Americans," she said. "Maybe Maddy's suffering from delayed Whales Reef Syndrome! WRS—that's what we'll call it. Or in her case, DWRS. Whatever it is, she is definitely changing!"

25

A SERMON TO REMEMBER

Lincoln Rhodes and Audney Kerr visited often throughout the rest of the week, so often in fact that the stranger to Whales Reef began to feel pangs of guilt for not divulging his identity. Fortunately his conscience did not have to prolong its turmoil much longer. The weekend finally came.

On Saturday afternoon David received an

unexpected visit at the Auld Hoose from Stirling Yates. The two men enjoyed tea and a stimulating visit together. As their time drew to a close, Yates finally broached the subject that had prompted his call.

"I have a request to make of you, David," said the minister. "If it is not inconveniencing either of you, I would very much appreciate it if you and Miss Ford could be at the church for tomorrow's worship service, if you think she would be agreeable as well. I can call her personally if you like."

"I'll be happy to talk to her," replied David. "We will gladly be there. Can you tell me what it's about . . . more surprise announcements?"

"I'm sorry," smiled Yates. "I am not at liberty to say more. I gave my word."

"Most mysterious!" laughed David. "But we will be there."

That afternoon as he paused on his way up to his room, Lincoln Rhodes made almost the identical request of Audney Kerr.

"I have a favor to ask," he said.

"Anything I can do tae make yer stay more pleasant."

"This is a personal matter," rejoined Rhodes. "Would you go to church with me tomorrow?"

Audney stared back in surprise. "I didna take ye for a religious man," she said.

"I hope I'm not. But I am a devout Christian, however different a thing that may or may not be in some people's minds. In any event, I would appreciate it, as a favor to me."

"Then I'll gae wi' ye," said Audney.

"Thank you. It will mean a great deal to me. Services start at ten-thirty, I believe. I'll see you at breakfast, of course. Then I'll come down about ten and we'll walk over."

The following morning, after making their way through the village and gradually joining the others walking up the hill, Audney was surprised when her new friend led her inside the church and up the center aisle where they sat down in the first pew. Behind them the church gradually filled to the music of Rinda Gunn at the organ. At twenty-five past the hour, Loni slid in beside Audney and they greeted warmly, David moving in at Loni's side.

Five minutes later Rev. Stirling Yates mounted the pulpit and the service began. The morning proceeded normally through hymns, announcements, Scripture readings, and prayers. At last came time for the sermon.

"I have something of a surprise for you now," said Yates. "I was contacted by our session a little over a week ago with the news that they had a young man to send us to see if he wanted to be part of our parish as my replacement, and if you were inclined to extend him a call as your new minister. As a favor to the man, I promised I would say nothing until this morning. So with that brief introduction, I would like to welcome to our pulpit Rev. Lincoln Rhodes from Edinburgh."

Her eyes as big as plates, Audney's gaze followed the young man beside her as he rose, left the pew, and walked to the front of the church and up the steps into the pulpit. Her emotions were flying in many directions—from stunned surprise to anger to confusion. All around her the church was abuzz with murmurs of astonishment. Rhodes and Yates shook hands and exchanged a few words. Then Yates stepped down, walked across the floor, and eased into the pew beside Audney. Before the wildly swinging compass of Audney's brain had stopped spinning, the young minister was speaking.

"I want to begin this morning," said Rhodes, "with two brief comments."

He paused to allow the last whispered flurries among his listeners to settle.

"First," he continued, "it is a privilege to be with you and to have been in your community this week. Whether or not you ultimately call me as your minister, my heart is full of gratitude to have met so many. In a few short days, your community has woven its charm through my spirit and I know that I would be happy, and I hope useful, here."

Again he paused, at last with the full attention of the congregation.

"Then secondly," he went on, "no doubt some of you may feel hoodwinked by my coming among you incognito, as it were, and not divulging why I was here. I apologize for that, and for allowing you to believe certain things about me that were not true."

He paused briefly before continuing. "I have learned," he went on, "that people are different around ministers. Their guards go up. It becomes nearly impossible to establish a true relationship. If you feel offended that I took liberties with your trust, of course you are free to vote against my appointment to your parish. The only explanation I can offer is that I neither said nor did anything to make you believe I was other than who I am. I wanted to meet you, and be met by you, simply as a man—nothing more, nothing less. I did not intentionally deceive you. That some might have drawn certain erroneous, and I must say humorous, conclusions about my reasons for being here, I'm afraid, is on your own heads. I did nothing to make you think I was a detective. You allowed that rumor to spread. That you succumbed to gossip places the responsibility for the misunderstanding at your own door."

As he listened, a slow smile crept over David's lips. This man was plainspoken! He was just what the community needed.

"Now it may be," Rhodes continued, "once I learned of what you were saying, that I should have stepped in. Honestly, I didn't know what to do. Gossip can be a cancer in a small community. It should not be allowed to gain a foothold. If I was wrong not to correct the story, again I sincerely apologize. If you decide to call me as your minister, I will promise always to speak the truth—bluntly if need be as I just have. I will never put on airs by pretending to be more spiritual than I am. When I do wrong—as I surely will—when I speak amiss, when I inadvertently hurt one of you—which I hope I do not, but if I do—I will apologize and hold my hand to the flame of my own faults, flaws, mistakes, and blunders. I will never try to be above you, because I am not above you. I will be one of you, because I *am* one of you.

"Having made my explanation and my apology, I would like to add one further personal apology to your own Miss Audney Kerr."

He glanced down at Audney with a smile he hoped would reassure her of his honorable intentions.

"Though I came as a mere guest to their inn, Audney and her family have shown me every courtesy and consideration. I have felt welcomed to your community as a result of their kindness and hospitality. As the Lord said, 'I was a stranger and you took me in.' However, as Audney and I had occasion to spend considerable time together, she in a sense was swept into the misunderstanding more completely. If I erred, Audney, I am sorry

155

and I pray you will forgive me. I only wanted to be known, by you and everyone else, as a *man* and not a cleric."

Rhodes took a deep breath, glanced around the small church, then turned his attention to his morning's message.

"It is only right," he said, "now that you know why I am here, that you be told something about me. I will not bore you with my full life's story but will give you a quick overview. Then for a few minutes I would like us to look together at the passage I alluded to a moment ago from the twenty-fourth chapter of Matthew's Gospel.

"As to my background, it is right that you be apprised of the fact that this would be my first pulpit as a fully ordained minister in the Church of Scotland. I am, as it were, a spiritual late bloomer. I did not decide to enter the ministry until I was thirty. If I am privileged to become your minister, therefore, I will come to you as a pastoral novice. I will rely on your help. I will come to you as a fellow sojourner in trying to discover what life is supposed to mean.

"I hold what is a somewhat unusual view that a minister, if he is to be like other men, ought to work for a living and not be dependent on the church. If I come here, I will therefore be looking for work. I come from a difficult background. I grew up on the streets of Edinburgh. I have nothing to hide. I am not proud of my past and

156

do not need to belabor the sins and indiscretions of my youth other than to express my gratitude to God for delivering me from that life. One thing my past taught me is how to work. I can work with my hands, and your chief here let me help in his garden yesterday. I can learn to do most things. I will work at any trade or profession that presents itself. I love the sea and it may even be that one of your fishermen will find himself in need of a raw recruit who doubles on Sunday as a minister."

A few murmurs and light laughter spread through the room.

"However, these are all considerations that will resolve themselves as the need arises. In the time we have left, I would like us to consider for a few minutes the Lord's words about welcoming strangers, and observe how this challenge applies to each one of us every day, not only when strangers cross our path—as this particular stranger came among *you* this week—but also in our daily relationships with family, friends, and acquaintances. . . ."

Fifteen minutes later, after the final hymn and benediction, the reverends Yates and Rhodes stood outside the door of the church shaking hands and exchanging greetings with the parishioners of Whales Reef. The comments on this day went beyond the usual bland praise for yet one more sermon they had paid but scant attention to. Whatever might have predisposed his listeners against young Lincoln Rhodes after learning his identity had mostly been met by his straightforward manner, and now evaporated altogether in the warmth of his friendly, smiling laughter toward one and all. He remembered every name and was so quick with questions about family and health and life's details, with self-deprecating humor about what he had done, that none could hold it against him.

At last Audney reached him and held out her hand.

" 'Twas a dirty trick ye played on us, Mr. Rhodes," she said with a twinkle in her eye. "Or should I call ye Reverend Rhodes?"

"Please, anything but that!" laughed Rhodes. "I meant no trick, and my apology was sincere. But vote against me if you think I was being duplicitous."

"I wouldna dream o' that, *Reverend*."

"Now who's being stubborn, *Miss* Kerr?"

Audney laughed. "Weel, I accept yer apology. An' I'll see ye back at the inn," she said. "By then maybe I'll hae made up my mind what tae call ye!"

Rhodes followed Audney with his eyes as she walked away with her mother and father, then turned his attention again to the line of men and women waiting to shake his hand.

PART 6
A Legacy Begins—*Island Explorations* 1924

26

A GRAY DAY

Brogan Tulloch wandered downstairs from his room in the east wing of the Cottage. The great clock on the landing struck 8:45 as he descended the central staircase. His father, stepmother, sister, and two brothers would be in the breakfast room. No doubt they would be shocked to see him awake, shaved, dressed—to all appearances in his right mind and ready for the day—at such an early hour. His normal custom was to shuffle in looking for coffee about the time Mrs. Baxter was setting out a light lunch for Sally and his father.

Sally glanced up from the table, as he expected, in obvious surprise. "Good morning, Brogan," she said as he entered. "You're down early."

"Don't know what got into me," laughed Brogan. "--Good morning, Dad."

"And to you, Brogan," replied Ernest. "Are you driving into the city today?"

"Hadn't planned to. Something you need me to do?"

"No, I just wondered if that's why you were getting such an early start on the day."

"No plans," said Brogan as he sat down and

161

poured himself a cup of coffee. "Thought I might go over to the Hotel for a spot of breakfast . . . maybe see how the new tour groups are getting on."

"I take it you were performing your customary duty yesterday evening—spreading cheer and goodwill mingling with the visitors to our little corner of the world," said his father good-naturedly.

Despite the fact that Ernest did not approve of his eldest son's drinking habits, he never preached at him about it. He was doing his best to treat Brogan as a man who had to discover his own way in life. Father and son thus maintained an amiable, even friendly relationship. Both men were growing, and thus more bonds of mutual affection were stirring within them than had been the case several years earlier.

"They had a shindig for the two groups," replied Brogan. "I spoke with a few people."

"The girls?" said fourteen-year-old Leith with a grin.

Brogan threw his half brother a wink. "Of course!" he said.

"If you're not doing anything, do you want to go shooting for grouse on the northern moor?" asked Leith excitedly.

"I don't know, Leith," answered Brogan. "We shall see. Does Father let you go shooting at your tender age?"

"I'll be fifteen in a few weeks!"

"That's not what I asked," laughed Brogan. "What about it, Dad—is the lad old enough to handle a shotgun?"

"As I recall, you were out on that moor by the time you were ten—sometimes without my permission!" laughed Ernest. "I'm not sure you were such a good influence on your brother."

"Exactly as I have always maintained—my corruptions of character are your doing!" chided Wallace, younger than Brogan by a year at twenty-two, now entering the discussion.

"What about you, Wallace?" persisted Leith. "Will you take me shooting if Brogan won't?"

"I'm afraid my answer is the same as his," replied Wallace. "We shall see. If the day turns warm and it doesn't rain, I might be up for a ramble on the island. With Father's permission, of course."

"Certainly," said Ernest. "But check with Baline at the Auld Hoose first. We mustn't interfere with what he might be doing with the grouse or the sheep. Most important, he will know the movements of the guests at the Hotel. If they are about on the island, you may have to plan your shoot for another day."

"I'm glad that's settled," said Brogan, taking a final swallow from his cup. "I think I will drive into the village and see about breakfast."

"Why don't I have Mrs. Baxter boil you a couple

eggs and make some fresh toast?" said Sally.

"Thank you, Sally," replied Brogan, "but I want to pick up a *Times* as well. Best of the day to you all!"

"Oh, Brogan," said Ernest, rising, "would you do me a favor? I've several letters I would like to post. I just finished them up. Would you drop them off?"

"Sure, Dad."

Ernest left the table, ran upstairs to his study, and returned a minute later. He handed three sealed envelopes to his son.

"Germany, eh?" said Brogan, glancing at the address. "And Norway . . . what's it all about?"

"Several friends I'm thinking of visiting."

"When are you going?" asked Sally.

"No definite plans."

"Maybe I'll accompany you!" said Brogan with an uncharacteristic smile, then turned for the door.

Leaving father and stepmother glancing silently at each other as if to say, *Why is he so chipper this morning?* Brogan exited the house by the kitchen door. He strode across the gravel drive toward two connected barns, a portion of one which now served in the capacity of garage for his father's two automobiles—a 1919 Mercedes Roadster and a newer 1923 Studebaker from Germany.

Automobiles were all the rage these days in Lerwick. But getting one to and from Whales Reef still proved a challenge. Had Ernest's father

William not so strenuously promoted his hotel and the island's tourism before the war by building a landing for a much larger ferry that serviced most of the smaller islands, it was doubtful even now that Whales Reef would have seen an automobile on its shores. As it was, tourist coaches regularly deposited forty or fifty people at the mainland landing through the summer months to be taken across the isthmus. There they either walked the half mile to the Hotel or waited to be taxied three or four at a time in the automobile William had purchased and brought to the island for that express purpose. The ferry across to Shetland had therefore made accommodation for the occasional transport of a vehicle, with a special gate onboard and planks on both landings for driving an automobile on and off.

It was only a mile from the Cottage into the village by the road. Brogan walked into the darkened barn and jumped into his father's Studebaker. A few minutes later he was bounding along the narrow road that skirted the island's southern coast at the breakneck speed of twenty miles per hour.

The village of Whales Reef had not been designed with automobiles in mind. Only one street was wide enough for the Studebaker—the main cobbled road leading through its center. Brogan braked in front of the Paper Shop, turned off the engine, hopped out, and walked inside. If any other traffic in the form of a carriage, buggy, or farm wagon came through before he was done with his business, which was unlikely, they would have to wait.

With the paper under his arm a minute later, Brogan walked along the main street, nodding to passersby as he went. The butcher and baker were both doing a brisk trade. Women with baskets in hand were coming and going from both shops and from another half-dozen small enterprises scattered along the central thoroughfare. That few men were about was easily explained by the fact that most of the men of Whales Reef had been out on their boats for hours. Besides the bakery, the busiest shop at this time of day was the post office. Brogan entered to the tinkling of the bell above the door, greeted everyone with friendly smiles and handshakes, stepped to the window, handed his father's letters through the glass to Ian Morrison, the postmaster, then left and returned to the car. All the villagers liked the son of the laird. He was, as some said, a "braw yoong chappie."

Driving out of town, Brogan walked through the Hotel's doors a few minutes later. The dining room was about half full. A hasty perusal of those lingering over coffee and tea revealed a number of faces he recognized from the previous night. Several greeted him, including a party of three handsome young women who, it was not difficult to see, would eagerly have made room for him

166

at their table. He had danced with several last evening. Oddly, their smiles on this morning failed to stir him.

After a few passing smiles, nods, and "Good mornings," Brogan sought an unoccupied table and sat down alone. He had just set his *Times* on the table when the Hotel's head waiter appeared.

"Good morning, Mr. Tulloch," he said. "It is good to see you."

"So early, you mean, St. John!" laughed Brogan. "Unexpected, what?"

"Very good, sir," nodded the waiter without comment. "Would you care for coffee or tea?"

"Coffee, I believe, St. John . . . and a spot of breakfast, I think. How are the eggs this morning?"

"Laid by contented hens, sir."

"And the bacon?"

"Quite toothsome, I am given to understand."

"Eggs, bacon, and coffee it is. And some toast and marmalade on the side."

"Very good, Mr. Tulloch."

The respectful St. John O'Malley, an Irish-born transplant and lifelong employee of the firm that leased the Whales Reef Hotel, evaporated away, returning a couple of minutes later with the coffee. Brogan made an unsuccessful attempt to interest himself in his paper. But he could not prevent himself from looking about every fifteen or twenty seconds to see if any new arrivals had wandered in.

O'Malley reappeared about ten minutes later bearing a steaming platter, along with a tray of sliced toast.

"Has the other tour group been down for breakfast yet, St. John?" asked Brogan as the waiter set his breakfast before him.

"They were mostly finished half an hour ago."

"Did they leave the island?"

"Their morning's session, as I understand it, will venture out on the eastern bluffs and tide pools along the shore."

"No doubt they are in search of puffins and whale sightings," smiled Brogan.

"You may be right, sir."

"When do you expect them back?"

"I really could not say, sir. In time for lunch, I would say. I believe they have another lecture planned in the Hotel's meeting rooms this afternoon. I overheard something to that effect."

27

STONE OF ANTIQUITY

In spite of a few minor frustrations, Emily Hanson was enjoying herself immensely. The atmosphere aboard the *Viking Queen* had been somewhat tedious for one of her social temperament and spiritual leanings. And now that the Northern

Adventure Tour had begun in earnest, Emily had to admit with more than a little vexation that most of the group's time was spent eating, getting dressed for meals, talking about food, or discussing trivialities after the meal was over. Precious little time remained for what she had come for.

Dr. MacDonald's daily lectures were limited to an hour each morning and another hour before that daily ritual of dressing for dinner began to intrude upon the collective consciousness. Coffee, tea, cocktails, and leisurely strolls about the Hotel grounds frittered away hours that, in Emily's opinion, could have been put to better use. This morning's excursion along the eastern shore of the island, with Dr. MacDonald's commentary as they went, had been the highlight thus far.

Emily was the youngest member of the group, the only one taking notes or asking informed questions, and probably the only woman among them not preoccupied with what dress and jewelry to set out for the evening's festivities. That afternoon, therefore, while Mrs. Barnes and the more elderly members of the tour rested in their rooms, and its younger participants lounged about the Hotel, Emily again struck out to explore her surroundings, this time overland toward the heart of the island.

Her path led away from the Hotel heading north, passing a cottage or croft with a small barn to her left, the only one of its kind she had seen outside the village, then continuing into barren moorland, rolling and hilly. Like all the islands of the Shetland archipelago, Whales Reef was virtually treeless, inhabited only by what hardy grasses and shrubs could exist in its chilly, rainy, salty, windy environment. The ground sloped gently upward as she walked toward a series of low hills. The highest of these, which could not legitimately be called a peak, rose some three or four hundred feet above sea level. It was high enough, however, and situated some two miles north of the village, to convey an impression of height. Without exactly planning it, Emily found her steps moving upward toward it.

The springy peat turf beneath her feet made walking pleasant. She did not understand all the complexities of peat formation. She knew only that the islanders cut brick-shaped wedges of the wet brown mass from moors in the north of the island. Their excavations extended deep into the earth, creating huge bogs that filled with rainwater and brown surface seepage after the peat was removed—dangerous pits that the island children were warned to stay away from. The soaking dark bricks were laid out to dry, which then burned hot in place of wood or coal. How the supply could be so inexhaustible was a mystery. But the sweet-smelling smoke rose from village chimneys day and night as it had for fifty generations. And still most of the island appeared unmolested from the shovels and earth saws of the continual subterranean harvest.

No fences of wood or wire barred Emily's way. The only boundaries consisted of stones piled in randomly crisscrossing lines across the moorland. These irregular lines of stone had far too many gaps and breaks and broken portions to prevent man or beast from going anywhere they pleased on Whales Reef. The laird's sheep roamed free. The cattle and chickens owned by the villagers were kept in pens and paddocks surrounding the cottages of their owners.

With the village well behind her, a delicious sense of isolation stole over Emily. Sea breezes blew constant in the Shetlands. Though it had no trees by which to make music, the unrelenting wind nevertheless made its presence heard as it passed over wiry grasses and shrubs, moaning in and around the stone dikes. On this day, with the temperature in the mid-fifties, Emily found the breezes tolerable and bracing.

She passed a large house to her left. It boasted several outbuildings and two pastures, where a dozen or more cows and horses were grazing. After another twenty minutes, becoming warm from the steepening climb, her attention was drawn to a peculiar shape at the hilltop in front of her. At last Emily crested the highest point on Whales Reef known as the Muckle Hill. The sight that rose before her struck wonder, curiosity, even perhaps hints of unspoken dread into her soul.

At the precise summit of the island, a gigantic irregularly shaped stone obelisk rose out of the ground, a great pillar of granite. It had obviously been set into the earth by human hands, though how many hands it must have taken was beyond comprehension. Its weight could not possibly be calculated in tons, but rather in dozens of tons. It projected some twenty feet above the ground and was surely sunk many feet below the surface. One flat face, apparently cut or chiseled, contained faint markings and symbols whose details had long since weathered away. It was of that mysterious type of ancient monument common to Scotland known as a "standing stone." No trace in legend or tale gave so much as a clue to what prehistoric peoples had dragged it to this location and managed to erect and anchor it so firmly in a foundation of peat that it had remained in place a thousand years or more. There were those who said it was druidic in origin, though in this part of the world *all* remnants of antiquity, perhaps with visions of Stonehenge lurking in the shadows, were considered druidic.

For several long moments, Emily stood staring up at the massive monument, trying to lure some sense of order out of the dim hints of man's hand in the shapes faintly discernable on the face of granite.

Slowly she walked toward it, reached out, and laid the palms of her two hands against the rough surface. It was as solid to the touch as the Rock of Gibraltar. The mere presence of the great pillar towering above the island filled her with veneration for the great unknowns of the past. How different, she thought, was life in the United States where *old* meant one or two hundred years. Here, such reckonings were measured in millennia.

28

HERBS ON THE MOOR

Lost in her thoughts in the breezy silence of the summit, a sudden motion caught Emily's eye.

Ten feet down the opposite slope, partially hidden from view by the stone, knees half buried in the soft turf, an elderly woman was bending low to the ground.

The sight brought a sharp breath of surprise to Emily's lips.

The woman straightened her back, rose, and turned. If the sudden presence of another human being startled her as much as it had Emily, she showed no sign of it.

"Best o' the day tae ye, lassie!" she said. "Oot for a wee walkie aboot the moor, are ye?"

"I'm sorry," laughed Emily, recovering herself. "I am afraid I didn't understand you."

"Then 'tis me who should be apologizin' tae yersel'," the woman rejoined, speaking more slowly. "American, are ye?" she added.

"Yes," nodded Emily. "I'm staying at the Hotel."

"Oh, aye. I should hae kenned."

"What were you doing on your knees?" asked Emily. "I thought you were praying, or maybe had lost an earring or something. Would you like some help?"

The woman laughed with hilarity. "My fat ears hae ne'er made the acquaintance o' an earring in a' my days, lassie. Sich a thocht's beyond imaginin'!"

She stooped, picked up a basket from the ground, straightened her back again, and ambled up the hill. "I've jist been collectin' some wee flo'ers an' herbs, ye ken," she said, holding the basket toward Emily. To have called its contents a *bouquet* would not have been accurate. Lying in the basket was an assortment of tiny blossoms, leaves, some grasses, and mostly what Emily took for weeds.

"What are they all?" she asked.

"Some for my tea, but mostly for my jars."

"Are they edible?"

"Only a few. But there's ither uses o' more o' the island's plants than folk ken. So they come tae me when they're needin' this or that or the ither.

174

'Tis why I keep a good stock on hand in my wee cottage. Perhaps ye'd like to see it. Would ye join me for tea, lassie?"

"I would like that very much," replied Emily. "Do you live in the village?"

"Aye. Come—we'll walk back t'gither. What's yer name, lassie?"

"I'm Emily Hanson."

"A good name. The nickums call me the Herb Woman, an' worse!" she said with a chuckle. "I'm Annabella Raoghnailt tae civilized folk. 'Tis a bit o' the auld Gaelic in my papa's name. He cud speak the Gaelic too. But 'tis nae mair nor less than jist *Roe-nall*. It sounds like a deer, ye ken, but 'tis really meanin' beautiful lamb. 'Tis a woman's name, but it was my husband's papa's name and they was both men's men an' I am prood o' it. I thocht the Annabella was aboot the prettiest name o' all the lassies on the island when I was yoong. But it doesna quite seem tae suit an auld gray woman the likes o' me noo," she added with a chuckle.

"I think it is a lovely name," said Emily. "What would you like me to call you, Mrs. Raoghnailt?"

"Naethin' the likes o' that. I'm no *Mrs*. I'm nae married. Annabella will suit me jist weel enough."

"I am very happy to have made your acquaintance, then . . . Annabella," smiled Emily. "Although I admit I was surprised when I saw you. I'm afraid I was so lost in looking at that great stone that I had no idea anyone else was within miles."

"Oh, aye—the Muckle Stane. When the mist blows awa', ye can see't frae a' the island. But maist o' the time, the rain an' fog's hangin' too thick."

"How was it ever erected up there on top of the hill . . . and by whom?"

" 'Tis a mystery, lass—not a soul kens hoo it came there or why."

The two new acquaintances continued down the uneven terrain chatting freely. Emily gradually accustomed herself to the older woman's speech, though it was sprinkled with so many strange words she was kept constantly guessing at more than half of what she heard.

Every so often Emily's colorful companion paused and stooped to the ground to inspect some plant or other. In some cases she rose and they continued on. In others she set her basket on the ground, took from it a pair of scissor snips, and clipped a handful of blossoms or leaves or grass and added them to the rest. Each addition came with a brief explanation to Emily of the plant in question. Though she could not remember them all, she learned about a half-dozen edibles that Annabella was collecting for her larder—including chickweed, water mint, fat hen, wild chives, sorrel, one or two members of the goosefoot family, and of course that species that grows everywhere, dandelion. She had been hoping to find a supply of nettles, Annabella said, to dry for tea. But it was surprisingly scarce on the island. Bogbean and wild mint were two of her other favorite collectables. The bogbean was medicinal, aiding digestion and circulation—though some also used it to flavor beer. The mint, she said, liberally placed on the windowsills, was the preferred method for keeping summer flies out of one's kitchen.

They reached the shoreline and turned south along the road. When they had covered about half the distance back to the village, a great stone building to their right gradually came into view through the undulating hilly terrain inland from the road. Its roofline bore traces of ornate design. Two wings sat perpendicular to each other and were joined by a central connecting wing angled into both. Emily had noticed the compound when out with the group that morning. Now she had the opportunity to satisfy her curiosity.

"What is that place?" she asked. "It is not like anything else on the island."

"Oh, aye—I daresay! 'Tis the Cottage, lassie."

"That hardly seems a fitting name. It's huge!"

"Aye. A castle's more like it—a plain man's castle, ye ken, as is oor laird, bless him. But the Cottage is what it's called. 'Tis the home o' the laird."

They continued past the drive that led off to

the quaintly styled Cottage. Spread with a thin layer of gravel, the road widened and showed the unmistakable ruts of automobile tracks.

Out of sight, the figure of a young man emerged from behind a wall, striding purposefully toward one of several outbuildings. Seeing the two women in the distance and recognizing both, though surprised to see them together, he slowed. Keeping behind what limited shelter the hedges, shrubbery, and a number of ornamental trees afforded, he crept furtively after them as they made their way toward the village.

29

COTTAGE OF INTRIGUE

Ten or fifteen minutes later Emily Hanson and Annabella Raoghnailt entered the outer precincts of the eastern lay of cottages of Whales Reef. Annabella led Emily off the central thoroughfare into a narrow lane. Their way led among a random conglomeration of stone cottages of seemingly infinite variety. They were set in no apparent order, some pointing north, others south, and the rest facing all the disparate degrees of a circle. A thin trail of white smoke floated up from every chimney.

Nearly all the cottages were surrounded by low stone fences, enclosing yards sufficient to accommodate a cow, perhaps a few sheep, and assorted ducks and chickens. A crude barn or "byre" stood somewhere on the premises, most often attached to the house, where the animals could be sheltered during the winter months. Colorful assortments of wash hung blowing and flapping in the wind on ropes ingeniously devised and strung. Wherever in their humble plots a few inches of soil might be cultivated, a patch of potatoes was growing, along with kale and what other vegetables could be coaxed out of the stubborn ground.

As they made their way through the maze, they negotiated so many twists and turns between cottages, fences, and clotheslines that Emily could no more have retraced her steps with her eyes open than blindfolded.

At last Annabella opened a rickety wood gate and led Emily into a yard and through the door of a stone cottage of the same appearance and construction as the others.

"Come in an' be welcome tae my bit hoosie, lassie!" she said. "Sit ye doon an' I'll hae tea along in nae time."

One look about the place filled her with fascination. She had not been inside an actual Scottish home since her arrival, much less the humble cottage of so fascinating a woman as her new acquaintance. A hundred mingled smells assaulted her as she walked into the large, dark single room that apparently served as sitting room, dining room, and kitchen all in one. Mint and bay were prominent, though she detected hints of dill and thyme, along with a few pungent spices to accompany the herbs. It was as though she had stepped into an herbalist's laboratory or the botany lab back at college. The furniture was sparse and obviously poor. The hearth was cold, but the remnants of a peat fire burned in a cast-iron stove.

Two walls were lined with shelves filled with an assortment of jars and canisters containing three or four dozen varieties of plant species, dried blossoms, crushed leaves, roots, cinnamon bark, and other barks along with diverse powders. On one of the low shelves sat a stone mortar and pestle.

Emily wandered about wide-eyed. Meanwhile, her hostess pumped water into a kettle, carried it to the stove and set it on the hob. She grabbed several fresh peats from a copper hod on the floor, opened the low iron door, and tossed them inside.

"Ye seem a mite curious aboot what ye see, eh, lassie?" said Annabella, reaching for a brightly colored teapot. "Ye'll be wonderin' aboot my herbs, I'm thinkin'."

"What a collection you have," replied Emily. "Have you gathered all these on the island?"

"Oor groun's too puir but for a few things the likes o' which I was gatherin' today. I go tae mainland Shetland, or hae other plants sent me for most o' it."

"Are they all for your own use?" asked Emily.

"Aye. But folk come tae me for what ails them too—those that arena feared o' me like the nickums!" she added with a laugh.

"I am astonished at the variety," said Emily.

"Half o' these or mair come from the Continent, some from the East."

"How do you get them?"

"I send for them, an' the laird, bless him, keeps an eye oot for what I might be needin' on his travels—seeds an' cuttings an' the like, noo an' then a wee seedling. He's got a keen eye for growin' things o' a plant nature as weel as wi' his four-legged creatures. An' o' coorse, some I grow mysel'."

"You have an herb garden?"

"Aye," nodded Annabella. "Come through an' I'll show ye."

She set aside the teapot she had filled with loose tea and led into a small room off the kitchen that opened onto her rear garden. It was clearly a later addition. Its sloping lean-to glass roof faced south. The top half of the three exposed walls were mostly comprised of windows. The little room was bright with sunlight, in stark contrast to the nearly windowless interior room of the cottage.

"A tiny hothouse!" exclaimed Emily.

On shelves filling every available inch sat pots of many sizes and shapes from which grew herbs and plants and bits of greenery.

"It's wonderful!" said Emily, walking slowly about and examining the shelves and their contents.

They made their way back inside the kitchen a few minutes later. The water was by now steaming up from the kettle. Annabella poured it into a porcelain pot on the plain pine table, then added two cups and saucers from a cupboard.

"Sit ye doon, lassie," she said. "We'll gie the tea two or three minutes tae git as broon as the peat water. Would ye like tae try it wi' a sprig o' dry watermint frae oot on the moor?"

"I will have my tea exactly as you do," replied Emily.

A jug of milk, a small bowl of sugar, and a plate filled with what looked like crackers of some kind followed. Within minutes they were seated sipping at aromatic cups. Emily had taken one of the crackers and munched at it with a curious expression.

"What are these?" she asked. "I've never had anything like it."

"Oatcakes, lassie. Milk, potatoes, an' oatcakes hae been the sustenance o' the Scots for generations."

"So these are oatcakes. I never knew what t
were like. They're rather plain and dry."

Annabella laughed. "Naethin' but oats, wate
an' salt."

"Do you make them yourself?"

"Oh, aye—a' the women make their own
oatcakes. None buys oatcakes at the bakery ither
than tourists. Butteries, aye, but nae oatcakes."

"Well, this day has been full of surprises," said
Emily. "Seeing your cottage and your herb garden
has been an education. I have taken many botany
classes. Though I am a biology major, plants are
not my field of study. I thought I knew a *little*
about herbs. Now I see I was mistaken."

"What do you study then, lassie?"

"My main area of emphasis is birds. That is why
I am here—to work on my senior thesis on the
birds of the North Atlantic."

"So ye're a scholar, are ye?"

"I don't know if I would say that. Let's just say
I am a student."

"An' a woman besides. I hae aye heard aboot
sich things—women votin' an' women gaein' tae
university an' the like. Weel, a' that isna for the
likes o' me. I hae nae interest in bein' nae mair
nor jist who I am. I'm content wi' things as they
be. I wouldna want tae stand in a man's boots. But
good for yersel', lassie, if that's what ye want."

Emily laughed. "I love to learn. College has been
exciting for me. It wasn't the kind of opportunities

mother and grandmother had. I guess times ve changed."

"Aye, though nae doobt mair in America than n Shetland. Naethin' much changes here. People stay where they are an' do what their parents did. I've ne'er been oot o' Shetland in my life."

"Not even to Scotland or England—mainland Scotland, I mean?"

Annabella shook her head. "I hae nae interest in a' that. An' it takes money tae travel."

"My father didn't altogether like the idea of my going to college," said Emily. "I come from a Quaker family, you see. Some people consider us old-fashioned. But in the end he allowed it."

"Weel, bless the dear man for that. Sometimes we hae tae grow an' learn in ways we dinna expect. So ye're a Quaker, are ye? I never met a Quaker in my life. Nor an American either. I always thought Quakers were a mite queer like, no the same as ither Christian folk. But ye're a pleasant an' ordinary enough lassie."

Emily laughed. "I hope so!" she said.

They continued to chat and sip their tea and munch oatcakes. At length Emily glanced at her watch.

"Oh, my goodness!" she exclaimed. "I had no idea it was so late. It's almost four o'clock. I'm sorry," she added. "I need to get back to the Hotel. We have a lecture at four."

She rose from the table.

"Thank you ever so much, Annabella," she sai
with a smile. "I have enjoyed myself more than I
can say."

"Will I see ye again, lassie?"

"Most assuredly," nodded Emily. "Our tour
leaves tomorrow for the big island. Then we
will be back in another several days.—Oh, but I
just realized . . . how will I find my way to your
cottage?"

"Just ask anyone in the village for the Herb
Woman. They'll point ye the way." She rose and
led Emily outside. "I'll walk ye back so ye can
find yer way tae the Hotel. Wudna want ye gittin'
lost on my account."

30

DINNER AT THE HOTEL

Brogan Tulloch wandered listlessly most of
the late afternoon after following Annabella
Raoghnailt and Emily to the village and watching
them disappear among its maze of cottages. He
returned home about 5:30 to dress for the evening
before setting out for the Hotel. He walked into
the dining room about 6:45. His spirits picked
up the moment he saw the young American at
a table alone. He strode immediately toward
her.

"Good evening, Miss Hanson," said Brogan as he approached.

"Mr. Tulloch," nodded Emily. "Would you care to sit down?"

"Thank you," replied Brogan. "I hope you will permit me to apologize again for my behavior when we first met out on the moor."

"Really, there is no need. I accept your apology."

"That is very kind of you. So how were your adventures today?"

"We had a fascinating lecture by Dr. MacDonald. And I met a charming woman—out in the fields in the middle of the island. Up on that hill with the big wedge of rock standing on end—what did she call it . . . an odd name."

"The Muckle Stane," said Brogan.

"That's it. Once she realized I was American she began speaking more slowly and using fewer words of dialect. Then I could mostly understand her."

"Yes . . . Annabella—I saw you with her."

"You did, where?"

"The two of you were walking past our house—"

"The Cottage, you mean? Annabella told me it was the laird's house. I didn't put two and two together that it was where you lived too. An odd name for such a large home."

"It's what everyone calls it," rejoined Brogan. "My grandfather built the place, though he didn't seem like the cottage type. I'm surprised he didn't call it Tulloch Castle. He cut a wide swath in his day, they say—the complete opposite of my father. So you had a visit with the village character, our own Herb Lady."

"I found her a dear and fascinating woman. She invited me back to her cottage—a real cottage— for tea."

"I saw you go with her into the village."

"You weren't following us?" said Emily, one eyebrow arching slightly.

"Only for a bit. I thought we might have a chance to talk. But I didn't want to intrude.—So tell me more about today's lectures."

"Dr. MacDonald spoke briefly about the wildlife of the North Atlantic," Emily replied. "He talked about Darwin's research on the Galapagos Islands and related it to the Shetlands."

After several more minutes of conversation, they looked up to see Emily's traveling companion approaching the table with their tour's guest lecturer, Dr. MacDonald.

"Mr. Tulloch!" said Mrs. Barnes effusively. "How wonderful to see you again. Are you joining us for dinner? Please do."

Brogan glanced at the other two. Emily smiled and nodded her assent to the invitation.

"Well then," said Brogan, "I would enjoy that very much. Thank you."

The next hour and a half passed quickly. At length Mrs. Barnes rose. "Would you excuse me," she said. "I think I need to freshen up." By then Dr. MacDonald was engrossed in conversation with several of the other guests.

A moment later Brogan and Emily were left alone.

"Would you like to go outside for a walk?" Brogan asked.

"That sounds nice," smiled Emily.

Brogan stepped around the table, offered his hand, and helped Emily to her feet, then led the way out of the dining room to the lobby and outside.

31

A WALK IN THE MOONLIGHT

Brogan and Emily left the Hotel. It was approaching nine o'clock but the gardens remained bathed in sunlight.

"So your tour is away from Whales Reef tomorrow?" said Brogan.

"To mainland Shetland," nodded Emily.

"Where are you bound?"

"I'm not sure exactly—to some puffin breeding grounds, I believe, the day after tomorrow. Somewhere in southern Shetland. Tomorrow we are in Lerwick all day."

"Well, you had better keep me far away while

you're about your puffin watching. I might scare them away!"

Emily laughed at Brogan's making himself the object of his own joke. They continued in silence for a minute. The sounds of the Hotel gradually faded as they entered the hedge-bordered paths of the garden.

"It always takes me by surprise how light it is," said Emily at length. "After being inside, then dinner . . . somehow I expected to walk outside and find it dark."

"Ah, but look," said Brogan, pointing to his left, "the moon is rising. So we can still call this a moonlit stroll. However, you're right, it is amazing when you're not used to it. If you look at a map of Scandinavia, its three countries all extend far into the Arctic Circle. We are *very* far north. The land of the midnight sun, you know."

"Now it's you playing the scholar," rejoined Emily. "And with a dry subject like geography no less."

"Just a bit of trivia I must have picked up somewhere!" laughed Brogan. "And though I would claim no geographic knowledge besides vaguely being able to tell north from south, I am surprised by what you were saying earlier about comparing the Shetlands to the Galapagos. Shetland is almost in the Arctic Circle, the Galapagos are on the equator. I would never have guessed there to be similarities in their respective wildlife."

"Obviously the climate is much warmer off South America," said Emily, "but the bird migrations tell a similar story. The species are entirely unique. But the developmental patterns are parallel. It ties in directly with my thesis."

"A thesis?"

"The graduates at my college write a senior paper. I am researching North Atlantic bird species."

"What college would that be?"

"It's called Wilmington."

"I'm sorry, and where is that?"

"It is a small Quaker college."

"Quaker—really? Why there?"

"They admit women for one reason. And I am a Quaker."

"*A Quaker!* How interesting—unexpected is more like it."

"You sound surprised."

"I suppose I am."

"Why?"

"I don't know, I suppose I always thought Quakers—"

"Were strange?"

"Maybe," he replied, laughing lightly. "But not *you,*" he added hurriedly. "You're—"

He realized that he had again taken a step in the direction of quicksand.

"*Normal?*" suggested Emily with a smile.

"That's not exactly how I would put it," said Brogan. "I don't know . . . you are lively and attractive and, I don't know—you seem fun. I suppose I considered Quakers dour and old-fashioned."

"That's something like what Annabella said when I told her. Anyway, I am here to get an early start on my project."

"What is your field of study?"

"Biology."

"Ah, right—the birds of the North Atlantic. So you get high marks in most classes, you study both biology and history, and you are on the vanguard of the new age of women attending university. You must be very proud."

"I never thought of being proud of study and learning."

"Surely you are proud of what you have done."

"I haven't done it *yet*."

"Will you be proud when you do?"

"It's more than that. I'm not sure pride describes what I will feel."

"What then?"

Emily grew pensive. "I love to learn," she answered at length. "Learning . . . discovering things you never knew before . . . don't you find it exciting?"

"I can't say as I found *study* exciting. I don't know about *learning* simply on its own merits."

"I love learning new things."

"Then I admire you, Miss Hanson. It is not a sentiment voiced in the circles I have been accustomed to move in. You and I are, at the end of the day . . . well, I suppose we are about as different as two people can be."

"Me the bookworm, you—what were you, Mr. Tulloch? You were probably an athlete. Am I right? Isn't that what all young men want to be?"

"Not all perhaps, but most."

"And were you a star athlete?"

"A mediocre one at best," replied Brogan. "I wasn't particularly talented, and didn't work hard enough to excel. I don't suppose I was a bad cricket player. I tried rowing for a time, but it is very hard work. And I ran a little too. I was no Eric Liddell, I'm afraid."

"I'm sorry, I don't know the name."

"Eric Liddell, the pride of Scotland."

"I have never heard of him."

"He is Scotland's most famous athlete at the minute. He will be competing at the Olympics in Paris next month. Actually they are already under way, though most of the track and field events come later. He and Harold Abrahams are our two stars, though they are going to have their hands full with the Americans."

"I'm sorry, I'm afraid I don't know much about sports."

"I've thought about popping over to watch Eric Liddell run, but I don't know if I will."

32

AMBITION, CHARACTER, AND FATHERS

"Do you still participate in sports?" asked Emily as the two new acquaintances continued to walk casually through the Hotel grounds.

"Not much chance after one leaves university," answered Brogan, "at least for someone of my modest skills. Not much cricket in Shetland—it's a warm weather sport. There are the Highland Games, of course, but I've not gone in much for that sort of thing. Maybe that's the advantage to being a bookworm instead of an athlete. One never outgrows books."

"So what are you now, Mr. Tulloch," asked Emily, "if your athletic and university days are behind you?"

"Me?" rejoined Brogan, seemingly unnerved by the question. "I don't suppose I know what I am.

"A wastrel, I suppose," he said after a moment. His tone was somber.

"That seems a rather strong dose of self-recrimination," rejoined Emily.

"What if it's true?"

"I doubt it's *entirely* true. Besides, you are too

young to be pronouncing such a judgment on yourself."

"But what if it *is* true—that I am a wealthy eldest son who hasn't made much of his life?"

"Then I would reply that most of your life is still ahead of you. You're only, what, twenty-four or twenty-five?"

"Twenty-three, actually."

"There, you see. You're hardly more than a boy!"

Brogan laughed. "What does that make you, then?"

"Why, a grown-up sophisticated woman of twenty-two," replied Emily with a playful smile. "But the point is," she added, "that it's never too late to begin moving in a more positive direction."

"Maybe you're right, Miss Hanson. I will consider myself reprimanded for being morose— good-naturedly reprimanded, of course.—But do you mind if I ask you a personal question?"

"I don't mind if you ask. But I reserve the right not to answer . . . if it is *too* personal."

"Fair enough. I agree to your terms. Here it is, then. Where does your drive come from?"

"My *drive?* Explain yourself, Mr. Tulloch."

"Your determination, your focus, your desire to do what you do. You have goals and dreams, you want to study and learn and write papers and graduate from college. *Why?*"

They walked on for a minute or two. "I honestly

don't know how to answer you," said Emily after some time. "I never thought about the why. But you're right—I suppose you have described how I am. I would not have thought to call it drive."

"Ambition, then?"

"That's worse. Women aren't supposed to have ambition."

"Why not?'

"It's unscriptural. At least Quaker women aren't supposed to be ambitious."

"I am sorry to be the one to break it to you, Miss Hanson, but from where I stand, I think you *are* ambitious. But it is *good* ambition, noble ambition."

"I still don't know if I like the word. But I thank you for the kind qualification."

"And as you are attending college and writing research papers, unless I miss my guess, you love every minute of it. Maybe that's what I mean by noble ambition—what you called learning for its own sake."

"I see what you are getting at. Maybe that's the *why*. And I *do* love it!"

"I did not enjoy school," said Brogan with a mordant smile. "I'm not proud of it, but it's a little late now. I only went to university because it was expected of me. But I did the least I could to get by, I'm sorry to say. Something tells me you do *more* than is expected."

"I try to. My father ingrained it in me."

"He sounds like a good man," observed Brogan.

"He wants his sons and daughters to grow up with integrity—what he calls *character*. He taught us to have high principles in morals and behavior, in loving the truth . . . in everything."

Brogan smiled, then glanced down at the ground. Emily had been gazing into his face as she spoke. She detected what seemed sadness in the smile.

"What is it?" she asked.

"I was only thinking that your comment reveals as much about you as it does your father."

"How so?"

"You obviously respect him."

"Of course. I respect my father more than any man in the world. I do not say that because I think him better than other men, but simply because he is *my* father. He is the father God gave to nurture me. That is reason enough for me to honor him."

"That is a remarkable statement. Not all young adults would say that of their fathers. Most want to be rid of the shackles of parental influence at the earliest opportunity. At least that was the case with everyone I knew at university . . . including me."

"I feel safe knowing that my father and mother are committed to doing their best for me."

It was quiet as they emerged from the gardens and began walking back toward the front entrance of the Hotel.

"I was also thinking of my own father," said Brogan at length. "I suppose I would say exactly the same of him—that he wanted his three sons and his daughter to grow up with integrity and character. Unfortunately, I have not been as receptive to that training as you have. I haven't honored my father as I should have. Once you get to my age, it's hard to know what to say . . . how to show it."

Emily did not reply. She did not know either Brogan Tulloch or his father well enough to offer comment.

33

TWO LIFE STORIES

Posting his letters to Germany and Norway earlier that day put Ernest Tulloch in a pleasantly nostalgic mood. The idea of visiting the Continent again, with the Great War and two marriages yawning as a bittersweet divide between the *then* of his youth and the *now* of today, filled him with many emotions.

His life-changing months on the von Dortmann farm in Germany had taken place twenty-six years ago, between 1897 and 1898, a year before his time in the army where he had met Winston Churchill. He returned to Germany for several visits after the loss of his first wife, during one of which he had met the farmer's aristocratic young cousin Heinrich, the future baron. But the war years of 1914–1919 had changed Europe forever. He had not been back since.

A warm front had moved in from the south yesterday. He went out for his evening ramble with only a cardigan. The air filled with sweet aromas from the sea, he struck out east from the Cottage, made his way across the dune, and descended the rocky slope to the beach. From there he kept to the sea path as it wound south and west, in and out, around rocks and up a few steep inclines, along a bluff, back down to the water's edge, until at length it led him to the outlying precincts of the village. He turned inland, crossed the road, made his way along a sheep track over the uneven moorland, and presently found himself approaching the church. He had no idea that about the same time he left home, his eldest son was walking through the Hotel's gardens in conversation with a visiting American girl less than a quarter mile from where he was now.

Ever since the divine commission, as he considered it, had come to him he had sought not merely to be a father who reflected the divine Fatherhood to his three sons and daughter, he had also tried to live in the reality of the other half of the fatherhood equation—by being all that a grown son should be to his own father and mother.

He knew how feeble and incomplete were his examples of both sonship and fatherhood. That he was a broken vessel, however, did not diminish the imperative of the command.

That neither of his parents were what could be considered "spiritual" individuals made it difficult to know how to honor them in the full scriptural sense. His father had been an ambitious and mammon-loving entrepreneur. His mother was a socialite, more concerned with appearances than character. Yet the command upon him was to *honor* them, and to discover what God had to teach him about himself through them.

That challenge had rewarded the son of William and Esther Tulloch in the development of his own character. He honored what he found to honor. Beyond that, he chose to honor them simply because they were *his* parents, and had been chosen by God to guide *him,* imperfectly as it may have been, into adulthood. Honoring them thus, he grew to love his father and mother during their declining years more deeply than he would ever have thought possible.

As many a son and daughter discovers, the diverse revelations of filial affection are accelerated after death. In their respective passings, Ernest was inexplicably loosed to know his father and mother yet more intimately than he had in life. His own continued maturity as a man no doubt contributed as much to this unfolding mystery as the fact that he must now know them after the manner of the spirit rather than the flesh.

His father had been gone nine years, his mother three. He visited their graves often to remind himself of the dual charge upon the men of the earth to be worthy sons to their forebears, as well as worthy fathers to those who came after.

He passed through the iron gate of the cemetery behind the church and came to a stop a few moments later in front of the family plot. *William Tulloch,* he read on the tall stone of his father, *1851–1915,* and beside it that of his mother, *Esther Walpoole Tulloch, 1853–1921.* Slowly his eyes drifted to the stone on his left where lay his first wife: *Elizabeth Clark Tulloch, 1880–1904.* Beside her grew a small expanse of green grass, below which he would one day be laid to rest himself, with Sally beyond him on the far side.

Being here always brought a smile of fond remembrance to his lips. The memories were part of his "second story," as he called it, the invisible saga of his inner life no one else could see.

Everyone is writing two life stories, his German mentor had told him during the summer of his spiritual waking. *Few, however, take in hand the authorship of the most important of the two, that inner autobiography it falls to each of us to write for ourselves.*

The one life story, Ernest mused fondly, remembering the old man's words, chronicled dates and events, times and seasons, and the visible circumstances of one's birth, education, relationships, marriage, finances, travels, successes, failures, and progress through the years of earthly existence.

The second marked the invisible, growing, progressive development of the soul.

He dated the genesis of his own inner story to that year of his encounter with the aging German. Was the man a seer or prophet, or simply a humble farmer sent across his path to plant seeds of hunger within him that would grow the fruit of wisdom in their chosen season?

Though he did not know it at the time, while he listened to old Erich von Dortmann's quiet call to life on a higher plane, his own inner biography was being birthed.

He returned from Germany in 1898 at the age of twenty-two a changed young man. As much as the German farmer had instilled within him during their long talks as they worked side by side in the fields, planting, cultivating, tending, and finally harvesting his plots of potatoes, sugar beets, and wheat, the book that had come home with him—his first and most treasured copy in German, *Das Leben am Zentrum*, well marked from several close readings until he had been able to locate an English translation—continued through the years to focus the life path on which he had embarked. Its original English title, simple yet profound, *Life at the Center*, could but faintly hint at the extent to which the message of an inner life, hid with God in the depths of the human soul, had changed him forever.

He was never the same after Germany. He was thereafter, as the author of "the Center" termed it, an *owned* man.

But he was to discover that the quest to know God intimately, and to know the true nature of the divine Fatherhood, was a solitary journey. He found not many companions who shared that journey.

He had tried to talk to his mother about it. Her focus, however, was too mired in the practice and traditions of church and society to see what the Church was supposed to mean. In a gesture of youthful optimism, Ernest had presented a copy of *Life at the Center* to his father on his birthday, signed and with a deeply personal inscription. With a melancholy smile he recalled finding the book among his father's possessions after the elder Tulloch's death, stuffed in a box with useless mementos, pristine and new, its binding stiff. It had never been opened past the title page.

Over the years Ernest would discover that the hunger to write one's inner biography on the hidden tablets of the heart was rare even among Christians.

At length he became more circumspect in sharing his journey with others. He realized that the hunger he felt could not be transmitted by enthusiasm or even by example. It must be birthed from within. Why such hunger had come alive in his heart in the years of his youth, when most young men were chasing much different dreams, was a mystery he had still not successfully answered. Whence came the hunger to know God?

During his months in the hospital in London after his wounding in Africa, he had made another profound discovery. Those months marked his introduction to the writings of the Scotsman.

As he stood, Ernest's eyes drifted again down to his mother's grave. He smiled at the memory. He had his mother to thank for that introduction. She had grabbed a random handful of books, none of which she had read, the Scotsman's along with a few others, from the shelves in the Cottage to bring him in London. She was more enthusiastic about her birthday gifts to him of a silk cravat and the gold-knobbed walking stick which was in his hand at this moment.

The greatest gift, however, had been those books of the Scotsman. With little else to occupy his time during the months of his convalescence, he had devoured them eagerly.

The writings of his countryman from Aberdeenshire propelled his quest for life at the Center into the high realm of Fatherhood.

PART 7
AUGUST 2006

34

New Friends

David Tulloch's morning walks were usually solitary. He had been an early riser since childhood. The day's first hours, whether in darkness or after an early summer sunrise, provided his touchstone to the inner realities that gave focus to his existence. With Loni now an intrinsic part of his life, though his dependence on solitude had changed, his spirit still needed that daily grounding anchor. He knew that Loni, too, was acquainted with the inner silences of what her Quaker ancestors called the Center. They were both now learning to bring another into their centering places, while preserving, each in their own way, the essential tranquility of their souls.

A quiet, self-reliant, and thoughtful man, David had had few true friends in his adult life, and none whose lives flowed in the same deep channels—who could have understood him, or would have wanted to be understood *by* him. He was coming to know Noak Muir in that way, though the man was old enough to be his father.

He walked into Coira MacNeill's bakery a few

minutes after six o'clock in the morning, expecting to see no one other than the proprietress herself. However, another figure stood at the counter with his back to the door, chatting with the shop's owner. As the bell rang announcing David's entry, the man turned. His face lit in recognition as he saw David walking into the shop.

"Mr. Tulloch . . . good morning!" he exclaimed, reaching out his hand.

"And to you, Mr. Rhodes . . . or should I say *Reverend* Rhodes!" laughed David, shaking his hand.

"No, please—I've been over that with Audney. No *Reverend* for me."

"Whatever you prefer to be called, you caused a bit of a hubbub yesterday. The village is talking of nothing else."

Rhodes laughed. "They have no one to blame but themselves," he said with good humor. "I told them it was their own fault for jumping to conclusions."

"You did indeed. I enjoyed your remarks very much. Our little community is far too prone to gossip. Your gentle admonition was needed.— Wouldn't you agree, Coira?" said David, turning to the woman behind the counter.

Where she stood listening, Mrs. MacNeill vouchsafed no reply.

"I hope I did not offend too many of my listeners."

"If anyone was offended, they are probably the ones who needed to heed your exhortation most of all.—Coira, I take it you have met our new minister?"

"I was in the kirk yesterday," answered Coira stiffly.

"Mrs. MacNeill and I are already friends," said Rhodes. "I have been visiting her every morning since my arrival and am her greatest fan. She is keeping this particular visitor to your fair community well supplied with oatcakes and butteries and biscuits and pasties. Between Evanna's meals and Mrs. MacNeill's treats, I've no doubt gained half a stone since my arrival."

The two young men left the bakery a few minutes later, each carrying a warm white bag.

"Which way were you going?" asked the minister. "That is, if you don't mind my tagging along."

"Not at all. I would welcome the company. I was on my way home through the village. I'll show you some of the back lanes that lead toward the moor north of town. In fact, why don't you come back to the house with me for tea?"

"I would love to—though I'm under a bit of a time constraint." He glanced down at his watch. "However, it's early yet."

David led off the main street until soon they were walking through the circuitous maze of alleys and narrow cobbled lanes that made up Whales Reef.

"So if you don't mind my asking," said David, "why *did* you keep your identity secret?"

Rhodes smiled. "For no other reason than what I said yesterday. People tend to act and react differently around ministers," he answered. "It's impossible to escape the baggage. There so often clings to clerics an indescribable air of mustiness and mildew. No matter how hard you try to guard against religiosity, when people meet a minister, they expect a subtle air of pomposity. They're on their guard. You would be amazed at how people change the instant they learn I'm a minister. It's one of the trials of the calling."

"It must make it difficult to enjoy the simple give-and-take of normal relationships."

"Precisely. People are always waiting for the moralizing homily, or some subtly self-righteous rebuke. I wanted my initial association with the people of your community to be free from those expectations. Whether I succeeded or not, only time will tell."

"How long will you be staying?" asked David.

"Actually, I'll be leaving this afternoon to fly down to Aberdeen. I don't want my presence to hinder a free discussion among the church leaders about my potential future here. That's why I'm watching the time."

"Do you want the job?" asked David.

"Absolutely," answered Rhodes enthusiastically. "I love it here. But I am young, inexperienced, and blunt. I may not be what they want . . . or need."

"I assure you that you have my wholehearted support," said David. "Most of the kirk's elders are good and honest folk—some my own relatives and men and women I have known most of my life. They will give you a fair hearing."

"I'm glad of that."

"I very much appreciated what you did yesterday," David went on. "Something very similar has been on my heart to say to our people—not as their minister like you, but as the chief."

"So we are thinking along the same lines."

"There have been so many rumors and innuendos swirling in the community for the past year, it's been all I could do to keep silent. Contrary to what many think, loose talk is not merely a pleasant pastime, it is a sin—a deadly sin. I love these people, but sometimes I am ashamed for how easily they believe whatever comes to their itching ears. But enough of *my* moralizing! Next thing you know, I'm going to sound like a minister preaching a hellfire sermon."

Rhodes laughed. "No worry of that. I agree with everything you say."

"Have you been to the manse?" asked David.

Rhodes nodded. "I had a pleasant visit and meal with Rev. Yates yesterday. He invited me to stay with him, but for my purposes I thought the inn best. So what can you tell me about this man who is charged with killing the Texan—your cousin, I believe Audney told me."

"Yes . . . Hardy—my third cousin."

"I realize I'm a newcomer, but my heart goes out to the man. I don't know why. Maybe from what I've been told, he reminds me of myself when I was young. I would like to meet him. Where is he being held?"

"In Lerwick."

"Perhaps I could get in touch with Mr. Sinclair and have him pick me up an hour earlier than planned. Do you think the fellow would consent to see me if I paid him a visit on my way to the airport?"

"I'm sure he would," replied David. "He wouldn't know who you were anyway. I have a better idea—I'll drive you into the city and then take you to the airport."

"That would be terrific. I would enjoy that."

"But prepare yourself," David added with a light laugh. "If he's in a bad mood, you never know what Hardy might say. He would probably be put off, as you say, knowing that you are a minister."

"Then I won't tell him to begin with. You can just introduce me as your friend."

35

FRANTIC REQUEST

By the time Loni was brewing her first cup of tea for the day, David and Lincoln Rhodes had walked through half the village and had been talking for over an hour in David's kitchen. It was obvious to both that a lasting friendship was in the making.

The morning's message from Maddy on Loni's phone, now that she had a dependable answering machine at the Cottage, sounded frantic. It had come through late the previous night from Maddy's D.C. condo.

I need to talk to you . . . immediately. Skype whenever you can, day or night. Maddy.

Unfortunately a storm had temporarily knocked out her internet and she was unable to comply with Maddy's request.

David walked Lincoln Rhodes back to the Whales Fin Inn about eight o'clock, agreeing to return for him in two hours. He walked straight to the Cottage to greet Loni for the day.

Maddy's urgent message and David's offer to Rhodes suggested the same solution. Such it was that two hours later, with Rhodes's single suitcase in the boot of David's car, that Loni and Audney, who was not about to be left out, piled into the ack seat of David's car. With David's passenger beside him, the four set out for the ferry and mainland Shetland.

An hour later, Loni and Audney were together at the Cappuccino Club to connect with Maddy, while David and Lincoln drove across town to the Sheriff's Court.

It was between six and seven in Washington. Maddy was dressed and ready to leave for work.

"Oh, Loni—you got my message," exclaimed Maddy, sitting down at her computer. "I didn't want to wake you in the middle of the night, but I've been desperate to talk to you."

"Hi, Maddy," said Loni. "Audney Kerr's with me—you remember her from the pub."

"Yes, of course."

"We're in Lerwick. I couldn't get through from the island."

"Best o' the day tae ye, Miss Swift," said Audney, poking her head next to Loni's in front of Loni's laptop.

"Hello, Audney—it's nice to see you again."

"Do the two o' ye need tae talk in private?" said Audney. "I can jist gae ootside if ye want."

"No, please stay," said Maddy. "Maybe two heads will be better than one.—Loni, you'll never guess what happened? Remember the guy I told you about?"

Maddy went on to describe the events of the previous week.

"What an amazing story, Maddy!" Lonr exclaimed. "And just after you bought that new dress you showed me."

"Yeah!" moaned Maddy. "But his first sight of me was in that horrible sweat suit. I can't imagine what I was thinking when I bought it."

"He obviously didn't mind. Men like active athletic girls."

"That's me all right! But seriously, folks . . . after what you said before about being afraid of falling in love, and the cheap advice I gave you—now it's my turn. I'm not as smart as I thought I was when it was you in the hot seat! I'm a wreck!"

"You gave me good advice, Maddy. You helped me take a step back and listen to my heart. It sounds as if this guy likes you. He hadn't forgotten you either. He's not married, I take it?"

"Gosh, you know I never asked. It didn't come up."

"Might be a piece of information it would be good to have. I can't imagine he would ask you out if he was. So what happened?"

"We went to lunch," Maddy went on, "and it was fine. I was nervous, but it wasn't so bad. He's easy to talk to. There were no awkward moments. It was just like two business acquaintances catching up. But he's asked me out again! It's hard not to be afraid. My adrenaline levels are spiking . . . sweaty palms, heart pounding, can't concentrate on work. I don't know what to do, what to wear. Lunch was different. But dinner in an expensive restaurant—like a real *date!* What if he brings me flowers? What if he tries to kiss me—what will I do?"

Loni couldn't help but laugh. "What are you asking me for? I don't know much about all that."

"You're ahead of me!"

"It's different with David. And don't forget how it started—with me chewing him out!" All three laughed at the reminder. "But eventually," Loni went on, "I was able just to be myself and one thing led to another. Before Hugh came along I had been on a total of about four dates in my whole life."

"If ye dinna mind me speakin' up, Miss Swift," now said Audney, "Miss Ford's jist told ye a' ye need tae know—jist be yersel'. Ye canna be other than that."

"Around him, I don't know what being myself means!"

"Remember what you told me before," said Loni, "that you talked too much. So if you find yourself starting to babble, just take a deep breath, slow down, and like Audney says, be yourself."

"That's easier said than done. I'm feeling too vulnerable to be myself. I don't want to get my hopes up and then blow it again. Hope and fear are two sides of the same coin and I'm bouncing back and forth between them."

"We are women after all," said Loni. "Aren't we supposed to be irrational at times?" she added, laughing.

"Not prim and proper businesswoman Madison Swift!"

"You should have seen me a few weeks ago when I exploded at David. It was mortifying, I was so stupid! Audney *did* see me, I am embarrassed to say."

"We a' done things we regret," said Audney. "Dinna say another word aboot it."

"So you see, Maddy," said Loni. "All part of the adventure of being a woman."

"But it's a new world for me," said Maddy. "I don't want to appear too enthusiastic. But neither do I want to make the mistake I did before of *not* allowing him to see . . . well, you know, that I like him."

"If a man takes a fancy tae ye," added Audney, "the worst thing ye can do is put on airs an' try tae be something ye're not. Jist be who ye are."

"I'm no longer sure who I am. Suddenly I'm a basket case."

"I'll tell you exactly what you told me," said Loni. "You said that I needed to come back here with David to find out how things stood, that I had to know. Well you have to know too. He has asked you out, so you need to take this opportunity to see what might come of it. True, you open yourself up for hurt. That's the vulnerable part. But if you don't take that chance, you will never know. Breathe deep and relax . . . then enjoy yourself."

36

A FOURSOME

The drive south from Lerwick to the airport at the southern extremity of Shetland known as Sumburgh Head was subdued. Each of the four sensed that a special bond had formed between them.

They lunched together in the city. Lincoln Rhodes's flight was at four o'clock. After his visit to Hardy, the young minister was all the more convinced that, whatever became of the murder charges, he was to reach out to David's cousin. When and how remained uncertain.

Parking at the airport, as they made their way into the terminal, David and Loni walked on ahead.

"I hope I will see you again soon," said Rhodes as he and Audney fell into step together.

"Hoo soon will it be afore the session gives ye an answer?" asked Audney.

"I don't know. Even if the vote goes against me, I will see you again. Perhaps next time I will come simply as a tourist."

"Come tae look at the puffins?" smiled Audney.

"Something like that. In the meantime, do you mind if I call you occasionally?"

"O' course I dinna mind."

Rhodes parted from the other three twenty minutes later.

"David . . . thank you!" he said, extending his hand. "You have opened your heart to me as a friend. I am more grateful than you can know.—And Miss Ford—"

"Please . . . *Alonnah*."

The minister smiled. "You informal Americans! Well, then . . . *Alonnah*—I wish you the best in your new adventure as an adopted Shetlander."

"Thank you, Lincoln—if I may return the informality."

"You may indeed!"

David and Loni stepped back. Rhodes turned to face Audney. She glanced at the floor. The next moment she found herself swallowed in his embrace.

"Good-bye, Audney," he said. "I have enjoyed our time together more than I can tell you."

Audney seemed to have lost her voice.

Lincoln released her and turned quickly away. In less than a minute he disappeared toward the departure gates.

The three made their way out of the terminal and back to David's car.

"Loni," asked David, "do you know about Sumburgh Head?"

"Not much, but it sounds familiar somehow."

"It's one of the most famous bird-watching sites in the Shetlands—huge cliffs, millions of birds—puffins and every other variety imaginable."

"Oh, of course. I just read about it in my great-grandmother's journal."

"Would you like to see it? We're practically there. It's something you have to see."

They left the terminal and were soon pulling into the Sumburgh Head parking lot, which at this time of day was filled with tour buses. Hundreds of people were milling about. They walked across one of several paths to the edge of the bluffs overlooking the sea.

"It's spectacular!" exclaimed Loni. "I thought the cliffs on Whales Reef were high. I've never seen anything like this. And the birds! No wonder the Shetlands are a bird-watching paradise. I don't remember reading about this in either of your books."

"I have a chapter devoted to Sumburgh Head in the book I am working on," said David.

As the three wandered about, David assumed the role of Loni's tour guide, pointing out various species of flora and fauna. Audney remained quiet.

After some time, a faint whir of a prop jet sounded behind them. Seconds later an airplane came into view, banking up steeply from the airport, arched around to the south, and came nearly directly overhead. They watched as it slowly receded into the blue and finally disappeared from sight.

Audney looked away and wiped at her eyes.

As if by common consent, the three turned from the cliffs and made their way slowly back toward the parking lot. David stretched his arm around Audney's shoulder.

"Ye hae yers noo, David," said Audney softly at length. "I was hopin' maybe I'd foun' mine as weel. But what if I ne'er see him again?"

"Ye need hae nae worry o' that, Audney."

"Hoo ken ye that?"

"I spent two hours wi' the man this mornin'," said David. "He's some taken wi' ye, Audney. I can tell ye wi' certainty—ye *will* see Lincoln Rhodes again."

37

EXCITED CALL

Loni set her alarm for 5:00 a.m., anticipating a call from Maddy the moment she got home from her fateful date. She was groggily sipping at a cup of strong coffee when her phone rang at 5:25.

"Hey, Maddy," she answered.

"You're up?"

"I was expecting you."

"What time is it there? I still get confused."

"Five-thirty."

"In the *morning!*"

"In the morning."

"Sorry—it's just after midnight here."

"So tell me everything."

"I had no reason to be nervous. Tennyson was a perfect gentleman. No advances. No innuendoes. I was fidgety but gradually settled down. We talked about everything under the sun. You and Audney were right—I tried to relax as if I was talking to you. I had a great time."

"When will you see him again?"

"You won't believe this—he's postponed his return to Alaska."

"He's from Alaska!"

"That's where he's living. His parents have a small ranch down in Virginia where he grew up. He wants to spend next weekend with me. He wants to take me there."

"Maddy—that's great."

"I'm a little stunned actually. I hardly know what to think."

"Will you go?"

"I'd like to. But meeting his folks—that is a little scary."

"Sounds serious."

"I don't know—I think mostly we're just having fun . . . like friends. I'm not sure he's got anything in mind. But it's definitely weird thinking that a guy just wants to have fun with *me*. You can't help the panic sweeping back in—especially the idea of meeting his parents! Let's face it, I'm not everyone's dream girl. The lingering fear of getting hurt is always there. I suppose all women feel it when they start getting close to someone. But what do I know? I feel like I'm in high school!"

"Who would have thought that we would be talking about falling in love," laughed Loni, "—both of us at the same time!"

"I hadn't allowed myself to say those words," said Maddy. "But I suppose that is it. That's what makes it so terrifying—realizing that I *am* falling in love again . . . for a second time with the same guy. If it ends up badly, I'm not sure I'll ever bounce back.—So what do you think I should do about this weekend?"

"You say he's being a gentleman. What is there to worry about? It's exciting, Maddy. It's a dream come true. You've been thinking about him all these years. Suddenly here he is. You told me that I had to see what would come of it with David. Now it's your turn to see where it leads."

"I know you're right. The magic from before—it's still there. Obviously I am thrilled. Still, it's happened so fast. Don't forget, this is Madison Swift you're talking to."

"The *new* Madison Swift."

"Maybe. But the old Madison Swift has almost finished her recommendations for the new laird of Whales Reef. We can talk about that later if you like . . . when it's daytime for both of us."

"Anything I need to worry about?" asked Loni.

"Not a thing. Your finances are on more solid ground than those of half our investors. You could leave everything as it is and you will have plenty of cash flow to keep the mill running and do whatever you want. The main question is whether you want to keep the investment portfolio as it is. It's very conservative—safe, dependable, almost zero risk. With a few changes, you could make it more aggressive and probably grow its value quickly. You know the kinds of things we tell our investors. Now *you* are an investor sitting on a portfolio that's not earning a fraction of what it could. It's what we tell our clients, it depends on your financial goals."

"You know me, Maddy—I never had financial goals. This is all new."

"Then you need to sit down with David—I assume you and he will be making these decisions together."

"He knows the needs of the people better than I do."

"Then the two of you need to decide what you

want long term. What do you want the estate's financial picture to look like in five years, in ten years? You could pretend that David is your client and that you are conducting an initial interview. You've done it with clients a hundred times."

"But you're saying there's no urgency, that if I do nothing, the estate's finances are fine?"

"More than fine—they're rock solid. Once you pay your inheritance taxes, which I believe Mrs. Bemiss has funds earmarked for, you will probably have to make decisions about what to do with the excess cash flow coming in. You could give the mill workers raises and modernize every home in the village with the income from the rents and oil leases. Unless oil suddenly dries up in the North Sea, money will be the least of your worries."

"And if David thinks it wise to diversify some of the investments, and grow the capital more aggressively, you would help me put together a plan?"

"Of course. But you can put together an investment plan as well as I can."

"Maybe we should consult your man Tennyson Stafford and look into some exotic hands-on adventurous investment that we get personally involved in."

"A great idea!"

"But not immediately. More important than the finances is what I intend to do with my life. I'm still not anxious to *live* in the Shetlands. And I don't want to give up my job with you. I also have to think of my grandparents. It's complicated. I have equal responsibilities there *and* here."

"You will figure it out. You'll probably travel back and forth for a while.—But I'm sleepy. I've had an exhausting emotional evening. I'm going to bed!"

"And I'm going to have another cup of coffee and start my day. We have a ewe we hope will give birth to a wee lammie or two today. And it looks like we may be in for more rain. Anyway, we'll talk about financial plans later."

"Give my greetings to Dougal and David."

"I will. Dougal always asks about you."

PART 8

A Legacy Begins— *The Friendship* 1924

38

STRANGE SENSATIONS

Brogan Tulloch stood at the window of his room gazing out on a twilight of colorful hues that would remain to usher in the dawn an hour or two from now.

He stood for fifteen minutes, then paced about once more. After another minute, like a fidgety child, he found himself in front of the window yet again.

It had been a long day of ups and downs. After breakfast at the Hotel, he had returned home midmorning, lounged about, had tea at eleven, lunch at noon, went out again, and nearly gone mad with boredom. Two or three times during the day he had perused the Cottage library, tried to interest himself in several books, had tea again at two, then wandered to the barn when, returning to the house, he had seen the two women on the road, and, like one possessed, he had followed out of sight.

And then tonight's dinner and the walk with Emily in the Hotel gardens afterward had been wonderful. Yet now that it was over and he had a chance to reflect on his peculiar behavior, he was more flustered than ever.

The night wore on. Below him the house was quiet. No noticeable disturbance of the air came to his face. Yet he was aware of a faint tingling of sea air about his nostrils, borne through the open window on breezes too light to be felt by the skin.

What was on his mind, he could not have said. He was unaccustomed to soul-searching. He didn't like it. He disdained the very idea that he was the sort of person whose soul required any kind of cleansing overhaul.

The only sounds coming from outside were the calls of a few nocturnal birds and, clearly audible through the silence of night, the sea. From the stables behind the house, the occasional stamp of horse's hoof or snort of pig or shifting of cows broke the stillness.

When was the last time he had been so sane and sober at such an hour? His senses felt keen and awake. Yet he was also strangely ill at ease, unnerved by invisible forces he could feel but not identify.

Whatever was going on was obviously due to the presence on the island of the American girl Emily Hanson. What on earth had possessed him to prattle on like he had in the gardens? He had behaved like a fatuous half-wit!

All that inane babbling about being a wastrel. What a fool he must have looked!

He wanted no one looking into his soul. Least of all himself!

A surge of insurrection rose within him. *I am who I am,* Brogan told himself indignantly. *I'm not about to change my life just because some silly American girl shows up on Whales Reef and—*

Suddenly he stopped.

Who was he angry at? No one had asked him to change. Certainly Emily Hanson hadn't. She didn't seem to care that much about him. After their first awkward meeting she had done everything possible to avoid him. He'd had to force himself just to engage her in conversation.

He turned from the window and took several restless paces into his room. Realizing there was no place to go, he turned toward the window for yet a third time.

Finally he slammed the window down with a bang—angry at the birds, angry at the cows and horses and pigs, angry at the fragrant air, angry at the sea.

39

MEMORIES IN MANY DIRECTIONS

The evening grew late. How long Brogan's father stood in the cemetery he could not have said. Father and son were sharing something profound during their respective midnight moments of solitude, though neither would ever know it—reflections that took each into that private sanctuary of the soul where few men and women dare to venture. For the father the paths into those regions were well trod. For the son, the experience was as unnerving as it was new. Coincidentally on this night, the thoughts of both revolved around young women. The elder was thinking of Brogan's mother, who would always be young in his memory.

Meeting Elizabeth Clark represented a third chapter in Ernest Tulloch's biography. Elizabeth was part of both his life stories. His earthly biography would read, *"Marriage to Elizabeth Clark in 1900 . . . birth of two sons, Brogan and Wallace, and daughter Delynn . . . death of Elizabeth in childbirth, 1904."*

The deeper and more significant story of the love that had blossomed between them, however, was highlighted by the mutual discovery of the intersection of their inner biographies. They had not merely "fallen in love." They had been united by common purpose, common vision. Their love was a shared quest to discover life at the Center of God's will and purpose.

His several returns to Germany in the years following Elizabeth's death gradually rekindled his vision. He walked the hills and roads and fields and byways of earlier times, carrying with him his worn German copy of *Das Leben*

232

am Zentrum, reading through it twice again, asking God to reignite his vision for life now that Elizabeth was gone.

The answer did not come all at once or in a blinding flash of revelation. But by degrees he knew that he had been shown Fatherhood that he might dedicate himself even more diligently to fatherhood. He would give himself heart and soul to his two sons and his daughter. He would pour everything he was as a man into them. As they grew capable of it, he would teach them of life with God. He would instill within their young hearts the seeds of hunger for the divine Fatherhood. Perhaps he could not change the world. Perhaps the world was not hungry for such an uncommon life. But he had been given three precious young ones. That life he could pass on to them, and, through them, to those who came after.

He threw his life into his three children. The injunction of Moses became the guiding principle of his life—to train them in the ways and outlook and priorities of God.

No man in Whales Reef spent more time with his children or enjoyed so much romping and exploring and traveling and hiking and riding with them. He was fortunate to enjoy a singular opportunity not given to all men—freedom of time, unencumbered by financial constraints, to be able to do so. And as they grew, he involved them as much as possible in his work.

When they were old enough, he read to them from the Scotsman's books. He took them on walks about the island, speaking of the natural wonders of God's creation and what it revealed about the divine Fatherhood. He instilled within them the necessity, as they grew older and would have families of their own, to pass on God's principles. He spoke to them of the commands of Moses to sons and daughters and fathers, pressing upon them the imperative to be God's boys and girl, who would grow to become his men and woman. He spoke to them of Jesus, of His life, of obedience to His commands, and of becoming Christlike men and women—the one purpose for which mankind was created.

When he met Sally Lipscomb, younger by ten years, Ernest was filled with more gratitude than he found it possible to put into words—both to God and to Sally herself. How could a man expect, for a second time, to find another companion to share one's spiritual journey as a helpmeet and friend of the inner life.

Knowing the propensity of a small village to gossip, and knowing the esteem in which Elizabeth had been held by the women of Whales Reef, Ernest kept to himself the courtship to the daughter of the landowner from north Shetland. He did not want Sally exposed to the wagging of tongues before he could simply present her as his new wife. Whether this was a wise decision might be questioned by the inevitable fact that tongues *will* wag and no preventative measures can stop them. Unfortunately Ernest's frequent absences and unknown romance, followed by Sally's sudden—as it seemed—appearance as the new mistress of the Cottage was such a surprise that it offended some of the village women to think that the laird had been courting a second wife in secret. To explain the thing, some of the low-minded among them suggested that perhaps *she wasna a true wife, if ye ken my meanin'*. Such rumors, however, quickly died away as the villagers grew to love Sally as they had Elizabeth.

Sally brought music and new life to the Cottage. All three children took to her as if she were their mother. Sally loved them as her own. The birth of Leith a year later in 1909 was greeted by his half siblings with no less joy than by his parents.

It had been Ernest's practice from almost the time Brogan could talk, even prior to Elizabeth's death, to begin instilling God's principles in the lad. As their walks about the island ranged farther afield and involved fun and laughter and exploration and animals and all the myriad pastimes so relished in by children in a rural setting, behind the scenes Ernest quietly instructed, challenged, and exhorted about God and His ways. Wallace and Delynn began similar walks with their father when they were old enough, until the four of them—Ernest with his three young ones—were often seen together in the village or about the island in animated conversation about everything from the origins of the universe to the color and shape of a seashell to the effect of the moon on the ocean's tides. By the time young Leith was old enough to be taken on the personal and private walks with his father, teenage Brogan had begun to grow distant and silent in response to his father's instruction.

Ernest Tulloch's thoughts returned to the present. He shivered momentarily. Though it was light as midday, night was drawing slowly down upon the island.

He turned, left the churchyard, and struck out over the hills toward home.

40

GONE

Brogan Tulloch awoke with sunlight streaming through the window. All he remembered from the night before was that he had been unable to get to sleep.

Gradually images returned . . . dinner at the Hotel . . . the walk in the gardens.

Now he remembered. He'd paced his room until after midnight. He was in a foul mood. He could hardly recall what it was about. Mercifully sleep seemed to have washed away the worst of its effects.

He rose from bed and again sought the window. He remembered slamming it shut in a fit of anger. The day was bright and sunny. What had come over him last night with all those ridiculous reflections? So there was a girl he had taken a fancy to—where was the harm in that?

He drew in a deep breath, then walked to his wardrobe. As he began to dress, his own words from the night before returned to his memory.

So your tour is away from Whales Reef tomorrow . . .

Seconds later he was throwing on the rest of his clothes, then flew down the stairs and out to the garage. A minute after that he was speeding in his father's Studebaker into the village and toward the ferry landing.

As he half skidded to a stop in front of the pier, he knew he was too late. Across the mile-and-a-half isthmus he saw the ferry chugging in the mist toward the opposite shore. Though the distance was too great to make out individuals, he could see the railings filled with members of the Northern Adventure Tour. The coach that would take them on the next stage of their "adventure" was no doubt waiting at the fog-enshrouded landing on the other side.

He stared over the calm waters of the sound, as if the mere rhythm of the ferry's engine was enough to keep him rooted to the spot. Gradually it slowed. He had taken the ferry to and from mainland Shetland so many times that he could envision every detail.

A few minutes later he heard a faint thud as the bow bumped against the opposite pier. He knew that its two-man crew was now tying their craft off to thick wooden pylons. He imagined that he could faintly make out voices and laughter coming across through the quiet morning as the group disembarked and began loading onto the waiting coach. They had paid the tour organizers a fat sum to attend to their every need. In his mind he could see the coach driver and his assistant lugging the suitcases and bags of Mrs. Barnes and her fellow adventurers off the ferry and to the luggage compartments.

Ten minutes later, Brogan heard the motor of the coach sputter, then roar to life. He followed the sound along the shoreline for another minute until a brief clearing in the fog revealed the tiny red shape bounding along. Finally it disappeared in the direction of Lerwick.

Brogan returned to the car. He was in no mood to go home just yet. Neither did the idea of breakfast at the Hotel appeal to him. The place would seem deserted.

He inched the Studebaker onto the road, turned toward town, and crept along still in first gear. Without planning it, but with no other destination, he found himself swerving onto the narrow road leading uphill to the church. The way was narrow, barely wide enough for the Studebaker. Had an automobile ever driven this way before? His father never drove to church.

He didn't feel like being around people right now. An empty church on a weekday morning ought to be a safe haven for solitude.

Brogan parked in front of the stone building and got out. Surprisingly he found the church door open. Slowly, almost on tiptoe, he walked inside. Though his father and Sally and the others were faithful Sunday after Sunday, he hadn't been to church since early in his teen years.

He sat down in one of the stiff-backed pews at the rear of the small building. Why did they make church pews so uncomfortable? Probably a remnant of that stern Scottish Calvinism that thrived on making religion unpleasant. He recognized every sight, every sensation . . . the stained glass, the pulpit, the smells of wood, mildew, plaster, and the faint reminder of fish coming from the fisherman's loft where the smell grew especially pungent on warm summer Sunday mornings. He had been coming here since his boyhood. It was all so familiar, yet on this day strangely different.

As he sat in the quiet dim light, from the distant past words and images began to rise into his brain of a time when all this—when, for lack of a better description, *belief, spirituality, faith* . . . when all that this church and its tradition represented had been intrinsic to his life. He had grown up immersed in its ideas and forms. His earliest memories were of walks with his father, his little hand in his as his father spoke about God and Jesus and the Bible and living in obedience to its principles.

As a child, then as a boy, even as a teen, he had taken it all for granted, assumed that he would grow up to be just like his father—that he too would be religious, and that one day he would speak to *his* children about God and faith and Jesus. He had believed it all then . . . or so he thought. He and his father had carried on many an interesting dialog about spiritual things. He had prayed with his father every day of his young life for thirteen or fourteen years. His father had been as close a friend as his brother Wallace. He had loved his father more than anyone in the world.

What had happened? When had he begun to resent his father's outspoken faith? And *why* had he soured on his father's instruction?

Was it merely what they called growing up?

He had not thought much about religion since leaving for university. He had not consciously stopped believing. The ideas of faith, if that was what they should be called, had simply drifted to the back of his mind until he was no longer interested.

Maybe such change was natural. That didn't explain, however, why he had in the process drifted away from his father.

A melancholy smile came to Brogan's lips. The image of his father's smiling face filled his mind. He missed his father. Yet how was something from the past, a friendship from his boyhood, to be rekindled now?

41

WHENCE AND WHY COME CHANGE?

A sound disturbed Brogan's reverie. He glanced up to see the minister walking into the church from a side door. Expecting no visitors at such an hour, he paused as his eyes adjusted to the dim light. He squinted to see who was seated in front of him.

"Good morning, Rev. Matthews," said Brogan rising. "I hope you don't mind. I needed a quiet place."

"Of course not," replied the pastor, "but is . . . Brogan, is that *you?* Brogan Tulloch!"

"Yes," laughed Brogan. "Your prodigal returns."

"That is not what I meant," rejoined Rev. Matthews, "though it has been some time. It is good to see you again."

The two shook hands. Brogan resumed his seat, and the curate sat down next to him.

"You are home from the university, I take it?" he said.

"Yes. Graduated and back to Whales Reef."

"Well, congratulations. How time does fly! It seems only yesterday that you were a young— well, none of that! You are quite the man now! What was your field of study?"

"Nothing too flashy, I'm afraid. Liberal arts, which is a fancy way of saying I couldn't make up my mind about a more focused educational objective."

"So, what are your plans? Business, high finance?"

"The options for a future laird of a small estate are somewhat limited," replied Brogan with a wry tone. "To tell you the truth, I haven't thought much about it. I'll have to find something to do with myself. At the minute I have no idea what that will be. I suppose just getting through university was my overriding goal. Now that it is over, I discover I hadn't thought much beyond it. Not much of a way to start one's life as an adult, is it?"

"Ah well, I wouldn't worry about that. We all find our path in our own way and our own time. I have no doubt you will find yours."

"Rev. Matthews, do you mind if I ask you a question?" said Brogan.

"Not at all," replied the minister.

"What do you know about the Quakers?"

"Not much, just what I learned in history books—bit of a wild sect back in the 1600s. Calmed down over the years, I understand. Are you thinking of converting?"

"Nothing like that," smiled Brogan. "Just curious. Have you ever known a Quaker personally?"

"I cannot say that I have?"

"What do you know about their beliefs?"

"Actually, not a thing. They are considered Protestants, if I'm not mistaken. Quite a large number went to America, I believe. Honestly, I thought they were more or less dying out."

"Well, that is interesting. Thank you, Rev. Matthews," said Brogan. Again he rose to his feet. "Maybe I'll have a stroll about the churchyard, if that's all right."

"Certainly."

"It was nice to see you again."

"And you, Brogan."

Brogan left the church, walked out behind the building, and soon found himself in the cemetery. Slowly he made his way to the family plot. He had been here many times with his father, but not for a long time, and never alone.

It all seemed so different today. Looking at the tombstones of his family amid the silence of the churchyard stirred up feelings of melancholy. He was suddenly aware of how fleeting life was.

For the first time he was looking at the stones in front of him through a man's eyes rather than a boy's. These were real people buried here, his own mother, his grandmother and grandfather, and other ancestors whose names he scarcely knew. One day he would join them.

He glanced northward toward the interior of the island, then struck out across the moor. Twenty minutes later he crested the Muckle Hill. There rose the Muckle Stane in front of him. How many times he had been here, too, as a boy.

He smiled as he remembered the legends and stories he and Wallace had spun together as they romped and played over the island. It had changed with his brother as well, just as it had with his father. He missed Wallace too. What had happened? Why had he allowed himself to drift away from everyone he loved?

From the Muckle Stane, Brogan continued on to the northern extremity of the island. He almost expected to see Emily sitting at the cliff edge trying to coax the puffins closer.

But it was only a memory. On this day the bluffs were empty of humanity. He continued to the cave, looked around briefly with the same feeling of desolation he had felt since arriving at the ferry landing. He meandered about the northern bluffs, made his way through the peat fields until he came to the western road, then slowly wandered back through the island's western moors.

At length Brogan returned to the churchyard and the Studebaker. It was now past one in the afternoon and he'd had nothing to eat or drink all day.

The rest of the day passed drearily.

42

COFFEE, LARKS, AND SNAILS

Brogan woke suddenly from a deep sleep. The idea that had filtered from the depths up into his conscious mind was so powerful that it had awakened him instantly.

For a second night in a row he had slept like a baby. It was light outside. He reached for his watch.

Unlike the previous night, however, his sleep on this occasion, though sound, had been brief. The hands on his watch read 4:39.

He lay back down. After the brainstorm that had woken him, he would never get back to sleep. He lay for another several minutes. Finally he rose and found his robe. He wandered to the bookshelf whose contents had been doing little in recent years but gathering dust. Maybe he would try one of the Scotsman's novels again. His father had supplied him, Wallace, and Delynn each with their own individual sets. Leith would probably soon be getting his own as well.

A little over an hour later, Sally, the early riser of the family, descended the stairs. Though the house was still quiet, she thought she detected the aroma of coffee. The house seemed warmer than usual for this hour. Her curiosity mounting, she walked into the morning room.

There sat Brogan at the table, dressed and ready for the day, coffee cup in front of him, reading his father's *Northern Scot* from the previous day. A bright peat fire blazed behind him.

"Brogan!" exclaimed Sally with an expression in which a hint of anxiety was mingled with obvious surprise.

"Good morning, Sally!" replied Brogan, glancing up with a smile of greeting to his step-mother.

"You're up early."

"Couldn't sleep," he replied. "So I got up with the larks and snails . . . I think those are the chaps Browning speaks of as being early risers. Can't put my finger on the exact quote, but it will come to me. "

"And a fire . . . fresh coffee! You have been busy."

"I'll pour you a cup," said Brogan, rising and walking to the sideboard.

He took down a cup and saucer from the cupboard above it, then walked to the stove and poured out a cup of the steaming black brew.

He took it to the table and set it in front of Sally where she had taken a chair opposite him.

"You like yours with cream," he said, "if I am not mistaken."

"One of life's little pleasures."

Brogan disappeared into the pantry and returned a moment later with a small earthenware jug.

"Thank you, Brogan. What a treat—being waited on like this. Ordinarily I have my first cup alone until your father comes in for his tea. And the fire! To walk into the morning room with the peat glowing and the coffee brewing . . . as I say, a treat. Thank you."

"My pleasure. Ah—I've got it! 'The lark's on the wing, the snail's on the thorn. God's in his heaven, all's right with the world.' Although I haven't been outside yet to see if Browning knew what he was about. But I fancy he did. Those poets were generally considered reliable in their observations, I believe."

"I would think so," laughed Sally.

"Not that you could prove it by me," rejoined Brogan. "It's not often I'm up with the roosters, or the larks and snails either for that matter. But my late nights are over. I've turned over a new leaf, Sally."

"And what, if I may ask, has brought all this on?" asked Sally, taking a sip from her cup.

"I don't know. I just woke up today and realized that it's time I did something with my life."

"And what would that be?"

"Ah, Sally—there you have put your finger on the nub. I don't know yet. That's always the problem for a young man, isn't it—knowing what to do with one's life?"

"I wouldn't know. I've never been a young man. I think it is more difficult for men. A woman's course is mapped out for her—once she marries, that is."

"How do you mean, mapped out?"

"Being a wife, managing a home, domestic duties, or, if they are so inclined and are of the aristocracy, keeping an active social calendar."

"Some young women don't see it that way."

"You sound as if you speak from firsthand knowledge."

"Not really. But there was a girl at the Hotel this week—on one of the tours, you know. She is certainly not waiting to get married and have her way mapped out. She is ready to take the world by storm."

"She sounds like one of those suffragette types who used to be in the news a few years back."

"That's just it—she wasn't like that in the least. There was almost—it sounds strange to say it—but there was a domesticity about her too, a sense of quiet and peace along with her goals and dreams. A girl of contrasts, one might call her."

"She sounds like a fascinating young lady. Is she at the Hotel now?"

"No, they're gone. Off with the continuation of their tour, leaving me no further along in figuring out life's quandaries. What is it they say about a journey of a thousand miles? Which reminds me—I'd like to go over to Shetland on the early ferry. Do you think Dad will mind if I take the Studebaker for the day?"

"Ask him yourself. I think I hear him coming down the stairs now."

Both glanced toward the door as Ernest's step descended the rest of the way down the main staircase. A few seconds later he walked into the morning room, glancing back and forth between wife and son, like Sally earlier, with an expression of surprise.

"Two of the four Tulloch men up with the roosters!" exclaimed Sally. "Or the snails and larks, if you prefer," she added, throwing Brogan a grin. "Look who made coffee for me, dear."

"I see that. Good morning, Brogan," said Ernest.

"I know, I know—I'm up early!" laughed Brogan. "Sally's already driven home that point."

"As are you, dear," said Sally.

"I heard voices," said her husband, walking around the table to the stove. "I didn't want to miss the party. Have we water for tea?"

"Just there, Dad," said Brogan. "Behind the coffee. It's been a while since I stoked up the morning's peats like you taught me. I can't guarantee whether the water's hot."

"It appears you haven't lost your touch," said Ernest, lifting the lid.

Ernest took his favorite teapot from the sideboard, filled it with a scoop of loose tea, poured out steaming water from the kettle, then sat down beside Sally to wait for it to steep precisely three and a half minutes.

"Say, Dad, I'd like to drive over to Shetland today," said Brogan. "Mind if I take the Studebaker?"

"Not at all. I have no plans. You might fill it with petrol while you are in Lerwick. I think the tank's down to about half."

"I'll take care of it. Anything else I can do for you in the city?"

"I'll think about it. What time are you leaving?"

"I'd like to make the first crossing."

43

THE CLIFFS OF NOSS

Brogan's first stop on the way to the ferry two hours later was at the Hotel. There he learned no more than that the Northern Adventure Tour would return to Whales Reef in four days. No one knew of their itinerary in the meantime, other than that they would spend one night at the Lerwick Hotel.

Not to be deterred, he took the ferry across and arrived in the Shetland capital about 11:00. No one at the Lerwick Hotel knew more details. The tour had departed early that morning.

Now what? thought Brogan to himself. He couldn't drive around the island aimlessly hoping to spot their coach. That would be like looking for a needle in a haystack. They might still be in Lerwick, though he doubted it. No, they were out in the country communing with nature somewhere. He was sure of it.

He thought a minute.

That's it—of course! he suddenly realized. Emily had mentioned puffin cliffs. All bird-watchers went to the towering cliffs on the Isle of Noss. It was called a "seabird city" during the summer months. They also said that it was one of the most spectacular overlooks to watch for whales.

Best of all, it was only five or six miles from here. Of course, it was two islands away. But there was no chance of missing them. Only one route led from Lerwick to Noss. Whichever direction they were going, he would be sure to see them.

Minutes later he was speeding on his way out of the city. A short wait at the ferry landing took him across to Bressay. Parking the Studebaker, he made his way the final half mile to the eastern shore of the island with a steady stream of hikers and bird-watchers. The tiny Isle of Noss lay across a hundred yards of water. It was accessible only during the summer months when enterprising fishermen from Bressay ferried tourists back and forth in their small boats for a nominal fee. Thus far Brogan had not seen the red coach or any sign of Dr. MacDonald's tour. Only one other group was about, but from what Brogan overheard they were mostly Italian.

He and his five fellow passengers bobbed their way across from Bressay, accompanied by the monologue of their fisherman skipper. The tiny island was crawling with tourists, most of whom were gathered near the edge of the high overlook on the opposite side. Below them, teeming colonies of puffins, fulmars, guillemots, and gannets were making such a racket in their roosts as to make hearing difficult. Everyone but Brogan had a pair of binoculars around his or her neck, most also had cameras. Those who were not gazing through their binoculars down into the cliffs were focused offshore, looking for porpoises or scanning the sky for great skuas.

Disappointed at seeing no familiar faces among the enthusiastic fowl followers, Brogan wandered about, then finally sat down on a large stone some distance from the main cluster of tourists. There he settled in to wait. Dr. MacDonald's tour was obviously not here yet. They must have made a stop or two in Lerwick.

It was truly a spectacular sight, he thought, gazing eastward over the expanse of the North

Atlantic. Across there somewhere was Norway, home to the fabled Vikings that had so captured his and Wallace's imaginations when they were boys.

The day advanced. Still there was no sign of them. The afternoon wore slowly on. By three o'clock he was famished and chilly. A swift breeze had picked up off the ocean. Why had he thought to bring no food or drink? He had not expected to be here so long.

Finally he rose and wandered back toward the western terminus for the small fleet of fisher ferries. He might as well head back over to Bressay. If they were coming to Noss this late in the day, he could spot them just as well from there.

Relieved to reach the parked Studebaker forty-five minutes later, Brogan climbed in and grabbed his coat. For two more hours he waited inside. At a little before six, he was ready to admit defeat.

Disheartened, he took the ferry back to the mainland, then drove into Lerwick while still keeping an eye out for any sign of the coach, though he knew well enough that they would no longer be sight-seeing at this hour.

Hungry enough to eat a horse, he booked him-self into the Hotel and then hurried to the restaurant for dinner.

44

SUMBURGH HEAD

Emily Hanson walked out of the small country hotel into the quiet evening. It was sometime after ten. She had just finished seeing Mrs. Barnes to bed. But sleep for herself was out of the question. She still couldn't get used to daylight lasting past eleven o'clock.

It had been a rich, full day, starting early in the city, traveling north for a sheepdog demonstration at one of Shetland's sheep ranches, followed by a nearby hands-on exhibition of peat harvesting. Then the drive around to the southern tip of the island had included stops and mini-lectures en route as Dr. MacDonald pointed out various examples of Shetland flora and fauna, as well as a few historic sites. A brief drive over the causeway to St. Ninian's Isle had followed, finally arriving at their hotel in the tiny village of Grutness near the southern tip of Shetland in time for dinner.

Emily had enjoyed the day immensely, relishing in Dr. MacDonald's lectures and taking copious notes. Tomorrow would be a highlight as they went in search of Picts, puffins, porpoises, and whales. She still had some reading she wanted to do before their visit to the prehistoric ruins of nearby Jarlshof. She should be in the room reading right now.

But Emily was distracted.

The night was more than just chilly—it was downright cold. She pulled her coat tightly up against the wool muffler around her neck. Thanks to today's demonstration she now understood more about peat and its miraculous properties. The white smoke from the village's handful of homes and cottages surrounding the Hotel was bent over at ninety degrees from the wind. They were only a mile north of Sumburgh Head, the southernmost extent of Shetland, surrounded by the North Sea and perched on a tiny sliver of land in the middle of a hostile ocean. It was fearfully exciting in a way.

A mile away, at the point itself, the tower of the Sumburgh Head Lighthouse rose in the night sky. In spite of the wind, she could hear the racket from Sumburgh Roost. The old Norse name of the place was *Dunrostar hofdi*, "The Head Onto the Thunderous Noise." The name derived from the legions of seabirds roosting at Shetland's southern tip during the summer months.

She still needed to finish her reading on the Neolithic and Bronze Age settlement of Jarlshof. Archaeological excavations had only recently begun at the site. The very thought that men had ventured to these remote islands as early as 3000 BC, and had forged a life in such an inhospitable clime, was remarkable.

Emily glanced back at the hotel. How did a hotel come to be here in the middle of nowhere? Compared to this place, Whales Reef was a busy metropolis.

That was all she needed, thought Emily, to be reminded of Whales Reef. As if she hadn't been thinking of it all day!

What was it about the laird's eldest son that so consumed her thoughts? She was embarrassed even to think it, but he was awfully handsome. What was he doing saying something to her like, *You are lively and attractive and fun.*

Young men like Brogan Tulloch didn't talk that way to Quaker girls.

It would be a relief to find him gone from the island when they returned. She was a simple Quaker girl. If she ever did marry, it would be to a young Quaker man, though she hoped it would be someone more interesting than Robert Wayland, the nephew of her mother's best friend.

Emily awoke the next morning after a fitful night's sleep. This day would be more leisurely. The three sites on their schedule lay within a mile or two of each other at the lower extremity of Shetland— the Jarlshof excavation site, the Sumburgh Roost and Cliffs, and finally a tour of the Sumburgh Head Lighthouse, designed by Robert Stevenson, which had been protecting ships with its light for more than a century. Breakfast was scheduled for 8:30. They would be away from the hotel by 10:00. A picnic lunch prepared by the hotel would follow at the Sumburgh Cliffs, giving everyone plenty of time to wander about. In all likelihood they would spot a few porpoises and whales offshore as well.

By one o'clock their coach pulled to a stop at the turnaround and parking area which signaled the end of the north-south Shetland road. The tip of the island lay about two hundred yards across a plateau, through which a well-worn trail led to the treacherously high cliffs. This was one of Shetland's most popular sites for naturalists.

Once the engine of the coach had stilled, Dr. MacDonald stood at the front of the bus.

"We have reached the southern end of Shetland," he said. "As you can see, we have a bright day and the view from the overlook should be spectacular. It will be windy at the point, so take your coats, and stand well clear of the edge—these are among the highest cliffs in Scotland. Our lunches and hot water for tea will be set up shortly whenever you are ready for them. We will be here about two hours. Our tour of the lighthouse is scheduled for three o'clock. All right then, follow me, everyone. Bring your cameras, your binoculars, and keep your eyes open."

Even as they exited the coach they heard a squawking tumult in the direction of the cliffs from what seemed a million seabirds of every imaginable species.

45

PICTS, PEAT, PUFFINS, AND PORPOISES

Brogan had spent a good part of the previous evening interrogating the staff of the Lerwick Hotel and its guests about sites a naturalist tour would likely visit to see puffins. The verdict was split about evenly between the Isle of Noss or Sumburgh Roost farther south. He debated whether to pay a return engagement to Noss the following day or cast his fortunes with Sumburgh. As he had already seen as much of Noss as he cared to, he opted for the latter.

After a good-sized breakfast and fortifying himself with a container of tea and sandwiches for lunch, he set out for the day. He arrived at the gravel parking lot adjacent to Sumburgh Head a little before eleven. Leaving his provisions in the Studebaker, he set off across the path for the fabled cliffs. Though he was a native Shetlander, and took high overlooks for granted, the sight as he approached the edge a few minutes later took his breath away.

The sheer drop-off to the sea was unfathomably high—twice the height of the cliffs at home. Standing five feet away, his stomach and knees were doing peculiar things.

Brogan backed away, then strolled about amid tourists and the overpowering sound of birds coming seemingly from everywhere. At length he found a sheltered patch of grass, reasonably dry, and sat down to wait. An hour later he had stretched out. In the warmth of the sun and somewhat protected from the wind, he began to doze.

Whether he fell asleep or not, Brogan never knew. What he did know was that he came to himself with a mechanical sound penetrating his sleepy brain amid the drone of the birds and the roar of the sea. It grew steadily louder until it became unmistakable: It was the engine of a coach chugging from the direction of the village he had passed through on his way here.

With a start, Brogan sat up and scrambled to his feet. There was the familiar red and yellow of the Northern Adventure coach pulling to a stop near where he had parked the Studebaker.

He broke into a run toward it. Suddenly he stopped. A wave of hesitation swept over him. How would he explain himself? His presence would be awkward in the extreme. All at once this madcap plan seemed positively idiotic.

He stood a moment exposed to view. Not a tree or boulder to hide behind. And there was the group disembarking from the bus . . . with Dr. MacDonald leading them straight toward him!

Quickly Brogan turned. There was nowhere to go! Behind him trooped Dr. MacDonald's tour. In front of him lay the cliff and the sea. He had run out of Shetland real estate!

He ran a few steps toward the cliffs, then turned and made his way along the path that skirted the line of the cliffs. Following it some distance, ahead he saw the terrain slowly change. The angle of drop to the sea eased and began to slope steeply down from the plateau. He crept toward the edge and saw that there was no longer a sheer drop-off. A path led down the incline, twisting and turning along the uneven ground toward a lookout point about halfway to the sea on a thin promontory jutting out from the cliffs. There a few bird-watchers were clustered and staring back up at the shoreline through binoculars.

Quickly Brogan descended the steep path until he was out of sight from above. A few seconds later he left the path, crept carefully through the thick steep-growing sea grass as best he could until he found a place to sit behind a small hillock of springy peat turf. When he was satisfied that he had eluded detection, he realized that he could not have picked a more spectacular hiding place. The blue sea spread out before him as far as he could see. Closer at hand the high cliffs swarmed with seabirds. Several hundred yards away, the lighthouse rose against the sky.

But he had little leisure to enjoy the view before his predicament was borne in upon him again. What was he to do now? How long would they be here? He supposed he could hide where he was for an hour or two. But of all things, he realized with a groan, his tea and sandwiches were back in the car!

There was nothing for it but to settle in to wait for as long as might be required. He leaned back against the hill and began absently plucking at a few weeds and wildflowers. A clump of white daisies was growing out of the side of the turf and he added ten or twelve to his tiny bouquet.

Slowly he closed his eyes. The sun felt good. At least he was out of the wind.

He heard the steps of a few hikers on the trail above him moving up and down between the plateau and the lookout point on the promontory. Again he grew drowsy.

Some minutes later voices intruded into Brogan's hearing.

". . . a better view . . . able to observe . . . you will see fulmars and gannets . . . a few guillemots, as well as puffins . . ."

Footsteps and muffled conversation grew louder.

". . . the more intrepid of you may want to venture down to the overlook . . . path is a bit steep in spots . . . completely safe . . . you will be rewarded with—"

Dr. MacDonald's voice was unmistakable. Was there no getting away from the man!

In the panic of a schoolboy about to be discovered behind the building with a gasper, Brogan hunched down against the turf to make himself invisible.

". . . I am certain Miss Hanson will go on down to the overlook," MacDonald was saying. "Others of you may want to join her. For those who prefer to remain above, this is about as far as—"

His voice stopped abruptly. The next words out of his mouth were the last ones Brogan wanted to hear.

"Good heavens!" exclaimed MacDonald. "There's someone . . . it looks like a man has . . . I say there! Sir . . . have you fallen . . . are you injured?"

Already the Good Samaritan had left the path and was scrambling down toward him. It was no use, thought Brogan. He had been seen. Obviously the professor thought Brogan was about to go toppling down the slope. He had run out of evasive maneuvers.

Slowly Brogan rose and turned. Dr. MacDonald stopped in his tracks.

"But . . . are you . . . ? Why—good heavens! Is that you, Mr. Tulloch?"

Brogan smiled. "It's me, Professor," he said,

brushing a few bits of grass from his sleeves and trousers.

Murmurs of surprise and astonishment spread through the group behind him. Everyone recognized Brogan.

"Why, look . . . I can't believe it . . . it's Mr. Tulloch!" exclaimed several of them. A cry of delight sounded from Mrs. Barnes.

"But this is most extraordinary!" said MacDonald. "I thought you had fallen. I say, what are you doing here?"

"Oh, just having a day out watching the puffins, you know," replied Brogan jovially. "You know me—Shetland's biggest puffin fan. Never happier than when amid a flock of birds, what?"

Even as the words left his mouth, Brogan knew how stupid they must sound.

He allowed his eyes to drift up the slope behind MacDonald to the group watching from the path. There was Emily in front, beholding the strange developments with an expression difficult to describe. Her cheeks reddened slightly as Brogan's eyes stopped on her and he smiled sheepishly.

"But . . . what an odd place to be," MacDonald was saying. "The cliffs are so much more visible from the overlook down there. Let me give you a hand back up to the trail," he added, stretching a hand toward Brogan. "I say, where are your binoculars? To see the cliffs most adequately, you really need a good pair of binoculars."

"Right, I seem to have forgotten mine," laughed Brogan lightly.

"Why don't you join us?" said MacDonald. "I'm sure the group would love to have you."

"Ah, right—thank you, Professor . . . just for a few minutes perhaps. I don't want to interfere with your lecture."

Seconds later, MacDonald and Brogan rejoined the group on the trail. Good-natured greetings with smiles and handshakes went through the gathering as if they had just witnessed their professor snatch a lost sheep from certain death and bring it back into the fold.

Emily had recognized Brogan the moment he stood, even before he turned and removed his cap, revealing his full crop of dusty brown hair, windblown in the ocean breezes. The sight of him standing there, obviously embarrassed, fumbling for words, then flashing that wonderful smile of his, was nearly enough—because the sight had come so unexpectedly—to make her knees buckle. Her heart gave a flutter as he glanced toward her.

As the professor led Brogan onto the path, unconsciously Emily retreated into the background as Mrs. Barnes was pushing her way excitedly to the front to greet the new arrival.

When the hubbub over Brogan's appearance died down, the group split between those who wanted to venture farther down to the overlook and those who decided to return to the plateau above. Hanging back between the two, Emily saw Brogan slowly approaching.

"Miss Hanson," he said, again with the sheepish smile.

"Mr. Tulloch," she said, returning his smile. "I must say, you have created quite a stir."

"That was not my intention, I assure you," laughed Brogan.

"So I gathered. It seemed as though you were trying to keep from being seen."

"Exactly."

"Why was that?"

"I don't know. I suppose all at once I was embarrassed at what I had done."

"Why? Have you been following us, Mr. Tulloch?" asked Emily with a hint of amusement in her tone.

"No, Miss Hanson," replied Brogan. "Actually, I was following *you*."

His words were so direct that for a moment Emily was left speechless. Quickly she recovered.

"Why in the world would you want to do that?" she said.

"Because . . . because, uh—I wanted to give you these," said Brogan, bringing his hand up from his side and giving her the bouquet of wildflowers, now half bent and crushed from the exertion of his rescue.

"Oh . . . thank you. They're lovely!" said Emily

as she took them. "But I cannot believe you came all this way for this. And how did you find us, anyway?"

"With difficulty!" laughed Brogan.

"Then why did you really come?"

"I . . . uh, I wanted to see you again," said Brogan, thinking rapidly on his feet. "I . . . that is—"

Suddenly a brainstorm flashed into his mind.

"—Because I wanted to invite you to have dinner with me when you return to Whales Reef," he added.

Emily stared back without expression.

"You came all this way for *that?*" she said in astonishment.

"It's not really so very far. Distances are not great in the Shetlands."

"You could have asked me when we returned in a couple days."

"I didn't want to wait. Besides, this is more adventurous, wouldn't you say?"

"It is surely that!" laughed Emily. "In that case, then, and as you have gone to such lengths, I accept your invitation."

"It is a date then . . . on your first evening back to Whales Reef.—And now, shall we join the others and continue down to the overlook?"

"I think we should," rejoined Emily. "Shetland's biggest puffin fan certainly ought to get the best vantage point of the cliffs he can!"

PART 9
AUGUST 2006

46

MADDY'S ADVENTURE

VIRGINIA, UNITED STATES

Tennyson Stafford picked Maddy up at 8:00 on Saturday morning. They arrived at his parents' ranch about 11:30.

They turned into a long, winding drive, with pasture on either side, and up to a lovely vintage Southern home. As she stepped out of his car, Maddy saw a handsome woman, tan-faced and with gray-black hair flowing from beneath a well-worn black cowboy hat, climbing over the rails of a paddock, where a half-dozen ponies scampered about. She jumped to the ground and walked toward them. She was wearing mud-splattered cowboy boots, faded blue jeans, and a blue work shirt, its sleeves rolled up to the elbows. Her face wore a bright smile as she approached and gave her son a hug.

"Hi, Mom!" said Stafford. "This is Madison.— Madison, my mother, Lucy Stafford."

"We're so happy to meet you, Madison," said Mrs. Stafford warmly, extending her hand. "Tennyson's told us all about you. We think it's wonderful how the two of you reconnected after working together all those years ago."

"*All* about me . . . what have you told them, Tennyson?" said Maddy.

"Just that you are a highly sought-after investment guru who passed me up years ago."

"Don't believe a word of it, Mrs. Stafford," laughed Maddy. "From what he tells me, Tennyson's investment packages are more ingenious than anything I do."

"Well, that is true," laughed Mrs. Stafford. "We're afraid to let Tennyson handle any of our money for fear of what he might make us do!"

"No mountain climbing in Nepal for you, I take it?"

"He told you about that? No, we were dreadfully frightened when it happened. They were on television—that's not the kind of news we were looking for. And we're trying to scale back our ranch work. We love the ranch, but it's hard work. We're anticipating no more hair-raising adventures in our lives. I'll be sixty next month. Clay's sixty-four."

"You don't look a day past fifty," exclaimed Maddy.

"And you, Madison, are a wonderful liar. But thank you for the sentiment."

"Enough of all this," interjected Tennyson. "Mom, take Madison to her room.—Madison, you did bring jeans?"

Maddy nodded.

"Then go get changed."

"Where are you off to?" asked Mrs. Stafford.

"Just up to the ridge."

"Her first time—?"

"She'll be fine."

"You haven't forgotten what happened to Melissa?"

Tennyson burst out laughing. "Actually, I had forgotten! I'll take the long way around. Could you throw together something for us to eat up there?"

"Sure, but don't you want to wait until your dad gets home? He'll be back in an hour."

"We'll catch up with him this afternoon.—I'll see you in a few minutes, Madison," he said, turning toward the barn.

"Where are you going?" asked Maddy.

"To get dressed. I'm staying in the bunkhouse. You'll be in the house."

He ran off. Mrs. Stafford hoisted Maddy's small suitcase as if it weighed less than a pound and led Maddy toward the house.

Twenty minutes later Maddy emerged again into the sunshine. She walked in the direction of the barn where she saw Tennyson sitting on the top rail of the paddock dressed just like his mother, complete with hat and boots. Two saddled horses stood next to the corral, their reins looped over one of the rails. Tennyson jumped down as she came toward him.

His eyes scanned her up and down. A gradual smile came to his lips.

"What!" laughed Maddy.

"It's just that I've never seen you in jeans before."

"You told me to bring jeans."

"Yeah . . . but—" At last he could not keep from laughing. "—But they look brand-new."

"They *are* brand-new. I didn't have a pair of jeans."

"And when I said jeans, I meant *real* jeans— Wranglers, Levis, or Lee. Those look like some designer brand."

"Yves Hardouin."

"You're kidding!" laughed Tennyson.

"No—he's a famous designer."

"And they probably cost a hundred dollars?"

"A hundred twenty-five."

"Oh my!" groaned Tennyson. "Well, they'll look better when we get them roughed up a little. And those jogging shoes—are those all you have?"

"Except for my pumps."

"Okay, come on—we'll find you a pair of boots in the barn."

"Why do I need boots?"

"Because you have to have boots for a ride."

"A ride!" exclaimed Maddy. "You don't mean . . . those horses aren't for *us?*"

"Who else would they be for?"

"I've never been on a horse in my life! I'm not really the horsey type."

"I thought your grandfather had a farm."

"He did—a *farm* . . . chickens and cows and pigs and fields of potatoes and wheat."

"No horses?"

Maddy shook her head.

"You'll pick it up in no time. It's easier than riding a bike."

"I'm not so good on a bike either!"

Tennyson laughed. "Like I said, it's *easier* than a bike."

Fifteen minutes later, Tennyson Stafford led Maddy, clomping awkwardly in a pair of cowboy boots a size too big, with a floppy-brimmed brown hat on her head, to the smaller of the two horses.

"This is Lizzy," he said. "She's ten years old and there isn't a gentler mare in Virginia."

He took Maddy's hand.

"Now reach your left foot up into the stirrup," he said. "Grab the saddle horn with your left hand. I'll boost you up into the saddle."

"Are you sure about this?" said Maddy nervously. "What if I fall?"

"I'll take good care of you."

A minute later, with a momentary shriek of terror as her right leg sailed over the horse's back and she plopped into the saddle, Maddy was in place. She grasped the saddle horn for dear life.

"There," said Tennyson. "Nothing to it. Just sit for a minute and get used to it. Here comes my mom with the saddlebags and our lunch."

They set off a few minutes later through an open gate leading along a wide trail through a grassy pasture.

"Keep hold of the saddle horn with the reins loosely in your fingers," said Tennyson. "Lizzy will follow me. No need for you to do a thing. After you're comfortable, I'll show you what to do with the reins."

47

TENNYSON'S RIDGE

To her complete disbelief, and profound relief, Maddy found that gradually she *did* become more comfortable in the saddle.

Lizzy was not, as Maddy feared, a bucking bronco, but rather a stately dame of advanced years who plodded dutifully along without a hint of inclination to kick up her heels. Tentatively Maddy began to relax her grip on the saddle horn, holding the reins lightly through her fingers, though still with no idea what to do with them. If she was not exactly feeling like Dale Evans or Annie Oakley, neither was she feeling like Madison Swift, investment analyst. A giddy feeling of girlish happiness swept through her to be doing something so brave.

Tennyson swung his mount out, slowed, and soon they were riding side by side. Gradually he instructed her in use of the reins, as well as voice commands and movements and pressures of her feet and legs.

"So tell me more about your grandfather's farm," he said as she began to relax.

"I loved going there," replied Maddy. "It's probably not far from here, a couple hours south. My grandfather was my father's father, so when my folks divorced, my mom cut off ties with him. I never saw him again."

"That's too bad. I'm sorry to hear that. No horses, but what else did he have?"

"I enjoyed the small animals. I was afraid of the cows– but the goats and dogs and cats and ducks . . . they were great. My grandfather died when I was in college. I never had a chance to reconnect with him. Part of me resented what my mom had done. My grandfather always treated me special. I suppose when I came to the city and grew up, so to speak, I steeled myself from those memories by becoming a workaholic."

By now they had entered woodland and were beginning to climb.

"Uh . . . we're not going up any mountains, are we?" asked Maddy.

"We already are," replied Tennyson. "But we'll

take the long way around—a nice gradual climb. There's a place I want to show you."

"By the way, who's Melissa?"

Tennyson laughed. "A girl I brought out here once—it was a long time ago . . . a college friend."

"Friend?"

"Okay, a little more than a friend. I made the mistake of taking the shortcut up to the ridge. We had to ford a small lake and the water was a little higher than usual. Melissa fell off into the lake. Once I got her back to the house, she left and that was the last I ever saw of her."

"But we're going a different way?"

"I assure you, I won't take you by the lake trail until you are such a horsewoman that you beg to see it."

"That'll be the day!"

"Actually, you look very good in the saddle, upright and confident."

"I don't feel confident!" laughed Maddy.

"That will come. Believe me, you're a natural. Next thing you know, you'll be going to the riding stables outside D.C."

Forty minutes later, after a climb steeper than Maddy thought she could survive, they emerged onto a high plateau. Spread out on three sides far below, fields of ranchland extended for miles. The pasture gave way in the distance to rolling haze-shrouded hills, though from this far away

276

one could hardly distinguish one interlocking ridge from another. The misty mysterious blue-gray vapor created the illusion that, if one could find the way into the distant hills, a fairy-tale world of wonder lay beyond them.

"Are those the Blue Ridge Mountains?" asked Maddy.

"They do have a bluish tinge," replied Tennyson. "But no, those are the Shenandoah Mountains. My folks' property borders the Shenandoah National Park."

"It's a spectacular view. And so quiet. Eerily quiet. I see why you like it here."

Tennyson led on for another five minutes, then reined in to a stop and jumped to the ground.

"I'll help you down," he said as he walked to Maddy's side.

A minute later she was again standing on her own two feet.

"Oh, I'm stiff!" she said as she got her legs beneath her.

"You're liable to be sore tomorrow. But your body will get used to it."

"You think I'm going to make a habit of this!" laughed Maddy.

"I hope so. But come over here—I'll get our lunch and then show you one of my favorite places in the world."

He removed the bags from behind his saddle, tied both horses to a tree, then led Maddy to the edge of a high cliff where the view to the Stafford property was almost straight down.

"That's our ranch there," he said, easing onto a large boulder ten feet back from the ledge. "I call this place Tennyson's Ridge."

"Why that?"

Tennyson thought a few moments. When he spoke, his voice was pensive and nostalgic.

"Every child has some special place where they go to be alone," he said. "Though they don't frame it in such terms, I've always thought that we all begin to contemplate who we are and what life means, in our special places. For some it might be high in a tall tree or on top of a rock, for others it's just the solitude of being in their room. It might be anywhere. Children are inventive in discovering their special places. This is mine, this ridge and this view of our ranch. When I discovered it I thought I was the first person in the universe ever to sit right here. I felt like Columbus or Lewis and Clark. That's why I named it Tennyson's Ridge. It was *mine*. I didn't tell my mom about it for a long time. I knew she would be afraid for me. I mean—look. It's a long way down. She knew I disappeared for hours at a time on my favorite horse. When I finally told her about my special ridge, she just smiled. I had the feeling she had known all along and even knew that the slight danger associated with the place was part of my discovery of what manhood meant. Anyway, I've never brought anyone here before. You're the first person I've ever shared it with."

"I'm honored."

"Looking down on the world like this, I feel as though my whole life is spread out in front of me."

"I see what you mean."

"Did you have a special place, Madison?"

Maddy thought a long while.

"I'd forgotten about it," she answered at length. "It was at my grandfather's farm. When I was there it was just like you say, I was thoughtful, alone, at peace . . . probably happier than at any other time during my childhood."

"Where was it?"

Maddy smiled. "Silly now that I think about it."

"Magical moments of childhood are never silly."

"Maybe you're right. We were visiting once when the corn was really growing. It had reached a few inches over my head. I don't remember how old I was. But a cornfield can be magical to a child. I went wandering into the stalks. I realize now how easy it is to get lost in the maze if you can't see over the tops of the stalks. But I just walked in amongst them like I had discovered another world. Then suddenly I came upon a little place in the middle where the seeds must have missed it somehow and no corn was growing. It was a little hole in the field no more than five or six feet wide. But as I walked into it and looked around, it was like you say—I had discovered my own private world. I sat down and just relished in the fact that I was *alone,* and that nobody in the world knew where I was. I guess at that moment it became, like you say, my special place. For the rest of that visit, I went back every day. I had to draw myself a little map and leave pebbles in a line so I knew exactly where to walk into the stalks."

Maddy smiled pensively and it fell silent.

"And?"

"That's all there is. The next time we went for a visit, the field had been cut and the corn harvested and it was nothing but a field of dirt. I never had another place like it. But the memory of it has been almost like having a special place. Sometimes my thoughts go back to that time, and I close my eyes and pretend I'm there again. I don't think I was very happy as a child. But I was happy then."

48

WHAT MANNER OF SHEPHERD

WHALES REEF, SHETLAND ISLANDS

When his uncle by marriage, Fergus Gunn, appeared at the door of the Auld Hoose, flanked by Evanna Kerr, Margaret Dalrymple, Sarff Fenris, Tevis Gordon, his cousin Murdoc MacBean, and Garth Kennedy, David knew it was no social call. These were the five men and two women who made up the committee of elders for the Whales Reef parish kirk. He immediately divined the reason for their visit.

"Hello, David," said Fergus, taking upon himself the role of spokesman, though technically Mrs. Dalrymple was chairwoman. "We'd jist like a moment o' yer time on behalf o' the kirk."

"Of course, come in!" said David, shaking the hand of each in turn. He led them inside and to the Muckle Room. "I'll just put on water for tea," he said. "Make yourselves comfortable."

Several minutes later they were seated with cups in their hands.

"We've come because we'd like tae canvass yer opinion on the matter o' the yoong minister Rev.

Rhodes," began Fergus.

"Why me?" replied David. "I'm not an elder, and it's no secret I have not been a particularly active parishioner."

"Aye, but it hasna escaped oor notice that ye been attendin' more often lately, an' as chief we want tae ken what ye think, if ye think the yoong man would be good for the island an' its folk."

"It is considerate of you to ask my opinion," replied David. He thought a minute. "I would say that it depends on what kind of minister you want," he began, glancing around at the seven. "There are ministers who feel it their duty never to say a controversial word and who are content for their listeners to nod off during their sermons. There are others who are more socially minded who talk every Sunday about doing good but never about the kingdom of God. There are others who shake things up and make their people uncomfortable at times. What do you want in a minister? If you want the social gospel, I doubt young Rev. Rhodes is your man. If you want bland sermons you can sleep through, I doubt he is your man. If you want someone who will challenge the people of Whales Reef to live as God's men and women, then he may very well be your man, and you may have discovered a true diamond in the rough. As I have no vote, however, and don't know what you feel the priorities of the church ought to be, I'm not sure how to advise you. What are your thoughts?"

"Our initial vote was split—five in favor, two opposed," replied Mrs. Dalrymple.

"And the rest of the church?"

"He stirred it up, just like you said," put in MacBean. "But most I have talked to liked the young man."

"Down-to-earth is what folk are sayin'," added Kennedy.

"We'd like tae ask the laird what she's thinkin' as weel," now said Evanna Kerr. "But she's new hersel' an' we dinna ken hoo long she'll be here, ye ken. So it's yersel' we wanted tae ask first."

"I appreciate that, Evanna. And," he added with a twinkle in his eye, "it may be that you have a more vested interest than the rest."

"On account o' Audney, ye mean?"

"Aye."

"I ken well enough hoo she'd vote!" laughed Evanna.

"And what do *you* think?"

"I dinna ken the yoong man weel," replied Evanna. "But I'd sooner hae a minister payin' his respects tae my daughter than Hardy!"

A few laughs spread around the room.

"Well said, Evanna!" laughed David. "If I had a vote, I would give the man two thumbs up."

They continued to chat for another fifteen or twenty minutes. When the committee left, though it had not been divulged to David which were the two opposing votes, all seven seemed favorably disposed toward the idea of Lincoln Rhodes's future in Whales Reef.

Several days later, David answered his phone to find that he was talking to the young minister himself.

"Have you heard anything from the session?" asked David.

"Not yet," answered Rhodes. "How about on your end?"

"I had a call from the church elders. They wanted to know what I thought."

"Uh oh!" laughed Rhodes. "Now I'm in trouble!"

"You are indeed, my friend," rejoined David. "I told them I wouldn't trust a scalawag like you with matters pertaining to *my* soul!"

Rhodes laughed again. "Well, let us hope they decide to override your presidential veto. Actually I called about something else. I have been thinking more about the plight of your cousin. Any news on that front?"

"Nothing," replied David. "I took his handgun to the police in Lerwick for testing. I've heard nothing about the results."

"With your permission I would like to look into the matter further, maybe investigate McLeod and the people around him."

"You hardly need my permission."

"I suppose not officially. Still, I wanted to talk it over with you."

"I want to help Hardy if I can. The ballistics report on the gun will certainly be important. Anything you can learn about what was going on at McLeod's company may be useful."

"Then I will look into it further. Carefully, of course. I would not want to make things worse for the man."

PART 10

A LEGACY BEGINS— *THE ISLAND* 1924

49

THE WHALES FIN INN

Technically speaking, the Whales Fin Inn was a hotel. It had been an institution in the heart of the village on the town square for a hundred years.

Once William Tulloch built the luxurious Whales Reef Hotel on the hill north of town, however, the local establishment saw few overnight guests. Like most entrepreneurs, the ambitious laird gave little thought to the livelihoods his monetary dreams might put out of business. Whether the small inn could survive became a topic of conversation. Everyone was happy to see the new influx of visitors to the island. But they did not like what it was doing to the fortunes of Nyssa and Donal Kerr. The owners of the inn were favorites in the village. Donal's great-grandfather had built the inn in the eighteenth century and it had been in the family ever since.

Nyssa and Donal were determined not merely to keep the inn limping along, but to invigorate it with new life so that it would remain a hub of village life. If its rooms were no longer in demand, they would focus their efforts on the pub. Donal came up with the catchy slogan upon which they would pin their future: "Shetland's Best Beer and Batter."

They used most of what small savings they possessed to remodel the pub area, to purchase new frying equipment for fish and chips, and for a large bright new blue-and-red sign in front of the building which read, *Whales Fin Inn—Shetland's best beer and batter: Lagers, ales, and spirits . . . meals and fish and chips . . . served all day.*

They knew that a new sign and interior to the pub were not enough. They had to deliver on their promise. Toward that end, they left the inn in the hands of Nyssa's brother and sailed for mainland Scotland. For two months they traveled about to find the best beer and the best batter for their fish and chips, whose recipe they would hope to buy. Donal sampled beer from every brewery large and small in Scotland. Meanwhile Nyssa visited chip shops and questioned owners, cooks, and chefs about every facet of the art of frying and serving the perfect slab of cod.

Upon their return, with great fanfare they announced an event no one in Whales Reef wanted to miss. In a month's time, every villager would be treated to a free pint and a free chip supper with only one stipulation: If they considered the Kerrs' new offerings worthy of the accolade, each one would agree to write a letter to some friend or relative on mainland Shetland, telling them where to find Shetland's best beer and fish and chips.

The strategy was an instant success. The recipe Nyssa had been able to buy from the owners of the Cullen Chip Shoppe in Aberdeenshire truly was the best fish and chips anyone in Whales Reef had ever eaten. And the beer on tap from the kegs Donal had arranged to have shipped from a small brewery in Snowdonia in Wales, with the stipulation that they could advertise it as the inn's "special home brew"—all his customers maintained—possessed *something* that set it apart from the rest. They continued to sell Guinness, Tennants, Caffreys, and Murphys. However, the home brew of the Whales Fin Inn soon established a reputation as notably above the rest. As the years passed, there were even those regulars from Lerwick who made the occasional pilgrimage to Whales Reef for the sole purpose of leisurely whiling away an afternoon while enjoying Donal Kerr's best. Nothing could completely ameliorate the trials and hardships of life, nor the disappointment of a poor day's fishing. But the beer purveyed by Donal Kerr unquestionably did its best.

And thus the Whales Fin Inn and pub had survived and thrived. It was as busy every late afternoon and through the supper hour as ever.

50
TEA AND WILDFLOWERS

Seated in her kitchen at the roughhewn table with her unexpected guest, Annabella Raoghnailt saw a shadow cross the window at the back of her cottage.

She glanced behind her as the back door of her hothouse opened. A moment later a tall familiar form strode in without the formality of a knock.

"Annabella," said her second visitor of the day as he walked into the kitchen. "I was in Lerwick two days ago and I—"

He stopped abruptly, staring back and forth between the two women seated with teapot, oatcakes, and a clump of wildflowers on the table between them.

"Brogan, laddie!" exclaimed Annabella, rising and planting an affectionate kiss on Brogan's cheek.

"—I didn't . . . I don't want to intrude," he stammered, unnerved at barging in so unceremoniously. "Emily!" he said finally. "I mean, hello, Miss Hanson. It is nice to see you again."

"And you, Mr. Tulloch," rejoined Emily, whose poise recovered itself while Brogan fumbled for words. "I suppose I am no less surprised to see you."

"I had no idea you were back on the island."

"We only arrived at the Hotel an hour ago. I came to ask Annabella the names of the flowers in my bouquet. You wouldn't expect me to press and dry them without knowing their names."

"Ah . . . right, I see," nodded Brogan. His eyes drifted again to the small gathering of plant life on the table, a little worse for wear but recognizable as what he had given her on Sumburgh Head.

"But what are *you* doing here?" Emily went on. "And with such an affectionate greeting!"

"The laddie an' me's auld frien's!" said Annabella, resuming her seat. "It's many a lang year since he first knocked at the door o' my wee cottage. But hoo do the two o' ye come tae ken ane anither?"

"A long story," laughed Emily. "I want to know how the two of *you* know each other so well that the laird's son walks into the home of one of his father's tenants without knocking and receives a kiss."

"Anither lang story," answered Annabella. "Sit ye doon, laddie an' hae a wee drap o' tea w't us while I tell the lassie hoo ye came tae the rescue o' an auld woman oot on the moor."

Brogan set a small paper bag down on the table as he took a seat. Annabella rose to bring another cup to the table and filled it with tea.

"I want to hear all about it!" said Emily eagerly.

"Weel, 'twas ten or twelve years syne," began Annabella. "I was oot on the moor gatherin' my plants, ye ken, when I came upon a pack o' nickums botherin' the laird's sheep an' fearin' them dreadful like. They were throwin' stanes an' there were wee lammies among them that they were tryin' tae grab, an' their puir mamas were bleatin' like they was cryin' for help. An' I came up til them an' I told them tae stop worryin' the puir things. They jist laughed an' hurled insults at me. They were a rum lot o' nickums. There's always nickums, but sometimes there's ain or two bad'uns in a village that make all the laddies follow, an' that's hoo it was wi' yoong Halvar Stein an' Robbie Stewart, ye mind hoo they were, laddie."

"Aye," nodded Brogan, "an' Robbie's nae sae much better noo, though he has his papa's forge tae keep his hand til honest work. Hopefully it will make a man o' him yet."

Emily glanced at Brogan with silent delight to hear his speech lapse into the island dialect.

"Aye," assented Annabella. "—So as I was sayin', I grabbed ain o' them, yoong Stewart it was, an' I took him by the scruff o' his neck, an' I said, 'If ye dinna stop worryin' the lammies, I'll gae straight tae yer papa an' he'll whip ye good.' The laddie jist laughed at me an' squirmed loose frae my haud o' him. An' he began taunting me an'

294

pullin' at my basket, an' he grabbed it an' threw it frae me an' the others began tossin' pebbles at me, an' they were callin' me all sorts o' evil names, which I been called worse an' no name can hurt ye anyway. I wasn't in any danger on account o' they werena aboot tae hurt me serious like, though worse has been laid at Robbie Stewart's door syne. But then all at once I heard a shout an o'er the moor yoong Brogan Tulloch came runnin' like a knight on his horse, an' he was yellin' an' callin' at them tae git back an' leave me an' the sheep be. He was yoonger than the maist o' 'em—what were ye, laddie?" she said, turning to Brogan.

"I think maybe eleven or twelve," replied Brogan. "Robbie's only a year aulder, but he was a big brute by then, an' Halvar was probably fourteen or fifteen. Some o' the others were yoonger, but they followed Halvar an' Robbie wherever they went. Ye're right—they were a rum lot. 'Twas good for a' when Halvar's family left for Norway."

"Weel, that was all they needed tae make them stop tormentin' me," Annabella went on. "They turned on Brogan an' threw him tae the ground an' hit an' kicked at him somethin' fierce. I did my best tae git them off o' him. I whacked at them wi' a stick, but they kept laughin' at me. Puir Brogan—by the time they had had enough, an' began tae think what the laird might do tae them, by then puir Brogan's face was dreadful bruised an' his nose bleedin' afore they finally ran off. I did my best tae git him tae his feet an' I helped him back here tae my cottage—we was closer tae here than tae the laird's Cottage, ye ken, an' I washed him an' bandaged his cuts wi' mint an' the squeezin' o' a leaf o' aloe that I had growin'. I was ready tae march straight tae his papa wi' the names o' the nickums, but the laddie wouldna let me tell the laird a word o' it. Ye made me promise, didna ye, laddie?"

"Aye," chuckled Brogan where he sat listening with a smile.

"I would hae gone straight tae the laird, an' then tae every one o' them nickums' mamas and papas. But Brogan said it would jist make 'em angrier an' that they might take it oot on me when he wasna aroun'. He was right. As it was, not a soul on the island e'er heard a word o' it. An' the laddie's been welcome at my door e'er since."

"Ye spin quite a tale, Annabella!" laughed Brogan. "I doobt it was quite so heroic as ye make it oot."

"No many laddies in the village would hae done what ye did yersel'."

"Ye were holdin' your own against them," laughed Brogan. "As I recall ye landed a few blows on ain or anither o' their heads wi' that walkin' stick o' yers!"

"Ah, weel—what hae ye in the bag?"

"Oh, right," said Brogan, reaching for it. "I was

296

in Lerwick two days ago an' I bought ye a new supply o' Earl Grey." He handed the bag to their hostess.

"Laddie, laddie, hoo can I thank ye!" said Annabella. "Jacksons or Twinings?"

"Only the original recipe for ain sich as yersel' wi' a trained nose an' palate for the precise herbal recipe—Jacksons, o' course."

Now it was Annabella's turn to chuckle. The two obviously loved one another as if they were grandson and grandmother.

Annabella turned to Emily. "The laddie takes good care o' me," she said, casting a tender smile in Brogan's direction. "Luik at this, will ye—he indulges me wi' the best tea tae be foun' . . . an' what's this!" she exclaimed, now peering into the bottom of the bag.

"Jist a few chocolates tae gae wi' it," said Brogan.

"The two o' ye will share them—wi' oor tea an' oatcakes," said Annabella, emptying the contents of Brogan's bag on the plate in front of her.

"We only have chocolate on Christmas," said Emily, reaching for one of the candies. "This is a treat!"

Half an hour later, Brogan and Emily left the cottage together and walked slowly through the village. Emily was carrying the crumpled bouquet of wildflowers that had prompted her visit to the cottage.

"Isn't this the usual time for your afternoon lecture?" asked Brogan.

"Everyone was so tired when we arrived that Dr. MacDonald canceled it. We had hardly settled into our room before Mrs. Barnes was sound asleep. So I thought I would come visit Annabella."

"Right . . . the flowers."

Emily smiled. "Thank you again, by the way."

"They're probably just weeds," said Brogan. "You didn't need to save them."

"Of course I did. When a girl gets flowers, she saves them. Besides, daisies aren't weeds."

"I suppose not. So are we still on for supper?"

"Just name the time and place."

"Tonight, then? I will treat you to the best fish and chips in the Shetlands."

"At the Hotel?"

"No, in the village. I'll come for you . . . six-thirty-ish?"

"I can't wait—formal or casual?"

Brogan laughed. "Definitely casual! There will be enough eyes on us already."

51

FISH AND CHIPS

Brogan and Emily walked down the hill from the Hotel a little after 6:30 that evening.

"Where are we going?" asked Emily. "Everyone was dying to know when I said I had plans for the evening."

"You told them?"

"I told Mrs. Barnes. In no time the whole group knew I was spending the evening with the laird's son and were pestering me with questions."

Brogan laughed. "Poor Mrs. Barnes. I imagine she is beside herself with curiosity."

"And jealousy," said Emily. "I must say she is rather taken with you."

Again Brogan laughed. "I am flattered. However, I think she may be just a tad old for me."

"So where *are* we going?"

"I am going to treat you to a little local color. By the time you return to the Hotel, believe me, not only your tour but the whole village will be talking about you."

"*Me,* why me?"

"Because you will be on display at the center of Whales Reef social life—the pub and inn and chip shop all in one."

"Now I am really curious."

"Have you ever had genuine Scottish fish-and-chips?"

"I don't think so."

"Then you are in for a treat."

"I still can't believe that you went all that way just to invite me for fish-and-chips."

"That was just a spur of the moment brainstorm. I suddenly realized, with you standing in front of me and having just made a gigantic fool of myself, that I needed some way to explain myself. The idea of supper blurted out."

"Oh, I see—well then . . . if you would rather *not* have dinner with me—" began Emily.

"That's not what I meant."

"I was just teasing. I am looking forward to it. And of course Mrs. Barnes will expect a full report."

They reached the end of the Hotel entry and turned toward the village.

"I've been along this road all the way through town several times," said Emily, "down to the harbor once, and to Annabella's cottage of course. But there are so many winding lanes and alleys and paths, it is a perfect maze. And there seem to be shops in every other house—look here is a cobbler's sign in this window—"

"Jock Buchanan, my third cousin."

"And there are so many things in the windows,

300

as if people are decorating their windows for passersby."

"Many of the women keep a corner of their cottage as a shop."

"Like Annabella's herbs."

"Exactly. See, there's Mrs. Urquhart's candies and sweets, and Mistress Sinclair with her yarns and tartans and threads—she is a seamstress and sells supplies and makes to order. Over there Mrs. Haye sells jams and jellies and canned fruits and meats.—Actually," said Brogan, "let's take this little lane here. We'll walk the scenic route."

He led into a narrow walkway. Emily had soon completely lost her bearings.

"They call this Shoppe Wynd," said Brogan. "Every house has a shop of some kind. You should see it at Christmas—they all try to outdo each other with lights and displays. It is very festive. For example, look there," said Brogan, pointing to a window ahead of them. "That is Mrs. Kennedy's. She lost her husband at sea ten years ago. So she began making handcrafts and discovered she had a knack both for creating interesting toys and for business as well. At Christmastime her little shop is filled with parents and children. She spends the whole year making things, and buying some from the mainland. Every child in the village comes to stare at her window to see what new she has."

"It sounds wonderful. I wish I could see it."

"Across the street is Mr. Gunnbjorn, a retired

fisherman. You wouldn't think that in a fishing village there would be a need for a fishing shop. But like Mrs. Kennedy, he has found a niche of unusual items that cater to the fishermen of the island—whistles and compasses, radios and maps, books, even specialty nets and traps and buoys and repair supplies and equipment. That's not to mention the summer recreational and tourist business. There are many who come to the Hotel to go line-fishing with the local fishermen. He does a brisk trade with them as well.—And over there is Mrs. Annar's curious shop."

"What does she sell?"

"Anything and everything. One day baked goods, wool yarn she has spun, aprons she has made, fresh apples . . . literally anything that strikes her fancy. But her specialty is used tools, small furniture, and clothes. Some people call it a junk shop, but to others it is a veritable treasure trove of interest."

"What fun!"

"And here is Dr. Jenkins's surgery."

"Now here's another tailor," said Emily. "And next door I see a clockmaker . . . and there a joinery shop down that lane.—What a fascinating collection of shops and trades. What is a joiner anyway?" asked Emily.

"A carpenter, cabinetmaker, a craftsman in anything to do with woodworking. That's Douglas Fletcher's place. He's getting on in years now, but he did most of the cabinetry in the Cottage. His son Thomas works with him now."

"Over there a smithy . . . and here's another baker—"

"The MacNeills. Yet another cousin."

"It sounds like you have cousins everywhere?"

"I'm probably related to half the village. The Shetlands are so insulated from the rest of Britain that it cannot be helped."

"I suppose in a way that's how it is with Quakers. Quakers marry Quakers. I am probably related in some way to half the Quakers in Pennsylvania, Delaware, and New Jersey. There is one line of Quakers, the Harlans, that married into Cherokee Indian royalty somewhere back in the 1700s."

"You mean you're part Indian? That would be exciting!"

"Not me," laughed Emily. "That connection between the Quakers and the Cherokees took place a long time ago. And your family are longtime Shetlanders?" asked Emily.

"For several generations," answered Brogan, "though the line of the lairdship came from the Highlands. My mother was a Shetlander who died when I was four. But we love Sally, our stepmother, as if she were our real mother—we three oldest, I mean."

"And Sally's a Shetlander too?"

"From mainland Shetland," nodded Brogan. "My father of course is of Whales Reef descent.

The lairdship and chieftainship always goes to the eldest son."

"What does a laird do exactly?" asked Emily.

"Mostly he is simply the landlord of the island property. The people depend on the laird in a way I doubt any American could understand. A greedy laird can make life miserable. A kind laird completely changes a community. As Scottish estates go, ours is tiny. For all I know it may be the smallest estate in Scotland. Our clan originated in the Highlands, but most Shetlanders trace their ancestry to the Vikings and Picts."

"We learned about the Picts, and then the Viking conquest," said Emily, "when we visited the archaeological site at Sumburgh Head where the Neolithic pottery was found, and the Bronze Age buildings."

"My dad's been keeping up on all that," nodded Brogan. "He is always reading about the latest findings."

"And all that landlord responsibility will fall to you one day when you are laird."

"I suppose so," shrugged Brogan. "It takes a special kind of man to do what my father does. My father is constantly encouraging the fishermen to buy their own boats and upgrade their equipment, even loans them the money to do so. He calls on every villager personally when their rents are due. They treat him like royalty. They always have tea ready and a spread of cakes and breads. He asks about their families and work and if they have any needs that are not being attended to. He used to take me with him, until I told him I didn't want to go anymore. I think it hurt him for me to say that. He was hoping I would see what he was trying to do. But I was a grumpy teen by then."

"They are glad to see him even though he has come to collect the rent?" asked Emily.

"You will understand more when I tell you how my father concludes every visit. They pay him their six-month rent—always in cash—whatever the rent on their property may be—thirty pounds, sometimes forty, I think the inn may pay sixty or eighty, being such a large building. Then after the villagers have paid him, as my father is leaving, he fishes about in his pocket and says something such as, 'That seems rather a high amount, don't you think?' and then he hands them back a five- or ten-pound note. It's all part of the ritual. They love him for it, and my father loves doing what he can for the people. Then he always adds, 'But not a word about this to a soul. This will remain just between us.' "

"But he does it with everyone?"

"He did every time I was with him. It makes rent day an event the people look forward to. The whole village knows of it, yet they are forbidden from talking about it. He wants it to be a special exchange between friends."

"I see why they love him. Will you continue the practice when you are laird?"

"I don't know," smiled Brogan. "I suppose that's one of the reasons my father took me along, so that I would learn by his example. I don't know how good a learner I have been. You always hear that the best learning comes from example. I wonder if that's true with children."

They came out onto the main street and arrived at the Whales Fin Inn.

"Here we are!" said Brogan.

He led Emily through the front door. A wave of warmth from frying fish and a clientele of customers assaulted them as they entered. The place was crowded at this hour and filled with the haze of smoke, pungent with the smell of beer and fish, and loud with animated conversation and laughter.

Gradually Emily was aware of glances coming their way, accompanied by a few whispered comments. A few of the young men greeted Brogan with friendly shouts and rose to shake his hand.

More greetings around the common room followed, with introductions to Emily as a colorful assortment of villagers welcomed her with friendly greetings she could scarcely understand. Everyone seemed glad to see Brogan. He was obviously a favorite with more of the villagers than Annabella Raoghnailt.

"Two fish suppers, Donal," said Brogan. "A little extra crispy on the chips—you know how I like them. And—" he turned to Emily, "would you like a beer—Shetland's best, you know?"

"Good heavens, no. I am a Quaker, remember. We are what I think you call teetotalers."

"Right, sorry. Two lemonades, then."

Brogan led the way to an unoccupied table. They chatted for a few minutes until they heard the proprietor call Brogan's name. Brogan retrieved their order and returned holding two packets wrapped in newspaper with oil seeping through.

"Here you are," said Brogan, setting one of the parcels in front of Emily.

He began to unwrap his portion. Laughing at the novelty of her introduction to this strange new custom, Emily did likewise.

"It looks delicious—and the smell is heavenly!" she exclaimed as she laid eyes on the golden slab of fish and fried potatoes inside. "Where is the silverware . . . what do you eat it with?"

"Your fingers, of course!" said Brogan, breaking off a generous portion of cod and lifting it to his mouth. "Watch out—it's hot!"

Brogan and Emily left the pub an hour later amid shouts and farewells to Emily and a few ribald remarks from those who were on to their third pint of Donal's best.

"You seem to be the toast of Whales Reef," said

Emily. "Though I suppose being the laird's son makes you popular."

"Not at all. That ruckus back there was all because of you."

"What did I have to do with it?"

"That you were with me, and that you are an American, that you were able to dish it out with the more forward blokes."

"Not bad for a Quaker girl, is that what you're saying?"

"Not bad at all!"

It quieted as they made their way back to the Hotel.

"Would you have lunch with me tomorrow?" said Brogan as he left Emily at the front entrance.

"My, an invitation for every meal. I don't know what to think. What is the occasion?"

"No occasion. It's just been a long time since I met someone so interesting. Actually, I don't know that I've *ever* met someone so interesting."

"You find me . . . *interesting?*" said Emily. "Is it because I'm an American?"

"I don't know. Perhaps that is part of it. We are under many misapprehensions about Americans over here. You are a mystery to us— still the rebellious cousins of the Revolution, you know."

Now it was Emily's turn to laugh. "Do I strike you as a rebel?" she said.

"Actually," chuckled Brogan, "yes . . . a little. You're very determined. And there is the added mystery of your being a Quaker. I find it fascinating. I don't know . . . you are a more complex young woman than you appear."

"I never thought of myself as complex. But I fear you are beginning to place me under the microscope a bit too much for comfort. It hardly seems that a man of the world like yourself would find a boring bookworm like me particularly interesting."

A peculiar expression came over Brogan's face.

"Maybe I am changing," he said at length.

This time it was Emily who became thoughtful. "Then I shall accept your invitation at face value," she said after a moment.

"Noon, then . . . or whenever your morning lecture breaks up? And . . . I have one more request," Brogan added. "Would you mind just calling me Brogan. The *Mr. Tulloch* sounds so formal."

"You *are* the son of the laird."

"Not to you. I am just Brogan Tulloch."

Emily smiled. "As you wish, then . . . *Brogan*. Good night."

52

LUNCH AT THE MUCKLE STANE

Emily was finding concentrating on Dr. MacDonald's lectures increasingly difficult. This morning's was particularly tedious knowing that Brogan would be waiting for her the moment it was over.

She walked out the front doors of the Whales Reef Hotel about 12:10. To her astonishment she saw Brogan standing across the entryway, holding the reins to two saddled horses.

She walked toward him with a laugh. "What is this?"

"I thought we would have a ride and then enjoy a picnic out on the island. As you can see," he added, pointing to a picnic basket strapped behind one of the saddles, "I have everything we will need. Do you ride?"

"A little. But I am hardly an expert."

"Lavender here is the gentlest mare in my father's stables."

"Sounds like fun, but I don't think this dress will be suitable for the occasion. Let me run back inside and change."

Twenty minutes later they left the precincts of the Hotel and rode slowly northward into the center of the island.

"This is the same way I came the day I met Annabella out collecting her plants," said Emily. "What is that house over there?" she asked, pointing to her left. "I noticed it before. It's much larger than any of the cottages in town."

"It's called the *Auld Hoose*, the old house," answered Brogan. "It used to be the laird's and chief's house. My father was born there."

"Who lives in it now?"

"My father's factor, Feandon Shaw. The barns and pens are more extensive than at the Cottage . . . it's where we keep the dairy cattle, also pigs and goats. The sheep of course wander the island. The produce—milk, cheese, yogurt, beef, mutton—is more than our families can use. My father gives most of it away to the villagers. Anyone in need can always come to him. No one will ever go hungry on Whales Reef, my father makes sure of that."

As the Auld Hoose with its barns and stables and fields of cattle and sheep faded behind them, the way ahcad steepened.

"Even though you've already seen it," said Brogan, "I thought we might enjoy the best view on Whales Reef along with the feast Sally helped me prepare."

"You helped her, did you?"

"I did. I spread butter on the bread and cut up the apples."

"You'll soon be on the Hotel staff as a chef! But

I thought lairds had servants to do such menial tasks."

"My father looks at things differently. As far as he is concerned, *he* is the servant. My grandfather and grandmother had a houseful of servants. But Dad and Sally keep one woman and one man, mostly, I think, simply to provide them employment. He kept on most of his parents' people until they gradually married or retired or left the island. Others he found positions at the Hotel. He and Mr. Shaw hire the village men from time to time to make sure people have work. The word *servant* hasn't been heard around here since my father came into the lairdship. He pays everyone a fair laborer's wage and considers them employees rather than servants."

They reined in at the top of the hill in the shadow of the Muckle Stane. Brogan tied the horses' reins to a stout heather shrub, then lifted down the basket.

"So, my lady," he said, spreading a tartan blanket on the ground and setting the basket on it, "for your dining pleasure we have dried smoked haddock, cheese, milk, oatcakes, jams, apples . . . and well-buttered bread."

"It sounds like a feast," said Emily. "How did this huge pillar of stone come to be here?" she asked as they began. "I can't imagine how it could have been dragged here or raised so perfectly into place to have remained erect for so long."

"The Legend of the Viking Stone is well enough known."

"Tell me about it."

"The Vikings were a nasty lot. They came to Shetland long before they went on to raid mainland Scotland and England. We grew up on Viking legends. Wallace and I pretended to be fighting off the Vikings one day, and to be Vikings ourselves the next."

"My brothers all played cowboys and Indians."

"I've heard about that," laughed Brogan.

"So tell me about the stone."

"Well, the greatest of all the Vikings was a huge Norseman some said was as tall as seven feet, though I doubt that. They say he stood more than a forearm's height above all other men. He was the first Norseman to arrive in the Shetlands and he made landfall on Whales Reef.

"The story goes that they had heard rumors of America, though it wasn't called that, centuries before Columbus. So Thor, that was the giant's name, outfitted a huge oceangoing vessel to make the voyage across the Atlantic, using as ballast an enormous stone pillar hewn from the sacred mountain of the gods in Norway, and carved with the lineage of Norse kings from time immemorial. They intended to claim the New World across the sea for Norway.

"They had scarcely set out when a fierce storm threatened to send them all to a watery grave.

When they had nearly given up hope, they managed to run aground here on Whales Reef. Knowing that this little island had saved their lives, they immediately claimed it for their own and set about to mark it with the monument they had intended for the New World. And that's how the Muckle Stane arrived on Whales Reef."

"But how did they get it up here?"

"Now that is a mystery. But I imagine in the same way that they had quarried it and gotten it into their boat in the first place, probably with fifty or more Vikings with ropes and rolling it on logs, I assume."

"That is an amazing story," said Emily. "Why would Annabella not tell me about the legend of the great Viking?"

A humorous expression came over Brogan's face. "Probably because she knows it for what it is."

"I am confused."

"She knows that Wallace and I made it up. It's pure fiction. No one knows where the stone came from."

"You had me believing every word!" laughed Emily. "It sounded completely plausible."

"Annabella was a tougher audience. When I told her the tale, she laughed all the way through that two young nickums—she calls all the boys nickums—could invent such a legend. But that's what boys do—invent their own adventures."

314

"So maybe you are not a scholar, by your own admission. But you are assuredly a storyteller. That was fantastic. You could write books!"

Brogan laughed.

"In your own way," added Emily, "you are a more imaginative individual than you let on, Mr. Future Laird."

53

THE ANGELS' HARPS

As Emily and Brogan rode away from the Hotel on their way to the Muckle Stane, a gray-haired woman of about sixty was calling at the Cottage. She was only a poor fisherman's widow. But she had no qualms about presenting herself at the chief's door. She would be treated with no less respect than if she were a queen.

Mrs. Baxter opened the door.

"I'm here tae see Lady Tulloch," said the visitor.

The housekeeper smiled and nodded. A minute later Sally came to the door.

"Hello, Margaret," she said with a warm smile.

"It's my mum, Sally," said the woman. "I think her time's aboot come, ye ken. I'd be grateful if ye'd play her through the veil."

"I will be happy to, Margaret," replied Sally. "You go back to her. I'll be along shortly."

As Sally turned back into the house and hurried upstairs toward her music room to collect what she needed, she heard Ernest fly through the door below, shouting for Brogan, Wallace, and Leith.

"What's happening?" she called down from the landing.

"Feandon just sent young Brodie across from the Auld Hoose. One of the bulls got loose and is making across the moor for the cliffs. The boys and I have to head him off."

"I was going to ask you to hitch up the small buggy," said Sally. "I have to go into the village. Poor old Diorbhall Taithleach has taken a turn."

"It's already hitched," replied Ernest. "I was headed that way myself. You take it."

Three sets of booted feet were already tromping down the stairs.

"Can I help, Daddy?" said Delynn, hurrying after them.

"The more the better. You're as swift as any of your brothers—"

"Hey!" objected Wallace.

"She's not as fast as me!" said Leith.

"Where's Brogan?" asked Ernest.

"He's having lunch with a girl at the Hotel," replied Leith, always captivated by his older brother's activities.

"Well, four of us ought to do it. But we'll have to run like the wind and encircle him."

Seconds later they were out the door. Sally

packed her harp and was soon on her way to the village and soon arrived at the Coyle cottage. Margaret's daughter had been watching at the open door. She ran out to take charge of the horse and buggy while Sally lifted out her clarsach.

"Mum's waitin' for ye," said the young woman. "She's in the hoose wi' my grandmum."

Sally carried the instrument through the door into the dimly lit cottage. Moments later she was at the bedside.

"How is she, Margaret?"

Margaret was well familiar with Sally's special gift to ease the suffering of the sick and dying of the village. "She hasna opened her eyes since yestreen," she said. "Her breathin's labored like, an' she's pickin' at the bedclothes, ye ken, the way folks do when their time's comin'."

Sally sat down on the chair beside the bed. Setting her clarsach on the floor in front of her and pulling it to her shoulder, gently she began to strum and pluck so softly at first that the sound could hardly be heard. Sally's eyes were on the strings of her instrument but Margaret's were fixed on the pale white face of her mother where her head lay on the pillow. At the first sounds from the harp, Margaret detected a flutter of her mother's eyelids, as if her eyes had moved beneath them. Sally continued, gradually moving into recognizable tunes from bygone years—hymns and folk tunes and Scottish favorites. She played for perhaps twenty minutes. By then Margaret's daughter Liusaidh had joined them at the bedside.

As the familiar strains of "Loch Lomond" began emanating softly from the strings beneath them, old Diorbhall's eyes throbbed again, then opened a crack. Margaret reached for her hand.

"Hoo are ye feelin' the noo, Mum?" she said.

"Middlin', ken," came a feeble voice from the bed. "But, aye, my man! The tune puts me in mind o' him. He an' me sang it t'gither when we was young, ken . . . an' it winna be long afore I'll see him again . . . my sweet man."

The speech had taxed what little strength she had left. She closed her eyes. A peaceful smile came to her face. She began to breathe more easily. Sally repeated "Loch Lomond" several times, then slowly moved into other traditional songs followed by hymns that she knew would be familiar from years in the church.

As the well-known tune of "Jesus Loves Me" filled the small cottage, again came a fluttering of the aging eyes. They opened briefly and darted back and forth, as if looking for some-one. "Aye . . . the bonny tune," she said softly. "It puts me in mind o' . . . I was a wee lassie, ye ken . . . the kirk an' the organ . . ."

A great smile spread over her face. Her eyes were wide now, wide but gazing straight ahead, as if beholding something in the distance, something

318

beyond the wall ten feet away, something far across earth's horizon.

Sally continued to play, first "It Is Well With My Soul," then "The Old Rugged Cross," followed by "What A Friend We Have in Jesus."

Still Diorbhall lay, absolutely still, eyes wide, staring ahead. The music seemed to enter into her heart and mind more deeply than any in the room, than even Sally herself could comprehend.

Sensing that eternity lay just beyond the cusp of her vision, but not beyond the reach of the strings of her harp, Sally gradually drifted again into the familiar melody of "Jesus Loves Me."

A holy hush descended. The music filled the air with nostalgic reminders for all four of the women present.

Suddenly a voice broke from the bed.

"Aye . . . the Bonny Man . . . 'tis the Bonny Man himsel'!"

Chills swept through Sally's body but she continued to play.

"He's comin' . . . he's sae light, all dressed in white like . . . the Bonny Man . . . an' there's music comin' . . . where's the music . . . aye, 'tis fae the angels! The angels at their harpies . . . aye, 'tis sich a peaceful tune . . . I canna put my finger on what . . . it puts me in the mind o' . . . aye, the Bonny Man's reaching oot his han' . . . an' if I jist . . ."

Her voice faded into silence. Sally glanced

down at the pillow. The eyes were closed even as a final breath slowly left her lungs in a long sigh. Upon her face still lingered a peaceful smile, and the light from her last earthly vision.

Softly Margaret began to cry.

Sally continued to play for a few moments . . . softer . . . softer . . . until the imperceptible vibrations faded into the trailing wisps of eternity.

Her hands stilled. Softly she rose, leaving the harp where it was, and tiptoed from the room, leaving mother and daughter and granddaughter alone to say their final good-byes.

From his vantage point with Emily on the Muckle Hill, Brogan saw the errant bull madly lumbering away from the Auld Hoose long before Feandon Shaw and his son and his own father and brothers and sister came into view chasing it down. He knew the danger if the mad beast kept on the way he was going.

He jumped up and was on his horse's back in seconds.

"I'll be back!" he shouted, and galloped down the north side of the hill.

Not to be left behind, Emily mounted and followed, though more slowly over the soft and occasionally treacherous turf.

By the time Ernest and the others reached the North Cliffs, they found the bull calm and in his right mind, his way to the bluffs barred by a horseman and a horsewoman, cautiously maneuvering the bull back in the direction of its home.

A peal of laughter sounded from Brogan's father at the sight of the two, who had kept the bull from the fate of the Gadarene swine.

"I'll let you take over from here!" laughed Brogan. "Our picnic basket is still waiting for us up on the Muckle Hill."

54

LAIRD AND AMERICAN

Emily lay on her bed wide awake. Across the room Mrs. Barnes's rhythmic breathing was deep and steady. She had hoped to work a little tonight on the notes for her paper. Mrs. Barnes had retired early, however, and she didn't want to wake her. She could try to work downstairs in one of the Hotel's sitting rooms, thought Emily. But there were always people about.

She drew in a deep sigh. She knew well enough that the other Hotel guests weren't the impediment to her concentration. She could not stop thinking about today's picnic and the episode with the runaway bull. Brogan's laughter still rang in her memory. It was such a contagious laugh—so spontaneous and full of life . . . exactly like what she had heard from the older Tulloch. Laughter must run in the family, she thought. How changed Brogan seemed from their first encounter on the moor. Was it really only a few days ago?

Her thoughts were obviously too full to concentrate on her paper. Nothing would do but to go out and walk off the energy of her preoccupied mind.

Emily rose, picked up a light wrap, and slipped quietly from the room. The clock struck ten as she crossed the lobby. Moments later she emerged into the open air. The evening's chill felt good on her cheeks. A flash of sunlight from the southwest took her by surprise.

Emily walked down the Hotel drive until she reached the main road. With no destination in mind, she turned away from the village. A few minutes later she found herself standing on the deserted ferry landing, staring out across the isthmus, waves gently lapping against the pillars and gravelly shore.

She would be here again soon, she thought, boarding the ferry for the last time to return to Lerwick, then Glasgow, then home to America. Suddenly her mind was full of strange new thoughts.

After a minute or two Emily left the landing and walked back the way she had come, pausing at a road leading to her left. Some two hundred yards up the hill, bathed in the low light of the sun off the sea, rose a small gray stone church with a bell steeple above. Drawn toward the reminder of her family and its spiritual roots, she turned into the drive and made her way toward it.

Reaching the solitary building a few minutes later, she gazed up at the solemn stone structure with its darkened windows of stained glass, red-painted door, and steeple stretching into the night sky. Seen at this hour, so stoic and stern, the cold, hard stones seemed lonely—a peculiar way to describe what was supposed to represent the living, breathing body of Christ on earth. If the church were truly made up of living stones, the granite blocks of which this church was constructed appeared anything but alive.

Emily read the sign on the front wall: *Church of Scotland.* She wondered what a devout Quaker like her father would think of this church and its doctrine. She would like to be here for a service.

She continued around the stone walls until she found herself approaching a small cemetery behind the church. The gate stood open. Seeing nothing ahead, she thought, but the inanimate stones of grave markers, she was suddenly startled by a movement. A tall figure, lean and in the garb of a working man, was walking slowly in her direction out of the depths of the cemetery toward the gate. He saw her, and his face registered equal surprise.

"Good evening," he said. "I didn't expect to

see anyone else here. I am afraid you took me by surprise."

"Hello," said Emily. "I was out for a walk from the Hotel."

"I surmised as much. You are American, I take it, with the tour staying at the Hotel?"

"It seemed too light to go to bed."

"Oh!" he said as a look of recognition dawned on his face, "—it's Miss Hanson, is it not . . . my son's friend from earlier today? I'm sorry, I didn't know you in the light of the sun behind you."

"Yes—Mr. Tulloch!" exclaimed Emily. "I didn't recognize you either!"

"It seems we are both suffering from the Emmaus Syndrome!" laughed Ernest.

"And I now realize that we had actually met, in a manner of speaking, even before that," said Emily, "on the moor a few days ago. I have to admit, however, that my attention was mostly drawn by the boy and his dying bird."

"Ah, yes of course," smiled Tulloch. "Young Sandy. That was a rather wonderful moment."

It was silent a few seconds as they reflected on their first brief encounter.

"Did you get the bull safely home?" asked Emily.

"Yes, thanks to you and Brogan."

"It was certainly the most exciting picnic I have ever been on!" laughed Emily. "But you appear pensive. Have you recently lost someone? Brogan mentioned no death in the family."

"Not recently," replied the laird. "But I come to visit the graves of my parents and first wife. Present grief does not bring me here as much as to remind myself of important influences from the past, and to pray, both for the past and the future. Of course, death is invariably accompanied by sorrows one cannot entirely escape. But I am a believer in eternal life, so my earthly sorrow has an eternal receptacle that I may pour it into."

"A colorful image. It is just like what my father might say."

"Your father is a believer?"

"We are Quakers."

"How fascinating!" rejoined Ernest with light in his eyes.

"Are you familiar with Quakers?" asked Emily.

"Only by reputation, you might say. However, one of my favorite authors is a Quaker. I find much in my spirit that resonates with his message."

"What is the man's name?"

"John Woolman."

"Really!" exclaimed Emily, then paused.

"I can see that I touched something," said Ernest with a smile.

"I am almost embarrassed to say it," said Emily. "You will scarcely believe it, but my family is descended from John Woolman."

"You don't say—that is extraordinary!"

"Believe it or not, we live on a parcel of land in Burlington, New Jersey, that has come down to my father from the original Woolman grant of land in the 1600s."

"I am speechless. I am doubly honored to know you, Miss Hanson."

"I don't know that we are to be honored because of a notable ancestor—least of all me. What is it they say about God having no grandchildren?"

"Yes, a perceptive insight," smiled Ernest.

"But my father is proud of his Woolman ancestry," Emily went on, "—for the right reasons, I would say—and a great admirer of Mr. Woolman and his writings."

The two new acquaintances continued to talk and walk slowly about the church grounds, then in the direction of the Hotel. An hour passed quickly. When Ernest saw Emily safely back to her lodgings sometime after eleven, she smiled at the reminder that it had been her preoccupation with one Tulloch man that had driven her out into the night. Yet now an hour later her mind was occupied with the father rather than the son.

55

HUSBAND AND WIFE

Sally Tulloch sat alone in the breakfast room of the Cottage and took a sip from the cup in her hand. Her husband, indeed all of Britain, continued its centuries-long love affair with tea. She, however, began every morning with two cups of coffee, sometimes with a splash of chocolate or peppermint added.

This was her favorite time of the day, Sally thought. It was about 6:30. The summer sun was already high in the sky. The house was quiet. All four children—from Leith the youngest to Brogan the eldest, were late sleepers, as was their father. In winter it would feel like the middle of the night when she rose in the darkness, stoked the fire and put on water for her coffee to enjoy with her morning's reading. Every day busied itself soon enough. But she looked forward to this hour as equally as important to her spiritual nourishment as eating and drinking were to her body.

She glanced up at the sound of footsteps from the stairway. A moment later her husband walked into the room, a well-worn book in his hand.

"Ernest!" exclaimed Sally with a smile. "You're up with the sun. What's the occasion?"

"None that I can think of," he replied. "I was up late too, but I woke rested and invigorated."

"It is a treat to have you join me. The water is hot for tea," said Sally, setting her book aside. She rose and walked to the stove where she had the teapot with tea ready. "Unless I am mistaken, I think I see an old favorite in your hand," she added as she poured steaming water into the pot.

"Your eagle eyes do not deceive you, my dear. It seems time for another reading."

"Has anything in particular prompted it?"

"I happened to meet the young American last evening out for a walk—the girl Brogan has been seeing and was riding with yesterday."

"He has certainly been different since she came to the island."

"It is an extraordinary thing. She strikes me as opposite to Brogan in every way—not at all the sort of young woman I would imagine him to take a second look at."

"What is she like?"

"Positively delightful. Personable, friendly, thoughtful. An engaging conversationalist . . . believe it or not, a deeply committed spiritual young woman—a Quaker."

"Really!"

"And an amazing coincidence—she is descended from old John Woolman, whom her father reads as avidly as I do. They live in Woolman's very locale near Mount Holly—a town called Burlington, if

I remember correctly . . . and on Woolman land."

"How astonishing. No wonder you are in a mind to read the journal again," laughed Sally.

She resumed her seat on the small couch with Ernest now beside her. A few minutes later, both with steaming cups in their hands, husband and wife were absorbed in their readings. They enjoyed their shared silences. Such times together, which they called "recreative solitude," provided the sustenance for their relationship. Occasionally one would share a thought sparked from what had just been read. At other times the silence would gradually drift into relaxed dialog.

At length Sally glanced up from her reading. Her face wore a thoughtful expression.

"The change in Brogan these last few days is all the more remarkable," she said, "now that you tell me more about the young woman. Is she really the cause of it, do you think?"

"Who can say? But when they were together on horseback out on the northern bluffs yesterday, I saw an expression in his face I haven't seen in years. I have to admit that the last thing I would have expected would be for him to take a fancy to a Quaker lass!" laughed Ernest. "But I am pleased that he has eyes to see her for who I believe she is. It is wonderful to see that the old spark of fun in his eyes and voice has suddenly returned. It's as though the true Brogan has returned."

"Maybe, as you say, something is waking up inside him."

"Whatever accounts for the change, I am grateful," said Ernest. "Brogan and I laughed and talked together yesterday like old times. If it is because of a girl, well, you know what they say— 'the Lord works in strange and mysterious ways, His wonders to perform.' "

They returned to their reading. It was Ernest who again broke the silence fifteen minutes later.

"And you were able to help old Diorbhall Taithleach through the veil yesterday?"

Sally nodded thoughtfully.

"I am going to call on Margaret today and see if there is anything we can do, if you would like to accompany me."

"It is always an extraordinary thing to witness," Sally said at length. "I feel like a bystander myself. And it seems that the harp is singularly suited to turn people's hearts toward eternal themes. It may be the subconscious association with angels and heaven. But it is nonetheless real."

"Why is music itself, do you think, so powerful when death approaches?"

Sally thought a moment. "I think I would say that every person has been created with strings that vibrate in harmonics to God's heartstrings. We have been created with the same spirit-harmonics that God possesses because we were birthed out of

His being. Most people go their whole lives and never feel the eternal music inside them."

She paused, obviously trying to find the appropriate words to answer her husband's query.

"When I play for someone who is dying," she went on, "I am trying to touch those places where the eternal music is waiting to come awake. Along with the music, I speak to them with a smile or a kiss or a gentle touch that gives dignity to their being. Honor prepares the way for the music. I want them to feel that death is the culmination of a good and worthy life. Someone like dear Diorbhall, in the eyes of the world, is just a wrinkled old lady, easily ignored, losing her memory, of little value. Such a one needs to know that I value the life they have lived.

"As I sat beside Diorbhall yesterday, though she was scarcely aware of my presence, I wanted her and her family to know that she had dignity as a child of God. It opens the way for the music to touch the spirit. She knew that death was near. As she walked through the door she left this life behind with my fading earthly music ringing faintly in her ears, even as she was being welcomed to the music of the angels' harps on the other side. My harp and the angels' harps blend as one. It's what I call, in the words of the old hymn, 'the music of the spheres.' "

"What a remarkable thing you are privileged to do, helping your fellow pilgrims die in peace," said Ernest, "with a smile on the lips and music in the heart. Promise me, my dear, that your harp will be at my bedside when my time comes to the strains of 'Whispering Hope.' "

"I promise. But what if I go first?"

"Very unlikely," laughed Ernest. "But if it should come to that, I will sing softly in your ear."

"What will you sing?" asked Sally.

" 'It Is Well With My Soul,' of course—your favorite."

56

A WARM TWILIGHT

Brogan and Emily walked out of the Whales Reef Hotel the following evening about 9:30. The evening was warm for the Shetlands, even in the summer. The mercury had risen to nearly seventy earlier in the day and it was still in the low sixties. By now everyone with Emily's tour had taken note of the interest the laird's son was paying to the young American. Gossip ran rampant, though in truth there was little to tell. Mrs. Barnes knew no more than everyone else did. Emily had confided nothing to her, other than that she found young Tulloch friendly, courteous, and interesting.

"So tomorrow is your last day in the Shetlands,"

said Brogan as they made their way slowly in the direction of the village.

Emily nodded. She knew that fact only too well. "We sail from Lerwick to Glasgow about noon . . . day after tomorrow, that is."

"And from there back to the States?"

Again Emily nodded. She was feeling strange sensations and did not want to talk about leaving. A long silence followed.

"I've enjoyed visiting with you," said Brogan at length.

"I have enjoyed it too."

"Do you suppose you will ever come back?"

"It is a very long way," replied Emily, her voice low. "My family doesn't travel like this—for pleasure, you know. My father is very frugal. We go to yearly meeting in Philadelphia. But that is all."

"Ah, right. Is that part of your beliefs? I mean, do Quakers . . . I'm sorry, I don't even know what I am asking?"

"Are Quakers frugal, do you mean?"

"I suppose that's it."

"I would say that Quakers focus their lives around church, family, and work. We generally keep to ourselves. I suppose there is a sense of frugality. Many Quakers are prosperous in business. It's just that we have simple values and don't believe in extravagance. I think it is simplicity of lifestyle more than frugality as such. Maybe the two go hand in hand, I've never thought about it."

"What do Quakers believe, then?"

"Much the same as other Christians. We believe that God speaks to every man and woman individually."

"Do you think God speaks to *you?*" asked Brogan.

Emily hesitated.

"I cannot say that I have heard His voice. I *believe* it, but I am waiting to experience it more personally. I realize that I am still young and have to make faith my own as I grow. And you?" she asked.

"What about me?"

"What do you believe?"

"I honestly have not thought much about it in a personal way. I dutifully went to church with my family when I was young. But I stopped as soon as I thought I could get away with telling my father I didn't want to go."

"When was that?"

"I was probably fifteen. I know it hurt my father."

"Did you ever talk about it?"

"With him?"

Emily nodded.

"No. We didn't talk much after I was a teen-ager."

"That's too bad."

"Do you and your father talk about serious things?"

"Yes, though I suppose a girl usually talks more to her mother."

"And you still go to church with your parents?"

"Yes."

"But you said you haven't made their faith your own yet?"

"That's not exactly what I said, only that I am aware my parents have a wider range of spiritual experiences than I do. My beliefs are *real,* but I know I am young. I am growing. I know my faith will grow deeper all my life."

"You *want* a deeper faith, I take it?"

"There's nothing in the world I want more. That's what I pray for."

"What an extraordinary statement."

"Why do you say that?" asked Emily.

"Because with all the things the world has to offer, especially in this modern day, for you to say that you want a deeper faith more than anything else . . . I have just never heard such a thing."

"What do you want more than anything in life?"

"I don't suppose I know."

"You haven't thought about it?"

"I guess not—not like you obviously have."

"It seems to me that there is nothing more important to think about."

"You might be right. But that is a new idea to me."

"I thought you said your father instructed you in spiritual things."

"You're right—he did. Maybe what I should say is that I haven't thought about faith since leaving home. I probably should have paid more attention when I was young."

"Maybe now is the time God wants you to start paying attention."

"Do you actually believe God has designs for our lives as specific as that?"

"I do."

"Again, you continue to surprise me."

"Surely your father taught you that."

"You're right," replied Brogan thoughtfully. "He believes that God is intimately involved in every facet of our lives. I assume that you believe that as well?"

"I do."

It was quiet a few moments as they continued to walk slowly.

"So I'll ask again," said Emily, "what do *you* believe, Brogan? You said you dutifully went to church. But what do you believe now . . . for yourself?"

"I never thought about belief as personal. I thought you were supposed to believe what the church said. So I suppose I believe what the Church of Scotland teaches."

"You don't sound very convinced. If that's all there is to it, how can you say you believe at all?

I asked what *you* believed, not what the church teaches."

"Maybe I'm not sure. I haven't thought about religion in a long time."

"Do you believe that a time comes in every life when a person has to make faith his or her own?" asked Emily quietly.

"Again, I haven't thought about it. You would probably say that it's time I made faith my own."

"That is not for me to say. Only you would know that."

Brogan smiled.

"What are you thinking?" asked Emily.

"Only that when we first met I accused you of being pushy and outspoken. But when it comes to faith and belief, you are just the opposite. You aren't one who pushes your beliefs onto others."

"I suppose you are right. I think Quakers in general are less evangelistic than some other Christians. We tend to believe that each person's walk with God moves along paths that no one can mark out for anyone else, that we each have to discover our spiritual journeys for ourselves."

They continued on through the village and eventually found themselves at the harbor staring out over the sea.

"Look, do you see that black smudge out there on the horizon?" said Brogan. "This warm

337

evening may signal a storm on the way. Unless I am mistaken, by this time tomorrow that little dark cloud will probably have engulfed us. It will likely be twenty degrees colder and we'll be under a downpour."

They turned and walked along the shoreline, then inland, crossed the road, and Brogan led the way behind the village back in the direction of the Hotel.

"Do you mind if I ask you something?" asked Brogan, his voice betraying uncharacteristic nervousness.

"Not at all."

"Would you mind if I wrote to you . . . after you're gone, I mean?"

"Of course not. I would like that."

Again they walked on in the quietness of the evening. Once more it was Brogan who broke the silence.

"Would you like to come to supper at the Cottage tomorrow evening?" he asked.

"The tour is planning a big send-off dinner for us at the Hotel."

"Oh, right . . . I didn't think of that. Mrs. Barnes will expect you to be there. It's just that I was hoping you could meet Sally and see the others again."

Emily thought a moment. "I'll talk to Mrs. Barnes. As keen as she is on wanting the book-worm to find romance on this trip, she might agree to dine with some of the others instead of me."

"Shall I pick you up?"

"I think I would like to walk over," said Emily, "now that I know where the famous *Cottage* is."

57

SUPPER AT THE COTTAGE

Just as Brogan had predicted, the temperature dropped all night. By morning it was in the mid-forties and the wind was blowing a gale. For the tour's last day on Whales Reef, Dr. MacDonald had scheduled one more sojourn out on the moor and along the coastline. The wind was so blustery by eleven, however, that they had to beat a hasty retreat back to the Hotel.

By the time Emily set out to walk through the village to the Cottage, the sky was black and threatening and the wind howling. She launched herself into it with relish. By the time she reached the village, she was enjoying the contest against the elements. The wind had whipped the sea into a boiling cauldron. Smoke from the cottage chimneys swirled and beat about the rooftops in a frenzy. Few were out. She continued past the village eastward along the road.

When she was about halfway from the village

to her destination, all at once the wind ceased. Suddenly Emily found herself in the middle of a great calm. From what had been a tumult of wind about her face and ears, all was quiet. The sound of the sea, frothing and foaming and pounding at the shore, came rushing at her in place of the hurricane.

Sensing that the change boded no good, Emily quickened her pace. Almost the next moment two or three huge drops hit her face. More came splattering onto the gravel beside her, isolated and heavy. They were joined by more. Within seconds the heavens opened and Emily knew she should have set out ten minutes sooner.

Inside the Cottage, impatiently waiting at the window, Brogan heard the first drops against the glass, then watched the downpour unleash itself on the island. Seconds later he was sprinting for the garage under a wide black umbrella. A minute later the Studebaker roared out into the deluge.

By the time Brogan led Emily through the front door of the Cottage five or six minutes later, the rest of the family was anxiously awaiting them.

Introductions and greetings were hasty and preempted by wind and rain lashing through the open door and Emily's dripping clothes.

The unceremonious beginning set the evening off in a festive spirit.

"Come with me, my dear," said Sally. "You are

soaked to the bone. We are not exactly the same size, but we will find you some dry clothes to put on regardless."

"She can use anything in my wardrobe," said Delynn, hurrying after them toward the stairs. "You and I are about the same size, don't you think, Emily?"

The women disappeared upstairs, leaving a trail of rainwater behind them.

"That storm certainly arrived all at once!" laughed Ernest.

"I told her it was coming," rejoined Brogan. "But she wanted to walk. She is a great one for the outdoors."

"And pretty!" added Brogan's half brother.

"You keep your observations to yourself, young Leith!" laughed Brogan. "Don't embarrass her."

Sally, Delynn, and Emily returned downstairs laughing, Emily wearing one of Delynn's dresses and her hair hanging straight and wet as she brushed at it with a towel. Sally was carrying the wet dress and shoes to hang in front of the fireplace where they would dry quickly. The three were laughing like schoolgirls. Wallace and Leith were soon pestering Emily with questions about America, Leith asking if he could come for a visit and if Emily knew any cowboys or gangsters.

Ernest remained mostly quiet through much of the meal, watching with a full heart as his three sons and daughter—nearly all now grown and interacting as young adults—laughed and talked as they hadn't for years. Occasionally his eyes met Emily's, and a quiet smile passed between them.

By the end of the evening, with many farewells, Emily felt as if she had been taken into a second family. She would not have traded the evening for anything, but it would make the next day's parting harder than ever.

The drive back to the Hotel beside Brogan at the wheel of the Studebaker was quiet. He pulled up as close to the entrance as he could get, then hurried her to the door under his umbrella.

They looked at each other and smiled.

"I will be at the ferry to see you off," said Brogan.

Emily nodded.

"Good night, Emily."

Emily smiled and nodded, then turned and hurried inside as the tears began to flow.

PART 11

SEPTEMBER–OCTOBER 2006

58

THE SCENT OF AUTUMN

WHALES REEF, SHETLAND ISLANDS

In northern regions like the Shetland Islands, temperate weather changes quickly. The only season that seems never to end is winter. Spring, summer, and autumn are fleeting and brief.

Thus it was, though heather still adorned Scotland's mountains, moors, and islands as August gave way to September, that nippy hints of change could be felt on the island breezes of Whales Reef.

The scent of autumn was in the air. The subtle shift in atmosphere affected various species differently. Migratory birds began thinking of warmer climes across the water to the south. The island's fishermen gazed with occasional concern toward the horizon, knowing what the coming months would bring.

And David and Loni sensed, though neither spoke of it immediately, that the approach of autumn signaled a new phase in their deepening relationship.

The two were often seen on the island together. They walked the streets of the village, along the

345

seashore, up the Muckle Hill, to the northern bluffs, and visited the chief's cave on several occasions. Many of the village women were reminded of those summer visits by the young chief during his student days when he was seen walking those same moors and coastlines with their own Audney Kerr. No longer, however, were they pining for what might have been. They had never seen their chief more at peace. If it was an American who had finally captured his heart rather than one of their own, she had shown herself in their eyes worthy of the honor.

One of the happiest for David was Audney herself. Her love for her friend and chief was deep and selfless. She rejoiced to see them together. David's obvious affection for Loni gave the final release to Audney's heart to love once more herself.

Though in Whales Reef Loni had discovered something she had yearned for all her life, she also found a longing reasserting itself to get back to her professional life. Overseeing the small Cottage household and becoming interested in the animals and the village and her responsibilities as laird were not *enough*. As seriously as she took her new role, she realized that she missed her office, she missed Maddy, and she missed the challenges of the business world.

Now that she was a woman of property and means, however—a *tycoon* as Maddy humorously dubbed her, it seemed doubtful that she would ever again be an executive "assistant." Would she still love that former life now that everything about her future had altered so dramatically?

On David's part, he knew that changes had come not only to the island of Whales Reef, but within himself. As those changes deepened, and as the weather began to turn and the nights of early September slowly lengthened and brought an occasional morning frost, his thoughts gradually coalesced into a resolve and a decision . . . both involving Loni.

The first he broached one morning when they were out with the sheep and dogs. He grew thoughtful.

"There are some things I want to talk to you about," said David at length. "Two things in particular. Much as it pains me, and though part of me does not want to say it, I sense that it may be time for you to go home—to your other home, I mean."

"Finally tired of me!" laughed Loni.

"Never."

"Why then?"

"Because you miss your work. Surely you sense it. I know you love it here. But part of you will never be completely fulfilled by all this."

They walked on as the dogs flew about and the sheep scampered over the ground, pausing to nibble wherever they could find grass.

"What do you suggest?" asked Loni.

"Everything is good on the island," David replied. "With everything at the Cottage back to normal with Isobel, Saxe, and Dougal, and with the mill humming along with Murdoc at the helm, there is nothing urgent or pending to keep you here. Obviously I would miss you, and the people are more attached to you than you have any idea. They really love you, Loni."

Loni smiled. "That's nice," she said. "Still a little unbelievable, but nice."

"As much as they, and I, would miss you, however," David went on, "I think you need to see how your two lives balance—get back into your work with Maddy and see how you feel about it. Now that you are laird of Whales Reef, and have had a good taste of what life here is like, you need to see how your former profession fits into it."

Loni smiled. "Funny. Sometimes I am sure you can read my mind. I've sensed the same thing."

"Not permanently, of course," David added. "But things are running smoothly here. You have thoroughly won the people over. Now you need to solidify your renewed relationship with your grandparents, as well as decide about your work with Maddy. I will hate to see you go, yet somehow I sense it is time."

"Like a season is drawing to a close." Loni paused, then added, "When we were in D.C., Maddy told me I needed to return with you to see what my future here held. Now maybe the reverse is necessary. I need to sort out things back home—to see what my future holds there. Past and future collide . . . and present too, I suppose."

"Along those lines," said David, "I thought it might be fun, if you'd like, for me to accompany you to Aberdeen before you fly back to the States."

"Oh, that would be lovely!" exclaimed Loni.

"I'd love to show you around mainland Scotland for a few days—take you to some of the historic sites, maybe to the Highlands where our clan, your ancestors, originated."

"I would love that!"

"Then I'll make some plans for us."

59

RETURN ENGAGEMENT

David Tulloch and Noak Muir were in the Whales Fin Inn one afternoon about one o'clock when a familiar figure walked unexpectedly through the front door.

David's face brightened. His mouth opened to call out a greeting when a finger to the new-comer's lips silenced him. With a grin, David watched as he crept across the floor to the counter, where Audney stood with her back turned.

"Beggin' yer lefe, miss," he said, "I ken ye dinna hae a chaumer redd for the likes o' an unco man wha's a veesitor tae yer wee inch—"[3]

Audney recognized the voice instantly, though not the thick Edinburgh dialect. She swung around, and her face lit into a radiant smile.

"Lincoln!" she exclaimed. The plate in her hand clattered to the counter as she flew from behind it. She ran and embraced him with a collision that was almost violent. An envelope he was carrying fell to the floor. Realizing what she had done, Audney's face reddened.

"My, that was a greeting worth waiting for!" laughed Lincoln Rhodes as he stooped to pick up the envelope. "It is wonderful to see you again too, Audney."

"I wasna thinkin'," said Audney, clearly embarrassed. "But we hae a couple rooms left."

"Nonsense!" said David, now coming forward. "Lincoln, my friend," he said with a vigorous handshake, "how good to see you . . . and you are staying with me at the Auld Hoose."

"It would seem that I have more invitations than I can accept. Rev. Yates is actually expecting me at the manse. He was the only one who knew I was coming, so it seemed best to accept his invitation. I appreciate the offer, David," added

3. "Begging your leave, miss . . . I know you don't have a room ready for the likes of a stranger who's a visitor to your small island—"

Rhodes. He hesitated as he glanced back and forth between David and Audney. "But it does seem that perhaps I should begin getting accustomed to my new home."

A sharp intake of breath came from Audney's lips.

"Are you saying what I think you are saying?" asked David.

Rhodes smiled and nodded. "I was notified by the session last week," he said. "Rev. Yates's resignation has been made official and he will be leaving Whales Reef in a few days to return to the mainland. Your kirk elders have called me to replace him, and the session has given its approval. As of this Sunday, you are looking at the new minister of Whales Reef."

"That is brilliant news—congratulations!" said David, again shaking his hand.

Audney's red face and blinking eyes revealed that she was suddenly at a loss for words. Whether Lincoln or David fully divined the depth of her reaction was doubtful. Rhodes, however, rescued her from further embarrassment by drawing her aside. David returned to his table.

"When the pub slows down later," said Lincoln in a low voice, "could I see you? Perhaps we could go for a walk."

Audney nodded shyly as she recovered herself.

"And I would like you to have supper with me at the manse," he added, "on Friday evening if you have no plans. Stirling will be spending the evening with Dickie Sinclair in Lerwick. It will be my chance to cook for you for a change."

Audney smiled and nodded.

After a few minutes in conversation, Audney returned to her lunch duties behind the counter. David rose and approached again, now with Noak Muir, who greeted Rhodes and likewise offered a hearty shake of the hand.

"There is another matter I need to discuss with you, David," said Rhodes with a serious expression. "I'm sure you will be interested as well, Mr. Muir."

They returned to the table.

"I have been investigating on my own into the McLeod situation," Lincoln began, speaking softly as the three leaned their heads together. "Has there been any news about the gun?"

"Actually yes," replied David. "I heard from the sheriff in Lerwick two days ago about the ballistics report. Hardy's gun was definitely not used in the McLeod shooting."

"I expected that," nodded Rhodes.

"How so?" asked David.

"I have several contacts with the Edinburgh Police Department. A detective there befriended me when I was a young, tough hothead. He took me under his wing and eventually led me to faith. We've been close ever since. He put me in touch with an FBI agent in the States, and I've learned that the McLeod company has been under investigation. Charges were about to be brought in both the U.S. and Britain—fraud, tax evasion, embezzlement . . . serious stuff. Some of the top executives could go to jail. There are rumors, too, of false evidence planted against one or more of them. I'm sure there's a motive for murder in there somewhere. McLeod himself was apparently a nasty bit of work, unscrupulous to a fault."

He opened the envelope he had been carrying and set the contents on the table in front of the other two men.

"I brought some photographs for you to look at," he said. "Do you recognize any of these men?"

"Who are they?"

"Executives in McLeod's company."

David picked up one of the photographs and eyed it carefully.

"You know, come to think of it," he said slowly, "I may recognize this chap." He examined the face intently. "I should show it to Loni—she was with me at the time."

"Where was that?"

"Believe it or not, on the same day McLeod apparently went missing, the day of the brouhaha at the town square—you remember, Noak? I think this man may have shared the ferry with Loni and me and Loni's friend on our way over to the island just before the fireworks in town, which ended with the altercation between Hardy and McLeod."

"That would put him on the island near the time of the murder."

"Who is he?" asked Noak.

"He was McLeod's right-hand man in the U.K.," replied Rhodes. "His name is Ross Thorburn. If you're right, that may put him in the thick of it."

"We should show this photograph to Hardy," said David.

60

THE PHOTO

LERWICK

David and Lincoln Rhodes paused on the pavement outside the building of the Lerwick Sheriff's Court building.

"I want to be in prayer when I talk to your cousin," said Lincoln. "You know him better than I do—what should be our prayer?"

"A good question," replied David thoughtfully. "Obviously in the matter of the murder, we do not know what happened so we can hardly pray for a specific outcome. We have to leave that in God's hands."

"Perhaps, then, we should simply pray that truth will come out . . . and will *win* out."

"Always one of the best prayers."

"As far as the man himself," asked Lincoln, "—what do you perceive to be his deepest personal need?"

"An even more probing question," said David. "Poor Hardy is so confused. He has no idea what life means."

He thought a moment. "I think if I were to pray one thing for Hardy," he said, "it would be that his heart is softened."

"Then, God," said Lincoln, bowing his head, "we join together in praying that truth will be known and will win out, and we ask that your Spirit would soften Hardy's heart. In the words of St. Francis, may be we instruments of your peace toward the softening of this man who is your child but doesn't yet know it."

"Amen," said David. "Melt Hardy's mind and heart to receive the gentle rains of suffering and the healing warmth of love, that your will in his life may be accomplished."

"Amen!" assented Lincoln. "Now may the Lord go before us!"

"Besides the McLeod situation, I think I should also tell Hardy about you and Audney," said David as they approached the building. "With Hardy's temper, it will be best that he has time to get used to the idea while he is out of harm's way, as it were. He is sure not to like it and may create tension with you."

"I can handle it," smiled Lincoln. "I'm usually

pretty good at diffusing hostility and winning people over."

"You may have your hands full with Hardy!" laughed David.

The two men continued inside. When Hardy walked into the visitors' room a few minutes later and saw them sitting at the table, he was noticeably less antagonistic than previously.

He sat down, and Rhodes set the photographs in front of him.

"Have you ever seen any of these men?" asked David.

Hardy pointed to the photograph and immediately identified Thorburn.

"I ken this bloke, all right," said Hardy. "Met him twice when McLeod was thinkin' I would inherit an' was tryin' tae involve me in his scheme."

"Did you see him the day of the meeting in the town square?"

"Dinna think so."

"Did you notice anything else out of the ordinary that day?" asked Rhodes.

Hardy thought a moment. "There was one queer thing," he said. "After the meetin' an' after McLeod took off in that big car o' his, when I was runnin' back home in the rain after chasin' him past the ferry, I saw a car drivin' slowly oot past yer place, David. I thought it must hae been someone payin' ye a visit."

"What kind of car did you see, Hardy?"

"Let me think . . . a light green Vauxhall—an Estate wagon."

"That's definitely the car that came across on the ferry with us," said David.

"But I canna imagine he had tae do wi' it," said Hardy. "The bloke's half crippled—walks wi' a cane, though he was strong enough . . . had a grip like a vise."

"A cane?" repeated David.

"Aye. Never saw him wi'oot it."

"Hmm . . . McLeod's body had a curious abrasion in the middle of his chest. The coroner didn't know what to make of it. It was almost as if he had been jabbed with the end of some kind of object . . . like the tip of a walking stick, perhaps . . . or a cane."

The three pondered the odd coincidence.

"Then I will look into it further," said Rhodes. "If we discover that Thorburn owns a green Vauxhall Estate, that would prove of great interest to the police."

"Are ye sayin' I'll be gettin' oot o' here?" asked Hardy, looking hopefully at Rhodes, then over at David.

"We will take this new information to the sheriff," said David. "Try to be patient awhile longer, Hardy. We're doing everything we can."

A thoughtful expression came over David's face. He looked across the table toward his cousin.

"There is something you should know, Hardy," he said. "When you *are* released—and we hope it will be soon—there are some changes in the village that you need to be aware of."

"What kind o' changes?" asked Hardy gruffly.

David hesitated. He glanced briefly at Lincoln Rhodes, then back toward Hardy. "Just this: Mr. Rhodes here has been called as the new parish minister."

Hardy shrugged. "All right by me."

"And . . ." David added slowly, "he and Audney are seeing one another."

Hardy glanced back and forth at the two men, obviously more keenly interested in this item of news.

"Audney takin' up wi' a minister," he said slowly, then began to nod with the hint of a smile. "Weel, maybe it's what she deserves at that. She's a bonnie lass—she deserves a good man."

He paused, staring down at the table, then glanced up again. He stared intently into Lincoln's eyes and reached his massive hand across the table.

"Ye take good care o' her, Mr. Rhodes," he said. "I offer ye my hand an' my promise that I'll make no trouble for ye. I think the world o' that lady, an' she *is* a lady too, better than I ever deserved. So ye be good tae her."

The two men shook hands as David watched the exchange in amazement.

"Before we go," said Lincoln, "as you may have to be here a little longer, is there anything I can do for you, Hardy?"

Hardy stared back with a blank expression.

"Do you need anything . . . anything I can bring you or do for you?"

"Not unless ye can skipper my boat an' git my crew back tae work," chuckled Hardy.

"Sure, I can do that," replied Lincoln as if there was nothing unusual in the request, "—tell me what to do."

"Ye're no serious—ye'd go oot wi' my crew?"

"Why not?"

"Do ye ken the fishin'?"

"I can learn. I've worked with these two hands of mine at more things than you would probably believe, Hardy," he said. "I can't say as I've ever made a tent, but I hope I am following in the tradition of the Tarsus tentmaker in my own way. To follow in the footsteps of the Galilean fishermen who first obeyed the call to fish for men would be a double honor."

Having no idea what he was talking about, yet realizing the young minister was in deadly earnest, Hardy's brain began to take in the practicality of Lincoln's offer.

"Weel then, if ye're willin', an' David could help ye—he's got fishin' in his blood as weel as I do, an' kens his way aboot a boat—ye could git in touch wi' Ian Hay and Gordo Ross an' Rufus

Wood and Billy Black—ye ken my boys, David—
an' ye could tell them tae show ye the ropes an'
git oot on the water. I need to pay the lads, they're
depending on me."

"I will get to work on it the moment we return."

"Thank ye, Mr. Rhodes, I'm indebted tae ye . . .
an' yersel' as weel, David."

61

Unexpected Visit

WHALES REEF

The event about to take place had been anticipated for a week.

Sandy Innes and Dougal Erskine had spent
the night with the expectant mother, taking
turns sleeping in Dougal's quarters. Sandy's
announcement at 5:30 on the fateful morning that
the time was nigh resulted in a hurried rush across
the island by the gamekeeper in his ATV. David
was already up with his first cup of tea and was
on his way to the Cottage with Dougal within
minutes.

The sound of the ATV's engine roaring away
from the barn, then returning twenty minutes later
at 5:50, roused Isobel, Saxe, and Loni from their
beds. By the time David came into the house with

360

a report shortly, Isobel had coffee and tea ready for an army and the household was abuzz.

"That coffee smells wonderful," said David.

"Is there news, Mr. David?" asked Isobel.

"All is well, Isobel," he replied. "Sandy and Dougal have everything well in hand. However, it may take longer and be more complicated than we expected. Sandy has never delivered twins before."

"Twins!" exclaimed Isobel.

"Can Shetland ponies really have twins?" asked Loni, walking into the kitchen.

"It is extremely rare," replied David. "But Sandy is certain of it. All we have to do now is wait."

"How exciting!"

"Sandy says it is in your honor. He says that you will have the privilege of naming them—the first two additions to the new laird's family."

Loni laughed. "That will be a privilege. Perhaps I shall sponsor a contest and ask everyone in the village to contribute ideas."

"You want to let yourself in for something like that?" laughed David. "They would absolutely love it. When word of this gets around, we will have a steady stream of visitors wanting to see the wee colties. This is huge—twin Shetland ponies!"

"How big will they be?"

"No bigger than sheepdogs. But they'll grow."

David's prediction proved accurate, the birth took a long time. Still no news was forthcoming from the hospital chamber by eight o'clock. By then word of the impending birth was circulating, and the village men had begun wandering out to the Cottage. Sandy, however, fearing the effects of a crowd on the young mother's nerves, insisted on visitors remaining outside the barn. Isobel kept coffee and tea hot, and oatcakes, digestives, scones, and butteries on the table. The back door of the Cottage remained opened all morning as villagers came and went. Loni walked into town about nine, returning with all the reinforcements from the bakery she could carry.

By ten o'clock a dozen or more men were clustered about chatting with David between the barn and the house. As they awaited developments, a small pen of newborn lambs and their mothers had been opened and was at the moment the object of their interest. Loni had just come out of the back door of the house bearing a tray of edibles when a tiny black-and-white lamb bolted between the men's legs and through the open gate.

"Watch yersel's, lads!" cried Fergus Gunn. "There gaes a live one!"

"Hold this, Noak!" said Loni, shoving the tray into Noak Muir's hands. She turned and ran after the lamb toward the front of the house.

"There's your new laird, lads!" laughed David. "She's not one to wait for someone else. Get him, Alonnah!"

As Loni dashed around to the front of the house,

a car turned into the driveway from the road and came slowly forward. The lamb scampered straight into its oncoming path.

Loni sprinted after it and managed to grab a clump of wool with one hand and maneuver the frantic thing, bleating in terror, off the road. As she did, she lost her footing and went sprawling into the dirt. The car came to a stop beside her.

Arms wrapped around the wriggling, shrieking ball of wool, her clothes splattered with mud, Loni struggled to stand. She heard the car door open as she turned.

Before her stood a man in business suit and tie.

Loni stared gaping. Her voice could only croak out a single word. "Hugh!"

"Loni!" he replied in a dumbfounded tone. "Is that really *you?*"

"It's me . . . but what . . . I mean, *you* . . . on Whales Reef? I can't believe my eyes!" She broke into disbelieving laughter at the shock of seeing her former boyfriend in front of her.

"You told me there were sheep and animals," said Hugh, looking up and down at her muddy clothes, "but you are quite the sight—a regular farm girl!"

"What on earth are you doing here?" Loni exclaimed.

"I came to find you," replied Hugh, "and talk some sense into you.—And look," he added, turning back to the open car door and pulling out a huge bouquet. "No chrysanthemums . . . they're roses," he added, holding them toward her.

"I can see that," rejoined Loni. "But I can't take them just now. I've got my hands full."

The interview was interrupted by the sound of footsteps running over the gravel entryway. Loni turned to see David hurrying toward them.

"I thought you might need help cornering the wee tyke," he said. "I see I shouldn't have worried."

His eyes strayed to the incongruous sight beside Loni—a man in a suit holding flowers. With equal humor Hugh beheld the approach of the manure-splattered rustic.

"Look who's here, David," said Loni. "It's uh . . . the man I told you about . . . my, uh, friend—he's come from the States."

"No kidding—from the States! You are a long way from home. Then welcome to Whales Reef!" he said. "—David Tulloch," he added, extending a dirty hand. "A pleasure to meet you."

Hugh hesitated, then shook David's hand. "Hugh Norman," he said. "You must be the gamekeeper I heard about."

A wry smile crossed David's lips.

"An' pursuant tae that," he said with a twinkle in his eye, "if ye'll jist gie me a grip o' the wee cowerin' beastie, Miss Ford," stepping toward Loni and laying hold of the lamb, "I'll git the wayward laddie back til his pen."

Their eyes met and Loni smiled.

"Will that be a', m'lady?" said David.

"Yes, David. I'll take Hugh inside and get cleaned up myself. But let me know if there is any news."

"I will, m'lady, ye can be sure o' that," replied David. He turned and walked away with the lamb over his shoulders.

"Come in, Hugh," said Loni, at last taking the flowers from his hand and leading him toward the house.

"What was that he was speaking? I could hardly understand him."

"Just a Shetland dialect of English. You get used to it. Lyrical, don't you think?"

"Backwoods is more like it. The fellow sounded like a hick. Though I suppose that's what he is, judging from the look of him.—So this is the famous cottage," Hugh added as he looked over the structure before him.

"This is it."

"A good-sized place. But what did he mean about news?"

"We are expecting the birth of twins to a Shetland pony in the barn in back. Everyone's excited."

"*Excited*—you've got to be kidding . . . about what?"

"Shetland pony twins. It's a major event."

Hugh laughed. "Whatever floats your boat."

"You could go join the men in back if you like," suggested Loni.

"Ugh, no—it sounds disgusting and messy. I'll leave that to the farmers."

They walked inside. Loni took off her muddy shoes, then led Hugh across the entry and into the Great Room. "Let me run upstairs and change my clothes," she said. "I'll just be a minute."

The short time alone restored Loni's equilibrium at the shock of seeing Hugh nearly on her doorstep.

She returned to find him seated and to all appearances not the least interested in the diverse contents of the room.

"Would you like some tea?" asked Loni.

"Coffee if you have it."

"Believe it or not, I have Starbucks. Come into the kitchen with me. The place is full of villagers and the coffee is on."

She led the way into the kitchen.

"Isobel," she said as the housekeeper turned toward them, "this is my friend from the United States, Hugh Norman."

"I am pleased to make your acquaintance, Mr. Norman."

"We are going to have some coffee."

"Would you like me to bring it to you in the Great Room, miss?"

"I'll take care of it, Isobel. I know just how Mr. Norman likes his coffee."

"Very good, miss."

"Please come get me the moment there is news from outside."

A minute later Loni and Hugh returned to the Great Room with their mugs.

"When did you get here?" asked Loni. "I mean, what a surprise—I am still reeling from the sight of you in Whales Reef. You flew up from Aberdeen, I take it?"

"Yes . . . this morning. I flew to London, then Aberdeen yesterday. But what's with the formal Mr. Norman stuff? Hardly what I would expect from someone who is almost my fiancée."

Loni let the comment go. "You came all that way . . . just to see me?" she said.

"Why else would I come to a place like this?" replied Hugh with a light laugh.

"It grows on you."

"I have no interest in giving it the chance to grow on me!" laughed Hugh. "Is it always like this, with people milling around all over the place?"

"This is a special occasion with the Shetland pony I told you about. The whole village may turn out by the end of the day. It's a rare thing.—But, Hugh . . . it's nice to see you, of course, but what in the world are you doing here?"

"I thought we needed to talk . . . face-to-face," he replied. "I got the packet with the ring and your note, but I didn't want it to end that way. I was hoping I could talk some sense into you. Look, Loni, I know I was abrupt on the way to the train. I apologize. I know it wasn't the kind of proposal a girl wants. But I promise to do better. Like with the flowers. I know I can be dense at times. I guess I don't always think about your feelings."

Hugh continued so rapidly, as if he was trying to get out everything he had planned to say in a single breath, that Loni could only sit and listen.

"I talked everything over with the congressman again," he went on. "He said I needed to explain to you what an opportunity this is for us, that I needed to change your mind, that if things were moving too fast for you and you didn't want to get married right away, that at least I needed to have a fiancée on the line. He said that would play almost as well. He calls you my gorgeous bombshell. Anyway, Loni, the campaign is in full swing. Surely you see what I'm trying to say . . . that you need to come home ASAP. And surely . . . I mean honestly, Loni . . . *sheep* . . . *horses* . . . rustics with manure all over them. Good heavens—what kind of joke is this place? Don't you want to be a congressman's wife?"

Loni sat speechless. It was more obvious than ever that she and Hugh were living in different worlds.

"Truthfully, Hugh . . . no," she said at length. Her tone was sad. Whatever tender thoughts the sight of Hugh might temporarily have evoked evaporated with the last words from his mouth. "I meant what I wrote when I returned the ring— I *don't* want to be a congressman's wife."

"But *why?* Who wouldn't want the opportunity to be at the center of power and influence? There is nothing for you here."

Loni did not reply immediately. When at last she spoke her voice was soft. "Hugh," she said, "there is *everything* for me here."

He stared back in disbelief. His expression registered complete bewilderment.

"Look around," she added. "Don't you see it?"

Hugh continued to stare at Loni as if he had not heard her correctly, then slowly shook his head. "No, I don't get it at all," he said. "The place is desolate. The houses are shacks. At least this place of yours is clean, but it's ancient and in need of some modern furniture. And driving through that village a few minutes ago—the place is a dump. I've come to rescue you from all this."

"*Rescue* me?" said Loni incredulously.

"I'm here to take you away from whatever spell this backward place has cast over you."

"You are under the impression that I need *rescuing?*"

Hugh could not help laughing. "It's obvious that you're living out some bucolic fantasy," he said. "It's a little soon for a mid-life crisis, but maybe yours has come early. But it can't last, Loni. It's time to return to the real world. Cash in on your good fortune and become the envy of every young woman in Washington."

Loni shook her head. Hugh was more clueless than she remembered.

"Hugh . . ." she began, though words instantly failed her. "I don't even know what to say . . . how could you think such things? I love it here. These are the most special people in the world. I mean . . . I just—I don't know what to say."

"Say you'll come home and marry me and we can get on with the campaign."

Loni was spared further awkwardness by footsteps behind them. David walked into the Great Room.

"Ah, your gamekeeper," said Hugh, glancing toward him with an amused smile.

"I am sorry for interrupting, m'lady," said David. "But the birth is imminent. I thought you would like to know."

"Thank you, David," said Loni, rising. "But we can dispense with the charade.—Hugh, I would like to introduce you again. Please meet the chief of our island clan, David Tulloch."

"*Chief?*" repeated Hugh, beginning to laugh. "Seriously!"

"I admit it is an anachronistic title," smiled David. "But we are traditionalists here. The people find comfort in the old ways."

"And what is that peculiar title you said came with the house, Loni?"

"She is our new *laird*," said David, answering the question on Loni's behalf.

"Right . . . so here are the laird and chief together—how quaint. But, Loni, seriously . . . you and I have to talk about all this. Surely you can see that—"

"I don't think you quite understand how the situation stands, Hugh," she said. "I have responsibilities here. This is not some idealistic fancy. This house and land is not just an inheritance, it is a heritage, a legacy . . . *my* legacy. Hugh, this is my *home* now, don't you understand?"

She set down the cup on the table beside her. "Now I am going out to the barn with David to attend the birth of my twins," she added. "You are welcome to join us. You are also welcome to stay here at the Cottage for as long as you would like. Maddy found the guest accommodations upstairs most comfortable. You are welcome to them as well. If you do not want to join us outside, I will have Miss Matheson show you to your room if you like. But let me be as clear as I can possibly be—I will not be returning to the States with you."

62

WITNESS

Hugh did not stay for the birth of the two Shetland "wee colties," nor did he avail himself of Loni's offer of accommodations.

Bowed but not broken by Loni's unambiguous clarification of her position, he returned to Lerwick. Only one more meeting took place between the two—lunch the following day. Hugh telephoned, inviting her to his hotel. He again did his best, as he said, to talk some sense into Loni. The result was the same.

Loni returned to Whales Reef while Hugh made plans to return to the States. Loni did not mention that she would soon be following him back across the Atlantic. On his return flight Hugh mapped out a restyled campaign strategy, promoting himself now as "Wisconsin's favorite son" and "one of the capital's most eligible bachelors."

Meanwhile, Hardy Tulloch's fortunes were about to take a new turn, and from the last quarter he or anyone would have expected. Knowing that her secret life was misunderstood by the village women, Odara Innes had never been one of Whales Reef's social gadabouts. She mostly kept to herself, a practice rendered easier in that she did not live in the village proper but with her father, Alexander, and widowed Aunt Eldora Gordon at the Croft on the moor, the former residence of the laird's gamekeeper. Carrying the silent pain of her heart, she had been seen even less than usual since the death of Macgregor Tulloch a year before. It was an unseen grief none but her father understood. The black rose at the old laird's funeral remained a mystery to the village auld wives. They still did not know what Odara had meant by it. Nor would they ever know.

Thus it was that Odara had been apprised of no details concerning Hardy Tulloch's plight. She and Sandy and Eldora had walked home after the fateful meeting at the town square several weeks earlier, hurrying the last quarter mile as close to a run as any of the three were capable of as the rain began to pour down. They heard vaguely that Hardy was in some kind of trouble, but it was hardly a surprise. Hardy was always in the thick of something. The significance of the fact that Odara had seen him galloping through the rain shortly after their return to the Croft was entirely lost on her.

It was a chance comment, made during a visit by David and Lincoln Rhodes to the Croft that led to the solving of the murder that had rocked the island. Hearing rumors about Lincoln and Audney Kerr, and observing Audney's regularity at Sunday worship of late, the three Inneses were full of interest in the new young parish minister. Keeping closer track of affairs than his daughter, it was Sandy who asked where the case against Hardy stood.

"He's a rum one, that Hardy," said Sandy's sister. "I always knew he'd come to an evil end."

"I would not be so quick to judge him, Mrs. Gordon," said Rhodes. "God may not be altogether finished with him yet, as the saying goes."

"Begging your pardon, Reverend," rejoined Sandy's feisty sister, "but I doubt there's much even the Lord can do for the likes of Hardy."

"I have to differ with you there, Mrs. Gordon. If you knew what I was once like, you may agree that there's hope for Hardy yet. His character has only begun to be formed. There's time yet. He may be a lonely man inside."

"Hardy Tulloch . . . *lonely?*" exclaimed Eldora.

"You may be surprised. I was once more like Hardy than you would know by looking at me now."

"What could the likes of him have to do with someone like you?"

"I ran with a rough crowd," replied Lincoln. "I was as tough as they came and was mixed up with a gang in Edinburgh. I grew up being beaten by my father, who was an alcoholic. I hated him and I hated the whole world, and I was out to show I could take on anyone. Then I woke up to what I was. I saw that I was either going to wind up in prison, or hurt someone, but that I was really only hurting myself."

The brief testimonial was sufficient to silence Eldora. Even David, who had heard fragments of his story from prior conversations, was moved by the honesty of his new friend.

"Will Hardy be convicted?" asked Sandy. "*Did* he kill the Texan, David?"

"I don't think so, Sandy," replied David. "His gun has been proven not to have been used. But the last anyone saw of him that day was running after McLeod just before the rain burst down. No one saw a thing of him after that."

"I did," said Odara.

David turned toward her with a look of question.

"Aye," she said. "I mind the day o' the meetin' an' the rain. We'd jist got home oorselves an' it was rainin' dogs an' cats an' I went oot tae the shed for more peats an' there came Hardy runnin' like the wind tae git oot o' the rain. I called after him tae see if he wanted tae wait at the Croft for it tae stop. But wi' the wind he didna hear me."

"Which way was he going, Odara?" asked David.

"Toward the village . . . along the path fae the road up til the Auld Hoose."

"And it was after the rain started?"

"Aye, not two or three minutes later."

David and Rhodes glanced at each other.

"Then he could not possibly have been out at the bluff," said Lincoln.

"Exactly what I was thinking," said David. He paused a moment, recalling what Hardy had said about the Vauxhall.

"I wonder if the police have questioned the ferry skipper who was on duty that afternoon," he mused, then turned to Odara.

"Odara, this is very important," said David. "Are you certain enough about what you saw, and when it was, to testify to it?"

"Aye. I saw Hardy wi' my two eyes."

"The police may want to question you."

"I saw what I saw."

After leaving the Croft, the rest of the afternoon David and Lincoln Rhodes spent in the village calling at every cottage in the vicinity of Hardy's to find anyone who might corroborate Odara's testimony that Hardy returned home within minutes of the storm.

Their inquiries resulted not merely in one eyewitness account of Hardy sprinting out of the downpour through the door of his cottage, swearing loudly at the elements to announce himself, but also in another neighbor's observing the smoke rising from Hardy's chimney ten minutes later, and Hardy himself running outside for fresh peats thirty minutes after that.

David's visit the following day to the detective

in charge of the case, while Lincoln went to apprise Hardy of developments, resulted in a new round of investigations. Two detectives spent the next day in Whales Reef taking testimony from all parties, establishing beyond doubt that Hardy was in his own house at the presumed time of the murder. Questioned also, the ferry skipper remembered the green Vauxhall on the short trip to Whales Reef, and its return an hour and a half later.

"Noo that ye put me in mind o' the day," he added, "I thought it a mite curious tae see the man drivin' toward the landin' fae the north o' the island, no fae the village."

By the end of the week, investigations were under way into Ross Thorburn's movements, including the search for a handgun which records revealed he had purchased some twenty years before.

Within days all charges against Hardy Tulloch had been dropped.

63

HOMECOMING

Whether or not Hardy Tulloch's two weeks in jail had in any way *humbled* him in the deepest sense of the word presented a fascinating query that would occupy the wagging tongues of Whales

Reef for many hours of profitless discourse in the coming days.

It would have been equally difficult to say whether Hardy's close encounter with the law had led to what is commonly known as *soul searching*. He had certainly had more time on his hands than he knew what to do with, with the result that his thoughts had wandered down many previously unexplored avenues. Some of these had ventured surprisingly close to regions of self-reflection. He had read David's book, *A Shetland Shepherd's Guide to the Islands*, almost twice through—a fact he might never admit. The begrudging recognition that David was a knowledgeable naturalist as well as a published writer was enough to pry open a tiny door of esteem toward his cousin. It was an infant seed of humility that, if nurtured by others and not squelched by Hardy himself when he returned to the real world, was sure to grow.

He was notably subdued walking out of the Sheriff's Court into the light of day, and feeling the fresh breeze and sunlight on his face. The drive back to Whales Reef in David's car, Hardy in the passenger seat, Lincoln Rhodes in back, was also quiet. David and Lincoln carried what conversation passed between the three.

What Hardy was thinking, in truth, only God knew. He realized well enough what he owed these two men. He was not accustomed to the feeling of indebtedness. Yet without their steadfast belief in him and their efforts on his behalf, he was well aware that he might have spent the rest of his life in prison.

If the strange sensations swirling within him were not enough, yet more changes were in store for Hardy Tulloch upon his arrival to the island of his home. Whatever he had expected riding across the isthmus on the ferry, it was not to see the entire village lining the shoreline.

"What are they all doin' there!" he said. "They canna a' be waitin' for the ferry. Somebody famous comin' til the island?"

David smiled and lightly patted his shoulder. "They're waiting for you, Hardy."

"*Me* . . . why me?"

"They've come to welcome you home."

The moment Hardy stepped out of the car onto the deck of the ferry as it bumped against the landing, a great cheer went up that could be heard all over the island. Hardy stood staring in amazement. Half the children of the island were holding balloons, many of the women flowers. Banners and hand-drawn posters all emblazoned variations of the same message: *Welcome Home, Hardy!*

Hardy stood bewildered, trying to take in the sight. At length he stumbled forward in a daze. Shouts, cheers, and applause rose around him as if the prime minister were setting foot on the island.

Loni came forward.

"Welcome home, Hardy," she said with a wide smile, stunning him further by planting an affectionate kiss on his black-stubbled cheek. "Your family and friends are waiting to greet you and congratulate you, as we say in the States, for beating the rap. We will be celebrating all evening at the inn. You will be the guest of honor."

Hardy could find no words. Keith Kerr now stepped to Loni's side and shook Hardy's hand vigorously.

"I ne'er thought I'd be sayin' this tae ye, Hardy," he said, "but tonight the beer an' ale's on me— a' ye can drink."

At last Hardy found his voice. "Does that include yer own special brew?" he asked with a suggestion of humor.

"Aye, it does. Ye're oor hero for a day at least, Hardy. Ye'll hae the run o' the bar."

" 'Tis mighty good o' ye, Keith," said Hardy. "But ye ken hoo I can drink!"

"I do, Hardy! An' I may live tae regret my offer."

Standing next to his car, David observed the outpouring of affection with a quiet smile. He was proud of the people of the community for putting old animosities to rest and coming together on Hardy's behalf. Such a time was healing on deeper levels than for Hardy alone.

Audney now stepped forward and embraced Hardy. "I'm glad ye're oot o' that place, Hardy," she said. "We've a' been prayin' for ye an' hopin' tae see ye wi' us an' home again."

Before Hardy could think what to say, Audney stepped back and joined Lincoln and David. Hardy walked off the landing into the midst of the tumult, at last entering into the spirit of the thing, raising his hands and waving to the throng. He continued toward the village with the mass of humanity behind him, quickly growing comfortable again in his former role as the center of attention.

Loni joined David with a smile. "Hardy seemed genuinely moved," she said. "That expression on his face was remarkable."

"There may be deeper changes going on inside him than we know," nodded David. "Time will tell."

A few hours later, during a lull in the festivities at the inn, Lincoln Rhodes saw Hardy draw in a deep breath and glance down briefly, closing his eyes momentarily and shaking his head. It was a poignant moment seen by none other.

Lincoln walked toward the table. "Hardy," he said, "let's go outside for a walk. I have something I want to talk to you about."

Hardy rose and followed Lincoln from the pub. Lincoln led him along the street, where more greetings and handshakes followed them, past the square and eventually down the street leading to the sea.

"Hardy, do you understand what happened

here today?" asked the young minister as they approached the harbor.

" 'Twas right nice o' the folk tae welcome me like they did," replied Hardy.

"It was indeed. You have Alonnah and David to thank for it. They organized the whole thing."

Hardy did not reply. He was not surprised. Yet Rhodes's words smote him with an unaccountable pang.

"Do you know why?" persisted Rhodes.

"Canna say I do. It isna as if I've given either o' them reason tae care a lick aboot me. I haena been much o' a cousin tae David, or Miss Ford neither for that matter."

"But they care about you, Hardy, in spite of whatever you've been to them. They forgive all the past, because they love you."

Hardy was silent. The words were too much to take in. He knew that David had always been beyond him. Perhaps this was why. Did *love* have something to do with it?

"It is not only your laird and chief, the whole community loves you, Hardy. You may not have given them reason to, but these people love you."

"I dinna ken why they would."

"There are no *whys* to love. Love simply loves. You are one of them—they are your family."

They reached the quay and stood looking out over the quiet harbor. A few fishermen were about.

But they sensed matters of import at hand and did not intrude in the conversation in progress.

"The love these people have for you, Hardy," Lincoln resumed, "is a picture of God's love for you. He is your Father. He too has forgiven everything in the past. You have not been all He has wanted you to be. Unless I am mistaken, up till now in your life you have cared about no one but yourself."

Hardy was staring down at the ground, a huge hulking man who was suddenly feeling like a boy again—yet for inexplicable reasons, the anger of his youth had left him.

"Ye're no mistaken, Mr. Rhodes," he said quietly. "That's exactly what I been, a self-centered bloke who cared aboot no one but mysel'."

"It may be time for that to change, Hardy," said Lincoln. "This thing that happened has come into your life for a reason. I believe that reason is that God wants you to wake up to what kind of man you have been, and ask what kind of man you want to be."

He paused to allow his words to sink in.

"Who do you want to be, Hardy?" he asked after a moment.

Again it was silent. When Hardy spoke, his words were not what Lincoln had expected.

"David's always been the one people liked best," he said. "I've ne'er been any good, always jist tryin' tae prove I was as good as him. But everyone loved David an' I canna say I blame them. Why should anyone care aboot me?"

"But they do care about you, Hardy—David most of all. So perhaps it is time for you to ask the Lord to make you the man He wants you to be. That won't be like David or anyone else. I'll ask you again, Hardy, what kind of man do you want to be? Everyone has to answer that question in his own heart. There are no accidents of character. I've told you about my past. I was a mean and angry young man. But there came a day when I had to decide what I wanted to make of myself. Now is that time in your life. No one decides to be angry, unkind, or selfish. But that decision is made a hundred times a day by the way we think and act and talk. I'll say it again—there are no accidents of character. What kind of man do you want to be, Hardy?"

64

A PITLOCHRY PROPOSAL

PITLOCHRY, MAINLAND SCOTLAND

Preparing to leave Whales Reef on this occasion was different for Loni than previously. She spent three days saying endless good-byes, with many hugs and tears and expressions of affection, and *Haste ye back, lassie!* from the women.

She *would* be back. She knew that now. Her two conversations with Hugh, though frustrating in their own way, had clarified in her mind what she had not actually put into words until they had popped out to Hugh: *There is everything for me here . . . This is not just an inheritance, it is a heritage, a legacy . . . this is my home now.*

The words had been playing themselves over in her mind ever since. They enabled her to say her good-byes with a peaceful heart. Whether she returned in weeks or months hardly mattered. Whales Reef would not change. The island and its people would be waiting for her.

On this occasion, she and David took the overnight ferry to Aberdeen. After a day in the city, they drove to the northern coastal village of Cullen where two rooms in the Seafield Arms Hotel were waiting for them. During the following days they completed a wide circle through northern Scotland, David acting as tour guide and history professor—from Cullen to Inverness, south along Loch Ness to Inchnacardoch—one of David's favorite hidden gems of Scotland, he said—then Fort Augustus, Fort William, Glencoe, over Rannoch Moor and south to historic Stirling and Bannockburn, east to Edinburgh and St. Andrews, and finally back north through the central highlands to Pitlochry. They checked into their two rooms at the bed-and-breakfast David had booked. Then David took Loni out for a walk along the banks of the Tummel before supper.

"Do you remember when I told you I thought it was time for you to return to the States for a while?" he asked. "I said I had two things to talk to you about."

"I do remember. You never told me the second thing."

"I wanted to bring you here for it," said David.

"To Pitlochry?" said Loni. "Why here?"

"There is a place I want to take you. It's called Heather Gems. It's a factory where they turn heather roots into colorful jewelry. It's really quite amazing."

"Jewelry from heather . . . I would love to see it!"

"And so you shall."

"I will show them my heather ring," said Loni, holding up her hand with the ring that he and Odara Innes had made of woven heather and sheep's wool. "I'm sure they have nothing like this!"

"Assuredly not," David laughed. "It is definitely one of a kind! I'm sure you remember, too, that first day I took you to the Chief's Cave," he went on, "when I told you I wanted to share my solitude with you?"

"How could I forget?" replied Loni softly. "That day is always with me."

David now took her right hand and gently

removed the heather ring from her fourth finger.

"I gave you this before as what I hoped would be a token of more to come," he said. "Things had been moving fast. There was more I wanted to say, but for your sake I couldn't. Your life had been turned upside down in such a short time. I didn't want to rush you toward another major change. We both had to be sure. We also had to wait for God to make His will known in the matter. At last I believe He has done so to my satisfaction. Hopefully that is the case for you as well."

He paused, smiled, then looked deep into Loni's eyes.

"That said," he went on, "Miss Alonnah *Tulloch* Ford . . . now that you are a full-fledged Scot, I would like to ask if you would be interested in changing your name—only slightly—by making your adopted middle name truly your own, and by doing me the honor of becoming *Mrs. David Tulloch?*"

Loni's eyes were glistening, her face radiant. All she could do was return David's smile.

"David—yes, of course," she whispered. "There is nothing I want more. I have been waiting my whole life for you."

"And I for you."

David slipped the handwoven ring onto the fourth finger of Loni's left hand.

"Then I would like to take you to the Heather Gems factory, where we will design a one-of-a-kind genuine heather gem engagement ring."

"Nothing will ever replace this one," said Loni. "I will treasure it for the rest of my life."

"Then you shall wear two heather rings!"

For the rest of their tour through northern Scotland until Loni's flight, she and David talked nonstop. As much as they had opened to each other before, realizing that they would spend the rest of their lives together unleashed an almost frenzied passion to know and be known in all aspects of their lives.

From Pitlochry, they backtracked before driving north through Glen Shee, past Braemar and Balmoral and along the Royal Deeside, through Banchory, visiting Crathes Castle and the Bridge of Feugh, then crossing inland again to the coast some miles north of the airport.

They spent their last night together at one of David's favorite haunts, the scenic village of Buchan Bay. Parking in the center of town, David led Loni across the square and into a tea shop overlooking the harbor. Painted lettering on the window read *Buchan Bay Bakes*.

"David!" exclaimed an attractive redhead about Loni's age. She rushed out from behind the counter and embraced David warmly.

"Hello, Sally," laughed David. "It is nice to see you again too! And," he added, glancing toward Loni, "I would like you to meet my, uh . . .

my *friend* Alonnah Ford from the United States."

"Your *friend,* David?" she repeated with a smile. "If I was the gossipy type like some of our village women, I might read more into it."

"No comment!—Loni," he added, "meet Sally Mackenzie."

"You are a lucky lady," said Sally, shaking Loni's hand, "to have a *friend* like David. There have been several lassies in our village who have had their eyes on him. If I hadn't been engaged myself at the time, that might have included me."

Loni's eyes flitted to her hand. At the same time she unconsciously slipped her own left hand behind her back.

"No," said Sally to Loni's unspoken question. "No ring. Let's just say things didn't work out.—Nab!" she called, turning behind her and shouting into the kitchen behind the counter. "Come and see who's here."

Nab Drummond, the owner of the shop, came through the kitchen door a moment later. His face brightened at the sight of David. More greetings and introductions followed.

"We need to get checked in at the hotel," said David at length. "We'll be back for a scone and tea after a bit. Then I want to show Loni all my favorite haunts in Buchan Bay."

"How long will you be staying?" asked Sally.

"Just overnight. We have to be at the airport in the morning."

Leaving the picturesque little village the following morning, the drive became subdued.

"What *are* we going to do about the future, David?" asked Loni as they approached Aberdeen. "We can't live separate lives."

"We will figure that out one step at a time," he replied thoughtfully. "We will probably have to travel between Scotland and the States with some regularity. We may have to maintain a home in both places."

"Are you saying you would be happy living part of the year in America?"

"To be with you, of course," smiled David. "You are my future now. Obviously if we are gone too much the people of the island will feel abandoned. You have an estate and properties and investments to maintain there. But we also have your grandparents to think of. What our lives will look like in five years, who can say? We need to be attentive to all our responsibilities."

"I know you had a reason for not proposing to me until we were away from Whales Reef," said Loni. "But it makes leaving all the harder."

"I know. But I didn't want to say anything on the island. Your grandparents deserve to be the first to know. And Maddy, of course."

"You almost spilled the beans to Sally back there."

"I know," laughed David. "That was a close one.

She obviously suspects. I noticed you casually hiding your ring finger."

"Will you tell the people when you get home?"

"Not a word. I'll have to be more careful than I was with Sally. The people at home will know nothing until you and I can tell them together."

"That's quite a secret to keep! Can you do it?"

"You know how I feel about being circumspect. Yes, I can do it."

"I wish we could tell Audney."

"All in good time."

"When will I see you again?" asked Loni.

"Actually, that brings me to another question," replied David. "What would you think of my coming over and spending Christmas with you and your grandparents? I need to ask your grandfather for your hand before we can make this *officially* official."

"Oh no—it's not official yet?"

"Let's say it's unofficially official. But we must have their blessing."

"They love you, David. They will be delighted."

"Nevertheless, I want to talk to him man to man and give him the respect due him as your guardian and grandfather."

"He will be honored that you do so. In any event, Christmas would be fantastic! I hereby invite you for Christmas!"

"Thank you very much, esteemed lady! I suppose we have to get used to our double lives sometime. An extended time away from Whales Reef will give us the chance to talk more about our plans."

"And set a date?"

"And definitely set a date!"

65

CHANGING HORIZONS

WASHINGTON, D.C.

Maddy was waiting for Loni at the D.C. airport.

"Maddy!" exclaimed Loni, embracing her affectionately. "You look fantastic!" she said as she stepped back. "You've lost weight."

"Fifteen pounds."

"Having a man in your life obviously agrees with you. I can't wait to meet him."

"Unfortunately that will have to wait," said Maddy. "He's back in Alaska."

"Are things serious?"

"I don't know. But I actually think he likes me."

Suddenly Maddy gasped in silent exclamation. She was staring at Loni's left hand.

"Loni . . . is there something you haven't told me?"

Loni smiled. "Yes," she replied. "David proposed to me—just three days ago."

"Oh my!" she exclaimed. "I'm so happy for you—congratulations! And then you had to leave him at the airport?"

"It wasn't easy. But our lives are going to be complicated, and probably involve a lot of travel. I suppose we have to get used to it. But he is coming over for Christmas."

"You won't see David for three months?"

"He wants me to get back to work. But can you believe what's happened to both of us—men in our lives . . . me engaged . . . you working out at a gym. What's become of us, Maddy? Are we turning into normal women?"

"I can believe it for you," replied Maddy. "It's harder to believe for myself. So David wants you to get back to work?"

"We agree that I need to see how my old life feels after this whirlwind inheritance and Shetland romance."

"He's not worried that you'll forget about him?" said Maddy with a grin.

"No chance of that! And speaking of work," added Loni, "what about New York? Have you given the brass an answer yet?"

"That's part of the pressure I'm under. My future is in limbo, as is Tennyson's. Here's the irony. He's been offered my job *if* I go to New York. But then we would be like you and David—working in different cities. Like you said—complicated. Now that he and I . . . you know, it's changed the entire look of the job scenario. What am I saying—it's changed the look of my entire *life!* Me—Madison Swift—putting a guy ahead of my job! Who is this new person in the mirror?"

Loni couldn't help but laugh.

"We have to make some decisions soon or they will offer New York to someone else," Maddy went on. "And actually Tennyson has been having second thoughts all the way around. He senses the investment world may be in for some bumpy times. He says the real estate market is in a bubble. He and I had a long Skype conversation yesterday evening. Now he is advising me against taking the New York job."

"That's a new twist."

"He thinks it may be risky. But I know you had your heart set on going."

"Maddy, you have to do what is best for you. Besides, my life is topsy-turvy now. I'm not sure New York is in the cards for me. I only wanted to go if you were going."

"Now I am wondering if it is right for me either."

"Really! Why is that?"

A smile came to Maddy's lips.

"It's really been special with Tennyson," she said. "I think there may be a future there. I have to play it out, just like I told you to do with

David. I can't commit to the New York job until I know."

"And if they offer the New York job to someone else?"

"That's a chance I have to take. Didn't one of us say that you don't get second chances with love? Actually, I think it was me who said it! Well, I *am* having a second chance. I don't want to blow it again."

PART 12

A LEGACY BEGINS— *THE VISIT* 1924

66

A Scotsman in America

He had done a few madcap things during his Oxford days, thought Brogan Tulloch. But never had he approached anything so crazy as this.

Brogan Tulloch stood on the foredeck of the *Mauretania*, gliding slowly by the shadow of the legendary Statue of Liberty welcoming travelers from far and wide to New York Harbor. Books and photographs of the iconic landmark could not compare with gazing up with his own eyes at Lady Liberty's countenance of resolve.

The mystery of America was a fascination to most Scots and Englishmen, especially after the United States had come into the recent war at the eleventh hour to help defeat Germany. Brogan had never actually contemplated setting foot in the U.S. Like most European youths, his was an intrigue with cowboys, gangsters, and flappers nebulously indulged from afar.

It was not America's reputation as a world power and home of Indians, daredevils, and gun-wielding criminals, however, that now brought him here, but rather the quiet and unassuming dignity of a certain young lady and her uniquely American religious faith. The moment his path had crossed hers on the far side of his island home, Brogan's world had shifted on its axis.

It was no secret that his father had not approved of the lifestyle of his collegiate days. Yet ever-supportive Ernest had voiced few criticisms, preferring instead to let time do its work in his eldest son. About this recent escapade, however, when the idea had been broached, Ernest had been nearly giddy at the prospect. He had been almost as taken with the girl as Brogan himself. Brogan never expected, however, for his father to support a visit to the States so enthusiastically as to foot the bill. The fact was that Ernest Tulloch was fascinated with Emily's Quaker heritage. That his son had been touched by the Light within her as well was a delight to his heart.

Now here Brogan was, with his father's blessing, on his way toward a meeting as improbable as their first encounter on the northern bluffs of Whales Reef. Would she consider him brash, arrogant, and too bold for his own good for having dared such an impertinent undertaking?

Brogan reached the New Jersey city of Burlington by train on the Saturday following his arrival. Now that he was so close he was unaccountably nervous, perspiring under his gray suit and fashionable matching felt hat. The natural self-confidence with which he had been endowed normally served him well in unfamiliar settings. It was with an uncharacteristic timidity, however, that he walked slowly toward the white two-story house whose address had been emblazoned on his mind since the first letter he had written to Emily on the evening after her departure from the Shetlands. He had imagined this moment for several weeks. Now suddenly it was all he could do not to turn tail and run.

He drew in a deep breath, then with tentative step walked up the stairs onto the porch, lifted the door knocker and let it fall. After several seconds of heavy silence, his knock was answered by the householder himself.

Miles Hanson found himself staring at a young man in his early twenties with a suitcase at his feet.

"Good afternoon," he said. "How may I help you?"

"Mr. Hanson?" said the stranger in an odd accent.

"That's right."

"I am Brogan Tulloch, sir," said Brogan, struggling to get the words past his dry tongue. He forced a smile and extended a hand.

The two men shook hands.

"I realize I am here on a great presumption, sir," said Brogan, his voice quivering. "But I have come . . . that is, I was hoping to be able to pay my respects to Emily."

Hearing her daughter's name from the sitting room, Mrs. Hanson rose and came to the door.

"Hello," she said, "I am Amelia Hanson. Did I hear you asking about Emily?"

"Yes, ma'am. I am pleased to meet you. I am Brogan Tulloch."

"You're not," she began, "—you cannot . . . but your accent . . . are you the *Brogan* Emily has been talking about . . . from Scotland!"

A sheepish smile came over Brogan's face. "I suppose I am," he answered.

"You have come all the way from the Shetlands!" she exclaimed.

"I know I should have written of my plans," said Brogan. "I apologize for the presumption."

"Then . . . goodness! This is remarkable— please, come in, Mr. Tulloch.—Miles, this is the young man Emily has been telling us about . . . the chief's son whose letters always cause such a commotion."

Brogan's apprehensions quickly dissolved in the exuberant reception from Emily's mother. She quickly ushered him inside.

Ten minutes later, disappointed to learn that Emily was gone, but warmed by the unexpectedly hospitable welcome from her mother, though Mr. Hanson remained aloof, Brogan sat enjoying coffee with Emily's parents.

"Now I see more than ever how foolhardy it was to come all this way unannounced," he was saying.

"I assumed that Emily's college—Wilmington, isn't it?"

"Yes," replied Mrs. Hanson. "It's in Ohio."

"We Brits are notoriously unknowledgeable about American geography," said Brogan. "We have no idea what distances are involved here. I assumed the college was nearby and that she still lived at home. We never talked about the details of her college life, and I haven't heard from her since she resumed her classes. How far is it from here?"

"Five hundred miles," replied Mr. Hanson. "It's a day and a half by train."

"My goodness—five hundred miles! I see now what a blunder I've made. Will there be no chance for me to see her, then?"

"She won't be coming home until Christmas," replied Emily's father.

"I suppose I might take the train out there."

Brogan observed the reluctant expressions that passed between the two Hansons.

"Unless that would be a problem," he added.

"It's just that . . . I don't know if you are aware—Wilmington is a Quaker college," began Mrs. Hanson, "and very conservative."

"Are *you* Quaker, Mr. Tulloch?" asked Mr. Hanson.

"I was raised in the Church of Scotland," replied Brogan.

Emily's father took in the information without

expression. In fact, he knew less about Scottish Presbyterianism than by now Brogan knew about Quakerism.

"It's just that . . . a young man, *alone,*" Mrs. Hanson went on with obvious hesitation, "paying a visit to one of the female students . . . it might seem—"

"I understand," interrupted Brogan, anxious to save her from embarrassment. "The last thing I want to do is cause awkwardness. Emily explained about her Quaker values. I understand that a visit would not be appropriate. I honestly did not realize she was so far away. It's probably best that I return to Scotland."

"It seems a shame when you have come so far," said Mrs. Hanson. "Where are you . . . that is, have you made arrangements? What are your plans? Are you here with a group or tour or—?"

"Nothing like that. I came alone," replied Brogan.

"You came on your own . . . just to see Emily?"

Brogan smiled and nodded. "I'm afraid I made no plans. Not very smart, I suppose."

Emily's mother did not speak for a moment. She was obviously thinking. The room grew awkwardly quiet. Miles Hanson shifted in his chair.

"In any event," Brogan added, beginning to rise, "I'm sure I will be able to find a room in your city, then take the train back to New York tomorrow."

"Nonsense, Mr. Tulloch," said Mrs. Hanson, with sudden resolve. "You've come a long way. The least we can do is invite you for a meal. Sit back down and let me get you another cup of coffee."

"Really, I do not want to intrude upon your hospitality—"

"There will be no more talk of your leaving," Mrs. Hanson went on now that her mind was made up. "In fact, you shall stay with us tonight. We insist—don't we, Miles?"

Though Mr. Hanson did not seem quite so eager about the invitation, he voiced no objection.

"It's settled then," said Mrs. Hanson. "Bring your suitcase in from the porch, Mr. Tulloch. We have plenty of guest rooms. We raised seven children here. With Emily off to college, and her next older sister married just last year, we find ourselves alone. The house seems rather too big these days. It will be nice to have someone to share it with."

Taken off his guard, Brogan looked first at Emily's mother, then over at her father. "That is very generous of you," he said slowly. "I know my appearance must have taken you completely by surprise—a perfect stranger showing up on your doorstep. Honestly, I have money and I can find—"

"We insist, Mr. Tulloch," repeated Emily's mother with a smile. "You are not altogether a stranger. We have heard about you. Quite a lot, in fact. As I said, your letters to Emily have been the cause of considerable excitement around here."

"I don't know what to say."

"Say you will accept our offer. Emily would want you to."

Brogan smiled. "I suppose she would at that."

An hour later, Brogan and Emily's father were walking outside behind the Hanson home on the land that had come down to Miles Hanson through his mother's side of the family.

Inside, Emily's mother bustled about with supper preparations and making a room ready for their unexpected guest. She was already revolving Sunday dinner in her mind for the next day when she knew Emily's two brothers and three sisters who were still in Burlington and their families would be eager to meet the young Scotsman. She knew, too, that wild horses would not keep her mother-in-law away.

Once recovered from the initial surprise, her innate hospitality had taken over. To this was added a mother's natural enthusiasm on behalf of a youngest daughter who had divulged to her more about her sojourn in the Shetlands than she had to her father. Once it dawned on her that this was the same boy—hardly a boy, nearly a full-grown man!—all hesitation about what to do vanished. The young man was every inch a perfect gentleman!

"This is a beautiful setting," said Brogan as Mr. Hanson led him across a field of wild grass studded with rocks and filled with low shrubbery and some scraggly species of trees. "Emily said that you have a sizable tract of land."

"Twenty acres," nodded Mr. Hanson. "Most of it hilly woodland, not much good for anything—no agricultural value, covered with oak and birch and maple trees—beautiful but useless."

Before Brogan could reply, the conversation shifted abruptly.

"So tell me, what are your intentions toward my daughter, Mr. Tulloch?" said Hanson bluntly. "No one sails halfway around the world unless he has more in mind than a casual social call."

Brogan smiled. "You are a man who gets to the point," he said. "It is a fair question."

"I hope you take no offense," rejoined Mr. Hanson, realizing he had blurted it out more brusquely than he had intended.

"Not at all," replied Brogan. "After all, you don't know me from Adam. You have every right to ask."

He paused thoughtfully. "To be perfectly honest," he went on after a moment, "I have no intentions. Emily and I don't know one another very well either. We shared many happy conversations when she was visiting on our island. And of course, as your wife said, we have written quite a bit since. When she was there, Emily met my family. Actually, my father and stepmother were quite taken with her."

"Your stepmother?"

"Yes, my mother died when I was three. I have but faint memories of her."

"I am sorry to hear that."

"My stepmother—Sally is her name—is a dear. We all love her as if she were our own mother."

"Your brothers and sisters?"

"I have a brother and sister who share my mother. I am the oldest—the *heir*, I suppose you would say," Brogan added with a light laugh. "Then we have a younger brother, Sally's son. Though she was on the island but a short time, they all became very fond of Emily. She is truly a remarkable young lady—strong in her convictions, intelligent, full of ideas and plans and vision for life. She is like no one I have ever met. I don't know exactly how to describe it other than to say that our talks together opened places in me that I hadn't looked at before. She helped me see myself in a new light. But her time in the Shetlands was so brief. I simply wanted to see her again."

Brogan paused again and smiled. "I suppose to the nub of your question," he added, "and to be equally blunt, I don't know if we have any sort of future."

"But you would like to find out?"

"I hadn't put it in exactly those terms," chuckled Brogan. "I have no idea what Emily thinks of me. But I suppose you're right—I would like to find out."

67

THE PENNSYLVANIA RAILROAD

WILMINGTON, OHIO

Later that night, after enjoying supper and an engaging evening with Emily's parents, the three getting to know one another better than any of them would have anticipated during the first awkward moments at the open door of the Hanson home that afternoon, Brogan lay in the bed of Emily's older brother reflecting on the eventful day.

Two corridors away on the opposite side of the large house, Miles and Amelia Hanson were engaged in quiet conversation.

"He is a nice young man," Emily's mother was saying, "—so refined and polite and educated and respectful. It seems a shame for him to come all this way and not see Emily."

"I hardly see that there's much we can do about it," rejoined Mr. Hanson.

"What would you think . . ." began his wife, "—it is an impulsive idea—but why don't you take a few days off from the bank and accompany him to Wilmington?"

"What . . . to see Emily?"

"That is why he came."

Mr. Hanson stared back at his wife with incredulity.

"Good heavens, Amelia," he said, "—I can't go running halfway across the country on a whim."

"He came all the way from Scotland, dear."

"I didn't ask him to come."

"What does that have to do with it? Think how happy it would make Emily. And of course she would love to see you too."

Miles Hanson was neither an unreasonable nor an unkind man. As a banker, he had learned to be a realist. He had come to the difficult realization in recent years that the women of his family— his mother, wife, and youngest daughter—were singularly determined. He would not call them strong-willed to their faces. But if that did not describe them to a tee, he was badly mistaken.

He had learned, sometimes painfully, that the consequences of resistance were more burdensome than to give his consent to their occasionally outlandish notions in the first place. It was not an easy lesson for a man to learn, but he was sufficiently a pragmatist to recognize the wisdom in such an approach. One could only hope that in the long run the greater good might somehow be served. If the Almighty had a hand in the thing as well—which he had to admit he often doubted where his wife's schemes were concerned—then hopefully his own good intentions would allow God's will to be accomplished. On this present occasion, it did not take him long to realize what the upshot would be for Emily to learn that her Scottish acquaintance had come all this way to see her and that her father had sent him home without allowing a visit. He would never hear the end of it.

Thus it was, three days later that Miles Hanson and Brogan Tulloch sat in the second class coach of the PRR on their way across central Pennsylvania toward Pittsburgh and Columbus, Ohio. In spite of his initial hesitations about finding a young man— –it would be going too far to call him a suitor—on his doorstep who had traveled five thousand miles to see his daughter, he found Brogan full of humor, engaging, intelligent, respectful, and a fascinating conversationalist. His was a stimulating worldview, a much different perspective than he encountered among his acquaintances in Burlington. He had not yet admitted it to his wife—it did not do to acknowledge the accuracy of her instincts *too* readily. But now that he was alone with Emily's young friend, he was thoroughly enjoying himself.

Brogan had eagerly accompanied them to

Meeting the day after his arrival, fitting into his Quaker surroundings with apparent ease. The extended family dinner that afternoon was a noisy, almost raucous affair. Emily's young nieces and nephews were mesmerized by the dashing Scotsman, whose mysterious tongue and infectious laughter, not to mention that his father was a *chief,* kept their eyes wide with wonder. He sat down on the floor and listened to their stories, displaying the keenest interest in the girls' dolls and the boys' toys. He was all eagerness as the youngsters took his hand and led him outside to see their grandparents' animals, pushing and pulling at him and taking him to all the animal pens and barn and their grandfather's locked workshop.

With a deepening sense that Emily had chosen this unusual new friend well, Amelia Hanson smiled from a window as her young brood of grandchildren clustered about Brogan like a Scottish Pied Piper, all chattering at once and clamoring to be heard, while Brogan laughed and teased and tickled and hoisted now one and now another onto his shoulders as the little crowd romped about the yard.

Nor was the Shetlander's spell over the household limited to the children. As youthful energies waned and the dishes were washed and put away and the extended family relaxed in the large living room, Brogan regaled Emily's parents and brothers and sisters and their husbands and wives with stories of Emily's Shetland adventure. Roars of laughter accompanied his recounting of their first meeting on the moor, followed by many nods at hearing Emily's feisty response.

"That's Emily!" laughed her sister Judith. "Can you imagine what it was like growing up sharing a room with her?"

"I was definitely not at my best that morning!" laughed Brogan.

"Our Emily is as forgiving as she is outspoken," rejoined Mrs. Hanson. "It appears she did not hold it against you."

"I suppose she forgave me at that," laughed Brogan. "But honestly, you have no idea how high the cliffs are in the Shetlands. Just thinking about it makes my knees quiver. I was sincerely afraid for her life. I'm also embarrassed to say that from a distance I took her for about fourteen!"

"She is a dainty girl," said Amelia.

"She's a little shrimp, Mother!" laughed Emily's brother Richard.

"Richard, what a thing to say."

"I definitely saw how wrong I had been," said Brogan, "when she came into the dining room that evening. She was stunningly beautiful. The sight took my breath away."

The room grew momentarily quiet. None of her family would have described Emily as beautiful. Without voicing it in so many words, most of the

413

adults in the room still considered her a girl, not only small but the youngest of the Hanson brood. She had grown up, gone away to college, and, without those closest to her realizing it, become a young woman. Hearing about her through Brogan's eyes was a revelation, especially for such a polished man of the world, a graduate of Oxford, to describe their little Emily as *beautiful*.

The only one in the room who did not seem surprised was Emily's grandmother. As she listened, it was almost as if she had expected it.

Many of his initial reservations long since put to rest, Emily's father was as fascinated as the rest to hear about his daughter, inwardly gratified at Brogan's report of how she had carried herself and of her outspoken defense of her Quaker faith. He laughed louder than anyone at Brogan's account of their unceremonious encounter at Sumburgh Head, and his embarrassment at being discovered following Emily's tour.

"Why did you follow her, Mr. Tulloch?" asked Emily's seven-year-old niece Sarah.

"Because I liked her, Sarah," Brogan replied simply. "I wanted to see her again."

"And is that why you are here, Mr. Tulloch?" now asked Grandmother Hanson with a twinkle in her eye.

Brogan smiled. It was quiet around the room where Emily's family sat looking at their guest, wondering what he would say.

"Yes, Mrs. Hanson," replied Brogan. "That is exactly right. I missed her and wanted to see her again."

And now as they sat together on the train two days later, Brogan and Emily's father chatted easily and even laughed a good deal together.

"The mere fact of sitting in a train watching the countryside go by," said Brogan, "is causing many of my perceptions of America to evaporate."

"How so?" rejoined Emily's father.

Brogan thought a minute. "We Brits have no conception of the sheer size of the U.S.," he said at length. "As you sit in a snug railway compartment in England, and even mainland Scotland to a degree, what meets the eye are small houses and trim gardens, chessboard hedgerows and green-carpeted meadows and pastures. But sitting here with you, I have not seen a house for an hour. It's endless forests and fields and mountains."

"And we are still only a stone's throw from the eastern seaboard," chuckled Mr. Hanson. "Two thousand miles from here, crossing the Great Plains and the Rocky Mountains or the Great Basin of Nevada, you might go five hundred miles and never see a sign of humanity."

"Remarkable! And the people are so unassuming, treating everyone else as an equal."

"Unfortunately most Negroes would not agree."

"I suppose you're right. But other than that, there seems to be no sense of station or class such as is prevalent in Britain. We're taught that America is a lawless wilderness full of arrogant, boastful men and loose women, without courtesy or morals or respect, money-grubbers and thieves and con men and gangsters and hoodlums. Unless I miss my guess, most of that is myth. The people I've met have been nothing but kind and courteous."

"Obviously every country has a thorough mix of good people and bad," rejoined Mr. Hanson. "America has its share of scoundrels, to be sure. But I think the longer you are here, the more you may discover that the U.S. is full of good and selfless people to a greater extent than many overseas realize."

Again it fell silent as the train clattered along.

"Emily speaks very highly of you, Mr. Hanson," said Brogan as their conversation gradually took a more serious turn. "She has the deepest respect and admiration for you. Believe me, you need have no fear for Emily about anything—certainly not on account of a man, whether myself or any other. She is completely circumspect. She would never do anything you disapproved of. She said she respected you more than any man in the world."

"She actually said that?" said Mr. Hanson, glancing toward Brogan as if he had not heard him correctly.

"Word for word," nodded Brogan. "I've never forgotten. It struck me as a remarkable thing for a young person to say about her father. A wonderful thing, actually. And now, knowing you and your family, I see what she meant. Respect and love flow between you all. You have a family to be proud of, Mr. Hanson."

By degrees Brogan thus won over the occasionally stoic American just as thoroughly as Emily had his own father back on Whales Reef.

"And Emily doesn't know we are coming?" said Brogan as they departed from Columbus on the final leg of their journey to Wilmington.

"I sent her a telegram saying I would be paying her a visit," replied her father with a smile. "I said I was bringing a surprise."

"She will probably faint at the sight of me!"

After checking into their favorite guesthouse near the college, Mr. Hanson and Brogan sought the office of Dean Wilson. She greeted Emily's father warmly.

"What a surprise, Mr. Hanson," she said, shaking his hand. "Have you seen Emily yet?"

"We wanted to speak with you first—two men on campus to visit one of your young ladies, you know. We mustn't raise eyebrows without your knowledge."

"That is very good of you. There will be no problem, I assure you."

"I would like to introduce you to Mr. Brogan Tulloch," Mr. Hanson said. "Whether you will find it as hard to believe as my wife and I did when we met Mr. Tulloch a few days ago, he has come from the Shetland Islands where he and Emily became acquainted during Emily's tour with your aunt. —Brogan, please meet Dean Wilson. It is she who made Emily's trip possible."

"I am happy to meet you," said Brogan, smiling and extending his hand. "And doubly appreciative if what Mr. Hanson says is true. Where would I be right now if I hadn't met Emily—well, I suppose obviously I would be back in the Shetlands!" he added with a laugh.

"It is a pleasure," said Dean Wilson. "You are a long way from home, indeed! There have been a few reports circulating that Emily met an interesting young man during her tour. Am I to assume that those reports concern you?"

"Perhaps so," replied Brogan sheepishly. "Unless she made acquaintance with someone I am unaware of. The tour guide seemed to have his eye on her."

"Somehow I doubt it was him," smiled Dean Wilson.

"So Mrs. Barnes is your aunt, then," said Brogan.

"That's right. You met her also?"

"We became good friends," laughed Brogan. "A delightful lady. She was most desirous that Emily find romance on the tour."

"That does sound like my aunt!"

"Whether she did, or whether she had to take me as a consolation prize—you will have to ask Emily."

He glanced toward Emily's father. "Nothing to be concerned about, sir," he said. "Sometimes I let my humor go too far!"

Hanson shook away Brogan's concern with a light laugh. He was by now accustomed to the young man's wit.

"Let me send Emily a message," said Dean Wilson. "I believe she is in class for another twenty minutes."

"She knows nothing of Brogan's visit," said Emily's father. "Please simply tell her I have arrived."

"Then this should be most interesting," smiled the dean. She rose, left the office briefly, and returned a minute later. "I will take you to the teacher's lounge. My assistant will get word to Emily to come to my office. I will bring her to you."

When the door to the lounge opened half an hour later, Brogan and Mr. Hanson stood. They saw Dean Wilson enter. Emily walked into the room at her side.

At sight of the two men, Emily stared blankly across the room as if she were seeing an apparition.

"Look who's here, Emily?" said her father with a wide smile.

"Dinna be frightet, lassie," said Brogan, a smile coming to his lips. " 'Tis only yer auld frien' fae Whales Reef."

At the sound of his voice, the spell was broken.

"Brogan?" Emily said in astonished disbelief. "Is it really . . . *you?*"

"It's me, Emily."

Suddenly heedless of everyone else in the room, Emily rushed forward with a shriek and threw her arms around Brogan's waist.

It took but a second for her to realize what she had done. She stepped back, glancing back between her father and Dean Wilson, her face and neck bright crimson.

Slowly her eyes drifted up and found Brogan's staring down at her.

"Hello, Brogan," said Emily softly.

She smiled, quickly recovering herself. "I'm afraid Shetland's greatest puffin fan won't find any puffins in Ohio," she added.

The room filled with the sound of Brogan's laughter. "On this particular excursion," he said, "I did not come in search of puffins."

68

Volunteer Laborer

BURLINGTON, NEW JERSEY

As happy as the two days of the visit were for Emily, they were more distracting than anything. Having to keep up with classes and studies, knowing that everyone on campus knew of Brogan's visit, and with her father sharing every conversation and meal, it was impossible to recapture the relaxed spontaneity of youthful dialog they had enjoyed the previous summer.

Despite that the surroundings were not so idyllic as a holiday setting far from home and free of responsibilities, however, their brief visit served this purpose, that neither Emily nor Brogan were disappointed. Even in dramatically different circumstances, the candle still burned within each of their hearts. If both had secretly wondered what the other was thinking during the intervening months, the mutual light in their eyes every moment they sandwiched between Emily's classes banished further doubts. After an inter-lude all too brief, when they said their good-byes, both knew that the flame would continue even brighter.

The train ride back through Ohio and Pennsylvania was subdued. The eyes of Brogan Tulloch and Miles Hanson had been opened to many things. Probably by now with some indication of what lay ahead, both men were thinking hard.

Brogan realized that he had nothing to return to the Shetlands for, no job awaiting him, no pressing duties. In truth, no responsibilities at all. That was his problem—he had nothing to occupy him. It was not until they crossed the border from Pennsylvania into New Jersey that he summoned the courage to lay before Emily's father the proposal that had been stirring within him throughout most of the trip.

He attempted to explain the reality of his situation, about the job in India that failed to materialize, and that there were no functions or obligations that fell to him as the eldest son of the laird.

"I know it may be presumptuous of me," he concluded, "though I suppose my entire trip here has been presumptuous. But is there anything I could do for you if I remained in the States awhile, work I might do for you or your family? Not for pay, of course—strictly to be a help. I'm sure I could find a room in town. I would like to stay in America for a bit longer, and hopefully be able to see Emily again. I would like to make myself useful."

Without divulging his thoughts immediately,

Miles Hanson found himself favorably inclined toward the idea. It was more than obvious that his daughter was smitten with this young man. What better way to find out what the amiable Scot was made of, whether he would make a suitable husband, and if he had spiritual depth to match his winning personality, than to invite him to live under his own roof and see how he handled himself in the flow and exchange of daily life. He supposed he was getting the cart before the horse, but if this young man and his daughter had a future together, he wanted to know everything possible about him before giving his consent to whatever might develop.

As might have been expected, Amelia needed no persuading, and the invitation was extended. Brogan could stay with them for an indefinite time, living with them, taking meals with them, the only provisions being that he give a reasonable though not a burdensome amount of work in return, as well as attend Sunday Meeting as one of the family. Brogan agreed heartily. He wrote to his father and Sally that same evening explaining everything.

One morning a few days after their return from Ohio, Emily's father found Brogan perusing the bookshelves of the small family library along one wall of the living room.

"An early riser, are you?" he said as he walked in.

"Good morning, Miles," replied Brogan. "Actually no—such has not been my custom, until meeting Emily, that is. You don't mind if I explore some of your books?"

"Not at all."

"I recognize some of these titles from my father's shelves."

"He is not Quaker?"

"No, but he is a great admirer of some Quaker writers, including John Woolman, your ancestor, Emily tells me."

"His grandfather was the original Woolman who came to the colonies in 1678, along with his friend John Borton from whom my wife is descended. This land has passed down through the family ever since. You might like to visit the Woolman home in Mount Holly. It is not far from here."

"I would indeed. My father reads the Woolman *Journal*."

"It is a Quaker classic. And you—what do you read?"

"I'm afraid I haven't been in the habit of reading spiritual books. My father is deeply devout—a great man spiritually speaking, I suppose I would call him, though I confess I have not taken my spiritual heritage as seriously as I should have. I am finally beginning to see how much I owe him."

"And you are members of the Church of Scotland?"

Brogan nodded.

"That is Presbyterian, is it not?"

"That's right."

"What do you know about the Brethren?" asked Miles.

"Not a great deal. It is probably the strongest religious denomination in Scotland besides the Church of Scotland. Every Scotsman is familiar with our two Johns—John Knox and John Darby. Why do you ask?"

"Only that I am curious. I find certain similarities in the origin of the Brethren and our own Society of Friends. There are just as many differences, I suppose one could argue. Still, it is a strain of the Christian faith I have been intrigued by."

"You would love to talk to my father. He is a great student, not only of devotional writers but of the history of spiritual movements. And as I will be attending Quaker services with you and have become interested on a more personal level, perhaps you could provide me some reading material to give me more of a foundation to understand Quakerism."

"With pleasure. I can certainly recommend an introductory book or two about the Christian life as seen through the Quaker lens."

A letter from Whales Reef several weeks later gave enthusiastic endorsement to the plan which was already well under way, and included a personal letter from Ernest to Miles Hanson, the contents of which Brogan never saw but which he could tell warmed the heart of Emily's father. It was obvious to Miles Hanson that in giving his consent for Emily to travel to the Shetland Islands, his daughter had become inextricably linked to a family of distinction and spiritual fiber.

And so it was through the warm and pleasant months of early autumn—usually alone, occasionally with one of Emily's brothers, and often for an hour or two in the evening and on most Saturdays with Miles himself—that Brogan began to clear and reclaim a portion of the Hanson land about a half mile north of the house that had been particularly hard hit by a blizzard two winters earlier. Trees were down everywhere and strewn in such disarray that a wagon could hardly get in to haul away the debris. Working steadily over the coming weeks, enduring sunburn and mosquitoes and a dozen initial blisters that gradually turned to hardened calluses, Brogan cleared that portion of the road, now mostly overgrown, that had once extended from one end of the property to the other, sawing and cutting and chopping enough firewood to last ten winters, piling up the scraps and brush that was good for no purpose other than the fire. It was a new experience for the Shetlander, where bricks of peat not chunks of oak were the fuel of choice.

"It is such a shame just to burn all this wood,"

he said one day, holding up a three-foot log of oak six inches in diameter.

Ten feet away where he was working, Miles set aside the ax in his hand and gazed over at Brogan with a curious expression.

"Just look at it—it's gorgeous!" exclaimed Brogan. "There is a fortune here."

"Hardly that," laughed Miles. "These oaks are nothing but giant weeds."

"Not where I come from. There is not a single tree on Whales Reef with a trunk like this. Wood is gold. Surely something could be done with it."

Often throughout the day it was Brogan and Amelia Hanson who sat talking in the kitchen for an hour or two after Brogan had come in, perspiring in the hot sun, face drenched in sweat, for a cold cup of lemonade, or the two of them enjoying a visit from Grandmother Hanson. In truth, as November approached and the days shortened and an occasional storm blew through curtailing Brogan's work, it was the two Hanson women who came to know Brogan better even than Emily herself.

Brogan also made himself useful attending to repairs and upkeep at the home of Emily's grandmother in town. He confessed himself woefully ignorant of carpentry, plumbing, painting, and other skills. But he was a rapid learner.

Owing to the scarcity of wood in the Shetlands, the woodworking craft was virtually unknown.

Indeed, the term was not one Brogan even remembered hearing. Though Miles Hanson was strictly an amateur, his workshop boasted many electrical tools that were a complete mystery to Brogan, as well as an abundance of fascinating hand tools, some of which dated back a hundred years or more and had been in the family for generations. Brogan was intrigued by the specific and unique uses for each.

"What is this contraption?" he asked as Miles showed him around for the first time.

"A lathe," replied Emily's father.

"And this?"

"A band saw."

And so it continued around the shop. With wonder Brogan examined various jigs and planers, saws, sanders, drills and augers and grinders and miter presses and glue clamps, and dozens of devices and contrivances for which purpose he could not so much as hazard a guess.

Under Miles's tutelage Brogan began spending his rainy days fiddling with the tools in the workshop. Gradually he began experimenting with scraps of oak to see what he could fashion from them. The results were crude to begin with. But he learned enough to tackle more complicated projects for Grandmother Hanson, who was so taken with Brogan that she devised more and more assignments to keep him busy when he was not otherwise occupied. Slowly he began to master a good many of the tools and displayed an unusual aptitude for their use. Well before the approach of Thanksgiving, Miles declared that they had a blossoming craftsman under their roof.

All the while, Emily was jealous of her family to the point of distraction. Her grades had not suffered yet, but her concentration certainly had. And work on her thesis languished as she spent much of her free time writing to Brogan.

Meanwhile, as they worked side by side, when Miles was not at the bank, he and Brogan talked easily and casually of increasingly weightier matters. What exactly defined the bond between the fifty-six-year-old Quaker banker and the twenty-three-year-old Scottish youth of privilege it was hard to say.

Emily had been counting the days until Thanksgiving. She had not planned to return home until Christmas, yet nothing could keep her away now. The reunion she and Brogan enjoyed at the Burlington station after she alighted from the train, while not as loud or exuberant as their meeting at Wilmington, spoke of yet deeper depths of feeling.

Amelia Hanson watched from across the platform as Emily slowly walked toward Brogan and melted into his waiting arms, neither saying a word as Emily laid her head on Brogan's chest for several long seconds. Amelia's heart skipped briefly at the sight. In that moment, the mother *knew*. Her youngest daughter had found her life's love.

Brogan was anxious to show Emily everything that had been engaging his time, what he had done out on the land and in the workshop and at her grandmother's house. Long walks on the property and along the river and into Burlington filled happy days that were all too brief.

The Thanksgiving feast in the Hanson home with all the family present was a bittersweet celebration. Brogan had already made clear that he felt it time for him to return to Whales Reef after the holidays. They knew it would be the last family gathering before his departure. The yearly family tradition was observed as Mr. Hanson told the familiar story, new to their British guest, of the pilgrims and Indians and first American Thanksgiving, followed by the passing of the basket with kernels of corn as each around the table expressed a "thanksgiving" for the day. All her younger nieces and nephews stealing her thankfulness for Brogan's presence among them, Emily was hard-pressed to add her own special twist to the tradition.

As the meal followed, Brogan was also given the opportunity to enjoy the story of the landing of the *Shield* on Burlington Island in the frozen Delaware River as the year 1678 came to a close, and of the arrival of their first Woolman and Borton ancestors in America.

Emily had secured permission from Dean Wilson to remain at home for several extra days. On the Monday following Thanksgiving she and her parents left Burlington to accompany Brogan to New York, where he would board the ship that would take him home.

Thinking how different this day was from the parting the previous June when they had seen Emily and Mrs. Barnes off on their adventure, Emily's parents moved off along the quay leaving the two young people alone.

Emily's face was red and her eyes swimming. Brogan took her in his arms and held her for a minute in silence. At length he stepped back and gazed into her face.

"I think I may love you, Emily Hanson," he said softly.

"Oh, Brogan, don't say such a thing!" said Emily, at last bursting into tears.

"Why not? It's true."

"It's bad luck to say something like that. I don't want to get my hopes up."

Brogan stared back at her.

"Your *hopes*," he repeated. "You don't mean . . . you're not saying you might actually love a wastrel like me?"

"Brogan, you're not a wastrel! Daddy says he has never seen a harder worker."

"What's that got to do with it? What did you mean by getting your hopes up? You're not saying that you could love someone like me?"

"Of course I do!" exclaimed Emily. "Why do you think I'm crying—because I *want* you to leave? Are you blind, Brogan Tulloch? I think I've loved you from the moment you frightened the puffins off the bluff."

"You sure had a funny way of showing it!" laughed Brogan.

"I'm a girl. I'm supposed to be irrational."

Again they embraced.

"You will write?" said Brogan.

"Just try to stop me!"

An hour later Emily and her parents stood watching as slowly the ship glided away until Brogan, his arm lifted high, could no longer be seen at the rail.

A few moments more they stood, then turned and walked away. Miles stretched his arm around Emily's shoulder and gave her an affectionate hug. Between the two, Emily slipped her hands through her two parents' arms.

"Thank you both for being so welcoming to Brogan," she said. "I'm dying to ask what you think of him . . . but I'm afraid to."

"You need have no fear, Emily," said her mother. "I think the rest of the family loves young Brogan Tulloch *almost* as much as you do."

69

JOURNAL OF LOVE

Alone in her room that same evening, Emily began a new chapter of the "Shetland Journal" her grandmother had given her the previous June. It was also a new chapter in her life that would occupy her for years to come and fill several more volumes. She dated the entry December 2, 1924.

Everything was a blur after saying good-bye to Brogan last summer on the ferry landing at Whales Reef, *she began.* I scarcely remember the next few days. I'm afraid I wasn't as attentive to Mrs. Barnes on the return journey across the Atlantic as I should have been, though she seemed to understand. I often came to myself standing on the deck of the ship in mid-Atlantic. I could think of nothing but Brogan Tulloch. I was certain I would never see him again.

How would I be able to tell my family what had happened, that I was on my way home completely captivated by the son of a Scottish laird and chief, who wasn't a nice young Quaker boy and was a self-described man of the world who said he drank too much?

I cried halfway home and tried to put thoughts of him out of my mind. Why would he care about someone like me? He had probably forgotten me already.

When the first letter from Brogan arrived after I had been home less than a week, I tore the envelope open in a frenzy. Before I went to sleep that night I had read it four times. Then came another two days later. I wrote back, and he wrote again, and our letters began passing each other on the ships crossing the ocean.

When I returned to Wilmington I was so busy that I didn't write for a few weeks. I heard nothing from Brogan either. Then suddenly came the day when Dean Wilson called me to her office. I knew it wasn't about a trip to Scotland this time, though what would be her reason for wanting to see me, I had no idea. She was acting very mysterious. But a strange smile spread over her face as she led me to the teachers' lounge.

The moment I saw Brogan standing next to my father, I'm afraid I rather lost my senses. I remember nothing other than coming to myself a few seconds later with my arms around him.

The two days were joyously happy, trying to squeeze the time since we had seen one another into hours that were all too brief. The next two months were agony knowing that Brogan was with my family, in our very house! Yet I could not see him, touch him, hear his voice, relish in his laughter.

Thanksgiving, too, was joyous beyond description. Yet it was fleeting . . . and over in what seemed like seconds. Then another parting . . . today . . . and I am crying again, and my heart is sick because now Brogan is truly gone.

Yet somehow at last my heart is filled with hope. I dare not think what I am hoping for. Again I am afraid I will never see him again.

Yet I think I will. I don't know how . . . I don't know when . . . I don't know where.

But somehow I know I will again lay eyes on the smiling, laughing, wonderful, handsome face . . . of Brogan Tulloch.

PART 13

WINTER, 2006–2007

70

NEW ADVENTURES AHEAD

WASHINGTON, D.C.

Loni had been back in Washington a month trying to reintegrate into her former job. She was going through the motions, but her heart was elsewhere.

Maddy, too, had been different since Loni's return. Once banking her future on the New York promotion, her continued delay was seriously jeopardizing her standing in the eyes of company president Adrian Chalmers. For both women, the highlight of any day or week was no longer landing a new client or putting together a snazzy investment deal, but a letter or phone call from David Tulloch or Tennyson Stafford.

A reprieve of sorts—a deadline beyond which Maddy determined she would not go—came in mid-November in the form of an invitation from Tennyson to fly to Anchorage and join him in Alaska for Thanksgiving.

"Are you going to do it?" asked Loni excitedly.

"You bet I am!" answered Maddy. "As I said—this is a second chance I do not intend to goof up. And like my world-traveling friend Loni Ford would tell me—hey, it's an adventure, right?"

"What will the weather be like? It's getting a little late in the year."

"Tennyson warned me it could be cold. He said to bundle up and bring winter clothes. But he said he wants to *talk* . . . about the future."

"Ooo—sounds serious! Will you stay . . . ?"

"What . . . *with* him? No way. Tennyson is a gentleman. He keeps a corporate apartment for his clients where he'll put me up. And one way or another, by the time I get back I am going to give Chalmers a definite up or down. As a matter of fact," said Maddy, rising from behind her desk, "I think I'll head up to the tenth floor right now and tell him that if he can extend his patience two more weeks, he will finally have his answer. Though he's so frustrated with me by now that he may not agree!"

"You're his star," laughed Loni. "That's why he's been so patient with you—he can't afford to lose you."

Two weeks later, on the Tuesday night following Thanksgiving, the buzzer from the outside door of Loni's apartment building startled her. She glanced at the clock. It was 10:30. She was already in her nightgown. She hurried to the intercom.

"Loni, it's Maddy," said a familiar voice. "I'm downstairs. I have to see you."

"When did you get back?"

"Just now. I came straight from the airport. I'll

explain everything. Come on, girl—let me in already!"

Three minutes later Maddy exited the elevator, pulling her suitcase behind her along the corridor, her left hand shoved in the pocket of her coat. Loni stood at her open door waiting.

"I could have picked you up," said Loni.

"I know. But I changed my flight and wasn't sure when I'd arrive. I took a cab."

Loni closed the door behind them.

"Would you like some tea or something?" she asked.

"I ought to get home and go to bed," replied Maddy. "But I'm wired—I probably won't sleep for hours. A cup of tea does sound good—maybe peppermint or something without caffeine. I'm sorry for keeping you up."

"Forget it!" rejoined Loni as she put the kettle on to boil. "I want to hear everything. How was Alaska?"

"Cold—though not as bad as I expected. Beautiful, of course. It snowed once, otherwise sunny and clear . . . just cold. And night comes early at this time of the year."

"Just like the Shetlands, from what I hear. So . . . ?" said Loni with a smile. "Does Alaska figure into your future? Is it a place you could envision living . . . *permanently?*"

Maddy returned her smile. "Thankfully that is a question I will not have to answer," she said.

441

Loni stared back with a quizzical expression. "You're not saying . . . the two of you didn't—?"

"What—break up?" laughed Maddy. "Just the opposite."

At last she pulled her hand out of her coat and extended it toward Loni. On her fourth finger glistened a dark red ruby. "Tennyson proposed to me," said Maddy, her face beaming.

"Maddy!" cried Loni, giving her a hug. "Congratulations!" She stood back and took Maddy's hand for a closer look. "It's gorgeous. I'm so happy for you."

"And I also bring news that will provide the solutions to both our dilemmas," said Maddy.

"You mean you *and* me?" said Loni.

"Exactly," answered Maddy excitedly. "Tennyson and I are going to start a new company. He's been thinking of a change for a while. He's leaving Alaska and moving back here—probably to Virginia to be closer to home, maybe even to D.C."

"So the New York promotion is off?"

"I will definitely *not* be going to New York," said Maddy. "I'm going to give Chalmers the news tomorrow, along with my thirty-day notice. Tennyson will announce the change to his clients on the first of the year."

"And what will the new company look like?"

"Tennyson will continue what he has been doing, and I will oversee their investment portfolios and add diversity to everything. We've got some ideas how to grow the company in keeping with his vision of hands-on personal investments. We will keep doing what we both do best, but we will do it together."

"That sounds wonderful! What a fantastic business model."

"And we want you to work for us."

"Really! As your assistant?"

"You're way beyond that now, girl! You're a tycoon, remember?"

"So you say!" laughed Loni.

"If you come on board, you will be our U.K. liaison and investment strategist."

"That sounds rather highfalutin."

"You will be free to travel and come and go as you like, and operate from here or Whales Reef or wherever you and David eventually land. Yours will be a floating assignment—on commission."

"You are too good to me, Maddy. I don't know what to say."

"You don't have to make a commitment immediately. We have plenty of time. I'm sure if you want to stay on at Capital, Chalmers would make you a lucrative offer. Maybe he would give you my job after all."

"I can't imagine working in the investment world without you, Maddy. You're my mentor."

Maddy laughed. "I think we're about equals by now."

"I'll talk to David," said Loni. "I'm sure he will love it. Any idea on a date for you two?"

"We're thinking sometime in the spring. In the meantime, we will spend Christmas at the Stafford ranch in Virginia. I'm sure Tennyson's folks will have some ideas about our wedding plans too . . . and I have to talk to my mom. That may be a little weird, but I want her to be part of it."

71

THE REDEMPTION OF HARDY TULLOCH

WHALES REEF

David departed the Shetlands in mid-December—carrying more cards and gifts for Loni from the villagers than he could well manage. His tentative plan was to be gone a month, spending Christmas with Loni and the Fords, as well as giving himself the opportunity to see how life in the States suited him. Loni would move in with Maddy for the duration of his visit, leaving her apartment for David's use. A big city high-rise would represent a change of epic proportions to the Shetland shepherd. But David was eagerly anticipating the new experience. The change of venue, he hoped, would enable him to complete work on his book. He was also eager for the research opportunities provided by proximity to the Smithsonian Institute.

The reunion between Loni and David at Reagan International was understandably exuberant. The drive back into the city continued their nonstop conversation from three months before. Skype and letters and emails and phone calls were no substitute for being together in person. Loni was eager to know about everyone on the island.

Along with news of Ross Thorburn's arrest for the murder of Jimmy Joe McLeod, the most surprising report brought by David from Whales Reef concerned the changes taking place within their mutual cousin under the gentle influence of his friendship with Lincoln Rhodes—now Hardy's full-fledged skipper on the *Hardy Fire*. Not so surprising was David's account of the deepening affection between Audney Kerr and the new minister.

Back on the island, with Loni and David gone, Hardy's exoneration and the reception from the village, and the acceptance shown him by Lincoln Rhodes, wrought a change on the hulking fisherman no one had seen coming in a hundred years. Hardy actually seemed humbled from his ordeal.

As life gradually resumed its former routine, Hardy found inexplicable thoughts, feelings, memories, images, and urgings stirring inside him. The inheritance was decided. The invisible lifelong burden of being compared with David, for reasons he could not explain, ceased to exert a hold on him. His deep-seated jealousies and resentments slowly drifted away like an outgoing tide. What David and Loni had done plunged straight into his heart. Without an ounce of his deserving it, they had done their best for him. They had not given up on him. They had believed him. At last David had his chance to laugh in his face, to exact a lifetime of well-deserved revenge. Yet he had done just the opposite. David's words rang in Hardy's ears for weeks: *We came to see if we could help you. Is there anything we can do for you?*

What would make a man who had been treated with the contempt he had shown David ask such a question?

Though the law didn't permit it, especially since he was the most innocent man on the island, he knew that if it were possible David would have taken his place in that jail cell and let him go free. That's what kind of man David was. David would give his life for him. At last Hardy realized it. He nearly already had during the episode at sea the previous winter.

The very thought was more than he knew what to do with. David had forgiven every unkind word, every lie, every attempt to deceive, all the

446

poundings he had given him through the years. The Ford lady, too, though he had attempted to steal the inheritance from her, had returned him nothing but kindness.

All around Whales Reef, the villagers were friendlier and nicer than Hardy knew he deserved. Rather than being glad to be rid of him, they actually seemed happy to have him back.

And the new minister—never a disparaging word, only smiles and friendly slaps on the back . . . eager to help, willing to do anything for Hardy and his crew, tackling the dirtiest and most unpleasant jobs with a smile, showing Hardy the utmost respect, asking questions and learning everything he could about ropes and engines and fish and their habits and tides and winds and nets and Shetland's weather patterns. From being adversaries with the other fishermen in the contest against the elements, during his absence Hardy's crew became known as willing to give any of the others a hand or lend a man to another crew that might be shorthanded for a day.

Hardy's homecoming and Lincoln Rhodes's appointment as the new minister infected the community with new spirit. All Whales Reef was energized by the obvious joviality between the two men. They were often seen laughing and joking or talking seriously with one another. Their friendship rubbed off on everyone. Throughout the village, the morning's greetings were more spontaneous, the smiles wider, the laughter heartier. Not even the darkness and cold of the season could extinguish the warmth of reconciliation that the change in Hardy had awakened. People are happiest when hearts are one, and that great truth was now flourishing on the island.

Some turning points in life come rapidly like a sudden sunrise, others emerge into the light of day like tender shoots poking tentatively out of the darkness. The unseen forces that till the inner soil and warm the buried seeds of being may continue for years without apparent result. All the while the suns and rains of a man's smiling, forgiving, sacrificing, praying, enduring, loving brothers and sisters reach deep, eventually, with God's help, bursting their hard shells in order that those seeds of personhood might sprout and send down roots into the softened soil of character.

As unlikely as the friendship might have seemed, their shared histories drew Hardy and Lincoln Rhodes steadily closer. Hardy found in the new minister a man who understood him, who had some idea what he had been, yet more importantly what he might become. Steadfastly and earnestly, man to man, friend to friend, he pointed Hardy toward the Hardy of God's vision, the Hardy that to be would bring a joy in life he had never known. Hardy was reluctant to set foot inside the church, knowing that people would gawk and talk. But he was eager for Lincoln's words, hungry to learn, hungry to become the man Rhodes saw but who was still a stranger to Hardy himself. Many an evening as the sun crept away toward the southwest, Hardy spent at the manse—questioning, listening, probing, thinking . . . coming closer by degrees to being able to look into the mirror and see a true reflection of the man he was, as well as the man he wanted to be.

Hardy grew out his beard and again marched in Lerwick's *Up Helly-Aa* Viking celebration on New Year's Eve. He did not, however, have more than two pints to drink throughout the entire evening, and was clean-shaven again within days after the event.

At last came an evening three weeks after Christmas, with the wind howling about the manse and the rain pouring down and the peat fire burning low in the grate, when Hardy went to his knees with Lincoln Rhodes beside him, and tearfully asked God to make a true man of him.

As they rose to resume their seats a few minutes later, the manse remained quiet. The air was thick with the import of eternity. Lincoln Rhodes was not a man to fill the silences with personal opinions or counsels. He preferred to give opening to the great Silence of the universe, as the still small voice of its Creator spoke to the man beside him over whom the angels were rejoicing.

Prompted to turn his friend's attention toward

the Word that would henceforth be his life's guide, he reached for the New Testament that lay beside him and opened it to the nineteenth chapter of Luke's Gospel. Slowly he began to read. At length he arrived at the conclusion of the great passage of redemption and reconciliation between man and God, and between man and man:

> So he made haste and came down, and received him joyfully. And when they saw it they all murmured, "He has gone in to be the guest of a man who is a sinner." And Zacchaeus stood and said to the Lord, "Behold, Lord, the half of my goods I give to the poor; and if I have defrauded any one of anything, I restore it fourfold." And Jesus said to him, "Today salvation has come to this house. . . ."

A few days later Hardy appeared at Noak's door. He removed his cap as one side of his mouth rose in an attempted but oddly nervous smile. The expression on his face was one Noak had never seen before.

"Good day tae ye, Hardy," said Noak.

"An' tae yersel', Noak," said Hardy, smiling again, almost sheepishly. "I'm here tae ask hoo much ye need tae clear off yer debts."

"I told ye, Hardy," replied Noak, "I'm no wantin' tae sell my boat."

"I'm no here aboot yer boat," rejoined Hardy. "I'm just wantin' tae ask ye hoo much ye need tae clear a' yer debts an' git ye wee boatie outfitted like it needs. I'm wantin' tae gie ye what ye need."

Noak stared back in perplexity. "I dinna ken if I'm understandin' ye, Hardy," he said slowly.

"I want tae help ye git back on yer feet, Noak—nae strings, no interest . . . jist one frien' helpin' oot anither. What ye need, I'll put intil yer acoont at the bank in Lerwick tomorrow. Ye'll sign no papers an' yer boat'll stay yer own. Ye'll be under no obligation tae me."

"That's right kind o' ye, Hardy," said Noak, still more than a little bewildered, but willing to take Hardy at his word. From inside called a woman's voice. "Arena ye goin' tae ask the man in for tea?"

Within a week it was all around town that Hardy had sold their boats back to Gunder Knut, Sandy MacGowen, and Iver Quinby for half what he had paid for them a year before, though without asking for so much as a farthing in return down payment, these amounts to be paid to Hardy without interest or monthly obligation. They would pay him what they could when they could, no matter how long it took.

Before the winter was out, Hardy was back to a single vessel, the *Hardy Fire*, still the biggest boat in the harbor. Having to trim his own crew as a result of the change, Billy Black went to work for Iver and Gordo Ross for Gunder. Hardy kept

Lincoln Rhodes as his own first mate along with Rufus Wood and Ian Hay as his crew.

Whenever Hardy came into the Whales Fin Inn now, for he still enjoyed his daily pint, he could not have been more the soul of courtesy toward Audney Kerr. When her engagement to Lincoln Rhodes was announced in early March, Hardy was the first to hear of it, and the first to offer his congratulations. He waited until the inn was mostly empty of customers, then walked toward Audney. She did not pull away when he embraced her affectionately.

"Lincoln told me aboot the two o' ye," he said quietly. "I want tae wish ye a' the happiness in the world, Audney. Ye've loved the two best men I ever kenned," Hardy went on. "That's David an' noo the man who's tae be yer husband. I ken ye waited a long time tae find him. But ye couldna do better than Lincoln Rhodes. I'm happy for ye both."

"Thank ye, Hardy," said Audney, smiling up at the big rugged face. "I ken that Lincoln thinks the world o' ye as weel. Ye'll always be a friend."

Hardy merely smiled, then turned and left the inn. Audney watched him go with a quiet heart. If good things came to those who waited, she was the living embodiment of that truth.

72

A PENNSYLVANIA CHRISTMAS

UNITED STATES OF AMERICA

Upon his arrival in Washington, D.C., Loni settled David into his new digs at her apartment. Then followed a much-anticipated visit to the seventh floor of Capital Towers, with happy greetings between David and Maddy and the rest of Loni's colleagues. They capped off the day of their reunion with dinner at one of Loni's favorite restaurants, one where Loni was confident they would *not* encounter the congressman-elect from Wisconsin, Hugh Norman, and his new fiancée, a beautiful New York debutante.

While awaiting the arrival of dinner, David pulled a small box from his pocket. "I wanted to show you the ring we ordered from Pitlochry," he said. He opened the lid and held it across the table to Loni.

"Oh my, David—it's beautiful! So full of vibrant colors."

"But you can't have it *quite* yet—sorry. I still need to talk to your grandfather. Then we will make this engagement officially official."

"You are so funny! With you everything has to be done just so."

"You know what Paul said," smiled David, " 'Let all things be done decently and in order.' "

"That's all well and good, but I doubt Paul had an engagement ring in his pocket when he said it!"

Snow came to the eastern seaboard on the eighteenth of December, a week after David's arrival. Two days later, under sunny skies and with cleared roads, he and Loni were on their way to Pennsylvania.

David wasted no time getting down to the business at hand. Within an hour of their arrival, he and Mr. Ford disappeared into the barn where their conversation was brief, though earnest, resulting in a manly shake of the hand and a few tears brushed back from the eyes of Loni's aging grandfather. Twenty minutes later, in the presence of the two faithful Quaker saints who had raised her, David proposed to Loni a second time, now "officially" with her grandfather's enthusiastic blessing, then gently placed the new heather ring on her finger. Mrs. Ford wept freely, embraced David, then took Loni in her arms for a lengthy squeeze. She had always hoped that Loni would marry a Quaker. She now realized that the Lord had something just as good for Loni, and might prove even better—a true *Christian* man in whom the inner Light burned bright.

An invitation had been extended to David's

sister Margaret and her fiancé, Malcolm Adams from Glasgow, to join them for Christmas at the Ford home. David and Loni picked them up at the Philadelphia airport on the twenty-first. It was a joyous reunion between brother and sister, who had not seen each other in over a year.

If Mrs. Ford had been elated with David's visit the previous summer, she was positively beside herself now to host such a festive Christmas gathering.

A great tree, decorated by more hands than their hostess dreamed of seeing again under her roof during the holidays, sat in the middle of the living room. The house echoed with carols and singing and laughter as the day approached, with multitudes of enticing smells of pumpkin, custard, pecan pies, and David's rice pudding all emanating from the kitchen. David and Margaret laughed and reminisced together like children, with stories of childhood keeping Loni and Malcolm in stitches.

Much last-minute shopping filled the two days prior to Christmas—with drives into Harrisburg and Lancaster, as well as excursions through the Amish country of southern Pennsylvania and its variety of shops.

The guests and their hosts gathered on Christmas Eve for more carols, enjoying eggnog and German pancakes, a Ford family tradition, before the highlight of the evening—Mr. Ford's animated rendition, complete with his Santa cap and white flowing beard retrieved from the attic, of "The Night Before Christmas." As the words *And to all a good night* fell from his lips, the small assembly broke into applause, followed by many fond girlhood reminiscences from Loni.

Christmas morning was as festive as if the house were full of children. These were her children now, given to her in her old age. Loni's stocking from another box in the attic had been hung above the fireplace after most of the household was asleep. Beside it three others had been hastily labeled and added. When Loni saw the reminder of so many years ago, her eyes filled with tears. She went to her grandmother and embraced her tenderly.

With steaming mugs of coffee and tea, and with the savory aroma of a roasting turkey filling the house, Mr. Ford read the timeless Christmas story from Luke, before the four eager thirty-somethings jumped into the piles of gifts under the tree like boisterous boys and girls, to the inexpressible delight of the Fords.

Mrs. Ford glanced toward Loni, where her granddaughter sat with eyes aglow. She had not allowed herself to hope that Loni would join them for more Christmases. Seeing her granddaughter so happy filled her with gratitude to the Lord for restoring the locust years, though not in a way she could have imagined.

After meeting and that afternoon's dinner, well

bundled against the December chill, Loni and David led Margaret and Malcolm over the fields and through the wood to the now swollen creek where Mr. Ford had taught Loni to fish so many years before. Watching them walk away along the driveway from the porch of their home, the two couples hand in hand, William Ford stretched an arm around the diminutive form of his wife.

"We thought we had lost our family," he said. "Now we have more family than we dared dream of. It wasn't only Alonnah who found a family when she went to Scotland . . . so did we!"

"The Lord has been good to us, William," said his wife. "I admit that I was sad for many years at what I thought we had lost. Now not only is Loni back, we have Alison's side of the family under our roof as well."

"Legacies come in many forms and enrich our lives in diverse ways," rejoined her husband, "if only we have eyes to see them."

David returned to Whales Reef in late January. As "Stafford Investments" got off the ground in the following months, Tennyson decided on Washington as his new company's headquarters for the foreseeable future. Besides the fact that Maddy and Loni were at home there, with comfortable apartments and a network of contacts, the location was central between the Stafford ranch and the Ford farm and would necessitate the least disruption to the lives of everyone involved.

Maddy and Loni made some changes to their apartments with an eye to having their husbands-to-be joining them. A new office was leased, and Tennyson's move from Alaska was completed by March with most of his belongings placed in storage at the ranch. They dubbed the new enterprise *Investatures*, adding the descriptive slogan: "Invest in *Your* Adventure."

Winter and spring passed with less drama and uncertainty for the people of Whales Reef than those of the previous year. Though the weather was severe, spirits were high. The anticipation of a wedding between their laird and chief the following June was as great as a royal celebration at Buckingham Palace.

By late spring the intimate discussions in front of the hearth at the manse had been joined by half a dozen, sometimes ten additional hungry souls. The discussions around the warmth of a peat fire were not limited to spiritual matters but ranged from favorite music to books, movies, politics, and philosophy, with occasional lectures from David.

Tennyson and Maddy were married in Virginia during the first week of May. Loni, Maddy's mother and sister, and a dozen Stafford relatives were in attendance.

A week later, Loni flew from Philadelphia to return to her "home" in Whales Reef.

Having completed her reading of her great-grandmother's journal during her months in the United States, Loni was anxious to get back and continue her explorations in Ernest's study. She was hopeful of picking up the threads of the correspondence between Emily and Sally that had sprung up during the war. She was confident that their letters would help piece together the final chapters of the story of her Whales Reef ancestry.

Arriving on the island, therefore, one of her first orders of business—after seeing David and the villagers and enjoying her favorite walks!—was to reacquaint herself with the contents of the letter box. There she indeed found what she was looking for—letters she had only but glanced through previously. In another envelope she discovered a tiny bouquet of dried wildflowers—surely the very clump that Brogan had hastily given Emily at Sumburgh Head.

A more thorough search of the study turned up a series of letters between Emily and Sally buried deep in an unlabeled box in the back of a drawer in one of the file cabinets.

With the correspondence between the two women before her, as well as the wartime letters between Emily and Brogan, everything she had read in her great-grandmother's journal about the years of misunderstanding and separation leading up to the war gradually fell into place.

She flipped through the stack of envelopes she

had retrieved, yellowed with time, their postmarks tracking the years in rapid succession . . . 1924, 1926, 1928 . . . then the great silence leading to the war years.

Along with the old journal, these letters told the history of the times. Taken together, they told a story, not merely of one family but of the century in which her ancestors had been born and grown and lived and loved and died.

PART 14

A LEGACY BEGINS—
THE LETTERS
1924–1953

73

RENEWED MEMORIES

AUGUST 7, 1943
BURLINGTON, NEW JERSEY

Dear Sally,

I hesitate to address you by your given name. It seems I ought to use the more formal "Lady Tulloch." I don't want to be guilty of the American propensity toward undue informality. However, as you did me the honor of speaking so personally and signing simply "Sally," I will take the liberty of addressing you in like manner. Though it has been years since we saw one another, somehow I think I still know you well enough to know that is what you would want.

It was more wonderful to hear from you than I can possibly convey! When the letter was delivered I did not recognize the return name. The circumstances surrounding our last letter from the Shetlands caused my heart immediately to seize me with dread. My first thought was that something had happened to Brogan and a stranger was writing to tell me. With quivering fingers I tore at the envelope. My heart leapt, suddenly with joy, as I saw your name. I'm afraid I cried all the way through your letter. With mail so slow and unpredictable, sometimes I don't hear from Brogan for weeks, even months. I confess it is difficult not to be fearful. It is war, after all, and England and Scotland are in constant danger, far more than we are here.

So your news about Brogan was doubly welcome. It was almost as good as receiving a letter from him. I will hear from him about everything eventually too, of course. Then I will rejoice all over again.

Oh, my! What wonderful news you bring. The minute I finished reading, I hurried upstairs to my mother and was crying and babbling so incoherently that I could hardly tell her why. I finally handed her your letter to read for herself.

I am just as eager to know everything about Whales Reef and your lives as you say you are to know about us. After so many years of silence between us, it is as if suddenly the floodgates are bursting open. Those lost years are pressing to rush through in a tidal wave!

You asked about our "little Grant." How time flies! He was but two, if I remember correctly, when we last heard from you—just beginning to talk. He was born in 1927, the same year, again if I remember correctly, that Wallace was married. Now our *little* Grant is a strapping sixteen-year-old—easily six inches taller than me!—and, with Brogan away, the man of the family. I lost my father five years ago. My mother is aging but healthy. She is seventy-two and we are living with her in the family home where I was raised just outside Burlington.

You also asked how the crash of 1929 affected us. As you know, my father was a banker and the financial world was hit hardest of all. My father's bank failed, so he and Brogan were both thrown out of work. However, my parents owned our home and its acreage was free of debt, so there was no danger of being foreclosed upon as happened to many. One of my brothers and one of my sisters and their families moved back to live with my parents. Brogan and Grant and I and my grandmother were already there. We had chickens and my father bought three cows. With an enormous garden, along with fruit trees and much canning and plenty of milk to make cheese, we managed. It was crowded, but it is a large home and there was a sense of adventure being forced to band together and make the best of hard times.

I cannot recall with certainty exactly when we last heard from you. We continued to write for some years, though, hearing nothing in return, we were never certain if you received our letters. Therefore, perhaps I should answer your questions about our lives by starting from the beginning. Well, not the beginning exactly because you know *that* part of my story! My adventure obviously began when I first went to Whales Reef and met Brogan and the rest of you. Then of course after I returned home to New Jersey, Brogan surprised me that autumn of my final year, appearing at Wilmington College with my father! Never have I been so shocked in my life!

Brogan and I wrote so many letters during the months following his visit, it was all I could do to keep my mind on my studies. I gathered from his letters that he was different, that people on the island were talking about the change that had come over him.

He said that he and his father, your dear Ernest, were enjoying long walks and talks again. How different everything looked, he said, than it had through his teenage eyes. The respect and honor in which he held his father often brought tears to my eyes as I read. He also told me briefly about Ernest's youth as a laborer on the farm in Germany, then joining the army and becoming friends with the young Mr. Churchill. I would love to know about all that. Perhaps you can tell me more of the story.

I did notice one difference in Brogan even from such a great distance. When we first met he poked fun at my scholarly pursuits, professing himself uninterested in school and learning. After returning from the States, however, he spoke of wanting to put the time to better use rather than lounging about accomplishing nothing. He said that he had decided to use the rest of the school year to study as diligently as I was at college. He would follow my example, he said. Imagine my surprise when I read that!

He spoke of books he was reading and ideas he was thinking about. He told me of the hours he spent in his father's study reading in various devotional books. He also said he had set himself to read as many of the Scotsman's novels as he could, along with rereading several history texts from his time at Oxford. He had squandered those years, he said, but was now determined to make the best of his education, even if belatedly. He was also, he said, reading the New Testament through for the first time.

I don't know whether you knew it, but he even began keeping a journal. I had explained to him about Quakers and their journals.

No doubt you and Ernest saw these changes more clearly than I did. I cannot imagine what a joy it must have brought to your hearts to see Brogan determined to redeem the time, as the Bible says.

I am sorry . . . my mother just reminded me that I need to walk to the pharmacy to pick up some medicine for her. There is much more I want to tell you! However, I am eager to get this off to you today. Though all too brief after such a long time, I will close for now. Please write again soon!

As you request, I will post this letter to your brother at the address you gave me on Shetland. Very mysterious!

Sending you much love,
Emily

74

CENTERING ROOTS

AUGUST 28, 1943
WHALES REEF, SHETLAND ISLANDS,
SCOTLAND

Dear Emily,

The joy you wrote of at my letter can hardly be greater than mine to receive yours. I relished every word! I have already read it over three times!

You are so right about the floodgates opening. If the years have been swept away in our hearts, however, their effects on our bodies have not. When you were here it seemed that I was so much older. I am, after all, married to Brogan's father. I am now fifty-eight, well on my way to a head graced with a full garland of gray. I am a *grandmother* for goodness' sake! I still feel young, but one look in the mirror tells me I am not!

Yet now we are almost of the same generation, a mere seventeen years between us. No one imagines that they will really grow old. Yet it comes!

Oh, that you were here, where we could talk and talk, and embrace and cry, and then talk some more. Especially with our men gone and war raging throughout Europe, and the darkness that has consumed the Continent threatening the world . . . to be with you and to have you here would be such a comfort and joy.

Alas, we must content ourselves to know that our hearts are again one in our Savior. I am so full of praise to Him for this new beginning. I am eager to hear more about your lives. I suppose the romantic in me wants to know more about your romance with Brogan! I can scarcely believe that it began in 1924, almost twenty years ago!

You asked many questions. I hardly know where to begin. How do we fill in the years! I laughed to read your observations about the changes in Brogan during your final year in college. So many times we glanced toward one another with raised eyebrows. We obviously noticed those changes as well. The entire island noticed! How often alone in our room did Ernest and I whisper to one another, *What has come over Brogan?* You should have heard Ernest singing your praises, speaking of the tiny American beauty who came to the Shetlands and tamed his son.

You also wondered about Ernest as a young man. Where to begin! Everything he is as a man has roots in his upbringing on Whales Reef and those pivotal years of his early twenties. In a sense, Brogan's personal history, and mine, and our entire family's, cannot be separated from what those years built into young Ernest.

It began when an opportunity arose for him to spend a year in Germany working on a dairy farm for an enigmatic farmer by the name of Erich von Dortmann. Ernest's eyes glow when he speaks of it. He describes the German as a Christian mystic in the guise of a man of the earth, and he took the young Shetlander under his wing. As they worked side by side, von Dortmann gently transmitted the truths about life with God that became an anchor for the rest of Ernest's life. Ernest returned to "the farm," as he always called it, on several occasions after that. But the first Great War put an end to travels to the Continent. The old German farmer died shortly after the war. Ernest visited the German's son once in the late 1920s, as well as a cousin he spoke of. But the rise of the Nazis and this new war has rendered further contact impossible.

Ernest dates his quest for what he calls *life at the Center* from that time—a phrase from one of several books the old German gave him. He wrote many letters home during that year. From my acquaintance with the two older Tullochs, it is probable that most of Ernest's reflections lay beyond the ken of his parents. However, I have read Ernest's collection of "Germany Letters" and they remind me of the contemplative mystics of old. From a young age, the compass of Ernest's heart was pointed toward God.

Curious as it has always seemed to me for such a devout young man, the following year Ernest joined the army and was sent to South Africa. He says it was something he felt God leading him to do. As he looked back later, he laughingly confessed himself puzzled by the decision as well. It was during the Boer War there that he made the acquaintance of a certain young aristocrat by the name of Winston Churchill. When Churchill was captured by the Boers, Ernest was instrumental in helping him escape. The two traveled three hundred miles to Portuguese territory in Mozambique. Ernest was badly wounded at the end of their adventure and sent back to England. While Churchill was rising to prominence and being elected to the House of Commons in 1900, Ernest lay in an army hospital in England.

He points to those months of recuperation as

the second great turning point of his life. His mother came from Shetland to visit him, bringing with her some novels by the Scots Victorian writer MacDonald. It was those novels, he says, that deepened even more his hunger to know God as Father. He eventually made a complete recovery and returned to the Shetlands. He and his first wife, Elizabeth, were married toward the end of that same year. Brogan was born a year later, in 1901.

By the time I met Ernest after Elizabeth's death, the strength of his devotion had been plumbed to yet greater depths by his years of grief. I must admit, at first I was a little in awe of him. He was ten years older than I was, quiet, reflective, with a kind spirit and humility that went straight to my heart. But a somber man he was not— just thoughtful. His laughter and humor were infectious. He courted me as the most genteel of gentlemen, with old-world courtesy and grace. At the same time, he was fun to be with. The sun was always shining in his presence!

Ernest and I were married in 1908. Though I was sad for the grief he had endured in losing a wife he loved, I yet considered myself the most blessed of women to be privileged to share my journey with him. God's ways are indeed mysterious, how grief and joy intertwine so intricately as He weaves His purposes through the tapestries of our lives.

I paused and set down my pen after writing those last words.

I find myself nostalgically reflective. Oddly, like you, though my mind is full of so much to say, my fingers and heart have suddenly stilled. Perhaps that is God's faint whisper telling me it is enough for now, and to end this letter with that chapter of our lives which seems so near, yet also now so far away.

I will therefore close with,
as you say, *much* love,
Sally

75

QUANDARIES OF CHANGE

SEPTEMBER 19, 1943
BURLINGTON, NEW JERSEY

Dear Sally,

Where to begin a reply is the hardest question after receiving your letter that arrived two days ago. Thank you for all you told me about dear Ernest. His letters from those years must indeed be a treasure. Brogan has told me of many of his father's favorite spiritual books. He has tried to locate copies of some of them here.

Did Ernest really call me a *beauty?* I do not

think anyone has called me that in my life! I am not so vain as to take it seriously. I laughed out loud to read your words.

I also smiled when I read your reference to my *romance* with Brogan. As time passes, the fluttering hearts of youth grow more thoughtful. I do, however, gaze back on those first months and years with fondness and quiet happiness.

I finished my thesis and final year at Wilmington and graduated in June of 1925. It was clear from the letters passing between us that Brogan and I were in love. I use the words now, from the vantage point of many years (at my ripe old age of 41!), though I would not have openly said it at the time. I had never expected to marry at all. Realizing I was falling in love with a Scot was frightening. I kept my deepest feelings secret. I did not dare allow myself to dream of marriage.

Brogan said nothing either, though afterward he confessed that he knew he wanted to marry me almost from the beginning. Yet without speaking of it in so many words, as I looked back I was able to read between the lines that he was thinking seriously about his future. He occasionally let some comment drop about his grandparents and the titles of laird and chief, and how different his father was from his own father. It eventually came out that the future laird and chief of Whales Reef—which everyone knew would ultimately be Brogan himself—must marry a Shetlander. I think when I was first there he had mentioned it, but it went right over my head. I thought nothing of the implications. It was clear Brogan was wrestling with that.

Where did I—an American—fit in? Brogan and I did not refer to it openly in our letters. Yet when he began to tell me about conversations with his father I was able to discern that the future of the lairdship and chieftainship represented a major unresolved issue. No one had anticipated someone like me coming along! In spite of the complications it had suddenly brought to his life, I could tell that Brogan respected Ernest for what he called his father's Deuteronomy vision for the land and its future.

I'm sure you knew of Brogan's plans when he returned for his second visit to the States that summer to ask my father for my hand. Afterward he formally proposed to me. At that point he told me more specifically about the inheritance. That's when Brogan explained the reasons for his father's conviction. I wasn't sure what to do. I loved Brogan with all my heart. Yet I wondered if it was my duty to turn down his proposal for the sake of the legacy that fate had placed on his shoulders.

I laid the matter before my father privately and asked him what I should do. He simply asked, "What does Brogan want? If he wants to marry you in spite of the difficulties, it seems that should be enough."

"What if that is not what is best for the future of the island?" I replied. "What if Brogan is too blinded by love to know what is best? Might it be my responsibility to say no?"

"That I cannot say," my father answered. "But if you wait upon Him, the Lord will speak to you."

Brogan and I continued to discuss it, and of course continued praying. As much as I loved Brogan, more than anything I knew we had to try to find God's will rather than what we might want ourselves. I asked Brogan if our marrying would break his father's heart. He said that he had two brothers who could take his place in carrying the family legacy forward. I replied that I did not think someone else could replace any child in the heart of a parent.

Almost as if he had known the quandary facing us, before I had given Brogan a final answer, a letter arrived from Wallace. It was warm and affectionate and in one sense took the pressure off us. Wallace expressed his enthusiasm for our marriage. At the same time he was adamant that Brogan should be the future chief and laird of Whales Reef. He wanted neither title, Wallace said. He recognized the difficulties involved if Brogan immigrated to America. But he offered to act as Brogan's future factor to make it possible for him to retain the titles even if we were living in the States.

Brogan was deeply moved by Wallace's offer. But in the end he decided not to avail himself of Wallace's offer, and at the same time take any further quandary about the matter out of his father's hands. He decided to relinquish his inheritance as first born, and in so doing also lay down future claim to either title. The best solution, he felt, was for him to step aside and let the property and both titles, at Ernest's death, go to Wallace.

Believing that God had indeed shown Brogan the way through the quagmire, and that God as well as both our families was supportive of our marrying, I gave Brogan the answer I had hoped to give him all along.

The letter I received from Ernest several weeks later went straight to my heart. Giving his unreserved blessing and his saying that he loved me as a true daughter meant the world to me. It was the final confirmation that we could move ahead with peace.

As you know, we were married in the spring of 1926. My father was able to arrange for a position for Brogan at his bank. It was such a joy to see Brogan and my father working together. It warmed my heart to watch them walking away from the house toward the woods, or when I heard them in the workshop talking away like old friends.

With all my brothers already gone, and the house being so huge, we lived with my parents in Burlington. I became pregnant toward the end of the year and gave birth to our son in 1927.

We always looked forward to the letters we received from you during those happy days. I remember Ernest greeting our news that we would soon be parents by reminding Brogan what a rambunctious two-year-old he had been. Brogan laughed about the curiosity of parents remembering children as they were when young. Now he and I are doing the same thing!

I believe it was in that same letter that we received a premonition of storm clouds on the horizon. Ernest indicated that Wallace seemed to have been bitten by love, adding that it was not an alliance he was comfortable with, hoping that wiser counsels would ultimately prevail.

I remember Brogan's response as he glanced up after reading it. "I wonder who it is Wallace is interested in."

Brogan continued to notice his father's concern in future letters. When he finally revealed the name of the young woman in Wallace's life, Brogan's countenance instantly clouded.

"Priscilla Hadle," he exclaimed. "I can scarcely believe it. Two more opposite individuals I cannot imagine. I fear for what Wallace is getting into."

"Who is she?" I asked.

"A woman who is up to no good," replied Brogan. "She once set her sights on me. And she was married at the time."

"Is she divorced?" I asked.

Brogan read further in his father's letter.

"Apparently she was widowed a year ago," he said at length. "She must be four or five years older than Wallace."

"Might she have some ulterior motive?" I asked.

"Priscilla always has an ulterior motive," replied Brogan. "She is as conniving as the day is long and was from the time she was ten."

But back to the beginning of our family.

When our newborn son was seven or eight days old, Brogan left the house carrying him in his arms. He walked out behind the house and disappeared among the trees. We still had not decided on a name. When he returned, Brogan's eyes were alive with a quiet look of peace as I went outside to meet him.

"I finally understand," he said.

"Understand what?" I asked.

"About my father and the land, why he loves it as he does. I used to think my father strange for being out of step with modern times. I would see him early in the morning or late at night out wandering the island. He looked so solitary, yet I see now how completely I misunderstood him. For him the land was life. It was a legacy that had been passed down to him and that was his responsibility to love and protect and pass along to his descendants with the same devotion. It is what he called the Deuteronomy legacy. The land was a biblical symbol for something deeper—a permanent family legacy that can only be passed down from fathers to their sons and daughters. He did not want to break that important chain in the ongoing generational link. It was that he tried to instill in us—in Wallace and Delynn and Leith and me.

"With our son in my arms, suddenly that legacy made sense," Brogan went on, "—everything my father stood for. I saw that our being here does not necessarily have to break that link. We can carry on that legacy just as my father had—the spiritual vision of life with God."

I find myself surprised as I write that so much of what happened so long ago is coming back to my mind like it was yesterday. It is all imprinted on my heart because of its meaning and significance, even all these years later.

But to continue, "*That* is the Deuteronomy vision," Brogan had said. "It is not one specific piece of land. It is what the land *represents*—a spiritual legacy with the injunction that parents pass it on to their children. Not only unto the third and fourth generation—God intends this legacy to be passed on by every generation to every next generation for all time. It's truly an *eternal* legacy."

He stopped and gazed back at the land that had come down through the years to my family through our Woolman and Borton ancestors. I almost saw the same look on his face as I could imagine on Ernest gazing out on the moors of Whales Reef.

"In those moments I knew that my home is here now," said Brogan after a minute. "I must look ahead. Our son will grow up as an American. We can carry on the legacy of both our fathers and do so here. The Quaker and the Shetland legacies will fuse into a new generational line that is both new, and yet continues the ancient legacies that have come down into us. We now have the opportunity and challenge and duty to transmit to our children the spiritual principles our parents built into us."

I think I can almost remember the words he prayed that day, if not exactly I think they are close to his very words.

"Lord, grant that my life here, in this new land, and our son, will worthily carry on the name Tulloch, continuing my family's heritage, yet also will establish the beginning of a new legacy, which is just a continuation of the ancient legacy

of Moses, to faithfully transmit your truths to the generations that follow. May this land and this son you have given Emily and me be blessed and fulfill the desires of my father's heart, and the desires of Emily's father's heart. May fruit grow from this tiny human seed in my arms, spreading down through time into sons and daughters yet unborn, who will grow to be the men and women of your eternally expanding legacy of life wherever you take them in the world."

And as he prayed, he said that the words of his prayer had given us our son's name. . . . *Grant Tulloch.*

I am still, years later, taking in the depth of Brogan's revelation that day.

Those were happy days for us. Letters flowing between Brogan and his father and brothers always brought us such joy. Brogan and Wallace and Leith reminisced by letter about their days as boys on the island, especially their adventures in the cave. Brogan told me about the three stones they set in place as symbols of their future responsibilities toward the people of the island and how he and Wallace had spoken to their younger brother about his duty as a chief's son. Though he was the youngest, they urged upon him that he must take that responsibility just as seriously as they did. Such memories were poignant for Brogan. In one way he felt that he had abandoned the threefold cord of that pledge in the Chief's cave. Yet neither did he doubt his decision to emigrate to America.

In the coming months Brogan and I talked about a visit to the Shetlands. We wanted you and Ernest to see our new son. Yet time moved quickly. With the pressures of a small family and Brogan's job, we obviously could not undertake such a trip soon. We felt no urgency because we knew we must wait until Grant was older. Unfortunately, unforeseen events prevented that day ever coming.

When word came of Wallace's engagement to Priscilla, Brogan was stunned. He had hoped that the thing would die out. He wrote Wallace immediately warning him against moving ahead. It was an excruciating letter for Brogan to write. Wallace had been so supportive of us. Brogan was loath to criticize Wallace or Priscilla. Yet he felt compelled to warn his brother in the strongest possible terms.

When the letter came from you soon afterword that the wedding had been hastily planned and carried out, Brogan was heartbroken. He felt that Wallace had succumbed to a great deception that would have far-reaching consequences.

Letters from Wallace stopped immediately. Brogan never heard another word. His heart nearly broke.

Dear Sally . . . I am sorry to end on a sad note. But it does make me sad to remember the breach between two brothers who loved one another. Surely there are few evils that so rouse the righteous indignation of God more than that of disuniters and separators, who foment discord and strife, and by subtle and selfish manipulations work division in families. I am sorry to speak so strongly!

Bless you!
My heart is full of love for you,
Emily

76

Relinquishment and Grief

OCTOBER 5, 1943
WHALES REEF, SHETLAND ISLANDS,
SCOTLAND

Dear Emily,

I felt such sadness in the final words of your letter. I nearly wept. It is a sadness I also feel. I know Wallace's marriage has not been what I'm sure he hoped it would be. I see occasional grief in his eyes. Perhaps being away from Whales Reef during these war years will help him gain perspective about it all. I continue to pray.

However, it was reassuring to hear more about Brogan's thoughts concerning the inheritance.

You have no idea how Ernest likewise wrestled with it. He was terribly torn. In the end he decided to release Brogan from the necessity of marrying a Shetlander. You cannot imagine how highly he thought of you. I knew nothing of Wallace's offer to Brogan. I do not think Ernest did either. God bless him!

I remember so clearly when Brogan told us his plan to return to the States to propose to you.

"What will you do there?" I asked.

"I am hoping that Emily's father might find me a place at his bank."

A great smile spread over Ernest's face. "My son . . . a banker," he said. "Not in my wildest dreams would I have imagined that!"

The night before his final departure for the States, Brogan and Ernest prayed and wept together. I've never seen anything like such love between father and son. Both were heavy of heart yet they knew that Brogan had to follow the love God had brought to his life.

Poor Wallace! As you surmised from Ernest's letters, we too were terribly concerned about the marriage to Priscilla so soon after the death of her first husband. Ernest is a trusting soul, but he feared that her motives were less than honorable. Though Priscilla had grown up on Whales Reef, daughter of the village postman, we had not seen much of her in recent years. We had no idea that she had set her eyes on

Wallace. Priscilla had married for money and prestige once and was apparently determined to do so again. Wallace is innately a good soul, but far too trusting. He was no match for her wiles. He was never the same after the marriage, as if he was under a spell.

I'm sorry, I cannot write more now. Too many emotions are stirring within me. That is not always the best time to commit words to paper.

Like you, I apologize to close on a sad note. These are heartbreaking memories.

Sally

77

THE WOOD AND THE LAND

OCTOBER 25, 1943
BURLINGTON, NEW JERSEY

Dear Sally,

With you, I will pray for Wallace, and all concerned. I believe that God can wake anyone, as I know you do. My father taught us when we were young that prayers are like arrows. We launch our prayer arrows up into God's care. But when He sends the answering arrows into the hearts and minds of those we pray for is up to Him. He may hold our prayer arrows for a long time, waiting for a perfect moment of readiness to launch their answers back down into the hearts of our loved ones. So I will pray for beams of light and wakefulness to be sent into Wallace's heart . . . in God's perfect time.

I cannot imagine the grief you and Ernest must have endured to watch Wallace marry unwisely, and then, if I surmise correctly, to grow distant from you. I know how it hurt Brogan that Wallace cut him off, as it seemed. He was certain Priscilla was at the bottom of it, though had no proof of it. He could not but suspect her of poisoning Wallace against him.

About a year after the letters from Wallace stopped, suddenly so too did letters from you and Ernest. All communication from Whales Reef simply ceased. We were utterly bewildered.

Closer to home, the stock market crash of 1929 changed everything in our lives. My father and Brogan both lost their jobs when the Burlington National Trust bank failed. Suddenly we were poor and the possibility of returning to the Shetlands was gone. As I told you, we were living with my parents, and the families of my brother and sister joined us. With a big garden and the animals, we managed to grow and raise most of our own food. Brogan was resourceful and found odd jobs around Burlington to bring some little cash to the family even if it meant working for pennies an hour.

Poor Daddy became terribly depressed. I know Mama was worried for him. He seemed to age quickly.

I don't know whether Brogan told you after his first visit here, but he was so taken with the trees on our property. In America we take trees and forests for granted. But sometimes he would stand staring at a tree, then whisper, "It's so beautiful!" He was fascinated with my father's woodworking tools and eager to learn about them. As it turned out, his simple love for wood and what could be done with it became a door for us out of the worst of the economic collapse.

While walking the circumference of our property, Brogan came upon an old dilapidated building from early Quaker days next to the stream. I had not thought of it in years. As children we were warned not to go too near it for the danger and the stream, which, though small, was quite rapid. I think my brothers probably played there, but I had only seen it once or twice and was afraid of it.

"Oh, that," said my father as Brogan mentioned it at supper that evening. "That's the derelict mill. Dates from the 1700s. The whole thing's ready to collapse."

"But it looks like there's still some equipment there," said Brogan, "rusted saws and belts, a water race and sluice. It's obviously in poor repair, but why couldn't we get it operational again?"

"I think it's too far gone for that."

But Brogan wasn't about to give up so easily. His excitement was that of a boy. My father had no objection to his plan, though remained skeptical. That is until Brogan took him out to the mill a week later. My father was astonished at the change simply from clearing away rubbish and debris, and making the overgrown road passable again. The next day he joined Brogan in the salvage operation. Within a week one of my brothers joined them and they were talking and scheming how they might barter for new timbers and roofing, floor planking and equipment to get the mill rehabilitated and operational again, even the possibility of running electricity out to the building. By the end of the year, they had begun milling a few trees from the property, which is lush with oak and birch and ash. Thus Hanson Hardwoods was born.

One day walking on his way back from the mill and showing young Grant the area he had cleared on his first visit to the United States, suddenly Brogan was seized with an idea. He came running back and into the house full of excitement. Within minutes he dashed back out, returning twenty minutes later with an armload of medium-sized logs. He disappeared into the woodshop for the rest of the afternoon.

Two days later he said he had something to show me and led me out to the shop.

"Look at this bench I made, Emily!" he said excitedly when we were inside. "All from scrap wood that otherwise would have gone for firewood."

"Brogan, it's beautiful. How did you know what to do?"

"Your father drew out a sketch and got me started. But I didn't save the two earlier attempts that did end up as firewood!" he added, laughing.

For the next few days the mill was silent. Instead, Brogan and my father were making more drawings and trying to create what they had envisioned. Sounds of sawing and other equipment came from the workshop nearly from dawn to dusk. Within another month "Tulloch Handcrafts" was added to our industrious little homestead. We had wood aplenty! If they could find customers for their milled lumber and small items of furniture, my father and Brogan began to hope they might be onto something.

From his earliest days, young Grant hung around both the mill and workshop. He loved the old-fashioned tools and the contraptions at the mill. By the time he was six he was making toys out of wood scraps. It was so wonderful to see three generations working together out on the land behind our house to support our family.

I often found myself thinking of Ernest's vision for the land under his care. I hoped that his prayers for Brogan were being answered. And I prayed that our lives would faithfully fulfill the vision of his father's heart, even though it had been transplanted to a new land.

The fledgling business never made a lot of money. But it kept Daddy and Brogan and one of my brothers and a brother-in-law busy making practical and sturdy furniture. Gradually as people heard of their work, they began to make custom crafted pieces. They developed the motto, "If you can draw it, we can make it." By the time Grant was ten, he was showing an aptitude for woodworking himself and was out in the shop with Brogan every minute he was not in school.

During the first few years of the Depression we continued to write to you and Ernest and Wallace and others. We assumed there must be some confusion with mail service. The longer it went on, however, the more bewildered we became. Our letters were never returned, but neither did we receive replies. We grew very concerned, yet had no way to get to the bottom of the mystery. Brogan wrote to friends and acquaintances in the village, but no replies ever came. All communication from Whales Reef simply stopped.

We never heard another word from Shetland

until the devastating letter from Priscilla some years later.

Warm regards, much continued appreciation for your letters, and with *great* love,

Emily

78

SILENCE

SEPTEMBER 3, 1943
WHALES REEF, SHETLAND ISLANDS,
SCOTLAND

Dear Emily,

Thank you for the image of prayer arrows of light! I have already begun praying differently as a result.

You can be assured that Ernest and I rejoiced at the many ways you and Brogan were indeed fulfilling the prayers Ernest had prayed for his children.

The confusion over the letters was equally great for us. Everything you say was mirrored here. Your letters suddenly stopped. We also continued to write, but heard nothing in return from you.

Oh, what a terrible and wicked confusion!

We were completely mystified at the abrupt

cessation of communication. Like you, our hearts breaking over what we wrongly assumed.

I feel my blood beginning to boil! How I would long to retrieve those lost letters. Alas, I fear they were probably destroyed. We must await Ernest's return to try to learn more. How much Wallace knows, and whether he was complicit in the duplicity, is a question that burns on my mind.

Of course, all this brings us to the source of the silence—Priscilla's letter to you which you mentioned. Ernest told me about it only vaguely from what he was told by Brogan.

What did Priscilla actually *say* to you?

The realization of what caused the estrangement—or should I call it the presumed estrangement—and these many years of silence, I must admit, fills me with indignation. If I was at liberty I would have been on my way before now to the Auld Hoose with the wrath of an avenging angel. I fear, however, that I would probably only be taking out my personal anger on one who, in Shakespeare's words, may be more to be pitied than censured—though I have difficulty believing that. Censured, certainly. Pitied . . . my heart is not there yet!

However, Ernest has strictly forbidden me to speak until he is home and he has a clearer sense of the Lord's mind in the matter. But my Old Eve with her half-eaten apple has her hackles up! Wallace is away from the island as well, with an army unit in North Africa, which adds another complication to how this should be handled. Leith is in the Royal Navy in the Indian Ocean.

For now I must content myself with corresponding with you in secret through my brother on the north of the big island. I have told him everything. Whenever he receives a letter from you, he will drive down and deliver it personally to me. When I have completed this, as I have done previously, I will take the ferry across to the mainland and have my brother post it so that I remain completely invisible. No one in Whales Reef will ever know that correspondence between us has resumed.

Reflecting on those times makes me nostalgically happy and sad at the same time. Probably those feelings are deepened by Ernest's absence, and by the underlying *angst* of the war. I do not like using a German word, but it is the perfect word to describe the oppression we are under. Ernest and Mr. Churchill, though not close, remained in contact through the years and have been involved in something secretive for more than a dozen years. Ernest began traveling to Germany and Norway shortly after the time you were here, though he could never divulge what it was about. When the war broke out in 1939, Mr. Churchill revived

Ernest's commission from the Boer War and appointed him a colonel, though the position is more like a civilian liaison than military one. While he wears a uniform, technically he is answerable to no one but the prime minister. He has papers which, on the rare occasions he finds it necessary to use them, invariably, he says, draw raised eyebrows and expressions of astonishment, followed by, *Yes, sir,* and, *Whatever you want, Colonel Tulloch.* He is still not at liberty to tell me what he does. He comes and goes, though I never know when I may see him again. Occasionally he travels to London to see Mr. Churchill personally. About half his time he spends attached to the naval base at Scapa Flow, where he remains special liaison to the prime minister.

I have been saving some newspaper clippings to send you. I thought you would be interested in what war news looks like from our side of the pond, as they call it.

Blessings and love,
Sally

79
DECEPTION

Dear Sally,

What a good idea to send newspaper clippings! I so enjoyed them.

I read the articles entitled: *Shetlanders Join Gordon Highlanders . . . RAF Banff Strike Wing Attacks German Positions in Norway . . . Rescue of Refugees from Norway Increase . . . Continued High Losses for Shetland Seamen . . . High Employment and Rising Wages Continue on Shetland from War Work . . . Local Population Aids War Effort . . . German Aircraft Bomb Skerries Lighthouse and Scalloway Civilian Bus . . . Floating Mines Off Shetland Coast Increasing Danger.*

It makes the war seem so real and close! We over here can hardly fathom what you must be going through. I will return the favor, though I doubt you will find U.S. news very exciting.

Remembering back to the wonderful letters that passed between Brogan and Ernest during the first year of our marriage reminds me with grief how much has been lost by the years of silence. Ernest was prevented being part of those treasured years in Brogan's life when he was becoming a spiritual man, and Brogan was denied the privilege of drinking from his father's wisdom at the very time he was most hungry for it. Priscilla will have much to answer for in the next life for what she stole from both men.

In any event, Priscilla's letter arrived in late 1931. We had heard nothing from Wallace in four years, or from you and Ernest in almost three. We were trying to go on with our lives, praying for you all of course, but not knowing what had happened. Our hands were full with young Grant and the difficulties of the Depression. That was just about the time Brogan and my father had set about reclaiming the old mill.

Then suddenly came the letter. When I realized it was from Whales Reef I was so excited, though I did not recognize the handwriting on the envelope. I restrained myself from opening it until Brogan came home that evening from a job in town. He tore into it and pulled out a single sheet. As he began to read, his face went pale.

I don't know why I saved the letter. I should have burned it because it nearly destroyed Brogan. However, I still have it and it is probably best that I just quote it to you. I don't want to be unjust toward Priscilla, though in my darker moments I wonder if that would even be possible.

"Dear Brogan," *he read,*
"I have the duty to inform you that your father Ernest is dead. Before his death he confessed that you had broken his heart by leaving Whales Reef. His obvious grief has been a great trial for Wallace, which I have done my best to alleviate. Wallace and I are married, and he requested me to write to you saying that he denounces you for what you did to your father. Neither he nor any of the family want to hear from you again.

Sincerely,
Lady Priscilla Tulloch"

I have never seen Brogan so devastated. That day was the low point of his life. He felt that he had lost a father and a brother on the same day. In one way, he never recovered. We of course wrote letters of condolence to you and attempted yet again to establish communication.

Finally, heartbroken, I'm sorry to say we gave up and stopped writing. Brogan gradually went on with his life. Yet something was always missing after that.

I pray that the many prayer arrows I sent into the bosom of God for my husband during those dark years will at last explode with light and life in his heart.

Bless you, dear Sally,
Emily

80

HEART OF DIVISION

NOVEMBER 1, 1943
WHALES REEF, SHETLAND ISLANDS,
SCOTLAND

Dear Emily,

To read those words of Priscilla's infuriates me all over again. How I will be able to hold my tongue until Ernest is home from the war I cannot imagine. But I shall try.

Poor Brogan! I cannot imagine his grief upon receiving such a letter. What woman can truly understand the love of fathers and sons? Yet I think I have some idea of the pain it must have caused him from the pain I observed in Ernest when we never heard from Brogan again.

Oh my, what deception has been leveled against this family . . . and from one of our own! We have tried so hard to be kind toward

Wallace's wife. I can scarcely believe that this was going on behind our backs.

After what we have now learned, I can only conjecture that Priscilla must have known that Wallace was hoping Brogan would one day resume again the mantle of firstborn and become the eventual laird and chief. Wallace may even have hoped that you and Brogan would return to Whales Reef. He probably confided as much to Priscilla. This was no doubt Priscilla's great fear, that she would lose the prestige she so coveted, and her control over the estate and its wealth which she assumed would one day be hers.

When she began to devise a scheme to work division between the father and his sons, I cannot begin to imagine. Growing up in the post office, she would know its workings and schedules. Since learning what I have from Ernest and you, and after instituting discreet inquiries, I have learned that the needy daughter of the current postman, a girl named Chloe, who has worked at the Post since she was fifteen, has been a pawn in Priscilla's hand almost that entire time. No doubt Priscilla came and went without raising the hint of suspicion on the part of Jamie Colquhoun, the current postman, who knew her as the daughter of his predecessor. He was probably gratified by Priscilla's friendship with his daughter, who is slow and without a mother. Somehow Priscilla must have contrived to get her hands on the letters. It is the only explanation I can think of.

What galls me almost to madness is the thought that Priscilla probably took the letters, opened and read them, laughing at what simple-minded fools we all were to pour out our hearts to each other. For all I know, she probably burned them. I cannot stand the thought of it! Doubtless Brogan's warnings against her made her hate him as much as she despised Ernest, knowing that both of them saw through her.

With all sincerity of heart, Emily, I do pray that God will develop Christlikeness of character within me. Oh, but I can become angry— God forgive me—in the face of duplicity and hypocrisy. How will I be able to stand next to Priscilla in church, singing hymns and listening to prayers as if nothing is amiss? I may have to make some excuse for being absent for the next Sunday or two. Hopefully it will not take me longer than that to get my attitude back in harmony with the Spirit of Jesus.

On a brighter note, Leith married a sweet village girl named Moira Mair. Though Priscilla looks down on her and treats her with condescension, the rest of us love her dearly. They live with us in the Cottage and have a son, Alexander, and two daughters, Aeileidh and Ailish—my own three grandchildren—though

Wallace's and Delynn's children consider me their grandmother as well.

Delynn married Jock Cauley, owner of two fishing boats. They live in the village and have a son, Fraser, and two daughters, Emma and Ava.

Wallace and Priscilla have three sons, Macgregor, Callum, and Cameron, and a daughter, Isla.

We are very fortunate in that all our grandsons are too young to have been conscripted into the war.

I think I shall close before saying anything I will regret. I know I need to go to my knees and pray for Priscilla. But it will be difficult, I must confess.

Yours,
Sally

81

THE DARK YEARS

DECEMBER 7, 1943
BURLINGTON, NEW JERSEY

Dear Sally,

What a day to remember—a day of infamy as President Roosevelt called it. We have now been at war for two years, just about the same

502

length of time Brogan has been away from home.

Thank you for your letter of November 1. How could a month already have gone by? I am trying not to think of all the might-have-beens of those dark years, but rather to rejoice that they are behind us at last. As you say, overlooking what has been done is not easy. Personally I would like to wring Priscilla's neck—figuratively, of course . . . we Quakers are supposed to be pacifists! However, I try to remind myself that vengeance is the Lord's. What she may have to endure in order for Him to turn her heart toward repentance I can scarcely imagine. In that sense, I am sorry for her. What grief awaits her when her eyes are opened to the suffering she has caused.

Life went on for us during the 1930s, as life does, with Brogan and my father working very long days getting their business off the ground. At first weeks would go by and they would not make a single sale or find so much as an hour's work in town. But they were glad just to be working. They were supremely confident that their hard work would pay off in the end. But during some of those years we lived on milk and eggs and cheese, apples and carrots and potatoes, all of which we had in abundance from our cows and chickens and garden and orchard.

We were vaguely aware of the rise of the

Nazis in Germany. But it seemed far away. As the Depression slowly began to release its grip on the country after Mr. Roosevelt's election, optimism began again to flourish. No one could see what dreadful things lay on the horizon. A young mother does not think much about world events.

Grandma died at the age of ninety-one. Mama and I were with her at the end.

We lost my father in 1938 at sixty-nine. By then he had recovered from his despondency and lived long enough to see the hardwood business begin to thrive and grow.

Grant grew, and though we hoped for more children, none came. I cannot say I *completely* lost hope. But once I passed forty it seemed obvious that Grant would grow up without a brother or sister.

Eventually the tensions in Europe could no longer be ignored, especially after Hitler invaded Germany's neighbors. Brogan saw the handwriting on the wall, that Britain and France would have no choice but eventually to go to war. Even then I think he was praying about what should be his own response.

After we were married, Brogan had converted to Quakerism and applied for dual citizenship. Though our church, or "Meeting," was not a conservative one, Quakers in general are against war. All my brothers and most of the young men of our Meeting are conscientious objectors, as was Brogan. However, as a citizen also of the United Kingdom, he felt the war more keenly than most Americans. At times I think he felt almost guilty being so far away when his homeland was under attack. He read about the Battle of Britain and Dunkirk with emotions few Americans could understand. When the HMS *Hood* was sunk in 1941, he hardly spoke for days. We heard that many Shetlanders lost their lives on board. I knew he was thinking of Wallace and Leith and feared for them. That's when he decided to volunteer, even before the U.S. entry into the war. Having just turned forty, he was obviously older than most young men who were going to war in the world— most of them mere boys. But with everyone in his homeland sacrificing so much, he felt he had to do something to help.

He volunteered for civilian medical service and began his training in the fall of 1941. I know he was hoping that in being sent to England he would have the opportunity to visit Whales Reef. He dearly wanted to see you and try to reconnect with the family. However, the suffering was still so acute in the south of England, even after the Battle of Britain, and with the ongoing threat of a German invasion he was sent to London.

Like all wives at the time I was worried to see

Brogan sail off to the war even if not as a soldier. Brogan tried to alleviate my concern with his characteristic joviality. But I couldn't help it. I cried watching the ship sail out of sight.

He had only been in England two weeks when the attack came on Pearl Harbor on December 7.

Eventually his Scottish connections made him ideally suited for an assignment in the Orkneys. Just a few months ago he was sent to the British naval facility at Scapa Flow to serve as a medical liaison between the Royal Navy and U.S. command forces in the north.

I will try to get a Christmas card off to you with some photos. If it is delayed, however, know that I will be thinking of you and your family and wishing you the best of Christmases possible under the circumstances. We will hope and pray that the new year of 1944 brings an end to this terrible war and brings our men home safe and sound.

Yours,
Emily

82

REUNION IN KIRKWALL

Dear Emily,

Believe it or not, it is your husband again taking pen to paper to write you what may be the most exciting letter I will ever write. When you will receive this I have no idea. We hear reports that mail is taking up to two months to the States.

I am still in the Orkneys and enjoying my expanded role very much. I was glad to help in London's hospitals, but it was gruesome work. It is nice to reach the end of the day without blood on my hands and clothes.

After three months in Kirkwall I knew the city and its haunts fairly well. As I told you, I have a room in the barracks with the U.S. naval officers who come and go from Scapa Flow. Obviously most activity in the Orkneys is naval. The sailors have quarters aboard their ships which are constantly returning from and being sent out on new assignments. As a civilian, I am accorded slight V.I.P. treatment, though the accommodations are basic and the food plain. My barracks are a ten-minute walk from the city. I have discovered two or three places in town where one can get a decent cup of tea, something my American colleagues wouldn't know if you served it on a silver platter with watercress round it. Also it is nice to be able to enjoy oatcakes and a true Scottish scone—neither of which I was able to find in London where the shortages of food are severe.

I hope you are sitting down for what I am about to tell you!

Three mornings ago I was walking along the sidewalk in Kirkwall toward my favorite tea shop. The lady who operates it, wife of an Orkney fisherman, bakes everything in their flat upstairs. It is an unassuming little place, but she makes the tea strong and her oatcakes are fresh.

It was early, about 6:15 in the morning. I had to be at Scapa Flow for a meeting at 8:00. I had my notebook and pen and planned to begin a letter to you over a pot of tea with a warm scone and raspberry jam—another wartime luxury I have surprisingly been able to find here. I don't know where she gets the jam, but until it runs out I am enjoying it.

The military barracks were full of activity, but the city was still mostly asleep and the streets and sidewalks deserted. Coming around a corner my eyes were immediately arrested when, about fifty yards ahead, I saw a man walking toward me from the opposite direction. The instant I saw him my eyes shot open.

The tall form . . . the slightly discernible sway in the man's gait . . . the erect head set high on broad shoulders!

My feet froze. I felt my face go white.

My eyes had to be deceiving me! I could only stare.

How could it possibly be? My first thought was that Wallace was stationed here and that the years had produced an uncanny resemblance to our father. And yet the man appeared sixty or more, and was in the uniform of a British officer, with abundant white hair flowing from beneath his hat.

It *couldn't* be Wallace!

Suddenly I was running along the sidewalk, feeling tears flooding my eyes.

He had seen me by now. He glanced quickly over his shoulder, thinking perhaps that I was running toward someone behind him. Nearly the same instant, however, his head spun back around as recognition dawned.

An expression of incredulity spread over his face. His lips quivered but no words came. He merely spread open his two arms.

I reached him and fell into his embrace.

I'm afraid I did not behave in very military

fashion—I sobbed like I hadn't since I was a boy. I could do nothing but stand with his arms around me, clutching him with mine and not wanting to let go.

"Dad!" I exclaimed. "What are you . . . we thought . . . we didn't hear anything more from you . . . we thought you were dead."

Gradually he also found his voice. We were both blubbering in an ecstasy of confusion and disbelief.

I have no idea what else he said. All I heard him whisper was, "My son . . . my son . . . my son!"

We finally stepped back. Both smiling from ear to ear, our glistening eyes roved up and down to take one another in.

Having lived for a dozen years thinking my father dead, it was like seeing a man raised to life. The expression in his tear-filled eyes is one I will never forget as long as I live. It was the look of pure love. What a thing it is—to be loved so deeply by one's father!

Questions and exclamations spilled out in profusion, as a river bursting a dam and rushing forth in a torrent.

"You're here!" said my father. "But not . . ."

It first now dawned on him that I was not wearing a uniform.

"I'm a civilian," I said. "I'm a conscientious objector, a volunteer working as a medical liaison. And you—a colonel! Goodness—how did you rise so fast?"

"Connections," he laughed. "I function more or less as a civilian too. The uniform is mostly for show. I'm what they call a personal liaison."

"I've never heard of that. Whom do you report to?"

He pulled a paper from the inside of his coat and handed it to me. One look at the letterhead and signature told me all I needed to know.

"Whoa, Dad—you do have connections! With this you could walk into Number Ten, no questions asked."

He laughed, and gradually we both recovered our equilibrium. Then Dad grew serious. "What's all this about thinking I was dead?" he asked.

"The letter from Priscilla," I answered.

He stared at me in confusion.

"What letter . . . ?" he said slowly.

"After you stopped writing," I added.

"We didn't stop writing," he said.

"About a year after Wallace's marriage."

"We wrote for a long time after that," he said. "It is true that eventually we stopped, but that was years later . . . after we heard nothing from you in three or four years. We assumed you wanted no more communication with us."

Now it was my turn to stare back with a bewildered expression.

"Goodness—not at all, Dad . . . we wrote and wrote, dozens of letters during that time. Nothing ever came from you in reply. Then three or four years after their marriage, Priscilla wrote saying I had broken your heart by going to America, that Wallace wanted nothing more to do with me, that no one in the family wanted to hear from me again, and telling us you were dead."

The thundercloud that gathered over my father's face was like nothing I had ever seen. For an instant I almost did not know him. From the intense joy we had both felt such a short time before, suddenly I saw the fury of a thunder-wielding Viking god rising within him.

He stood stunned for a moment. Then he turned away as if hiding from me what he was feeling, not from shame but not wanting me to see the anger he was capable of. When he turned toward me again, his face was red but his voice calm.

"The evil has spread further than I dreamed," he said quietly. "I had no idea. How she managed to keep such a plot from everyone I cannot imagine. I repent for trusting her too much, for trying to be a father to her when it is obvious she has despised everything I stand for."

Again he fell silent. It gave me the chance to take him in more thoughtfully. He was in his late sixties and had aged noticeably. Yet I recognized the look on his face as an expression of strength, dignity, and perhaps resolve. In the next few seconds I saw him cross some inner Rubicon, reach some decision. I think it was in that moment when I knew that he would eventually confront Priscilla, and perhaps even what he would say.

I was the next to speak. "So I didn't break your heart?" I said.

"Oh, Brogan!" exclaimed my father as if the question nearly broke his heart. "Every letter I received from you, our sharing of ideas, all your news about yourself and Emily and dear little Grant—it rejoiced my father's heart for the man you had become, for the woman you had married, for your hard work to establish a life for your family, for the choices you were making, for the wisdom I could see the Lord building into you. I was proud of you! You had become everything I had prayed during the years of your young life that you would become."

I had no words. How do you reply to such an affectionate outpouring?

"I don't know if I ever told you this," he went on, "but when you were only days old I sat and held you to my chest as you slept. I was nearly bursting with joy to hold my own precious son. In those moments I prayed that everything I was as a spiritual man would somehow be transmitted to you, that you would grow to be a man after God's own heart. A bond was established with you that has never left me."

He paused and smiled. "We had some rocky years," he went on with a smile.

"Dad, I am sorry about that," I said. "I don't know what came over me. I was stupid and foolish. I know I hurt you. I am sorry."

His only response was to laugh. "It's part of life!" he said. "No worries. We came out of it, in no small measure thanks to God sending Emily to you at exactly the right time. And indeed in your adulthood you did grow into the fulfillment of those prayers I prayed during your first hours of life. My love for you as a son to make a father happy and proud could not be stronger."

How many sons—probably not many—are privileged to hear such words from their fathers? Again we embraced. I felt that I literally melted into him as he wrapped his strong fatherly arms around me.

When we stepped back a second time we were at last ready to move forward and begin a new relationship together—now as men.

"I was on my way to Mrs. Nicolson's for tea and a scone," I said.

"You know Mrs. Nicolson!" Dad exclaimed. "Brilliant—hers are the best oatcakes in the Orkneys."

"I'm surprised we haven't met before now,"

I said as we fell into step toward the tea shop. "I try to come every few days."

"I've been down in London recently. I'm only just back. Bit of a secret mission, you know."

"A spy too, are you?"

"Hardly that," laughed my father. "But there are a few things the PM has me do that have to be kept out of the public eye."

A few minutes later we were enjoying the delectable aroma of strong tea brewing in front of us, continuing to piece together what must have happened with Priscilla and the communication breakdown, as well as rapidly filling in the high spots of the intervening years.

Shaking his head at one point, his expression grave again, my father spoke more forthrightly than I had ever heard him speak about another soul.

"As loath as I am to say such a thing about another human being," he said after a long sigh, "I fear that there is true evil in that woman. It is a grief to me to realize that she is the wife of my son and mother of my grandchildren. It is not lack of love that makes me say such a thing, but that her heart is impervious to the penetration of love. Sally and I have tried for years to win her over, to be all we could for her. Yet man-haters can develop such hearts of stone that true humanity cannot break that shell. What God will do with them in the end I cannot imagine.

My heart ached for Wallace the moment I heard of his secret marriage. I wept, not because I saw myself losing a son, but for the anguish that would one day be visited upon him if she ever turned against him."

It was silent as we both sipped at our tea.

"We will have to get together this evening," I said, glancing at my watch. "I'm afraid I have a meeting down at Scapa at eight o'clock," I added. "It's nothing critical. What are they going to do if I'm late, court-martial me? I'm not military anyway. But I do need to be there."

"They won't give you any trouble," said my father. "I'll drive you down."

"You have a car!"

"I am treated pretty well. Once I flash my papers, and tell them you're with me, you'll have no problems whatever."

"If you say so!" I laughed.

"Then I am going straight to headquarters and pulling whatever rank I have to arrange a telephone call to Whales Reef. Sally has to know I have seen you! I don't think Winston will mind a little personal business."

It turned out he was right. Wherever he went Dad was treated as a bigwig. That same day, he set in motion getting my quarters transferred. He had a nice apartment of his own, and within two days I was setting up my new lodgings with him. We both had our duties, of course, but we spent every free minute possible together. We had almost fifteen years' catching up to cram into whatever time we had. Neither of us wanted to lose a minute of it.

So much more to tell, but I need to get this off. I will write again soon.

I love you so much!

Brogan

83

CHRISTMAS AND A NEW YEAR

JANUARY 11, 1944
WHALES REEF, SHETLAND ISLANDS,
SCOTLAND

Dear Emily,

Suddenly in just three weeks' time I have received three letters from you! I am hopelessly behind in replying. Yours of early last month was followed by your long account of Brogan's letter. Ernest's call to me about their meeting was brief, and was followed by a letter full of emotion. I am waiting to ask his permission to copy it out by hand and send it to you. The outpouring of his heart was poignant. I cannot imagine what it must have been like for our two men that day.

Before I had a chance to write you again, your card came a few days after Christmas. Thank you for the photographs. What a joy to see you all, and Grant and your home and parents! I treasure them. I will see what I can gather to send you.

Christmas was something of a melancholy affair, as you can imagine. So it has been in Britain throughout the war. There is little money for gifts. Food and small handmade trinkets pass between families, but little else. No one feels like celebrating with the men away and with so many families suffering the grief of loss. I found the holidays doubly distressing visiting with our families and hosting Priscilla and Moira and Delynn at the Cottage, with all their children, for Christmas Eve and dinner the next day. Pretending that nothing was wrong, when inside I was feeling anything but charitable toward Priscilla, left me completely exhausted. The only gift she deserved was a lump of coal, yet I had to endure her subtle condescension toward Moira and Delynn. Her kiss on my cheek and bland expression of gratitude after opening the scarf I had knit for her was enough to turn my stomach. I'm sorry to sound petulant. I am not proud of it. No one would know from my example that I was a Christian. I hope you pray for me, as I do for you—I certainly need prayer these days!

Of course, we also have our "Boxing Day"

after Christmas when we take gifts around to the less fortunate in the village. Delynn and Moira and I did so. Mostly it is a chance to visit. Our gifts are too simple even to mention. But it is a tradition and the people appreciate it. Priscilla did not accompany us. Though she grew up on the island, I think even from a young age she felt superior to everyone around her. She still does. She rarely mixes with the villagers.

At last the holidays are behind us and the new year has come, and with it the long, long hours of winter darkness for which the Shetlands are known. It is a dreary time.

Every day seems to bring good news to some, heartbreaking news to others. Two hundred fifty Shetlanders have died in the war. Most of those have been lost at sea. The great majority of them are not even soldiers but merchant seamen. Just last week young Graham Muir returned home. He lost an arm in the Italian invasion and has been recovering in hospital. Seeing him with his sleeve pinned up and walking with a limp stung my heart. Yet the young men of many families will never come home. Many of us were waiting for him at the ferry landing. Graham's mother rushed forward with joy as she took her son in her arms. He was alive! At that moment, nothing else mattered.

I received letters from Wallace and Leith for Christmas, both mailed months before. Wallace will be transferred to Egypt shortly, something to do with the Suez Canal—perhaps he is already there—and Leith is still on duty in India. So many ships are being sunk that I cannot help worrying. I wonder if war is worse in some ways for wives and mothers than for their husbands and fathers. I suppose that can't really be true. But the men at least have something to do, as frightening as it must be. I think the danger gives them courage to withstand much that would seem insurmountable to us. All we can do is wait . . . and hope . . . and worry . . . and pray.

Curiously, the war has brought an economic boon to the Shetlands. The men who are here have more work and better wages than ever. They can make as much in two days as in a week before the war. Many women have gone to work as well. The jobs are mostly in construction—new roads and buildings and barracks are being built everywhere, harbors improved, radio towers going up. There are also jobs on farms and in food production for anyone willing to go to the mainland. The steady stream of refugees from Norway has also increased the need for living accommodations and medical services. Shetland is positively bustling! Of course, we would trade it all to have the war over.

Bless you, my friend! Your letters have become such a joy helping sustain me through these dark days. How I long to share them with Moira and Delynn. I know they suspect *something* from the light in my eyes. But for now no one must know of Priscilla's duplicitousness until Ernest has returned. So I keep my secret correspondence with you to myself, and, like Mary, treasure it in my heart.

Yours,
Sally

84

OFFER OF A SECRET MISSION

APRIL 9, 1944
KIRKWALL, ORKNEY ISLANDS, SCOTLAND

Dear Emily,

I dream of you often, then wake up with the terrible reality of war filling the darkness. But things have been happening too fast for me to dwell on my loneliness for you. And being with Dad makes it bearable.

The war is shifting. The Allies are moving up through Italy and it is only a matter of time before Italy surrenders. The Russians are dealing the Germans heavy losses on the eastern front. With Eisenhower in command of the forces in Europe, big things are in the wind. There has been talk of an invasion of the Continent for two years. It is so top secret no one knows any details, but the sense is that it may be imminent.

However, I have become involved in one of the least known efforts of the war that probably few will ever hear about. It started several months ago when Dad asked if I would like to accompany him on a mission he was about to undertake for Mr. Churchill. He could arrange it, he said, with the people in naval operations I report to.

"You know about Dunkirk?" he asked.

"Of course," I said. "British soldiers stranded on the coast of France rescued by thousands of boats whisking them across the channel before they could be captured."

"Right you are. It is one of the great stories of the war. What few outside northern Scotland and the islands know," Dad went on, "is that a similar operation is under way between Norway and Shetland."

"I've heard something about it, though vaguely."

"Actually, I was involved getting the network set up years ago. I went on several unofficial scouting missions to the Continent in the late twenties and thirties."

"I remember a trip to the Continent the year after Emily came."

"I've not been involved much since. The network has grown more extensive than anyone envisioned. The missions are for younger men and fishermen."

"So what's it all about?" I asked.

"A secret fleet of Norwegian fishing boats is sailing under cover of night to avoid detection by German aircraft, chugging back and forth from Shetland to Norway, supplying the Norwegian underground with weapons and supplies, food and fuel and all manner of materiel. On the return voyages they ferry refugees from Norway to safety in Shetland. Many are then transported to mainland Scotland."

"How long has this been going on?"

"Almost for the entire war. Germans ruthlessly patrol the coast from Norway to southern France fearful of an Allied invasion. That's why the boats mostly operate in winter when darkness conceals a good part of the voyage and especially the landings on the Norwegian coast. But losses have actually been minimal."

"You're not thinking of going on one of these missions?" I asked.

"I'm afraid I am," replied my father. "Hopefully not a dangerous one. I'll be on one of their largest and safest vessels. Churchill needs me to make contact with a man who possesses information that could be vital to a possible invasion of the Continent."

"A spy . . . a German?"

"I am bound to secrecy. Actually I know

very little. I will only say that my knowledge of German may be helpful."

"Why you, Dad?"

"The identification of this man is one of the most closely guarded secrets of the war. No one else will have any idea who he is. He will have no identification. He must be met personally by someone who knows him by sight and can escort him safely to the Shetlands, and from there south to meet with Churchill."

"And that individual who knows him by sight . . ."

"Correct," Dad nodded. "That would be me."

"And if I asked how you know him by sight, that would probably also be beyond my security clearance?"

"I hate to pull rank on you, Brogan, my boy," smiled my father, "but I am afraid so. It is so top secret that even I don't know everything. Churchill tells me what to do and I do it. In any event, I will sail on a merchant vessel to Scalloway. There I will rendezvous with a Norwegian fishing crew that will take me across to Norway and back. It should be routine. I wondered if you would like to join me."

I stared back hardly knowing what to think.

"I don't know, Dad, it hardly sounds routine. I think you may have more courage and appetite for danger than me."

He laughed. "It will be an adventure. With you

living in America, how many adventures will we have together?"

Needless to say, I decided to join him—though the mission turned out less "routine" than he expected!

I am sorry, but I need to sign off for now. I will give you the rest of the story later. I want to write it all out in detail, though when I will have the chance, who can say. Maybe it will have to wait until I see you . . . which I hope will be soon.

All my love,
Brogan

85

THE SHETLAND BUS

FEBRUARY 5, 1946
WHALES REEF, SHETLAND ISLANDS,
SCOTLAND

Dear Emily,

I can hardly believe that I am writing to you from the Cottage on Whales Reef with the war over! For two years in my letters I have been promising to tell you the whole story of my Shetland bus adventure with Dad. But there's never been a time when I could sit down and write it all out until now. Being here at home, reliving it all again and laughing with Dad about all that happened, telling Sally and the others everything, it's like it happened yesterday. And with the war over and not having to worry about the mail, I know this fat packet of pages will get to you safely. I will be on my way home soon as well! Perhaps I will get there before my story does!

With that said, I will embark on telling you of our adventure. The conversation with Dad when he invited me to accompany him on the mission took place in February of 1944.

We set out the following week, reached Shetland, and sailed for Norway about midnight, hoping to be a third or more of the way by nightfall later that afternoon so as to approach the Norwegian coast during the darkness of the following night. I was fearfully sick for the first half of the trip. The quarters were cramped and the smell of fish and diesel as sickening as the movement of the sea. But my father was in great spirits, the oldest man on the vessel probably by two decades, talking and laughing with the men, even taking a turn at the wheel. I had no idea he even spoke Norwegian. Notwithstanding his age, the crew must have been told he was someone important because they treated him with an almost uncomfortable show of deference.

In spite of being sick, the sea wasn't as bad as it might have been for February. It was the North Atlantic, however, with all that implies. We bumped and swayed through the daylight hours. We heard aircraft above us twice. But maneuvering through patchy fog, the skipper kept us out of sight. As evening descended and feeling better, I drifted to sleep and thankfully slept on and off most of the night.

When I next awoke I could tell from the sound of the engine that we had slowed. I went up onto the deck into the chilly gray of dawn. We were making our way through the placid waters of a narrow fjord somewhere on the Norwegian coast. The crew was busily pretending to be coming in from a night of fishing in case we were spotted. No one spoke. We crept along at three or four knots. The air felt pregnant with danger. The mere sight of the shoreline seemed ominous knowing that it was patrolled by Nazis, and that a German lookout might be watching us through binoculars at that very moment.

We rounded a bend of the channel which by then was as narrow as a river. A village lay ahead. We entered a small harbor. The skipper cut his engine, and the crew quickly jumped onshore and tied off the boat. A man in a dark overcoat stood on the quay. The captain stepped off to meet him. They spoke a few words. The captain turned and motioned to my father.

"That's our contact," he said to me.

We stepped onto the quay. The man had already turned and was walking toward the village. We hastened after him. He did not speak as he led us through several narrow streets, into an alley, finally turning into a narrower lane. Halfway along it he stopped, opened a door into a nondescript row of connected houses, motioned us inside, then himself disappeared.

We were standing in complete darkness. A moment later a candle flickered. A woman appeared at the end of a hallway. She motioned us to come. We followed her around a corner, up a flight of stairs, and into a room. She lit another candle sitting on a table in the center of the room, then another in a stand attached to the wall.

"You wait," she said, "comfortable here."

My father said a few words in Norwegian. She nodded and left us.

"These would appear to be our day's quarters," said my father. "We will probably see no one else until night falls again."

I glanced around. Two mats lay on the floor, generously supplied with blankets and even the luxury of pillows. A door stood half open, revealing a closet-bathroom—another luxury we might not have been so fortunate to find. On the table was spread a feast—rolls and bread, with meats and various cheeses. We sat down on two wooden chairs. A minute or two later the door opened and the woman appeared again. She set a tray on the table in front of us, complete with cups, sugar, a jug of milk, and a steaming pot from which emanated the unmistakable aroma of tea.

To our profound expressions of gratitude, she smiled and disappeared for good.

"It appears we have everything we could wish for," said my father.

"Now what?" I asked.

"I'm not sure. We must wait to see what comes next."

While I still felt slight effects of nausea, we made a wonderful breakfast and talked for a while, keeping our voices to a whisper. Though having slept on the crossing, I grew drowsy and was soon asleep on one of the mats. When I awoke, Dad was also asleep. I had nothing to occupy myself but my thoughts until he awoke. Whenever we were together the conversation flowed so rapidly that the time flew by.

The room had no windows. We had only the two candles, beginning to burn low but still with several hours of light remaining. Sometime after three we began to hear occasional dull noises elsewhere in the house.

"Nightfall is probably at hand," said my father. "We should probably have something to eat. We might not have another meal for some time."

What was left of the tea was cold. However, I must say, now that I was over the lingering effects of my seasickness, the rolls and goat cheese were as enjoyable as anything I have ever eaten.

Forty-five minutes or an hour later, the door opened again. A man appeared and motioned to us to follow. He carried a single candle that flickered as he led us through a narrow hall, up another short flight of stairs and along a hall until we came to what appeared a solid wall. The man knelt on the floor and rapped lightly. From the opposite side a portion of the wall began to open, revealing a low doorway surrounded by molding that rendered it invisible and without knob or other indication of its purpose. He crawled through. We knelt and followed. Another man met us on the opposite side. We found ourselves in an enormous attic among rafters, cobwebs, dust, and virtually no light except from a few scattered chinks in the roof above. The man closed the hidden door behind us. We crawled on our knees behind our new leader along planks laid across the joists. We made our way slowly for the entire length of the house adjoining that where we had been, finally emerging through another hidden door into the corridor of what might have been yet another dwelling.

We climbed to our feet. In the light of a dim

bulb hanging from the ceiling I saw that our guide was the same man who had met us at the harbor. We followed along several hallways, up and down more flights of stairs and around innumerable corners. At length he opened a door and we proceeded down a long, dark narrow stairway. From the dank smell I knew we were below ground. Having descended from the attic regions, we were entering the basement of a building, for all I could tell perhaps two or three houses removed from where we had waited.

Finally our guide stopped. A closed door stood before us. He motioned for us to enter, then entered himself and closed the door behind him.

The sight that met my eyes took my breath away.

We were indeed in the huge room of a basement, lit with electric lights, and filled with twenty-five or thirty people huddled on the floor around the room in groups—old and young, single men and women of all ages, and several families with small children. The warm smell of confined humanity was pungent. Every eye in the place rested on us as if we represented the salvation they had been waiting for.

I heard my father gasp involuntarily.

"They arrived two days ago," said our guide in perfect English. They were the first words he had spoken since meeting our boat that morning.

"They are desperate to get off the Continent. Their leader believes the Gestapo is following their movements—he has no idea why a small group such as theirs has attracted notice."

"They are Jews?" said my father, glancing around the room. "If so, that would be reason enough."

"He thinks there is more to it. So far from the centers of power, the few Gestapo we encounter are generally after important military personnel, as well as we of the underground, of course. This is simply a ragtag group of refugees."

"Perhaps it is you the Gestapo hope to find. Do you think they were followed?"

"Not when they reached us. They have been here two days. We have seen nothing untoward."

"Why have they not been transported?"

"They insist on remaining together. We have not had a vessel large enough since their arrival."

Dad glanced about the room again.

"Is the man you were sent for here?" I whispered.

"I will have to see," he replied softly. "This is not what I expected."

"What should we do?"

"I'm not exactly sure.—Lord, give us wisdom . . . and quickly," he added in a soft voice, obviously not speaking to me. "We may have to improvise. Our faithful captain is probably already waiting for us at the harbor."

As we had been whispering, a man from amongst the group approached.

"You are English," he said, "from Shetland?"

My father nodded.

"These people are with me," the man said. "We have come from Deutschland from those who know the fragrance of the rose."

A peculiar expression passed over my father's face at the words.

"Do you know what he means, Dad?" I asked.

"It is an escape network begun by a cousin of my old farmer friend," he whispered. "My debt to that family is more than I can ever repay. If I can complete what he began I will do so, especially with these lives depending on us."

"Those who love roses helped us across the Baltic and into Norway," the man went on. "I must get these people to safety. We are in grave danger. The Gestapo has hounded us from Denmark. If we are discovered, we will be sent to the camps."

"They are Jews, then?"

"We are all Jews . . . except for one who joined us in Hamburg."

"What do you know about him?"

"Nothing. But these are times one must trust. He has not betrayed us. He seems as fearful as the rest."

"I see," nodded my father. Dad thought a moment. "I would like to see everyone's papers before we decide what is to be done," he said.

The man turned and called softly into the crowded room. *"Zeigen Sie diesem Mann Ihre Papiere. Alle."*

A great shuffling took place, followed by a rustling of documents. My father walked slowly through the room, glancing at the papers shoved nervously toward him. He paid little attention but simply wanted to see who had papers and who did not. The room was silent except for the occasional murmur of a child as he made his way among them.

He came to a man standing toward the back, bedraggled and unshaven, looking like what I would have taken for a beggar on the streets of London. My father paused in front of him. He held out his empty palms and shook his head.

"Kein Papier?" said my father.

Again he shook his head. My father stared intently into his face, then moved on.

After a few minutes he returned to where I stood with the Norwegian who was apparently in charge.

"They will all come with us," said my father.

"The *Bergen* cannot hold so many," replied the Norwegian. "Larsen will not agree."

"Take me to him," rejoined my father. "Then

begin getting these people safely to the harbor by whatever means you do so."

"We move them in twos and threes, and by different routes. It will take an hour or more."

"Then begin immediately. I will take two with me."

He turned back to the Jewish man.

"Tell your people to get ready," he said. "You must split into small groups to be taken to the boat. They must be absolutely silent, and do exactly as this man tells them."

The German nodded.

"Two of the eldest will accompany me immediately. Organize the others as this man directs you. Come last yourself. When you arrive, we will know everyone is on board." He turned to me and added, "You come with the second group."

Within minutes Dad and the Norwegian left the basement with an elderly Jewish man and woman in tow. By then the room was in a considerable state of excitement. It was with difficulty that the German and I kept the noise to a minimum. The Norwegian returned half an hour later. He was accompanied by two women. It had been decided that an older man and his daughter, carrying her young son, would accompany me next.

"This woman will take you to the harbor," the Norwegian said to me, indicating one of the two. "She speaks no English, but you may trust her with your life."

He turned to the Jew in charge of the group. "Do your people know they must not breathe so much as a sound?"

The man nodded, then spoke a few words in German to the old man and woman. They nodded vigorously. With that, the five of us left the basement.

The woman led us up the flight of stairs, followed by the mother and her son, then her father. I brought up the rear. When we emerged into the chilly air a few minutes later, the village was quiet and dark. A heavy mist was so thick it felt like a light rain. The woman glanced back, pressed a finger to her lips in final warning, then we set out. She led through back streets and alleys, making more turns in so many directions that it would have been impossible to remember. After a much longer walk than Dad and I had taken after our arrival, we emerged from the cover of buildings and saw the harbor in front of us. She pointed toward the boat that was waiting for us. I now took the lead. When I looked back to make sure the man and his daughter were following, our guide had disappeared.

We reached the boat. My father stood at the rail. He helped the man and woman aboard with her son and led us below, reminding the three again that silence was imperative. There the two who had preceded us sat in the dark hold.

"Anything you need me to do, Dad?" I whispered.

"Actually . . . yes," he replied. "Wait up top and bring the others below as they arrive. Since I speak German, I will stay here to make sure they don't get talkative."

I went back up onto the main deck. The captain and his crew made no appearance. They were waiting in the wheelhouse, anxious to get under way. I wondered how my father had persuaded the captain to take so many refugees. He later told me that to the captain's original refusal he had reminded him that his explicit mission was to get my father safely to Norway and back to Shetland with whomever he had with him. If that meant twenty-five Jews, the orders stood. If he refused, my father said he would stay behind and await a vessel that would transport them all. The captain was free to go without him, and then explain to British naval authorities in Scalloway why he had returned empty-handed. The man had apparently grasped the force of my father's argument since he was now cooling his heels until the entire consignment of human cargo was aboard.

That process took eighty or ninety minutes. At last the German appeared with the final three of his group, including the beggar-looking man.

Even as they were stepping off the quay onto the deck, our Norwegian guide was disappearing into the night. The engine exploded into life, and slowly the *Bergen* inched away from the pier.

As quiet as we had tried to be, the slow *tonk-tonk-tonk* of the single-cylinder engine was so loud it seemed it would wake the countryside for miles. If a German patrol had been nearby, our voyage might have ended before it began. But the vast coastline of Norway, with its innumerable fjords and inlets, was impossible to patrol in its entirety. That thousands of fishermen continued to fish the waters offshore for the legitimate purpose of helping feed a nation disguised to some degree the activities of the Shetland bus. There were spies everywhere of course. Loyalty to homeland had been replaced in most Nazi-occupied countries by fear and the instinct to survive. German sympathizers and informants therefore probably outnumbered those willing to risk their lives in the underground resistance.

The Arctic whaler, one of the fastest boats in the rescue fleet, gradually picked up speed. The whole idea was to get far enough out to sea during the hours of darkness as to be beyond sight of the German planes patrolling the coastline. Once under way, the ban on talk was lifted. The engine was making too much noise for our voices to be heard anyway. The refugees in the hold were now in a bedlam of excitement at last to be on their way to England—as they called all of Britain. Though the idea was an anathema to most Scots, in their eyes we were all "Englanders." There was little food on board. No one had expected so many. But there was plenty of water and enough bread and apples and dried fish to satisfy the hunger of the children.

We were well out to sea by midnight. Those of the Jews who were not sick were dozing. I felt like a seasoned seaman now that the nausea of the first crossing was past. The hold was full, and as fishing boats such as the *Bergen* had not been designed for comfort, what sleep I managed, which wasn't much, was in lying down on the deck against a pile of damp, salty, smelly nets.

Dawn found us in the middle of the North Atlantic under gray skies that threatened rain. The boat's passengers came and went from below all day, if for no other reason than to stretch their legs and breathe fresh air. Concerned parents kept the children below, though many of them were sick and the smell of confinement was anything but pleasant.

Another night came, longer and more monotonous than the first. Hunger was more noticeable. The crew doled out what rations were available.

By the morning of our second day at sea we

were approaching Shetland from the northeast. Most of the men were on deck, spirits generally high in the knowledge that we had made it safely this far. Midway through the morning, however, suddenly the captain cried out, "German battle cruiser off starboard! All passengers below deck! Crew—nets out!"

I glanced about as we hurried below. On the horizon the cruiser was unmistakable, apparently returning toward Norway from duty in the North Atlantic. Wherever it had been, it must be off course to be sailing so close to Shetland, unless it was on a surveillance mission. The crew scurried to adopt their fishing disguise in hopes that the cruiser would take no notice and pass us by.

The next hour was tense. Above us we heard the crew shouting and bustling with their nets as if nothing was out of the ordinary. The cruiser had veered toward us, came within two or three thousand yards, then steered away back in the direction of Norway. About the time it was out of sight and the captain gave a shout of all-clear, one of the crew called out that the Shetland coast was faintly visible ahead.

The hold emptied. We all clambered up into daylight, with shouts of rejoicing spreading through the small ship. For another hour we inched closer as everyone stared at the slowly enlarging coastline.

Gradually, however, another sound came faintly mingling with our engine. Several of the crew stood at the stern railing, peering with binoculars toward the horizon behind us. Conversation stilled. It did not take long before the sound of aircraft could clearly be heard.

"The cruiser must have radioed ahead!" shouted one of the men. "Everyone below deck. Prepare for attack."

Beside me, my father did not seem to hear. He was scanning the coastline in the opposite direction, now probably about two miles distant. Glancing quickly about the boat, his eyes fell on two life rafts. He ran up to the wheelhouse to confer with the captain. By then I was scrambling below.

Two minutes later my father came hurrying down into the hold. He glanced about the mass of humanity, signaled to the bedraggled man without papers.

"Brogan," he said, "come up top."

We both followed him up the steep stairway into the daylight. Across the deck two of the crew were lowering a life raft into the water.

"I need you to get this man to shore," Dad said to me. "We're in too much danger exposed like this. He has to get to London. The dinghy has a motor with enough fuel to make it. The plane will concentrate its attack on us. If you are far enough away, they may not see you at all."

"I'm no sailor!" I laughed. Then I realized my father was deadly serious.

"Nothing to it," he said. "You're a Shetlander. We were born with webbed feet. Just point toward the shore and steer with the handle of the engine. It's impossible to sink these rubber dinghies."

"Why not you, Dad? You're more likely to get him through. I'll stay with the boat."

"If only one of us is going to live through this, I want it to be you," he replied. "Your life is ahead of you. You have a wife and a young son. My family is grown and I am at peace."

I stared back as the reality of what he was saying finally sunk in.

"Once you're ashore, find anyone to help you get to Scalloway," Dad continued quickly, "then back to Orkney. In my briefcase in our flat you will find my document of identification from Churchill. Guard it with your life. Find a transport, use your influence, and mine, and get to London. Present yourself at Number Ten. You *must* get this man to Churchill. With my letter of identification, tell whoever is in charge, 'Ernest Tulloch has brought a message for Mr. Churchill.' When you are allowed to see him, tell Winston, 'This is the man you sent Ernest Tulloch to Norway to bring you.'"

"But Dad—"

"You will be fine. Get to shore and get this

man to London. Do not let him out of your sight. Now go. I love you, and Godspeed."

I blinked hard, realizing, if worse came to worst, that he was saying good-bye.

Further objection was useless. Dad hugged me. I'm afraid I rather clung to him. But he stepped back quickly. To delay endangered my life as well as his.

Already someone was throwing a life vest over my neck and strapping it to my chest and bustling us into the dinghy. One of the crewmen had the small motor whirring. "You, front," he said to the German. "You, back," he added to me. "Hold handle . . . turn slow . . . not capsize."

Within another two minutes we were sputtering away from the *Bergen*. I was still almost in a daze at the sudden developments. But I had no choice but to do my best. I clutched the handle and inched the motor gently to the right and left, feeling the sensitive maneuverability of the small craft. Quickly we were bouncing up and down in the waves. A pang of terror shot through me as we went sailing up over a swell, then crashed down into the trough beyond it. I hoped Dad was right about not being able to sink these things!

The moment we were away, the captain of the *Bergen* veered sharply north. I watched as she powered away. By the time the plane reached the site, we were separated by hundreds of yards.

Explosions of gunfire burst out as the plane dove toward the whaler. I saw no sign whether or not she was hit. The gunfire stopped. The plane arched up and circled back for another attack. By the time gunfire echoed out again, we had covered enough of the distance that I was peering ahead for a suitable landing site.

I spotted a narrow stretch of pebbly beach that appeared free from jagged outcroppings or reefs, and made for it. Twenty or so minutes later we slid up onto the rocks. I cut the engine and we jumped out and together pulled the dinghy well up the shore. I glanced back and was just able to make out the *Bergen* in the distance. A thin trail of smoke rose from it, though if it had been hit it still had power. So close to the coast, the airplane had by now broken off the attack.

We ran up onto the plateau and glanced about. A croft lay about a mile inland. What a sight—white smoke from a peat fire rising from the chimney! We set off at an easy run. I had no idea where we were. It turned out we had struck the eastern shore of Whalsay Island, which lay only about five miles south of the small harbor of Lunna where the Shetland bus had originated four years earlier. The elderly crofter saw us coming from some way off and was naturally wary. A few words from me, however, in thick

Shetlandic made him instantly our friend. I told him we had abandoned a whaler bringing refugees from Norway, telling him where we left our dinghy.

From his proximity to Lunna, the man knew all about the rescue fleet. He brought us inside to his gray-haired wife, who gave us tea and bread and cheese. I stressed my urgent need to get to the naval base at Scalloway or Lerwick. In a cart hitched to two small ponies, we were soon on our way the two miles to Symbister on the south of the island. There the man's cousin was enlisted to sail us in his twenty-foot fishing boat across the sound to Voe.

Without going into the details of our journey and all the people who helped us—Shetlanders will do anything to help a fellow Shetlander—we arrived in Lerwick before nightfall. I went to the U.S. naval headquarters, identified myself and told what I was at liberty to say about my mission, which was that I had to reach Kirkwall as soon as possible.

Fortunately the admiral in charge believed me. My strange companion, who had still not uttered a word, and I were on a ship bound for the Orkneys that same night. We arrived in Scapa about daybreak. All this time I had no idea where my father might be, if he was still alive, or what had been the fate of the *Bergen*.

I retrieved Dad's document from our flat.

My immediate superiors in Kirkwall had been shown the paper when Dad requested my leave to accompany him. They did not doubt me when I now stressed that it was a matter of the utmost urgency that I get to London. Without saying so explicitly, I hinted that Dad and I were on a mission for the prime minister. They arranged for a flight from Kirkwall to Aberdeen. Before leaving Orkney we both had showers and a meal and we were able to get into fresh clothes. By evening we had landed in Aberdeen and were on an overnight train bound for London.

As Dad had instructed me, I went to Downing Street. Obviously I could get nowhere near the place. I asked to see the highest ranking man of the guard detail. I pulled out Dad's paper. "I have a message that must be delivered to Mr. Churchill immediately," I said. "Tell him that I am the son of Ernest Tulloch and that I bring him a message from Mr. Tulloch."

Expressionless, the man glanced over the paper, then left us. We waited perhaps thirty minutes for his return.

"The prime minister is at naval head-quarters," he said. "I have been instructed to take you to him."

We were promptly spirited away, deposited into the back of a black car, and were soon speeding through the streets. When we stopped, the door of the car opened and several guards took charge of us. They led us into a heavily guarded nondescript building, through a maze of corridors, and finally deep underground into a labyrinth of rooms crawling with high-ranking personnel of the Royal Navy. At last we were shown into a room where the first sensation to greet us was the smell of cigar smoke.

From behind a desk, a familiar form rose and gestured for us to take seats.

"So you're the son of Colonel Tulloch," rasped the voice I knew well from the wireless.

"Yes, sir. I am Brogan Tulloch. This is the man you sent my father to Norway to bring you."

"Well, young Tulloch, you have done well, as I would expect from Ernie's son."

"Thank you, sir."

"Actually, I was expecting you. I received a cable from your father just about an hour ago."

"He's safe, then!" I exclaimed.

"Yes, but it was a close one. The vessel was hit by German fire . . . one of the crew was killed actually, and your father received some nasty wounds from shell splinters. The ship was rather badly damaged, but they returned fire long enough to keep the plane at bay until it gave up the attack. The rudder was crippled, but they limped into the waters between Yell and the mainland of north Shetland. They just arrived a few hours ago, and your father cabled me immediately."

"And the refugees?"

"All safe. They managed to put in at Lunna and should be to Lerwick by tonight."

"That is good news," I sighed. "Are my father's wounds serious?"

"You know Ernie," chuckled Churchill. "If they were, he would not tell me so as not to worry you. But from the sounds of it, not so bad."

Churchill now turned to the human cargo I had delivered.

"So, Herr Schmidt," he said, extending his hand, "welcome to England."

"Thank you, sir," said the German in perfect English. "I was not sure I would get here at all. The Gestapo has been sniffing at my heels ever since I went missing in Berlin. I'm afraid I put a party of some Jews in more danger than I liked. But for the sake of defeating the madman calling himself Führer, I felt I had no alternative."

The man turned to me with a smile. "Thank you for helping bring me safely through," he said. "Please also thank your father for his courage on my behalf."

"Well, young Tulloch," said Churchill, "there is a war on, and this gentleman has risked his life and come a great distance to speak with me in private. I have arranged for you to be put up at one of our fine hotels."

"Mostly I am anxious to rejoin my father in Kirkwall."

"I understand. In the meantime," he said, "this pass will get you to the front of the queue for railway transport or for anything you need at no expense." He handed me a card that read, *On the business of the prime minister,* with Churchill's seal and signature emblazoned on it. "You have my heartfelt thanks on behalf of the war effort."

"Thank you, sir."

He shook my hand, then opened the door. I was taken charge of by a guard, who led me out of the building and to the hotel they had arranged for me. I had a nice dinner that evening, slept for ten hours, and was on a train back north the following morning.

By the time I reached Kirkwall, Dad was at the flat. His arm was in a sling but otherwise he looked fine. Our reunion was almost as emotional as our first meeting outside Mrs. Nicholson's tea shop!

It had been quite an adventure. I think we were both ready to resume our normal duties. As it turned out, my "normal duties," if anything in a war can be called normal, soon involved arranging for U.S. naval assistance to the activities of the Shetland bus in the form of American submarine chasers. This made the crossings to Norway much safer. I've actually made the crossing myself again twice—but more on that later.

86

SERIOUS INTERVIEWS

FEBRUARY 8, 1946
WHALES REEF, SHETLAND ISLANDS,
SCOTLAND

Dear Emily,

I am still on Whales Reef! Hopefully the account of our adventure reached you. Now I am back to the present and will tell you about my visit here.

Everyone is well and sends their love. Sally went on and on about her correspondence with you. She said it made the final years of the war endurable. I shared some of your letters to me these past two years—I hope you don't mind. I have met Leith's wife and more nieces and nephews than I can count, and renewed many old friendships—especially with Delynn, Leith, and Wallace. It is humbling to realize how much they truly love me . . . and of course, I them. Sadly my time here will be all too brief. However, I have been waiting too long already for a spot on one of the transport ships back to the States. I do not intend to miss my chance to return home . . . and to you! The evacuation of GIs from Europe has been as massive an undertaking as getting them here in the first place. Hundreds of British wives have also been waiting months to join their new husbands in the U.S.!

After the armistice I was back in London most of the time, helping with transportation logistics for the American wounded. Dad returned home soon after V-E Day. My volunteer obligations came to an end a week ago. I immediately took the train north. Neither Dad nor Sally had breathed a word of my reunion with him in Kirkwall. Not a soul knew I was coming.

Dad had been thinking and praying since our meeting about how to handle the situation with Wallace and Priscilla. He had been seeking the *right* response, not an easy thing to discern in such circumstances where human emotions obviously run high, and misinformation colors everything.

When I arrived on Shetland, Dad met the overnight ferry from Aberdeen in Lerwick. Before going to the Cottage to greet Sally and the others, he told me there were two calls he wanted us to make.

In order to confirm his and Sally's suspicions beyond a shadow of a doubt, our first stop was at the village post office. Dad got out, glanced up and down the street to make sure no one would see me, then we went inside.

"Hello, Jamie," he said as the postman greeted him. "I don't believe you know my eldest son, Brogan.—Brogan, say hello to Jamie Colquhoun. He bought the shop from Ian Morrison about the time you left for America."

"I am pleased to meet you," I said, as we shook hands.

My father quickly spoke again. "I would like to ask you to close the shop for a few minutes," he said. "I need to have a talk with you and your daughter."

The serious expression on my father's face was enough to cause the man noticeable concern.

"Aye, laird," he nodded compliantly. He went to the door, locked it, and pulled down the shade. "She's jist upstairs, I'll fetch her for ye."

We waited as the man disappeared through a door behind his counter. "Chloe, come doon!" he called as he ran up the stairs. "The laird's here tae see ye."

I could see in my father's eyes that the interview with the girl would be as unpleasant for him as for her. He did not relish what the responsibility of his position occasionally required of him.

When she followed her father into the shop a minute later, the look on the girl's face as her eyes flitted between us was the fear of an animal suddenly finding itself trapped. Though in her late twenties, she carried herself with the bearing of a young teen, as my father had given me to expect.

"Hello, Chloe," said my father. "This is my son, Brogan Tulloch. He lives in America. I believe you recognize the name."

"I, uh . . . I dinna ken, sir," she said slowly.

"You may not remember his face. But I believe you have seen his name . . . on letters coming through the post, haven't you, Chloe?"

She looked down at the floor and remained silent.

"You are a good friend of my daughter-in-law, Priscilla, aren't you, Chloe?" my father continued.

"Yes, sir," she answered in a soft voice, still staring down.

"If she asked you to do something, you would want to do it, wouldn't you?"

"I dinna ken, sir."

"Chloe, you have to tell me the truth."

"What mischief hae ye been up til, Chloe?" began her father. A quick glance and gesture from my father, however, silenced him.

"Chloe," my father said, "you *must* tell me the truth. Tampering with the mail is a serious matter. It is a crime, Chloe. You and your father could face unpleasant consequences. Now tell me why you recognize my son Brogan's name."

Her lips began to quiver. The girl looked at me, but her eyes quickly darted away.

"They was on the letters, sir," she blurted out, beginning to cry.

"What letters, Chloe?"

"Letters tae yersel', sir, an' Lady Sally an' Mr. Wallace, an' letters that ye sent til him in America."

"What did Priscilla tell you to do?"

"Tae bring her the letters!" the girl wailed, bursting into a fit of sobbing.

By now Colquhoun himself was fairly in a rage. I think he was anxious for us to leave so that he could give his daughter, in spite of her age, a whipping she would not soon forget. My father, however, continued to exude calm and did not allow him to intervene. If vengeance was the Lord's, in this case it was also the laird's.

"Do you know what she did with the letters, Chloe?" asked my father.

"No, sir?"

"Do you know if she still has them?"

"I dinna ken, sir."

"What did she do when you gave her the letters?"

"Patted me on the heid, sir, an' gae me a bob an' said I was a good girl."

"I see. All right, then."

Dad thought a moment. After a few seconds,

as she stood trembling in front of him, he again returned his gaze into her eyes.

"What you have done is very serious, Chloe," he said. "Do you understand that?"

"Aye, sir," she whimpered.

"Do you know what accountability is, Chloe?"

"I dinna ken, sir."

"It means taking responsibility for your actions. It means being honest and admitting what you have done. It means being willing to face the consequences. It means more than just apologizing, it means being sorry. What do you want to do now, Chloe?"

"I'm sorry, sir."

"Good. That is the best starting point for righting any wrong—saying you are sorry. Are you sorry inside, Chloe?"

"Aye, sir."

"*Why* are you sorry, Chloe?"

"Because I did wrong, sir."

"Who did you do wrong to, Chloe?"

"Yersel', sir."

"And who else?"

She sent a quick glance in my direction. "Tae Mr. Brogan, sir."

"Do you have anything to say to him?"

"I'm sorry, Mr. Brogan."

I smiled and nodded.

"But, Chloe," my father went on, "what you have done was not just wrong toward us—

you broke the law. That could get your father into a great deal of trouble."

"You winna let them put me in jail, will ye, sir?" she said, beginning to cry again.

"I do not think that will be necessary, Chloe. But you will have to make restitution."

"What's that, sir?"

"You must pay back what was stolen from all of us, and apologize to those you wronged—that means Lady Sally and Mr. Wallace and Brogan's wife in America." He paused. "That includes Lady Priscilla as well," he added. "You wronged her by allowing her to do wrong. When we help another person do wrong, that is just as wrong as what they have done. You need to apologize to everyone, either in person or by writing them a letter. You need to tell them what you did, that you know it was wrong, then ask their forgiveness. You must also apologize to your father. He trusted you to work for him and you wronged him too—not only for what you did but also keeping it a secret from him. This will be a very hard thing to do. But it is the only way to be clean. You will feel much happier after you have apologized. Do you think you can do that, Chloe?"

"I will try, sir."

"Then you will have to pay back the money for all the stamps that were used for letters that were not mailed or delivered. You will not be able to work in the post until that debt is paid. And you need to pay back all the shilling coins that Lady Priscilla gave you. That was dishonest money. Altogether it could be ten or fifteen pounds, Chloe. The debt has to be paid. That is part of accountability and restitution. Whether the debt of our wrong toward others is a farthing or a thousand pounds, it must be paid so that we can be clean again."

"But I haena ten pounds, sir."

"I understand. But I believe Lady Sally could use some help at the Cottage. And I may need help with my ponies. We will pay you for your work for us."

"Wi' the ponies, sir?" she said, immediately brightening. "The wee ponies?"

"Aye, Chloe, the wee ponies. Would you like to help me feed and clean up after them?"

"Oh aye, sir!"

Dad turned again to the girl's father. "We shall speak of this no more, Jamie," he said. "I would consider it a personal favor to me for you to have no words about it with your daughter. Leave her to me. I will let you know when her debt is paid and she can go back to work."

"Thank ye, laird, sir," nodded Colquhoun.

"But remember, Chloe," my father said as we turned toward the door, "you must apologize to all you wronged. When you are ready, you must go to them and ask forgiveness. If you need help knowing what to say to Lady Priscilla, especially when you take the money to pay back what she gave you, you and I will have another talk and I will help you. I will go with you if you want me to. You may forget much of what I have told you just now, but we will talk about these things again. For now, come to the Cottage tomorrow morning at ten. Then you and I will get busy feeding the wee ponies."

"Yes, sir," she said, for the first time looking up into my father's face with the hint of a smile as she wiped at her eyes. "Thank ye, sir. I winna do anythin' like it agin."

"I know you won't, Chloe. I will see you at the Cottage tomorrow morning."

A sad Colquhoun opened the door, and we left the shop.

"Hearing you speak to her so gently but firmly," I said as we returned to the car, "was like being a boy again. That's exactly how you spoke to us about serious matters—kindly, slowly, gently . . . always pointing us toward higher truths that it would take us years to understand, and always providing us with a way to make restitution. Even with your punishment, you gave us the means to make things right and move into forgiveness. Thank you for that, Dad. It was a great example. I've wanted to tell you that for a long time."

My father merely smiled in gratitude. It was a knowing smile, as if he already knew I had internalized that lesson from my early years.

Turning the Studebaker around, Dad drove back through the village the way we had come. Our next stop was at the Auld Hoose. Dad wanted to confront Priscilla before she found out I was on the island.

He parked in front of the house. We walked toward it and he lifted the brass knocker. A girl of six or seven scampered to the door and opened it.

"Hello, Isla," said my father. "Would you please tell your father and mother I would like to see them?"

She turned and ran into the house. "Mummy," she called out. "Grandfather is here with a man. He wants to see you and Papa."

We stood at the open door and waited. Footsteps approached. A moment later Priscilla was standing before us.

She had clearly aged since I had last seen her. Streaks of gray were visible in the dark brown of her hair. I was stunned at what a handsome and imposing woman she still was in her late forties, yet cold and hard. At sight of us, one eye squinted, and her cheeks blanched slightly. Otherwise she retained her poise. Flashing daggers at my father, her gaze drifted toward me. For a brief instant her eyes bored into mine almost, I thought, in challenge, as if warning me not to start anything. All this took place in a mere heartbeat.

"Wallace," she called into the house. "We have visitors."

The three of us stood and waited.

I don't know exactly what I had expected. In spite of the eighteen years that had elapsed since we had seen one another, Wallace knew me immediately. His face lit in a radiant smile.

"Brogan!" he cried. The next instant I was smothered in his embrace.

"But why . . . what in the world brings you here?" he stammered, stepping back and looking me over. "Were you here in the war?"

"I was," I replied. "I'm heading home next week. I'm only here for a brief visit."

"It is so good to see you. I have missed you!"

"And I you."

"How long have you been on the island?"

"Only just. Dad picked me up in Lerwick. My bags are in the car—I haven't even been to the Cottage."

"Gosh . . . we have so much to talk about! Come in, come in! And the question I've been wanting to ask for years—why did you stop writing? What did I do to hurt you?"

I glanced toward my father.

"That is actually why we are here, Wallace," Dad said soberly. "You and Brogan will have opportunity to catch up on the lost years. First, however, we need to inquire into why those years were lost."

Priscilla had been standing, calmly listening to our reunion with an expression that made it obvious she did not share our joy. If she knew what was about to come out, she gave no indication of it. Presumably she thought the secret of her postal shenanigans still safe.

"Therefore," Dad went on, still speaking to Wallace, "it is to your wife, not your brother, that you should perhaps direct your question."

A puzzled expression came over Wallace's face. Priscilla remained implacable, staring venomously at my father as we stood in the doorway.

Dad turned toward her. "We came here first, Priscilla," he said, "to speak primarily to you."

Still perplexed, Wallace looked toward Priscilla for some glimmer or hint of what this was all about.

"The truly remarkable thing," I now said, "must be Priscilla's seeing you and me and Dad together. She was under the impression that Dad was dead and that you never wanted to speak to me again."

"What!" exclaimed Wallace.

Priscilla did not so much as glance toward me. She continued to stare daggers at my father, as if she could cow him by sheer force.

He returned her stare calmly, then addressed her again. "We have come to ask you, Priscilla, if you are ready to repent?"

The silence that followed was long and heavy with ominous forebodings.

"You dare ask me such a question?" she said at length, spitting out the words with slow precision.

"Are you ready to repent?" my father repeated.

"It will be a cold day in hell before I will be subject to your inquisitions, Ernest!" she shot back. "What do I have to repent of?"

"I think you know that rather better than the rest of us," replied my father.

"Get out—leave my house! I'll not repent to you or anyone. I've done nothing wrong. I've got nothing to repent of."

Wallace at last found his voice. Emerging from his befuddlement, his first instinct was to come to his wife's defense. "What's this about?" he said. "Repentance . . . is such language really called for? A bit strong, isn't it?"

"I will let you decide whether it is called for, or is perhaps not strong enough, when you learn the truth of what she has done."

"But what has she done?"

"For one thing," I answered him, "telling me that Dad was dead and that you wanted nothing more to do with me."

Wallace stared blankly at me. He could make no sense of my words.

"She has sinned against us all, Wallace," Dad added, "yourself included. She has sinned against the universal Fatherhood and the universal brotherhood. As to specifics beyond what Brogan has just told you, I will leave her to explain for herself.—Priscilla," he added, turning again to his son's wife, "I am going to give you one more chance to make a clean breast of it. We know everything. Further pretense is useless. Now . . . will you repent of your sin?"

"Burn in hell, Ernest! You and your arrogance deserve the flames before I will ever repent to you!" She spun around and stormed into the house, slamming the door and leaving the three of us standing there in silence.

My father turned and walked toward the car.

"I will be at the Cottage," I said, offering Wallace my hand. He shook it, though he was clearly in shock and confusion. "It is truly good to see you," I added. "I'm sorry it had to be like this. When you know everything, you will understand."

I joined my father. No words were spoken until we reached the Cottage. I would not have relished being in Wallace's shoes when he returned inside.

He walked across the moor about an hour later. By then the Cottage was in an uproar over my presence. Word was quickly spreading through the village that the prodigal, so-called, had returned.

Priscilla divulged nothing to Wallace. My worry that she would unleash a torrent of verbal abuse on him turned out to be unfounded. My father remained taciturn, but Sally did not mind filling Wallace in on her correspondence with you and everything else. It turned out he knew nothing. He had been manipulated by Priscilla's confiscation of my letters into thinking I had cut him off. His apologies were sincere and heart-felt, though I detected what seemed a worrisome tendency to make excuses for his wife. His eyes had begun to open, yet I sensed that she still had a hold on him that would probably be difficult to break.

We later learned that Priscilla was on her way to the post office within thirty minutes of our visit. The ensuing interview with Jamie Colquhoun can have been no more pleasant for her than ours, culminating with his refusal to allow her to see his daughter. Priscilla was furious, but there was little she could do.

Hearing from other sources that Chloe Colquhoun spent the following day at the Cottage, she surely divined the truth. However, not another word was spoken about the letters. So far from being repentant, Priscilla carried herself more haughtily toward my father and Sally and Moira and the rest of the family than ever. She did not speak a word to me throughout my entire visit.

My days with Wallace and Leith and my father, however, have been rich beyond measure. To be in my father's study again, as a grown man—I cannot describe the emotions. Such talks we have had! He is eager to give me all his favorite books and half the Bibles from his collection. I will need an entire suitcase just for books! I think I am finally beginning to really know the man he is. One of the most astonishing realizations is that he seems as hungry and interested in my ideas and thoughts as I am in his. Though I am light-years behind him, he treats me as a complete spiritual equal.

I will be sailing for the States next week. Who knows, I may get there before this letter! I cannot wait to see you. I love you.

Your loving husband,
Brogan

87

Passing of an Era

SEPTEMBER 28, 1953
WHALES REEF, SHETLAND ISLANDS,
SCOTLAND

Dear Emily and Brogan,
  With deep heartache must inform you of death of Ernest Tulloch. *Stop.* Passed peacefully yesterday. *Stop.* Please reply via telegram soonest. *Stop.* Will delay funeral. *Stop.* Will have room at Cottage waiting!

Sally Tulloch

SEPTEMBER 29, 1953
BURLINGTON, NEW JERSEY, UNITED STATES

Dear Sally,
  Deepest heartfelt condolences. *Stop.* We grieve with you for a great man. *Stop.* Will arrive Southampton 8 October, Lerwick 10th. *Stop.* Possible delay funeral until 11 October? *Stop.* Emily sends best.

Much love,
Brogan

PART 15
MAY–JUNE 2007

88

THE LOCKET

Loni glanced up from the journal in her hand toward the stack of letters beside her. Together they told the same story. Tears filled her eyes at the final words she had just read. She had never dreamed that the two Shetland stories she had simultaneously been living in for the past year would merge with such a touching conclusion to the one and beginning of the other.

At last Emily's story had come full circle up to the day of Ernest's funeral, which she had heard about from Sandy Innes, and then further into the future until the day at last it crossed her own life. She had been totally unprepared for the final entry in the book she was holding.

It was early May. She had been back in Whales Reef a week.

Still conscious of preserving this room of the Cottage as much as possible as she first found it, she had yet moved a few things in the study around to make it more to her liking. The reading chair now sat angled slightly toward the window so she could look out toward the northern expanse of the island. From where she sat she gazed about the room. Her view offered a multitude of reminders of the spiritual legacy of her great-great-grandfather—his photograph on the wall, his favorite books lining the bookcases, his collection of Bibles that hadn't gone to the States with Brogan, the rolltop desk with its treasures, the files of his journals and writings.

She would never tire of simply *being* in this room. In manifold ways it represented the *Center* in the full Quaker sense. Like all deep spiritual truths, it had been long out of sight, a treasure buried and awaiting discovery.

And now that legacy, hidden for so long, had come down through Ernest's posterity to rest on her. How could she have dreamed during her early years that such a rich family tradition awaited her?

A small stack of books on a nearby table had become her greatest treasures—full of Ernest's markings, some signed to his sons and daughter, two among those she had discovered in Pennsylvania. Especially meaningful were the two identical copies of *Life at the Center*, each full of notes and underlinings, one in Ernest's hand and the other in Brogan's, revealing how remarkably the son had come to reflect and embrace the spiritual "center" he had been taught to seek by his father, and with the touching inscription from Ernest to Brogan: *From a father's heart to a son's, with the prayer I have prayed for you every day of your life, that you would discover and live in the center of God's love and purpose.*

Beside the books sat the letter box, with hers and Emily's journals and the box of letters next to it. In so many ways, the pages of her great-grandmother's journal had provided the touchstone for her own journey of discovery. How could Emily's story and her own and their experiences and discoveries of the two Tulloch men who changed their lives have been so remarkably parallel? Only one question remained: Where was Brogan's journal that Emily had mentioned? What a treasure that would be!

Loni's eyes drifted across the study to the framed photograph of Brogan and his father, Ernest, in his colonel's uniform, dated 1945. In spite of the serious business in which they were engaged, both faces wore broad smiles.

Gradually Loni's thoughts returned to the present. It was hard to believe that she would be married in a little over a month. The people of Whales Reef, though they had suspected it since last year, had finally been told of their plans. David had saved the actual announcement for Loni's return.

No one was surprised, though their hugs and congratulations were nonetheless enthusiastic. One after another of the women, each with winks and smiles, privately made sure Loni was aware that *she* had known how it was all along.

Loni continued to look about the room fondly. This study and this Cottage would no longer be hers alone. She and David would share all of life. Though they were still discussing whether to start their lives together at the chief's Auld Hoose or the laird's Cottage, and what to do with the second of the two family homes, one thing was certain—they would share *this* room.

Loni now reached for the letter box and removed the necklace with its gold locket, a gift she now knew that Brogan had brought for Emily from London when he returned from the war. Carefully she unclasped the locket and squinted down at the photograph of Emily Hanson Tulloch.

As she gazed again at the tiny miniature, the years seemed to fade away. Loni could almost hear her great-grandmother speaking, her voice distant, as if to Loni herself, of those years of long ago.

Loni looked down again on the last page of Emily's journal that had sent her reflections along so many deep emotional pathways.

When Brogan and I left Whales Reef in 1953 after Ernest's funeral, how could we have known that we would return only once more, for a single visit in the early 1960s? It was sad for Brogan in a way to see the village of his boyhood changing. The tumultuous sixties extended their influence even to such a distant place as Whales Reef. The young people were listening to Elvis and The Beatles. Even I could see the change. There were fewer shops than thirty years earlier.

By then Priscilla's health was failing. She had suffered a stroke and was never the same afterward. Bitterness, greed, and anger all take their toll on the human body as well as the soul. As far as anyone knew, she never repented nor apologized for the division she had sown in so many lives. Indeed, for a time she tried to persuade Wallace to claim the chieftainship for himself from his younger brother. For once, however, Wallace stood up to her. Knowing Priscilla as he finally did, and as surprising as it may therefore have been for Ernest to pass control of the island's affairs over to him, Wallace did his best for the people and gradually grew impervious to Priscilla's attempted manipulations. After her death in 1964, Wallace seemed to blossom. What followed were probably the happiest years of his adult life.

Grant grew and took over the furniture business, was married to our dear daughter-in-law Mary, and they had a daughter, Alison. How quickly the years speed by. There is so much one dreams of doing, yet all too suddenly the bones ache, the steps slow, the face in the mirror becomes lined with the creases of age, the hair turns white.

Where does life go?

I hope it goes into the heart of God where nothing is forgotten. I have no serious regrets because I have indeed lived most of my dreams. If one pang saddens my heart it is that somehow the years caused us to lose touch with Brogan's family on the Shetlands. Grant never came to know that side of his family. By the time his young family was sending down roots, they were thorough Americans and I feared that Brogan's Shetland heritage was being lost sight of to those who followed us. But life moves too rapidly, and the past drifts into the mists and fades from view.

Our dear granddaughter Alison met a Quaker boy by the name of Chad Ford. He was from a devout Quaker family, though there were strains with his parents that Brogan and I knew little about. Grant and Mary were circumspect. All we knew was that there was an estrangement and that Chad had not seen his parents for some time. How do estrangements between Christians come? Why do families allow separations to keep them apart? Surely few things grieve God's heart more than disunity among his people.

Whatever the difficulties, Chad and Alison were married. The joy of their marriage was of course marred by the fact that it was not shared by Chad's parents. And for me the year was bittersweet. Only a few months later my dear Brogan, the love of my life, went to his true home.

I now wait to see him again. I feel my earthly frame weakening as the years take their toll. My hand is feeble as I write these words. I do not think it will be long before we are reunited on the great expansive moorland of heaven—what the Scotsman calls God's high tableland where there are no separations. I wonder if there will be puffins there!

Three years later Alison gave birth to a daughter.

Though age brings pains and griefs, it also brings the perspective to know what is important, the inner vision to sift life's wheat and chaff, and to know joy in the simplest of pleasures. Truly one of the happiest days of my life came when Alison put my tiny great-granddaughter into my arms, her precious little Alonnah. What a privilege to hold one's great-grandchild! It is a joy not all women are given to know.

I thank God that such a moment came to me.

My eyes filled with tears to behold the tiny face, all her years ahead as mine were now behind. What would this life bring, what stories would it tell? And I prayed that she would know life in all its fullness, that she would discover her Scottish heritage, and know God as her Creator and Friend.

"Dear Alonnah," I whispered, "you are precious in God's sight. You are greatly loved. Now live life, dear one, for you are God's daughter. Live and become all that lies in God's heart for you to be."

How poignant to realize that this dear lady, her own great-grandmother, went to join her Brogan on God's high tableland only a few months after holding her in her arms and praying for her and writing these words. She belonged to this family, Loni thought—not only to her grandparents who loved her and raised her but also to this island family who had shown her such love and acceptance.

She *belonged*.

Blinking back tears, Loni closed her eyes with a heart full of gratitude and peace.

89

NOSTALGIC MEMORIES

As the greatly anticipated wedding between the laird and chief approached, the whole village was in a frenzy of excitement. Nothing like this had *ever* been seen on Whales Reef. Interest in Loni's unlikely inheritance had gradually widened to encompass not only the Shetlands but also many on mainland Scotland. Her engagement to the young clan chief—anachronistic in the eyes of some modernists, yet deliciously romantic to those of more traditional bent—heightened interest in the wedding all the more. Journalists from newspapers and magazines and a half-dozen Sunday supplements descended on the small island, each with an angle he or she was anxious to explore. All Lerwick's hotels and bed-and-breakfasts were booked nearly to capacity. At David's request, the MacFarlane sisters were among the select few to have a room at the Whales Fin Inn. The two Americans had been dying to meet Loni since hearing the news of David's engagement. The rest of the inn had been reserved for the bride and groom's friends and relatives.

Loni and David picked up Loni's grandparents and two of Loni's cousins at the airport and brought them to the Cottage, where newlyweds Maddy and Tennyson Stafford were already settled. For two days, Maddy had eagerly been showing Tennyson all about the island and mainland Shetland, and renewing her friendship with Dougal Erskine. The gamekeeper was as taken with Maddy's new husband as he had been with Maddy herself, especially once their animated discussions turned to horseflesh, where each man was eager to learn from the other.

Though understandably fatigued after the long trip, William and Anabel Ford assured Loni they would not have missed this wedding if the trip killed them. The next morning William accompanied David out with the sheep and dogs and was enjoying the sea air immensely. That afternoon he and Loni spent an hour together in old Ernest's study. Thereafter, for the remainder of their visit, if Mr. Ford was not seen for a while, everyone knew where they would find him. Before their flight home, he had a dozen of the Auld Tulloch's books he had asked Loni to borrow, adding considerable extra weight to his and his wife's suitcases.

David would host several more of Loni's extended family from Pennsylvania at the Auld Hoose when they arrived, along with Margaret and Malcolm and a few other mainland relatives. Stirling Yates had returned to the island and was staying at the manse with Lincoln Rhodes.

When the day before the wedding arrived, the island's population had swelled to double its normal size. Excitement was in the air.

With the final preparations made and all the guests on hand, the food for the reception and every detail attended to by a platoon of village women, with the outlook calling for sunny skies, with the church filled with flowers, and with the massive white tent and all needful accouterments for the reception celebration set up in front of the mill, Loni left the Cottage and struck out in the direction of the sea. There were not many places on this island to be alone, especially with it swarming with visitors. But she wanted to find a few minutes to herself to reflect on the unlikely journey that had brought her to this moment.

Full of memories of her first visit to the island a year before, in her mind's eye as she walked away from the Cottage she saw Sandy Innes standing along the road. She could still hear his first words to her.

Are you waiting for someone? she had asked him.

Aye, miss, Sandy had replied. *I've been waitin' for yersel'... I knew ye would come... though ye're a mite taller than I expected.*

Loni smiled as she recalled Sandy's cryptic words.

Her spirit's been here all these many years.

I see her in yer eyes . . . yer grit-gran'mither, as near as I can make it oot . . . Over eighty years syne I first laid eyes on her . . . I was but a wee tyke back then. But I mind the day weel. . . .

Loni walked on, pleasant nostalgic feelings sweeping through her.

A few days later had come her first fateful meeting with the man who would soon be her husband. Again she smiled as she recalled opening the door to see him standing and holding the tiny sprig of heather. His voice in her memory was was clear as if he were speaking at this moment.

It seems a rather paltry gift now, but it is all I have to offer. I am David Tulloch. I came by to welcome you to Whales Reef.

Almost as if her reminiscences about Sandy had produced her out of her own thoughts, ahead on the stone bench where she had spent so much time and where Emily had written her first journal entry, Loni now saw Sandy's daughter.

"Hello, Odara," said Loni as she approached. "You are a long way from home."

"Not such a long walk, if I dinna hurry," said Odara. "So, lassie, hoo are ye feelin'? Oot for one last walk in the Summer Dim afore yer big day?"

"A good time to reflect, wouldn't you say?" replied Loni, sitting down beside her. "So much has happened in a year. Occasionally I need to slow down and try to take it all in."

"Are ye ready tae be a chief's wife?"

"If I'm not ready now, I never will be!" laughed Loni. "But if you're asking if I have any doubts—no, none at all."

"Are ye happy, lassie?"

"Do you need to ask? Yes, happier than ever in my life."

"Let me see yer ring again—yer *two* rings."

Odara gazed down at Loni's finger. "You appear almost as deep in thought as I have been," said Loni.

"Aye," smiled Odara pensively. "Your weddin' puts me in mind o' many things. I never married ye ken. We might hae done, I suppose. Sometimes lookin' back I wish we had. But at the time he thought it best the way it was."

"*We* . . . who do you mean?"

"Why, Macgregor, lassie."

"*You* . . . and Macgregor Tulloch?" said Loni in surprise. "But I thought . . ."

"Ye've heard o' the black rose at his buryin', nae doubt."

"I confess, I have been curious. People still talk about it."

Odara did not reply immediately.

"If I tell ye the meaning o' the rose," she said at length, "ye must promise tae let no word o' it leave yer lips. I winna hae the auld wives trample on my memories wi' their palaverin'."

"I promise," said Loni seriously. "Whatever you have to tell me will remain between you and me."

Odara drew in a long and thoughtful breath. "There are many tales told aboot Macgregor," she began, "but there's only one who kens the whole truth 'o the man he was, an' that's me. . . ."

90

A Laird's Secret

Ye would never know it tae look at me noo, lassie, *Odara began,* but I was a pretty girl when I was yoong—too pretty for my own good. I suffered fae that curse o' pretty girls who ken that laddies look at them twice—I'm nae prood o' it, but I tried tae make them look at me, an' there's nothing worse tae character than wantin' tae be the center o' attention.

Like half the girls on the island, I took a fancy tae the laird's son Macgregor. That's Laird Wallace, ye ken. The laird was a kindly man, though Macgregor's mama, Lady Priscilla, was a mean-hearted woman, an' wasna kind tae Lady Sally after the Auld Laird died. But Macgregor took after his daddy not his mama, an' everyone on the island liked him, especially the lassies. Handsome tae make a girl go weak in the knee an' set her heart a-flutterin'. But he was eight years aulder than me an' what twenty-year-auld laddie would look twice at a twelve-year-old lassie like I was then?

It nearly broke my heart when he married the Norwegian woman. Her brother'd come til Shetland as a refugee in the war an' stayed. She came later an' bided wi' him an' then met Wallace. I was nineteen an' my friends knew that I'd been hopin' that he'd look at me one day an' take notice. I couldna be angry wi' him, but my friends hated him on account o' me, an' they spread dreadful tales aboot him tae spite him. As time went on there was never another laddie I fancied. Macgregor an' his new wife were mostly gone, travelin' an' the like. An' by then I wanted tae git off the island where folk insisted on talkin' aboot me an' my broken heart. I jist wanted tae forget an' I didn't like the other lassies feelin' sorry for me.

My daddy knew some wealthy folk in Lerwick whose ponies he took care o' who were needin' a lady's maid. He took me tae meet them an' I was hired an' went tae live wi' them. Gettin' oot o' Whales Reef was a relief, an' the family was good tae me. In a few years, seein' that I had an aptitude in the kitchen, they put me helpin' their cook, who was an elderly woman an' wouldna be workin' many more years. They sent me til a cookin' school for domestics doon in Perth. I took tae the cookin' like my daddy did tae animals. In another few years I became the cook o' the hoose. They gave me a flat o' my own, an' I was able tae see my family almost as often as I wanted, an' it was the kind o' job any poor girl like me would dream o'. An' they sent me back tae Perth tae learn new things every year or two. It was their way o' givin' me a holiday an' showin' me hoo they valued my cookin'. It was somethin' I looked forward to.

O' course I knew aboot poor Macgregor's divorce an' the terrible things bein' said o' him on account o' his wife . . . even that he killed her. It was all nonsense. I didna see him for years, but I never forgot him, an' I kenned it was all lies they were sayin' aboot him.

Sometimes growin' up in a small place where folk talk is a burden that canna be got rid of except by leavin'. Macgregor finally left Shetland an' went oot til India or someplace as a diplomat or somethin' in business. I never heard more than that he'd gone til the East. The witch Priscilla, while she was still alive, was so auld an' bitter an' decrepit that most o' the venom had gone oot o' her fangs, though her heart never repented for all the evil she had done an' all the divisions she had caused in the family. An' then after livin' as a widower for a good many years, an' happier he seemed as weel, wi' Priscilla gone, then his daddy, the laird Wallace, died an' Macgregor became laird.

Macgregor came back fae India an' took up the lairdship. He was forty-eight by then, though I hadn't seen him since afore he was married. I was still livin' in my flat in the city.

Then came a day I'll never forget, though I've told none but my own daddy aboot it in a' the years. I was at the farmer's market gittin' my fresh vegetables for the week. An' doon the street walkin' along came the handsomest man I'd ever seen. It was Macgregor himsel'. He was fifty-three an' I was forty-five. It was five years after he'd become laird.

I couldn't help starin' at him wi wide eyes, an' he saw me though I could tell he didna recognize me at first. His step slowed an' he came toward me. I smiled an' curtseyed like I'd been taught. He came an' stood in front o' me. Then slowly his face brightened.

"Odara?" he said like he still couldn't believe it was me.

"Aye, good day tae ye, Macgregor," I said.

"You're here . . . in Lerwick?"

"Aye, I'm cook tae the Bergrens, oot north o' the city."

"Yes, I know the family. Sandy mentioned it after I returned from the East. I was out in India before my father died."

"Aye, I heard aboot that."

"But, goodness . . . it is good to see you again! You are looking very well—and as pretty as ever."

"Thank ye, Macgregor. I'm sorry tae hear aboot yer wife leavin'."

A look of pain passed over his face, but he quickly smiled again.

"A long time ago," he said. "Water under the proverbial bridge. But enough of all that. Would you have time for a cup of tea with me? I'd love to have a visit."

An' we did. My heart skipped a bit, I admit, but I thought no more aboot it, until the next week at the market, an' I looked up an' there was Macgregor again. This time he had a sheepish smile on his face, not at all like what ye'd think o' a laird, ye ken.

"I hoped I might see you again," he said. "I've been waiting an hour."

"Ye've been waitin' for me?" I said, surprised like.

"I have indeed. I thought maybe we could have tea again."

This time we visited even longer an' I told him aboot the cookin' school an' that the Bergrens sent me til Perth every two years for a week an' hoo much I enjoyed it. He asked lots o' questions and where I stayed there, an' I told him that I'd be travelin' tae Perth at the end o' that month.

Again I thought little more o' it an' I didna see him at the market again. But imagine my surprise when he appeared at Perth.

"He went there to see you?" asked Loni.

Aye. I didna ken what tae think. An' he stayed the whole week an' we saw one another every evenin' an' it was like livin' in a dream tae be wi' the very man I thought I'd loved as a wee lassie.

That's hoo it began, an' we met like that in Perth every two years from then on. Somehow he always contrived a way tae see me. No one on the island ever knew. I dinna want ye tae git the wrong idea—we stayed in separate rooms. There was never any o' that kind o' thing, if ye follow my meanin'. He was a gentleman, an' wouldna lift a finger in an unseemly way til a woman.

I looked forward tae my trips til the mainland more than ever, for I had a secret that the auld wives o' Whales Reef woulda died for.

Odara began to laugh as she went on. Loni continued to listen, enchanted with the clandestine love story.

Every time he came til the Hotel where I stayed, he met me holdin' a deep blood-red rose for me. We had more fun than ye could imagine. We often went intil Edinburgh, sometimes took the train doon til London an' went tae the theater an' a' aboot the city. He'd buy me a new dress every time for some special evenin' oot on the toon. Afore long I stopped attendin' the cookin' classes a'together, an' we jist spent the week together. Twice we went over til Paris an' Macgregor treated me like a queen, though I was jist a puir Shetland lass, daughter o' the island veterinarian. He taught me tae dance an' we always went dancin' an' he took me tae the best restaurants. In my heart I thought that he had made a lady o' me. I was prood tae be seen walkin' along on his arm.

He finally told me aboot his wife an' the troubles they had. He'd managed tae keep some track o' her. She'd married again in Norway but never had children an' died yoong, in her fifties I think it was. Talkin' aboot her made him sad. I could never tell if he loved her or not. I know he thought he'd made a mistake marryin' her, but he blamed her for nothin'—that's the kind o' man he was. He wasn't the blamin' kind. But the pain and sadness never left him, an' sometimes I was almost worried for hoo it would seem to overwhelm him.

When I decided tae quit my job an' gae back til Whales Reef, we talked aboot what tae do an' contrived a plan tae keep meetin' on the mainland. By then I'd told my daddy aboot it. That was when my aunt Eldora was stayin' in toon wi' her husband. So Macgregor was free tae come til the Croft, bein' laird an' my daddy bein' the vet. When he did, Daddy'd leave us an' go oot an' we were free tae talk an' hae tea together. We jist had tae be careful that none o' the auld wives came callin'. But Daddy kept his eye oot an' not a soul ever knew. An' as I was sayin', we contrived a plan for me tae fly doon or take the boatie til Aberdeen where Daddy an' me spread the story, though in sich a way as we werena lyin' exactly, just leadin' folk tae believe that I was visitin' a cousin. An' jist by coincidence the laird would happen tae be gone at the same time. We made it so that my make-believe cousin lived in Edinburgh so that we could be at the festival most summers. Every time I came back from Edinburgh I had a new dress. I told people that my cousin was wealthy, an' never allowed the slightest blush tae come tae my cheeks as I said it. I didna hae much I could do for him like that, but I made him a heather ring, like yers, lassie, an' that's when I first began tae weave the heather an' the wool together.

Odara paused. A smile, almost a glow, shone on her face at the fond reminiscences.

"If you don't mind my asking," said Loni, "why didn't you ever marry?"

Odara thought a few seconds, then drew in a deep breath and continued.

Weel, the main reason is that he didna ask me. I would hae married him, for I loved him a' my life. But knowing the things people said o' him, he didn't want folk thinkin' ill o' me. As I say, there was always a strange kind o' sadness aboot him, though we had fun an' laughed together. I felt tender toward him, almost like I had tae protect that part o' him that still hurt from afore, an' not intrude on it mysel'. A' those years when he was helpin' the villagers that they never knew, and keepin' the mill an' providin' work for the widows an' keepin' rents low, an' people thinkin' o' him so different than he was . . . I knew it hurt him. His daddy had modernized the auld Hotel but then after he was gone the mill fell on hard times, but Macgregor never told a soul an' kept hirin' anyone needin' work, an' payin' them good. No one knew all he did for the island. An' he wanted tae protect me fae all the evil o' loose tongues an' gossip. An' he was enough o' a traditionalist, though folk think o' such things differently noo, but he didna think a divorced man ought tae marry again, an' he wanted tae protect me fae the stain o' marryin' a divorced man. We enjoyed something special together an' maybe he was afraid o' spoilin' it. Our weeks, sometimes two, every year, more than made up for the rest o' the year when we only saw one another occasionally. He didna come by the Croft often for fear o' settin' folk talkin'. An' in a way, maybe it was best as it was, because the love that grew in my heart was deep an' quiet an' I treasured it even more. What we had together was honorable an' we were happy sharin' it. Oor secret became oor delight. Sometimes I'd find a dark red rose oot on the moor, for he knew where I walked, an' my heart would leap an' a smile would come tae my lips. I knew he'd left it for me.

An' that's the story o' the black rose, lassie. When I dropped the rose intil his grave, the tears that fell doon my cheeks were the tears o' love.

Loni reached over and took Odara's aging hand and gave it a squeeze. "Did David ever know?" she asked.

Odara smiled. "I think so," she replied. "I told him not long ago that I loved his uncle—that's Macgregor, who was really his cousin—an' it seemed like he already knew. But I also told him I'd deny it if he told a soul," she added, chuckling.

"Well, thank you for telling me, Odara," said Loni. "I am honored to be part of what is a very special love story. No one on the island will ever hear of it."

91

THE WEDDING

The morning of the wedding dawned bright and clear. To everyone's relief there would be no rain. The day would not be particularly warm, but for the Shetlands warm enough.

By now she was accustomed to sunlight through the windows at three in the morning. However, Loni managed to sleep until a little after six. Even before she left her room, she heard the Cottage stirring. Soon it was abuzz below and around her. Before making her appearance, the bride-to-be crept to the Bard's Chamber for a few minutes of "centering down," as her grandfather would have described it. She gazed at the photographs that so deeply represented the legacy she had discovered here, then perused the bookshelves, and finally walked to the window and looked out over the island. At last she was ready.

She descended the stairs where she found Isobel scurrying about the kitchen. Maddy and Tennyson were already enjoying coffee and heading out for a walk to the shore. Loni's grandparents were soon down, declaring themselves well rested. Before long the kitchen and breakfast room were noisily filled with the rest of the guests.

Loni knew that this wedding truly belonged to the entire community. She belonged to the village, the island, and these people. She wanted to give everyone the opportunity to participate in it. Accordingly, she had devised a unique processional involving all the village ladies.

She and her ladies in attendance, which in one way or another involved half the village women, began to gather inside the mill by ten. With pins and hems and slips and stockings and curls and braids and fasteners and shoes and much making over the bride herself, with infinite fussings over every woman's preparations from head to toe, the next two hours passed busily and joyfully.

Meanwhile the village men, barred from setting foot near the mill, were carrying out their own pre-wedding rituals at the Whales Fin Inn. All the women, including the MacFarlane sisters, had been run out of the place by eleven. The boisterous attempts by the village men to get the principal players in the drama suitably outfitted in their tuxedos, David in the kilt of his clan with matching blue tuxedo coat, were singularly masculine in nature—laughing and ribbing and poking fun, with an occasional mildly ribald joke from the coarser elements. All was taken in good fun as part of the age-old rite of sending a bachelor off to his fate as a married man. It was early in the day for drinking, yet a few final toasts were required. David's cousin was no longer inclined to make fun of kilt or clan. To all appearances he and the groom might have been lifelong best friends. Clean-shaven and remarkably well turned out, Hardy took upon himself the honors of leading several toasts as the morning progressed.

At 12:30, the female bridal party made their way to the church, accompanied by a dozen or more chattering women. The parish minister, Lincoln Rhodes, attempted to offer a few words to settle and prepare them for the solemnity that befitted the occasion. But the village women were far too excited and talkative to be solemn about anything.

About ten minutes before one, Lincoln disappeared. A minute later the great bell in the steeple rang out. The whole island had been awaiting the signal. The gong echoed as far as the North Cliffs.

Lincoln returned and led the feminine procession, Loni and her grandmother and bridesmaids talking and laughing on their way, back toward the huge tent pavilion that had been set up two days before outside the mill. By now the route between church and mill had filled with many more lining the way. Through their midst came the bride and her retinue. The village women and their daughters, all in their Scots finery, closed around them as Loni passed, and now accompanied her on the final stage of her journey, a great cloud of witnesses moving behind her like a flowing human veil.

Back in town, at David's request his other two minister friends each offered a few words to the men outside at the square. As the bell tolled its summons, David and Loni's grandfather and cousin Jacob, led by Stirling Yates and Dickie Sinclair, set out. A somewhat boisterous melee of village boys and men made their way up the hill behind them. Some who followed, it is true, had by now enjoyed two or three pints and were in high spirits indeed. The swarm of men did not make quite such an orderly procession as they went to meet their counterparts, more resembling a host going forth to battle than a wedding party. Yet as they approached the pavilion from the opposite end, they quieted and order gradually descended over the chaos.

The human tides slowly met and merged like the coming together of two living rivers. Wives and husbands and children found each other, spreading out and settling into place.

David and his men took their positions at the makeshift altar in front of the pavilion where the vows would be exchanged.

Loni's grandfather continued to the opposite side to await his granddaughter coming from the church. Lincoln Rhodes left the women to join the groom and his attendants. The guests and relatives were seated under the great tent, with many also standing surrounding it. The trail of women melted away to find their places, leaving

Loni alone with her bridesmaids at the open end of the pavilion. William Ford walked toward her beaming with pride.

With everyone in place, music from a lone violinist began to the soft but triumphant tune of "Caledonia." Down the aisle now came Loni's best friends Madison Stafford and Audney Kerr. The bridesmaids were attired in light teal gowns with scarf and sash—matching Loni's Whales Weave scarf that kept her warm on her first crossing to the island a year before.

Awaiting them, David stood with Hardy Tulloch and Noak Muir beside him.

When the bridesmaids were in place, a hush descended. The lonely cry of a single bagpipe broke the silence. A Highland rendition of Wagner's "Bridal March," scarcely recognizable at first, floated over the island. Loni took her grandfather's arm. To the haunting strains of the melody, grandfather and granddaughter started down the red swath of carpet laid between the rows of guests. As she made her way through their midst, those seated under the tent rose and turned to face the radiant bride. She was dressed in a simple white dress, a sash of the Tulloch family tartan over one shoulder and pinned to her opposite side. Loni carried a small bouquet of heather and baby's breath.

The pipes dissonantly convulsed into silence. After Lincoln's welcoming *Dearly beloved* . . .

and the ceremonial passing of the paternal hand, William Ford sat down in the front row beside his tearful wife. Both instinctively reached for the hand of the other.

The happy ceremony continued to its appointed conclusion.

"And now," said Lincoln in joyful culmination, "may I present the laird of Whales Reef and the chief of Clan Tulloch . . . henceforth jointly known as Mr. and Mrs. David Tulloch."

Clapping and music rose as David and Loni walked down the carpet of red, extending hands to greet those about them who were within reach, at last emerging into the sunlight. The surrounding throng went wild with applause and congratulatory cheers. That same instant the piper filled the bag of his pipes and let loose with the traditional wail of "Scotland the Brave."

It took at least fifteen minutes for the wedding party to get inside the mill. There a few formalities were attended to and photographs taken. While they were thus engaged, an army of men moved chairs and tables and assembled the wooden dance floor in preparation for a festive afternoon of cake and more food and drink than could be imagined, to be accompanied by music and dancing. The piper was joined by a four-piece box and fiddle ensemble. Meanwhile, dozens of women scurried off to their homes for the platters and dishes they had been preparing for a week.

By the time David and Loni reemerged from the mill to begin the long process of shaking every hand on the island, music filled the air while a stream of food-bearers hurried back from town.

92

SWING TIME

After a celebration marked by many of the island's couples renewing their youthful enthusiasm for country dancing to the lively jigs, reels, and strathspeys provided by the band, the unexpected highlight of the afternoon came during a break between dances when William Ford approached the bandleader.

"Do you know any Glenn Miller?" he asked.

"Nae too many," replied the fiddler, "though I think we might mind enouch tae stumble oor way through 'In the Mood,' the 'Brown Jug,' an' the train song."

"Yes, 'Chattanooga Choo Choo,' " smiled Mr. Ford. "Any of those will do nicely."

After a few words to his comrades, the music began again. The style was decidedly unique, but the swing beat was prominent and that was what mattered. Around the dance floor expressions of bewilderment spread among those too young to remember the music of the war years.

Into the midst of their perplexity, eyes turned toward a white-haired American couple walking hand in hand onto the floor. And with great fanfare and whoops and cheers, the crowd was treated to a visual display of Lindy and Swing like nothing any of them had ever seen. Loni's two grandparents kicked up their heels, turning and spinning to the lively music like twenty-year-olds, as indeed they had been during the 1940s when they had secretly taught themselves to dance to the big bands playing on the radio.

After a few minutes where she watched, Loni's astonishment mounted yet higher to see her grandparents joined by Maddy and Tennyson, who had taken dancing lessons prior to their wedding. Then surprising the villagers all the more, former parish minister Stirling Yates, as nimble on his feet as the four Americans, grabbed a laughing Audney Kerr and led her onto the floor, improvising as he attempted to teach her the moves to the delight of the crowd, which was soon clapping and whooping in "swing time."

"Grandma, Grandpa," exclaimed Loni as her grandparents left the dance floor flushed and breathless a short time later, "that was fantastic! I had no idea."

"I didn't know if I would remember," said Mrs. Ford. "It's been years."

"Like riding a bicycle," laughed Mr. Ford. "But if either of our parents had discovered what we were doing out in the barn sixty years ago . . . oh, my goodness!"

As energies began to flag about five o'clock, it was time to say good-bye to the bride and groom. Their bags were packed and already aboard the worthy craft that would take them to Lerwick and the Kvelsdro House Hotel.

Their plans were to depart the following morning for Iceland. There a combination honeymoon and research trip for a grant David had recently been awarded would occupy them for two weeks. As recently as the previous evening, even with the wedding looming, David had been scrambling to gather notes, books, and articles on the mysterious disappearance of starlings on mainland Britain throughout the nineteenth century. He hoped to discover evidence that they had remained plentiful on Iceland as well as on Shetland, and investigate whether the wide-bill Shetland subspecies—which offered a potential solution to the riddle—could also be found in Iceland.

Slowly David and Loni began to move away from the pavilion and down the drive toward the road. The clustering throng accompanied them into town and to the inn. Attended by Hardy and Audney, they changed clothes, then reemerged onto the street and continued toward the harbor, still with the throng of wedding celebrants behind them.

Outfitted with banners and ribbons and decorations—and scoured with bleach by Hardy and first mate Lincoln Rhodes to remove all traces of fish—the *Hardy Fire* awaited. Not only had most of the aroma of its trade been removed, so too had all unnecessary machinery and equipment, leaving the deck mostly clear for a dozen chairs. The bride and groom now boarded, along with the wedding party, absent the Fords who did not feel up to the trip. Hardy's passengers would accompany the chief and laird on the short forty-minute jaunt to Lerwick, then return to Whales Reef.

Once aboard, Loni stood and waited for the spectators lining the harbor to quiet.

"Thank you all for a most extraordinary day," she said loudly, trying to be heard over the lapping of the sea along the shoreline. "David and I will treasure the memory of it forever. You are in our hearts and we love you."

Shouts and applause rose over the harbor.

"I thank you again also," Loni went on, "for welcoming me into your hearts and your community. Who could have imagined when I first came planning only to spend a day or two that it would end in this?

"I have one brief announcement before we are off. I want to take this opportunity to tell you that during my absence Hardy Tulloch will act as my factor. If you have needs or concerns, you may talk to him. You may trust him entirely just as

David and I do. Hardy will know how to reach us if need be.

"Now God bless you all! We will see you again very soon!"

A huge cheer went up as David stepped forward beside Loni. They raised their arms to the crowd of well-wishers as Hardy fired up his powerful engine. Moments later he was guiding his craft toward the narrow opening between the concrete walls.

As the *Hardy Fire* slowly slipped out of the harbor, David and Loni continued to wave to the crowded quay and shoreline. Again the piper began to play. By degrees the melancholy strains of "Lerwick Harbor" quieted the human clamor.

As they cleared the thick walls, the melody gradually modulated and a new familiar tune arose over the subdued and watching crowd. Slowly their voices joined in. The words of the Scottish anthem of memories and hopes drifted across the waters as the *Hardy Fire* gained speed.

> Should auld acquaintance be forgot,
> And ne'er brought to mind.
> Should auld acquaintance be forgot,
> In days of auld lang syne.

David smiled at Loni and stretched his arm around her. They continued to wave back as faces

faded into the distance and their singing grew
fainter—

    . . . auld acquaintance . . . to mind . . .
      forgot . . . in days of auld lang syne . . .
    . . . days of auld lang syne . . .
    . . . auld lang syne . . .

—until at last only the skirl of the pipes
remained.

93

THE LEGACY

David had lived every day of his existence at
the Auld Hoose. His entire perspective of life
was rooted in that ancient seat of the chief. Now
he found himself somewhere else. He awoke on
their first morning after their return to Whales
Reef in momentary confusion. He glanced about
the master bedroom, turned over, and realized
he was alone.

He rose, wandered to the window, and drew
back the thick curtains. By now thoroughly awake,
his subconscious nevertheless expected to see
the ocean in the distance looking west, with the
open moorland of the island inland and east.
Instead, everything was backward.

He threw on a shirt and trousers and left the room in his bare feet. The alluring smell of coffee filtered up from below. He found Loni in the great room, a peat fire blazing away in the fireplace.

"Good morning, my dear!" he said, walking into the room. "You're up early."

"We're home. Can't lounge around in bed," said Loni. She set aside the book in her lap, rose and greeted her new husband with an affectionate kiss.

"I'm not used to anyone being up *before* me," laughed David. "I'm usually up with the sun."

"No doubt our normal patterns will reassert themselves soon enough—coffee?"

"It smells great," replied David, drawing in deeply of the aroma. "I think I will set aside my normal custom of tea first and join you."

They walked to the kitchen where David poured himself a fresh cup. Two or three minutes later they were seated together in front of the fire.

"Speaking of old habits," said David, "I was completely disoriented when I woke up. When I looked out the window the sun was coming from the wrong direction. This move across the island is playing tricks on my brain."

"It is traditional for a woman to follow a man to his home. We *could* rethink this whole thing."

"No, I will be happy here. This is the fitting place for the lairdship and chieftainship to reside. It's what the people expect. And I love the Cottage. But what brought you down so early?"

A thoughtful expression came over Loni's face. "I was perusing my journal," she answered.

"And pondering many things," added David. "I know that expression. Not having second thoughts about marrying me, are you?"

"You know better than that," laughed Loni. "No, I was just thinking about where I've come from, how everything has changed. I suppose with the wedding and honeymoon behind us and this representing, as they say, the first day of the rest of my life, I needed to look at my journal again. The first thing that struck me when I opened it was that I don't need it anymore."

"Not need your journal—a self-respecting Quaker like you!"

"I don't know about that," laughed Loni. "When I originally began I was trying to figure out where I belonged in life. It was my way of sorting through the confusion of not knowing who I was. Most of those questions are resolved. Reading these early pages a few minutes ago . . . they sound like a different person."

"I would like to read it someday . . . if you would ever be willing to share that chapter of your life with me."

"I think I would be embarrassed. I'll have to think about that.—By the way," Loni added with a smile, "I don't think I ever told you about my Husband List."

"No, you never did!" laughed David, looking

surprised. "That is definitely a story I need to hear!"

"Here—I'll show you," said Loni, flipping to the back pages.

"Look—how could I have known. *Kind . . . Treats women with respect . . . Good looking . . . Likes children and animals . . . laughs easily and often . . . knows how to make others laugh.* I've been adding to and crossing out from this list for years. Without knowing it, all my life I've been compiling a character description of a certain David Tulloch of Whales Reef. I think I may have begun falling in love with you the moment I heard your laughter."

As if on cue, David burst out laughing again. "What about me?" he said. "I found the woman I've been waiting for without even knowing it."

"Speaking of which," said Loni after a minute, "how amazing is it coming home to two more engagements announced while we were away?"

"Our wedding must have started something!"

"Actually it was Maddy and Tennyson who started it. I am especially happy for Rakel—the dear girl—as you must be for Audney."

"I'm happy for them both," nodded David. "I've known them all my life. They both deserve being loved by two good men. Is there any word on dates yet?"

"Audney said she thinks it will be in the fall. I don't know about Rakel and Armond."

Again it fell quiet as Loni stared deeply into the fire in front of them. At length she rose, still holding her journal, walked slowly forward and knelt in front of the hearth.

"What are you doing?" asked David.

"I think it's time to say good-bye to my past," replied Loni softly. "Before you came down I was planning a little ritual to burn this book of reminiscences. It's time to move on."

David set down his coffee cup and hurried to her side. "You can't do that!" he exclaimed.

"Why? It's done its work. I want to look ahead now."

"But what is contained in your journal is an intrinsic part of who you are."

"Who I *was*."

"Then let me rephrase—who you were *becoming*. Those years were part of that growth. They helped make you who you are today."

"But I don't want to look back at them anymore."

"I get that. But what about those who come after, your posterity . . . our children—we *are* going to have children, aren't we?"

"Absolutely! But why would they care?"

"Look how much your great-grandmother's journal has meant to you. What if she had burned it, thinking no one would care?"

"I see what you mean. That would have been a catastrophe."

"You have been helped to know who you are by Emily's story. You have no idea who might be helped in some way by yours. You have to keep that legacy for whoever will come after you."

"I can't imagine that."

"I'm sure Emily didn't imagine that the little baby she held in her arms, as you told me, a few months before her death would be changed by *her* story. In a way, maybe Emily was writing her story for you. Who can tell who you have been writing for? You discovered your legacy from the past, and now you are part of a legacy that will go on into the future."

Loni smiled nostalgically. "You feel strongly about this, don't you?" she said.

"Yes . . . I do," replied David seriously. "There is nothing so valuable in life as each individual man's or woman's story of growth and becoming. I told you about Stirling Yates's story. I shared my struggles with you and your grandparents. Look how Maddy has changed. Noak Muir's is a remarkable story of becoming. And Hardy more than the rest! Every story of growth is amazing."

"I hadn't thought of it like that."

"You have to preserve the legacy of your life for those who will come after," he went on. "And I hope one day, with your permission, to read both your legacy journals—yours and Emily's. The story they tell is a treasure."

Loni continued to stare into the fire. At last she

drew in a deep breath, then stood and walked across the room, her journal in hand, and picked up Emily's from the coffee table beside the couch where it lay. She carried the two journals to the wall of books.

"I will do as you suggest," she said, "and save them together, with the letter box, here on the bookshelf. They will remain as *our* legacy."

She and David sat down again beside each other on the couch.

"I don't suppose my written journal is the important thing anyway," she said. "It was just my record of the journey. The important thing is that I now know who I am."

"And who is that?" asked David with a smile.

"I admit that the *Loni* and *Alonnah* were confusing for a long time—two people in one body. That's the story of my journal—the story of Loni and Alonnah and how they were trying to figure out who they each were."

"And now you have a new surname to add to the confusion," said David.

"Which I am honored to have. But it has not added to the confusion. My new name has *resolved* the confusion of my past."

"You said a minute ago that you know who you are," said David. "Do you remember when you asked me to tell you in twenty-five words or less the results of my spiritual journey?"

"I believe I offered you a hundred," smiled Loni.

"You did—and very generous of you it was. How about if I give you a hundred to tell me the results of your journey to know who you are?"

"I won't need that many. I would say that who I am is Alonnah Loni Emily Ford *Tulloch*."

"How will you keep them all straight?" chuckled David.

"Easy—they're all the same person."

"And who is that?"

"It's *me*."

94

ENDING FRAGMENTS

That Tennyson Stafford would hit it off with David was scarcely a surprise, especially in that their wives were best friends. Both men were adventurous outdoorsmen eager to learn of all the places the other had been and what they had seen and done. Their conversations during the months leading up to their respective marriages were lively and animated, full of many questions and much laughter, with plans and ideas thrown out to get together here, there, and everywhere for some shared exploit.

But during the wedding week on Whales Reef, Maddy and Tennyson also struck up a surprising friendship with Audney Kerr and Lincoln Rhodes.

The result on the day following Loni and David's departure for their honeymoon was a brainstorm which was immediately put into effect—Audney and Lincoln accompanied the Staffords to Aberdeen where they showed the two Americans around the city before seeing them off on their flight back to the States. Their farewells were full of many promises to stay in touch.

Rakel Gordon and Armond Lamond were married in October of that same year.

Audney Kerr and Lincoln Rhodes exchanged vows the following month. Maddy and Tennyson Stafford returned to Scotland for the second of the two ceremonies.

David and Loni remained in Whales Reef throughout the autumn months, to the delight of the villagers, and were integral participants in both weddings.

Before the week of the wedding reunion in November was over, the Tulloch, Rhodes, and Stafford trio had agreed to join in a holiday at the earliest their busy schedules could accommodate it. Much discussion took place via letters and phone calls and emails over the course of the next few months, with the result of four days together in London the following May, almost exactly coinciding with Maddy and Tennyson's first wedding anniversary. While the three women enjoyed shopping together, and spent almost an entire day in Harrods, the men confessed the noise and traffic and congestion somewhat tedious. They agreed amongst themselves that Tennyson would plan their next outing.

Such it was that, two years later, the three Scots were treated to a singularly American adventure—whitewater rafting on the Colorado River.

Thus began a tradition of meeting every two years. Their reunions included visits to New York and San Francisco, but also to such diverse destinations as Disney World in Florida, deep-sea fishing off the coast of Maine, a driving tour of the U.S. National Parks of the Southwest, a camping trip on horseback in the Adirondacks, a week in England's lake district, a tour of the Galapagos Islands, a trek up the Andes to the Inca ruins of Machu Picchu, and a train trip across Canada. Loni had been trying to plan a crossing of the Atlantic by ship, in memory of Emily Hanson's first visit to Whales Reef, but had not yet been able to fit it into their schedules.

Their conversations around campfires, in hotel rooms, or while driving to one or another of their destinations were always stimulating, probing, and thought-provoking. When the subject turned to matters of spirituality, as it often did, Maddy did not offer many thoughts. What exactly was her condition of mind and soul it would be difficult to say. She would probably not have professed to belief, but in her heart she believed more than she once had. As David would say, she was growing and *becoming,* which was the best thing that could be said of any man or woman. Above all, she was *listening.* And surrounded by friends like David and Loni, and Audney and Lincoln Rhodes, and with a husband who loved her as did Tennyson Stafford, that is saying a good deal.

William and Anabel Ford lived to be ninety-three and ninety-five respectively. Both were fortunate to die in their own beloved home, and drifted away toward the eternal sunrise with Loni at each of their bedsides.

David and Loni had three children, a son, Chad Ernest Tulloch, and two daughters, Emily and Madison.

Cousin Hardy eventually married village lass Gunna Ewen. As Loni's traveling with David kept her away from the island on and off throughout the year, Loni promoted Hardy from temporary to permanent factor on the island.

Hardy and Gunna, and their eventual energetic brood of six laddies and lassies, took up residence in the Auld Hoose.

Of necessity Hardy had to scale back his fishing, though he did not completely give it up. Along with his duties as the parish minister, Lincoln Rhodes shared with its owner the responsibility of keeping the *Hardy Fire* pulling fish from the Atlantic at least four or five days a week.

All his life Hardy remained devoted to his laird and his chief.

ABOUT THE AUTHOR

Michael Phillips is a bestselling author of a number of beloved novels, including such well-known series as SHENANDOAH SISTERS, CAROLINA COUSINS, CALEDONIA, THE JOURNALS OF CORRIE BELLE HOLLISTER, and THE SECRET OF THE ROSE. He has also served as editor of many titles, adapting the classic works of Victorian author George MacDonald (1824–1905) for today's reader, and his efforts have since generated a renewed interest in MacDonald. Phillips's love of MacDonald's Scotland has continued throughout his writing life.

In addition to his fifty published editions of MacDonald's work, Phillips has authored and coauthored over ninety books of fiction and nonfiction, ranging from historical novels to contemporary whodunits, from fantasy to biblical commentary.

Michael and his wife, Judy, spend time each year in Scotland but make their home in California. To learn more about the author and his books, visit FatherOfTheInklings.com. He can be found on Facebook at MichaelPhillipsChristianAuthor@ facebook.com. To contact Phillips, write to: macdonaldphillips@sbcglobal.net.

Books are produced in the United States using U.S.-based materials

Books are printed using a revolutionary new process called THINKtech™ that lowers energy usage by 70% and increases overall quality

Books are durable and flexible because of smythe-sewing

Paper is sourced using environmentally responsible foresting methods and the paper is acid-free

Center Point Large Print

600 Brooks Road / PO Box 1
Thorndike, ME 04986-0001 USA

(207) 568-3717

US & Canada:
1 800 929-9108
www.centerpointlargeprint.com